D1539992

HOROWITZ & MRS. WASHINGTON

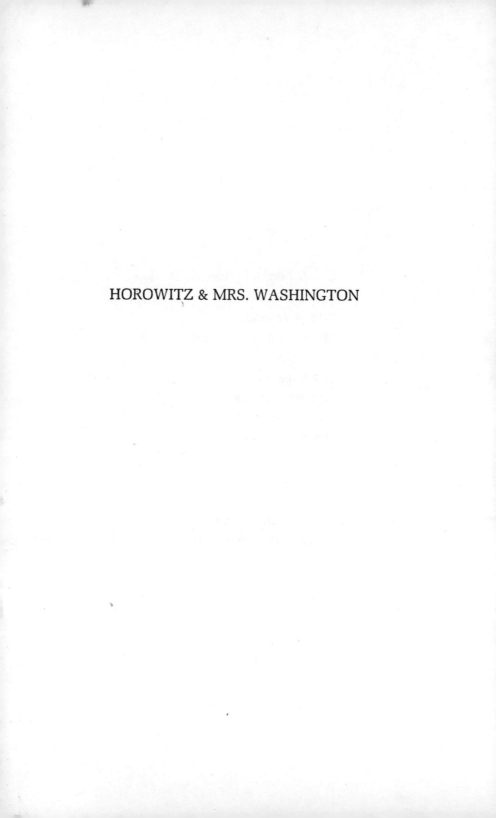

Other books by Henry Denker

THE ACTRESS

THE SCOFIELD DIAGNOSIS

THE STARMAKER

THE EXPERIMENT

THE PHYSICIANS

A PLACE FOR THE MIGHTY

THE KINGMAKER

THE DIRECTOR

THE FIRST EASTER

SALOME: PRINCESS OF GALILEE

MY SON, THE LAWYER

I'LL BE RIGHT HOME, MA

Henry Denker

G. P. PUTNAM'S SONS
New York

Library of Congress Cataloging in Publication Data

Denker, Henry.
  Horowitz and Mrs. Washington.

  I. Title.
PZ3.D4175Ho   [PS3507.E5475]   813'.5'4   79-1114
ISBN 0-399-12341-5

To Edith, My Wife

The opinions expressed by
Samuel Horowitz are solely
his own and do not necessarily
reflect those of the author or
the publisher.

PART
I

Chapter One

"Mister, a man your age does not resist muggers! You could have got yourself killed!" the irritated cop rebuked Samuel Horowitz in a quite forceful tone.

Horowitz sat silent while the nervous young black intern attempted to suture the ugly wound. But he could not keep from thinking, Some doctor! Where did anyone ever get the idea that a black kid could be a good doctor? To be a good doctor, a man had to be Jewish. History, from Maimonides on, proved that the best doctors are Jewish. Kings, emperors, even some popes, insisted on having Jewish doctors. No wonder this young black intern is nervous. He knows his work is being judged by an expert, a real *maven* on doctors!

So Samuel Horowitz had been thinking when a strange, terrifying feeling overcame him. Then he lost consciousness. The last thing he remembered was the young intern saying, "Christ! Not this! Not now!"

*   *   *

Horowitz came to and he found himself in bed, in a private room. He asked the nurse what had happened. She avoided his question, gave him a shot, and he went off to sleep. He woke hours later to find his son, Marvin, staring down at him with considerable concern.

"Marvin?" Horowitz asked, puzzled by his son's sudden presence. Marvin should be in Washington, in his big law office there.

"You're okay, Pa. Don't worry. It's going to be all right," Marvin reassured.

Whenever anyone volunteered to reassure Sam Horowitz before he asked, his first reaction was always "What's so bad that they have to tell me it's going to be all right?"

Marvin could read his father's eyes. "You had what the doctors say was a minor stroke. In a way, it's lucky you were in the emergency room at the time."

"Some *gedillah*! That's certainly the luckiest thing that ever happened to me," Horowitz said bitterly. "Imagine, there I was, bleeding like a stuck pig from a razor slash and I was lucky enough to have a stroke at the same time. I should be the happiest man in the world!"

"Pa . . ." Marvin tried to interrupt.

"That black intern, did he discover that I had a stroke? Or did he give me one? Just to finish up what his dear 'brothers' failed to do with the razor?"

"Pa, please . . ."

"Of course. I am lying here, wounded, sewed up like a repaired old shoe, suffering from a stroke and one 'please' is supposed to wipe everything clean."

Sam Horowitz was silent for a moment before he dared to ask, "So what's the damage?"

"Well . . ." Marvin began.

"I don't like reports that start out with 'well'. That means it's very bad. So never mind introductions and preambles. Give me the straight honest facts. Don't lie to me, Marvin."

12

Marvin Hammond, partner in the New York and Washington law firm of Judd, Bristol, Crain and Hammond answered his father, Sam Horowitz, "Look, Pa, it's going to sound worse than it is."

"Just tell me the truth. I'll figure out if it sounds worse that it is," Horowitz grumbled.

"They haven't been able to do a complete evaluation yet. But they think there's a minor involvement of your left leg and arm. If that proves true, you've got a good chance of recovering almost complete mobility with the proper kind of physical therapy. You haven't suffered any loss of vision. And it's obvious you haven't lost your power of speech. You're still as sarcastic as ever."

Marvin smiled, hoping to lighten the moment. But his father did not reciprocate. Instead, he stared off, grimly.

"That's all? You told me the worst?"

"As far as they can tell without a complete evaluation, that's all," Marvin reassured.

"Hmm!" was all Horowitz would say until he asked, "And my face?"

"A slight twist on the left side. Hardly noticeable."

"I meant about the . . . the stitches," Sam Horowitz admitted, self-conscious about his vanity.

"They expect that to heal very well. Won't leave much of a scar. Oh, by the way, I called Mona. She's planning to come."

"Tell her not to bother," Horowitz said. "There's nothing she can do here. And she has so much to do back there. How are they going to run San Diego without Mona Fields?" Sam asked bitterly, reflecting on the three times he had seen his daughter in the past four years.

"She suggested your going out there to recuperate," Marvin informed, hoping to soften his father's attitude.

"I will recuperate in my own home!" Sam Horowitz said staunchly. "Charity she can do through one of her organizations. Not through me!"

"Pa, please . . ."

13

"I have raised a daughter who can only respond to disaster. She should be the first Jewish president of the Red Cross. Before your mother died, we hardly saw her. Once she died, Mona came flying East that very night. And such a crier. Funerals were invented for your sister Mona."

Marvin knew it would do no good to try to talk his father out of it. So he remained silent, waiting for Horowitz to make the next move.

"Look, you call your sister. Tell her that I'm not in danger of dying so I am not a disaster. There is nothing she can do here. She better stay home and take care of her husband and San Diego. When I am all recuperated, if I feel like taking a little trip, I might go out to California for a few days."

"But she wants to come," Marvin persisted.

"And I don't want her to!" Horowitz said with finality.

"Okay," Marvin agreed reluctantly.

It was obvious Marvin was anxious to leave. Before he could, Horowitz asked, "Marvin? Do something for me?"

"Of course, Pa. Anything!"

"Go to the apartment. Find my reading glasses. And my toothbrush. Bring them."

"Sure, Pa."

After Marvin departed the hospital Sam Horowitz lay stiff and straight before trying to move his left leg. It responded only partially, as if some overwhelming force gripped it, preventing it from carrying out its normal function. He tried to diminish the importance of that. After all, he argued, he was exhausted from the entire experience. The suddenness of the attack. The struggle. The wound which could have been fatal. The slight stroke. He persisted in calling it slight. He tried to raise his left hand to his face, to find the wound, to assess the length of it. But his hand could not reach it. Again, the

14

invisible force weighed on him, preventing him from carrying out a motion he used to do a hundred times a day without thinking.

He tried his right leg. It functioned as usual. His right hand and arm. No problem. So he reached to the bedside table and found the button. He pressed it. He waited. After what he impatiently considered a reasonable time no nurse appeared. This time he pressed his finger down on the button and deliberately kept it there.

Soon he heard an angry female voice approach his door demanding, "Who's the maniac in 724 who keeps ringing?"

The door was thrust open aggressively. A large woman, red-faced, red-haired, of obvious Celtic extraction, demanded, "What seems to be the emergency in here? And take your finger off that button!"

Sam Horowitz bristled, but withdrew his hand. He knew when he was outgunned. He felt a bit sheepish as he asked, "I would like a mirror."

"A mirror, is it?" the nurse responded hostilely, more angry now than she had been. "Even at two hundred and eighty-five dollars a day, you do not ring like that just to ask for a mirror! You can damn well wait! We have some very sick people on this floor!"

"I would still like a mirror," Sam Horowitz insisted quietly.

"When we have time," the nurse replied, trying to slam the door behind her. The air-pressure doorcheck prevented her.

Sam Horowitz was alone. Helpless. Yet his need to see the wound the muggers had inflicted demanded to be satisfied. He grasped the bedside table for leverage and was able to roll himself onto his side despite his left leg and his left arm, which refused to cooperate. He pushed himself up until he was in a sitting position. He was sure now he could make it to the bathroom. There must be

15

a mirror on the cabinet door there.

He slid his right leg onto the hard shiny tile floor, then, with an assist from his right hand, he eased his left leg down. He pushed himself up from the bed. And, for the first time in his life, discovered that his legs would not sustain him. He toppled forward, letting out a shrill cry of alarm. He struck the floor, unconscious.

When he came to he was back in bed. The red-haired nurse was standing over him, staring down angrily. Horowitz opened his eyes, blinked a time or two, then closed them to blot out her reproving stare.

"You're not fooling me," she accused. "You're conscious. You can hear what I'm saying. So listen good. Don't you ever, ever, get out of bed without assistance! Do you understand, Mr. Horowitz?"

Finally opening his right eye, Sam Horowitz responded, "I have been getting out of bed for sixty-eight years by myself. I don't need lessons from you or anyone." Then he asked less defiantly, "What's your name?"

"Copeland."

"Copeland?" Horowitz questioned. "You look Irish."

"I am," she declared belligerently, as if any question was an invitation to a fight. "My maiden name was McMennamin."

"Then, Ms. McMennamin, go blow up some buildings in Belfast and leave me alone!" Sam Horowitz declared.

Ignoring his jibe, Copeland ordered, "You just stay in that bed!"

"Then give me a mirror!"

"This is a hospital, not a barbershop!"

"I want to see my face," Horowitz insisted.

"You've got a two-day growth of beard. You need a shave."

"I want to see what they did to me."

That seemed to soften the burly belligerent nurse.

16

"They'll take out the stitches in a few days. And it won't be bad. Not bad at all."

"Can I see?" he asked, then meekly added, "Please?"

"Okay. If you insist."

Nurse Copeland returned moments later with a small hand mirror. He brought it slowly up to his face. For reading or other close work he needed glasses. But to see the patch of gauze that almost covered his entire left cheek he needed no aid.

"Can I . . . can I uncover this?" he asked.

"Better if you didn't. Those things always look uglier than they are."

"I . . . I want to see."

"Okay." She reached over and gently lifted the taped edge of the gauze pad.

He stared into the mirror, shocked by the angry red scar and the black thread of the sutures crisscrossing it. That was what that intern must have been doing when Horowitz passed out.

She was sensitive to his shock so she consoled, "It follows the crease in your cheek. When it heals, it'll fold right in. You'll hardly notice it."

"Railroad tracks," Horowitz said. "Looks like railroad tracks."

"Once the stitches are out and the swelling resolves you won't notice them." When his eyes challenged her, she was forced to concede, "Maybe a few white lines. Faint ones."

"My whole life, sixty-eight years, without a scar on my body. Not even one operation. Now this." Horowitz shook his head sadly. "It's no longer a world for people. Only for animals. Those bastards!"

"I hear you tried to fight back," she said disapprovingly.

"What else? I should give up without a fight? That's a lie that Jews don't fight back. We've had too much experience with savages. We fight!"

"Of course," Copeland agreed quickly, to prevent Horowitz from becoming overwrought.

"It's not only you Irish who fight," Horowitz protested. "And what's more *we* win! Remember what happened in 1967? The Six-Day War? And then in '73? They hit us with a sneak attack on Yom Kippur but in the end we had both Egyptian armies surrounded. And it took the Russians and the Americans together to force us to let them go. And don't you forget it!"

"Okay" Copeland conceded, hoping to end his tirade, "I won't forget it."

"And as for the English!" Horowitz continued, "We didn't just threaten, bomb, then run away and hide. We got rid of them!"

"Yes, I know," she agreed wearily.

"So don't give me lectures about fighting or not fighting! You hear?"

"I hear," she said, turning to leave.

"Where are you going?" Horowitz demanded.

"I have some patients who are really sick," she said pointedly.

"What's the matter? I'm not sick?" he demanded, offended at being placed in a lesser category of any kind.

"In just thirty seconds you beat the British once and the Arabs twice. How sick can you be?"

Horowitz glared at her. She glared back. Then her vivacious hazel eyes could no longer maintain their angry gaze. She relented. He smiled.

"You're pretty fresh. But I like that. My Hannah, she was fresh too. Sweet, but I couldn't get away with anything with her. She always had the last word. She had a sense of humor, too. Like you."

He beckoned her closer with the forefinger of his still functioning right hand. When she remained aloof, he winked, gesturing again. "I want to ask you something."

18

"You're an old letch. I wouldn't dare come too close to you," she joked.

"Listen, in my day . . ." he began to boast pridefully. But he stopped when he realized "*In my day . . .* those are very sad words. They mean my day is over. There's nothing left but to die."

"Come, now," Copeland protested.

"That's what I wanted to ask," he admitted softly.

"What?"

"Doctors lie. Relatives lie. But someone like you, an honest woman, I would believe. You've seen cases like me before. What's going to happen to me?"

"They'll make an evaluation of your condition. Then give you physical therapy. You'll slowly regain the use of your leg, your arm, your hand. After a while it'll be like it never happened."

"Honest?"

"Honest."

"It always works, this physical therapy?" he tried to pin her down.

"Well, in medicine, nothing 'always' works," she admitted uncomfortably.

"Aha," Horowitz absorbed his unhappy prognosis.

"Listen, Mr. Horowitz, you're in pretty good condition for a man your age. You can overcome almost anything. If you try. The main thing is not to give up."

"Of course," he said, not in agreement but in sarcastic disparagement.

"Look, I do have other patients. . . ."

"Go, go," Horowitz urged. "And thanks. For trying to make me feel better."

Once she was gone, he picked up the mirror in his good right hand and stared at his face. Samuel Horowitz. Sixty-eight years old. With a big bandage on his left cheek, and a left hand and arm that would not respond to his simplest commands.

19

He studied his face and realized that since Hannah's death he had lost considerable weight. Where he had always seemed a healthy man, almost plump, his loss of weight had caused his face to become so lean that one might now call him gaunt.

He frowned, studying his image in the mirror. He smiled. In both instances his cheeks were cleaved by two sharp creases which slanted from below his cheekbones down toward the corners of his mouth. Gaunt, indeed.

Yet he was still a fairly handsome man. At least, Hannah had always thought so. And he appeared quite benign until impatience betrayed itself, as it did now, in his pursed lips and deep blue eyes, which were his most expressive features. He had always been a stubborn man. But since Hannah's death he had grown irritable as well. He was quick to argue, easy to antagonize, and had appointed himself the arbiter of all public questions.

He read his *Times* every morning mainly for the sheer enjoyment of disagreeing. He was given to a loud singsong *Ho-ho-ho!* every time his view of common sense was egregiously violated by *The New York Times*. Sam Horowitz had his own opinion of what constituted all the news that's fit to print.

With people, he was the same. Stubborn, argumentative, suspicious, and given to his singsong warning when he was about to disagree. His *Ho-ho-ho* was not delivered with Santa Clausian jollity, but intoned as a prelude to some dire, dogmatic prediction or criticism, both of which he possessed in abundant supply.

Horowitz was a man of great pride. He had come to this country as a child, lived in poor circumstances, vowed to learn the language, the ways of this new land, and to work his way up in the world. Poverty had forced him to leave school at an early age. He had secured a job as an errand boy in a small wholesale paper and twine business. He had gone into business on his own when he was barely twenty-three. He had succeeded well enough to marry, live very comfortably, raise two children and send both of them to very prestigious colleges. He had provided well for Hannah all during her life. Which meant a steady maid, a vacation in the mountains every summer, a trip South almost every winter when business pressures allowed, and a new mink coat every fourth year.

Once the children had gone off on their own, Samuel Horowitz's life consisted mainly of his business and Hannah. They took frequent trips, having been to Europe three times in the last six years of her life. There was no comfort or convenience he ever denied Hannah. When she died, he had only one consolation. Everything that money could provide had been done to save her life. And he was proud that all during their marriage Hannah had never known want, or wanted for love.

Being a prideful man, Horowitz never found it easy to apologize, even when he knew he was wrong. Forced to do so, he could not be direct, but always had to find a roundabout way, which he usually couched in a manner reminiscent of the Talmudic logic of the rabbis of old. He had a habit of closing both eyes as if in deep thought. Then finally he would open his right eye to glance at his opponent as if to make sure he or she were still there. Thus, one eye open, one closed, Horowitz would worm his way into an apology that usually ended short of confessing his error or declaring he was sorry. He employed the same one-eyed technique when making any request that he hesitated to present forthrightly.

People who knew him well were aware of this habit, and of his singsong warning ho-ho-ho. They could judge, in advance, the degree of his dissent by the musical accent on his final ho. The more attenuated that syllable, the more rising tonal variations he invested in it, the sharper and more intolerant his dissent was sure to be.

21

*　　*　　*

Horowitz had been lying alone for a long time. Hours, it seemed. He kept thinking, Damn it, damn them, they are going to put me in a cage. They'll call it a wheelchair. Or a nursing home. But it will be a cage. Like in a zoo. Who wants to live like that?

And my son, his wife and children will come, out of pity or duty, to stare at me at decent intervals. Not to assure me, but to salve their own consciences. Mona will come from her San Diego and her Hadassah and her ladies group at the temple. And she will cry. Of course, Mona will cry. It's the thing she does best.

Or perhaps Bruce and Candy will come down from Boston to visit him during school breaks. Leave it to Mona to send both her son and her daughter to school in Boston. Harvard yet. It was a mark of distinction in Mona's circle. Like the four-hundred-thousand-dollar house, the Rolls that Albert drove, and the M-B SL that Mona drove. To have two children who could make it at Harvard was the ultimate in West Coast distinction.

Mona, Mona, Mona, he lamented. All her life she had had pretensions. Still, in the end, she made them work for her. She had achieved everything in this life that she had ever wanted.

Then why did Horowitz regret what had happened to her? Why did he always think of her with a touch of sorrow? He would never know.

Right now he had other, more pressing, problems to concern him. What would happen to him?

If only Hannah were still alive . . . he started to say, realizing the thousands of times his thoughts had started that way ever since she had died.

If only Hannah were still alive . . . she would be by his side every moment now. Not out of duty, but love. Not for appearance's sake, but because of devotion.

If only Hannah were still alive, he thought sadly, this

22

whole thing would never have happened. He would never have gone shopping. Never been burdened with a bag of groceries when he was mugged. Never have been slashed. Never had a stroke. None of those things would have happened if Hannah were still alive.

Suddenly he felt a sharp pang. If Hannah were still alive she might have gone shopping, she might have been attacked, possibly even slashed, or killed.

He was relieved that she was dead. At least she had been spared that terror, that indignity. She had lived out her life without being defiled by the animals. That was something to be thankful for.

It was the first time since her passing that he found some solace in it. As for himself, he did not have long to go. He could recall reading somewhere that in a large percentage of cases, once one mate died, the other was sure to follow shortly thereafter. And why not? What was there to live for? To become a prisoner? An inmate in an institution? A slave to a wheelchair? Dying was easier, and certainly more dignified.

So, Mona, don't come and cry for me. Bruce and Candy, don't make any duty calls on your way back home to the Coast. Marvin Hammond, my dear son, I gave you a good education, a good start in life, but you owe me nothing. So don't feel obligated to take care of me. I will go peacefully and quietly to my grave without your help or Mona's tears.

Only one thing I regret. I am the last of the Horowitzes. There will be Fields. And there will be Hammonds. But no more Horowitzes. I am the last of an undistinguished but proud line.

Chapter Two

Two days later a young black man wearing glasses and attired in a starched white hospital uniform came to see Sam Horowitz.

"What are you, another intern?" Horowitz began belligerently.

"I'm the physical therapist," the young man said. "I'm here to do an evaluation."

"Evaluation of what?"

"Of you."

"What about me?"

"I'm here to assess how much of an insult has occurred."

"When they grab you from behind, and hold a razor to your throat, I don't call that an insult. I call that a mugging. An attempted murder. So don't give me words like 'insult.'"

"Mr. Horowitz," the young man explained, "I was using insult as a medical term. It means the body has

24

suffered a trauma. My job is to see how much of an insult, how much damage. So I can prescribe the proper course of therapy."

"Okay," Horowitz said. "Insult me. Evaluate me. Do what you have to."

The young man threw back the cover, exposing Horowitz, who was attired in only a short hospital gown.

"What are you going to do?" Horowitz demanded, trying to cover as much of himself as he could.

"I'm going to exert some pressure on your leg. I want you to push back. Hard as you can."

He lifted Horowitz's left leg, pushed against it, waiting for Horowitz to resist. The old man tried but did not succeed too well. The young therapist nodded gravely.

"What's the matter, I didn't push hard enough?" Horowitz asked. "Try me again."

The young man did. Horowitz exerted his maximum effort. But even he realized that he had succeeded no better the second time than the first. Again the black therapist nodded gravely.

"Let's try the hip now." The young man put him through the same type of test to discover the degree of mobility and resistance in his left hip. He seemed no more pleased.

"Well?" Horowitz asked.

The young man did not respond but proceeded to carry out the same tests on Horowitz's right leg and hip. Horowitz responded very well. But that only seemed to make the young man more pessimistic.

"Now the left hand, Mr. Horowitz, close it. Make a fist."

Horowitz had to assist his left arm with his right to raise it sufficiently to project his hand forward. Then, with all the will and effort at his command, he tried to carry out the simple function of closing his left hand until it formed a fist.

25

"That as far as you can go?"

Not wishing to be judged and found wanting, Horowitz replied, "No. I can do better."

He made another great effort, but his fingers would not respond as he wanted them to. He stared at the hand which now resembled an open claw.

"How does it feel?" the young black man asked.

"Like . . . like rubber bands are attached to my fingers and won't let them close. If you could release those rubber bands I could do it. I could."

The young man nodded but proceeded to put Horowitz's left arm and his shoulder to similar tests. At the end he uttered an almost silent, contemplative, "Uh-huh."

"That's all you can say?" Horowitz demanded. "That's an evaluation? How long did you go to physical therapy school?"

"Two years," the young man informed.

"And that's all they taught you to say? Some school! They give classes in uh-huh!"

"I'll map out a course of exercise that will begin tomorrow."

"You didn't tell me. What's the evaluation?" Horowitz insisted. "After all, I'm the patient. I am entitled to know. I'm paying for all this."

"Okay," the young man conceded. "You seem to be suffering no loss of proprialception. But you do show the effects of a transient ischemic attack, which has left you with a degree of loss of function of the left leg, hip, arm, hand, and shoulder. There is apparently a lack of ability to dorsiflex the foot, which will create drag in attempting to walk. We will design a course of exercise and activity that we hope will mitigate those conditions."

"Propria . . . whatever that word was, means what?"

"Proprialception," the young man explained. "It means sensation. You have not lost sensation in your arm

26

or leg. And that's good. But there is loss of mobility, which we must begin to overcome at once or else spasticity will set in."

Although he did not understand much of what the young black man had said, Horowitz was too proud to admit it, so he responded with an agreeable, "Now, that's what I call a civil answer."

To himself, he said, Smart aleck! Give a *shvartzer* a little education and he right away becomes better than anyone. But Horowitz kept that opinion to himself.

In the days that followed, every time the resident arrived to make his cursory rounds, Horowitz would ask, "Well, doctor?"

Always he received the same comfortless answer: "You're doing fine, Mr. Horowitz, fine!"

That's not what I want to know, he would protest in his mind. What's going to happen to me? I don't want to be dependent. I don't have to be. I have a little money saved up. I can manage. Just tell me honestly what my situation is. That's all I want to know.

Yet no matter how he phrased it, the doctor's answer was always the same: "You're doing fine, Mr. Horowitz. Fine. Time will do the rest."

Time, Horowitz argued, time? You're saying time to a man who, the one thing he hasn't got much left of, is time.

He received his first bitter taste of the reality of his situation when they rolled the wheelchair into his room. Mrs. Copeland and an orderly assisted him out of bed and into the chair. She gave him instructions on how to use his good right hand to operate the chair to make it go forward and back and how to steer by using his right foot.

She left him to practice, saying, "When you feel up to it, you're free to go down the hall to the solarium. It's a

27

nice bright day. You'll enjoy talking to other patients."

Left alone, Samuel Horowitz sat motionless in the wheelchair. His right hand rested in his lap. His left hung almost useless over the arm of the chair. He tried to raise it. He could not quite make it all the way. So he lifted it wih his right hand and laid it in his lap. He thought to himself, This left hand is an orphan, a cripple, a sick child that I will have to baby the rest of my life. I will have to drag it along, or wait for it to catch up. But whatever it is, I no longer consider it part of me. It is a stranger, an inconvenient hindrance of a stranger that, unfortunately, I cannot ever leave behind.

After some minutes of sitting still, hating the chair, his arm, his condition, and the world at large, he reached his right hand to the wheel. He was able to make the chair move forward slightly. He reversed the action and the chair responded, moving back but describing an arc. He would need the aid of his right leg to make the chair move in a straight line or turn when he wanted it to.

Then he stopped suddenly, thinking, If I learn to do this well I'll be doomed to do it for the rest of my life. I want to walk! By myself. With a cane, if I have to. But I refuse to become a prisoner of this chair! I refuse!

But in moments, he sat helpless and defeated. A prisoner. Tears slowly traced down his cheeks. He had not cried since Hannah died. His tears burned when they reached his sensitive healing wound. They followed its course slowly, painfully, permitting him to count the stitches.

Afterwards, he learned to operate the chair proficiently enough to get out of the room and down to the solarium. It was a slow, crablike journey at first. But he made it. There he could look out over Central Park and the buildings beyond. He could even see his own home.

When other patients tried to engage him in conversation he was curt or unresponsive. In every way possible, he chose to dissociate himself from the sick and helpless. He had been an active man all his life. If he could not become so again, he saw no reason to survive. He would not be content with less than the man he had been.

But by the end of day, when Mrs. Copeland or some orderly helped him back into his bed, he had to admit, only to himself of course, that he welcomed that refuge. He should hate this bed if he ever hoped to triumph over invalidism. Yet, he welcomed it instead.

Eventually they tried to encourage him by introducing a quad cane into his day's activities. It was a shiny metal cane with a padded black handle. Instead of a pointed tip, like an ordinary cane, it rested on a small square platform, supported by four rubber-tipped metal feet, which gave him a broader and more secure base on which to lean. Grudgingly he exercised with it several times a day until he was able to take as many as ten steps. Emotionally, he was never able to accept it at all. The odd-looking contrivance became only another reminder of his present deficiency, his inability to do something as simple as standing securely on his own two feet or moving his left foot without it dragging awkwardly.

The day had finally come when, after due and costly consultation, the doctors agreed that Samuel Horowitz was ready to go home. He would be glad to get out of the place, despite the fact that he had formed a deep affection for feisty Mrs. Copeland. He would miss her. Behind that outward domineering brusqueness, she was so sensitive that if she could not pretend to be brusk she would have no defenses at all.

He would even miss his grudging, labored journeys down the corridor to the solarium. And his acerbic, monosyllabic conversations with the other patients, who seemed too willing to tell him their life stories, their triumphs, and troubles. For himself, he preferred privacy. Yet, he would miss them, because here, at least, he could compare himself with those worse off. But out there, in the world of the healthy, to whom could he feel superior?

He had to make plans for himself. Many people his age were going South to live. He had always resented that as the acceptance of defeat by old age. Besides, the South was a land inhabited by scavenging, predatory widows looking to pounce on the first widower who came along. He preferred to stay in New York.

But first things first. Get home, to his own apartment, to familiar places, objects, habits. He would be relieved just to be there.

But when his son, Marvin, came to claim him, Horowitz realized that simply going home was also a complicated and difficult matter. He was not permitted to go home by taxi as he had expected. It would require a special car called an ambulette, which would accommodate his new collapsible wheelchair. And he would not be able to make it into the building lobby without the assistance of Juan, the doorman, whom he had hoped to avoid and whose help he would like to be able to refuse. No, he realized, as they were loading him into the ambulette, it would take the doorman and Marvin to carry him and the chair down those three steps into the lobby.

He dreaded the whole idea.

Chapter Three

The ambulette pulled up before the canopy of the old apartment house on Central Park West. The door on the passenger side opened and Marvin Hammond stepped out, while the driver came running around to curbside to assist.

Together, they lifted out the wheelchair. While Marvin and the driver settled financial matters, Horowitz slowly turned himself about to face the building.

He was home again.

He stared up at the facade of the building but was disappointed; coming home failed to have the welcome and familiar feeling he had anticipated.

He continued to stare up at the building. It had been almost new when he, Hannah, and the two children had moved in twenty-nine years ago. Now, it appeared old, shabby, and in disrepair. The canvas canopy was frayed in places, whipped by the winds and the rains that came sweeping in across the park during heavy storms. One

wall bore traces of an almost eradicated bit of por-
nographic graffito, another sign of how the neighborhood
had deteriorated, especially the side streets, where most
of the buildings were no better than slums.

Still, this old building had served them well. Mona
and Marvin had both grown up here. From here, they had
gone off to college. Here they returned with their degrees.
Mona with a husband, too. A bright young man. He
would be a good provider, Hannah had predicted after
the wedding. She had been right, as usual. In a bold
decision, the newlyweds had gone off to California. San
Diego. There Albert went into real estate and amassed a
fortune. Now Mona lived extremely well. She raised two
children of her own. She used to come through New
York twice a year when she and Albert went to Europe.
But since Hannah died, they took the over-the-Pole flight
so Horowitz had not seen them in more than a year,
despite Mona's insistent invitations to visit them. He had
seen his two grandchildren only once during that time.
When they stopped in New York on their way up to
Harvard.

Bruce. And Candy. Some names from Jewish children,
Horowitz thought. Bruce? An extrapolation from Baruch,
which had been Horowitz's father's name. Candy was
from Candace, which was from his mother, whose name
had been Chana. Still, the names Bruce and Candy went
well with the name to which Mona's Albert had changed
just before they moved to San Diego. From Feldstein to
Fields. Not a bad name, Fields. Fields. Fields. Sam
Horowitz had to admit that if you said it often enough it
came to sound almost Jewish.

He was quick to remind his conscience that neither
Mona nor Albert ever denied being Jewish. Quite the
reverse, Mona was extremely active in Hadassah. Albert
was a heavy contributor to the United Jewish Fund out
there in San Diego. It just rolled off the tongue better, and

sounded more distinguished, when the dinner chairman announced, "From Mr. and Mrs. Albert Fields, twenty thousand dollars!"

Mrs. Albert Fields, Horowitz considered. He could recall Mona when she was only sixteen, coming out of this same building on her way to high school. She was pretty. And bright. And, thank God, in those days a father could send his daughter off to school without worrying whether she would be robbed, raped, or mugged. Nowadays they were not safe even in private schools or colleges. Nowadays no one was safe.

Especially not on side streets.

In the moments Samuel Horowitz had to wait for his son to pay the driver of the ambulette, all those memories flashed through his mind, including the moment of his mugging, the struggle, the slashing of his cheek, his stroke, and the consequences that had followed.

But those were memories. Now, Horowitz had to address himself to the immediate present. In a moment or two, as soon as Juan, the doorman, realized they were there, he would come rushing out to greet them. Juan would smile and appear cheerful, though Horowitz knew that secretly the Cuban refugee resented having to do menial work.

How different, Horowitz thought, from the days when my father brought us over from the old country to escape the danger of the First World War. No job was too menial for him. Jews were used to deprivation and the bitter reverses of an unjust world. They did not hold themselves to be above any honest work. But these new immigrants, the ones from Cuba and Puerto Rico, they wanted to start at the top. As for the blacks from the South, don't even mention their pretensions. And the government was agreeing with them! Some world!

At the same time, Horowitz realized that what he really resented most was having Juan see him in his present condition. The last time Juan had seen him, Horowitz had left the building in his usual buoyant manner, making some innocuous comment about the weather and turning the corner to head down to Columbus Avenue to get the few groceries he needed for the next few days. When Hannah was alive, he never had to bother about such things. Since she was gone, and he was not home during the day, he could not order food and have it delivered. Instead he would fetch it for himself. Besides, in person, he could shop more economically. Not that he had to count pennies. But it annoyed him to overpay. It only encouraged inflation.

So, that day, he jauntily strolled out of the building on his way to Columbus Avneue. The last time Juan the doorman had seen him, he was healthy, vigorous Samuel Horowitz. Now Juan would see a sick, frail Samuel Horowitz, who could not even walk from the ambulette to the elevator but had to be carried down the three steps like an infant in a baby carriage. Damn it, why couldn't Marvin have arranged to bring him home when Juan was off duty or on his lunch hour? Why did Marvin force him to endure this indignity?

Ah, but there was Juan now, smiling, and seeming so friendly, helpful, and delighted to see him.

"Mr. Horwitz!" Juan exclaimed warmly in his heavy accent.

Horwitz, Sam commented to himself, after two and a half years you would think Juan could learn his name. There are two *o*'s in Horowitz. But then it had taken Juan months even to master Horwitz. And damn it, stop smiling! Sam fumed to himself.

When the driver of the ambulette volunteered to assist Marvin with the wheelchair, Juan would not hear of it. He grasped one wheel of the chair. Marvin took the other wheel and together they carried Samuel Horowitz down the three steps into the lobby of the building.

34

Another crisis of confrontation, Sam Horowitz suddenly realized. Angelo, the elevator man. A Puerto Rican. What had happened to elevator men named Pete and Eddie? In the old days, doormen and elevator men were all Irish, pleasant, correct, and knew their place. Now the Juans and Angelos were so damned obvious in their phony warmth you would think they wanted to be adopted. When all the while they hated their jobs, the tenants, the whole country, and the system.

He resented bitterly appearing diminished or pitiful in their eyes. He wanted to be the Sam Horowitz of only four weeks ago, whole, unwounded, jaunty, self-sufficient.

He felt himself perspiring freely. Another reminder of his new condition. These days mere thoughts could bring on the same flood of perspiration that activity used to. He would be glad to be out of Juan's hands, past Angelo, and back in the privacy of his apartment.

His present deficiencies would seem more bearable if he were free of the staring, commiseration, and pity of other people. Most of all he wanted to be alone. Soon he would be. That was the thought that enabled him to endure Juan's insistence on helping with the wheelchair right into the apartment. When Marvin offered Juan a tip, the man refused.

"Not for somethin' like this," Juan said, as if it were a labor of friendship and affection.

He's faking, Sam Horowitz thought bitterly. He's faking because he can see me as the source of lots of big tips from now on. He thinks I'm a helpless invalid. That I'll be dependent on him from now on. For my newspaper. My mail.

Finally, Juan was gone. Samuel Horowitz was free to look about the apartment he had inhabited for twenty-nine years. Though it had only been four weeks since he had left, it seemed like many months, even longer.

35

Instead of feeling relieved, he was depressed.

"Pa . . ." Marvin began, with a rising inflection which made it quite clear that this was the preamble to a serious discussion.

Horowitz thought, He better not lay down the law to me. I've seen it too many times. A parent grows old or sick and right away his children start to treat him as if he were an idiot, incapable of making his own decisions. Marvin, he silently warned, you better watch your step. If you start telling me what you and your sister decided to do with me, I'll throw you out!

Instead of voicing his threats, Horowitz replied with a barely indulgent, "Yes, Marvin?"

"We talked it over and for the time being . . ."

"Who talked it over?" Horowitz demanded.

"Mona and I, who else?"

He said it, Horowitz thought to himself, he said those terrible words. Mona and I. But aloud, Horowitz said, a bit too sweetly, "Yes, and what did you and Mona talk over?"

"Well, we think this apartment is too big for you now. You don't need a dining room. Or such a large living room. But for the time being you'll be better off here in a familiar place. So we'll let moving go till later."

Thank you, thank you very kindly, my dear children, Sam Horowitz observed to himself. Aloud he said, "And?"

Puzzled, Marvin responded, "And? And what?"

"When any conversation starts off like that, there's got to be more. What else did you and Mona 'talk over'?"

"You're going to need a woman," Marvin said.

"That's very thoughtful. I would like a nice *zoftik* twenty-two-year-old blonde," Horowitz taunted. "Your mother could tell you that I always liked a woman with a little flesh on her bones. Lately, the new type woman, so skinny with hips barely wide enough to hold up their jeans, they're not women at all."

"Dad, be serious!"

"I am serious. You call them women? In my day . . ." There was that unfortunate phrase again. "Okay, I'll be serious."

"After talking to the doctors, Mona and I decided that what you need is a woman who has experience both as a practical nurse and a maid. A woman who can help with your physical therapy yet won't mind doing housework, preparing your meals, things like that."

"So?" Horowitz asked belligerently.

"So," Marvin ventured, "Mona and I decided to look for such a woman. They're not easy to find. I had to call dozens of nurses' registries before I found one who, for personal reasons, wanted this kind of job."

"I see," Horowitz said. "And what's wrong with Bernadine? She worked for your mother eleven years and then for me ever since your mother died!"

"Bernadine is a very competent cleaning woman," Marvin granted.

"She doesn't cook so bad when I ask her to!" Horowitz defended.

"But Bernadine doesn't know anything about physical therapy," Marvin explained.

"And you found a woman who does?"

"A very fine woman. Capable. Good references. With hospital experience."

Horowitz did not respond at once. Finally he asked, "What's her name, this gem of a woman who has all the qualifications of an experienced saver of human life?"

"Dad, it won't help if you start off resenting her," Marvin advised.

"Okay. So I'll start off by loving her. What's her name so I can write her love letters," Horowitz grumbled.

"Harriet Washington," Marvin said.

Resentful of being saddled with a stranger, a woman

37

whom he had no voice in choosing, Horowitz improvised sarcastically, "Dear Harriet Washington, I love you! I have never seen you, but if Mona and Marvin love you, I love you. No, that's too bold for a first letter. Why not, Dear Miss Washington . . . is she married or not?"

"She's a widow," Marvin replied.

"*Ho-ho-ho!* Save me from widows! I had enough of them in the months right after your mother died."

"When you see her it will become quite obvious that she has no designs on you. She is a widow, a mother, a grandmother, and she has other things on her mind than marrying a man like you."

"Okay," Horowitz accepted. "As long as we get that clear. Now then, Dear *Mrs.* Washington, I . . ." He paused suddenly, the bitter sarcasm went out of his voice as a fresh and more disturbing thought occurred to him. "Washington. Washington. That's not a common name. She's not related to . . . no she couldn't be. Hey, wait a minute, *boychick!* Washington *is* a common name. In certain places."

"What do you mean?"

"Washington is a very common name among colored people. Tell me, she's a *shvartzer?*"

"Yes."

Horowitz exploded, "I don't want her in this house!"

"But, Pa, Bernadine is black, too."

"Bernadine is different. She's a fine, warm human being. Bernadine you can trust. You don't have to count the silverware when she leaves at the end of the day. I don't want any black strangers in my house! That's final!"

"Pa . . ."

"Don't 'Pa' me. And don't argue with me! I don't know what arrangement you made with her, but pay her off! I don't want her here! Clear?"

"Pa . . ."

"One more 'Pa' and I'll throw you out, too!" Horowitz said, beginning to spin his chair around to present his back to his son.

"Pa . . . please, keep your voice down."

"I will not keep my voice down!" Horowitz shouted. "I will yell it from the housetops."

Addressing the front door, Samuel Horowitz called out, "Mrs. Washington, don't you dare come here! Not in my house! I don't care if you are a practical nurse. I don't even care if you are a brain surgeon. I don't want any black stranger in my house! I have twenty-two stitches in my face because of black strangers. I don't want to see one more black stranger as long as I live!"

"Pa, please," Marvin pleaded desperately.

"And you get out. Now!"

Horowitz swung his chair about so that he stared at the wall to show his son how completely cut off from him he wished to be.

At that moment, Samuel Horowitz heard a different voice. A woman's voice. It was soft, but quite firm. And a bit angry.

"Mr. Hammond, may I talk to you?" the voice asked.

Out of sheer embarrassment, Marvin did not answer at once. Slowly, and with great effort, Samuel Horowitz turned his wheelchair about. Standing in the archway that led to his bedroom he saw a small, mature black woman. Her shiny ebony hair was braided and wound about her head like a glistening tiara. Her face was neatly featured behind silver-rimmed glasses. She was compactly built, which belied her age. She was attired in a white nurse's uniform and she carried a fresh pillow case in her hand, betraying that she had been making up the bed all the while Horowitz had been arguing with his son.

Horowitz cast a quick glance at her, too embarrassed to take a long look. She stared at him, not angrily, but almost full of pity. He resented that so much that he turned away again.

"Mr. Hammond?" the woman repeated.

"Yes, of course," Marvin Hammond said. With a glare toward his father, he pointed the way toward the dining room where he and the woman could talk privately.

Meanwhile, Samuel Horowitz, who had pretended anger to cover his embarrassment, tried to overhear what they were saying. When he could not, he attempted to wheel himself closer. But he had maneuvered himself into an awkward position, his chair had one wheel on the foyer carpet, one wheel off.

"I didn't know you were already here," Marvin was saying by way of apology. "I thought I'd talk with him before you arrived."

"You had no right to do that," Mrs. Washington said.

"I apologize," Marvin tried to ameliorate the unhappy situation.

"I mean you had no right to do that to *him*," she responded. "This should have been explained to him before today. You shouldn't have thrown it at him so suddenly."

"I'm sorry."

"Now, if it's going to cause a problem, I'll tidy up the place, give him his lunch, and leave. Or if it would help, I'll stay a day or two until you can find a replacement. Some white woman. He'd feel better."

"It won't be easy to find a woman equipped for this particular job, white or black," Marvin explained. "I know. I had one secretary in our New York office do nothing but call registries for a whole week."

"Well, I don't know what to do," she said.

"Give it a try, please?" Marvin begged.

"That depends more on him than on me," she pointed out.

"I'll talk to him," Marvin said.

40

"Okay. But I have to know now. I have another offer and I have to give them my answer this evening."

Marvin Hammond wheeled his father into the living room, despite Horowitz's protest that he was quite capable of doing it himself. Marvin wheeled him close to the window that faced east. He raised the window shade to allow the mid-morning sun to stream into the room and at the same time give access to an extravagant view of Central Park that had always been one of Horowitz's great pleasures.

"For that view alone it is a delight to live on the West Side," Horowitz had always said. That was before he had been mugged. On the West Side.

Despite the warm sun and the pleasant view of the park, which was rich and green again after an unusually punishing winter and a late spring, Horowitz felt no more disposed to listen with any degree of reasonableness. When Marvin tried to make eye contact with him, Horowitz turned his head to stare out the window and avoid him.

"Pa, this time you have to listen to me."

"I'm listening," Horowitz declared impatiently, giving every evidence that he did not intend to be convinced.

"The situation is more serious than you think."

"How do you know how serious I think the situation is?" Horowitz demanded, still staring out at the green park below. "I don't know why I can't still have Bernadine. She's practically a member of the family. I like her. She likes me. We get along fine. I don't want any stranger in this house!"

He realized he was raising his voice again. So he reached out with his good right hand, seized Marvin by the coat and drew him close so he could whisper. "Are you going to give that woman in there, that stranger, a set of keys to this apartment? She'll come in some night and

41

rob me blind. You can't trust them. Bernadine, I trust."

"Pa . . ."

"Again with the 'Pa'?"

"You need physical therapy."

"I'll get that at the hospital. They said to come back once a week. So I'll go back once a week."

"You need therapy every day. Here. At home. She can do that. You need someone to keep the place clean. To make your meals."

"We eat too much!" Horowitz protested. "A whole civilization based on eating. I only need a little Sanka in the morning. And one meal in the evening. Who needs lunch? Not me!"

"Pa, you need three balanced meals a day. You need physical therapy. You need to be looked after by a competent person. Now, Mona and I agreed . . ."

"Ho-ho-ho," Horowitz exclaimed sadly at the mention of his daughter's name. "So what did the pride of San Diego agree?"

"If you can't get the care you need at home, and if you refuse to go out and stay with her . . ."

Horowitz interrupted, "Parents take care of children. Children are not supposed to take care of parents."

"Pa, will you listen to me and stop arguing?"

"Who's arguing? I am only pointing out certain facts," Horowitz said.

"There is only one fact of importance now. Based on what the doctors told me, Mona and I decided that if you won't agree to this arrangement, we will have to put you in a nursing home."

"*You* will put *me* in a nursing home?" Horowitz scoffed. "If it were not so insulting I would laugh. A nursing home. I think I *will* laugh." He made an attempt at sarcastic laughter, which sounded just hollow enough to betray that deep down he realized the possibility of such a fate. "I'll go back to the hospital first! Mrs.

Copeland will take care of me there. A fine woman. Even though she is Irish."

"They won't take you back. You're not sick enough to occupy a hospital bed. You need therapy. You need activity. You need to resume a more normal life."

"Some normal life. In a nursing home," Horowitz demeaned.

"You're not giving us any choice," Marvin pointed out.

"And what about giving *me* a choice?"

"We are."

"Some choice. A nursing home. Or Martha Washington."

"Her name isn't Martha," Marvin corrected.

"What difference does it make?"

"Pa, we don't want to do anything to make you unhappy. But we have to follow Dr. Tannenbaum's orders."

"I'll get another doctor!"

"The orders will still be the same."

"A nursing home," Horowitz considered. "I never thought in my whole life that would happen to me. I'd rather be dead."

"Pa, dying is easy. Living takes a little effort."

"Ho-ho-ho! A whole philosopher suddenly. The Talmud according to Reb Marvin. Oh, forgive me, my dear son, you don't like to be reminded. Marvin Hammond, philosopher!" Horowitz scoffed.

"Pa, you're not facing the situation."

"I am facing the situation," Horowitz protested. "But I don't like it."

Once he had softened sufficiently to admit that, Marvin continued. "Pa, one of the things I've always admired about you is your sense of independence. It was no great trick for me to become a partner in an important law firm. Because you handed me my education on a silver platter. But you don't know how many times I've asked myself, if

I came over here, a refugee kid, a foreigner, with no money, no advantages, would I have had the guts and the ability to eventually set up my own business and make a success of it?"

Making a pretense at modesty, Samuel Horowitz protested, "IBM I wasn't."

"But you did it by yourself. And it was yours. A free, independent spirit at work in a free economy. And you made it. On your own. I've always admired that. But changes do occur. It happens to every human being, if he lives long enough. There comes a time when he can't be independent any longer. He needs help. There's no shame in admitting it or accepting it," Marvin pleaded.

"Believe me," Horowitz began with great determination, "if I had my strength back in my arm and my leg . . ."

"Pa, that's the point, you don't have it back. You have to accept that."

Horowitz was silent for a moment before he asked, "Marvin, what did they say? Really say? The doctors."

"Exactly what they said to you. I told them, my father is a tough man. You can tell him the truth without any nice little lies. Give it to him straight. He can take it."

"Thank you, Marvin, I appreciate that. So what they said to me is true? I can get better. Maybe not all better, but a lot better."

"Right!" Marvin said. "But you'll need help until you do."

"Or else a nursing home?" Horowitz contemplated sadly.

"It's the only alternative," Marvin said, a bit more firmly now. "Of course, there's always Mona's home."

"Oh, yes, Mona, the Queen Esther of San Diego," Horowitz dismissed that possibility.

"Pa, what do you say?"

"I won't do it!" Horowitz rebelled at the last moment.

44

"I'm a mature individual. In full possession of my faculties. I won't be put away!"

"Pa, you should know that if forced to I can get a court order," Marvin pointed out, without any attempt to minimize the possibility.

"I'll get a lawyer. I'll fight you!" Horowitz raised his voice in anger.

"Pa, how are you going to prove that you don't need a nursing home? By wheeling into the courtroom in this chair? No judge would rule in your favor under those circumstances. So the issue is clear. It's either this woman or a nursing home. Make up your mind."

Horowitz was silent for long moments. Then, "Why can't we find a different woman?"

"I told you, it's impossible to get one who's qualified and who'll take such a job. It's really a step down for her to do any housework."

"There must be another woman somewhere. . . ."

"We weren't able to find one."

"Besides she hates me," Horowitz declared.

"How do you know?"

"She must. After all," Horowitz confessed, "she heard what I said about her, about all blacks."

"She doesn't hate you," Marvin insisted.

"If she said things like that about me *I* would hate her."

"Pa, I've got to get back to Washington. I don't have all day," Marvin said. "If you don't say yes now I'll have to scrounge around for some nursing home that'll have room for you."

Horowitz considered bitterly. "All my life I promised myself I would not end up in an institution."

"And you don't have to," Marvin pointed out. "So?"

"So . . ." Horowitz contemplated. Then he asked, "You're sure she'll stay?"

"She said she would."

"She has good references?"

"The best."

"She's . . . she's not a bad-looking woman. I mean, from just the little I saw of her she seems *ballabatish*, decent, clean."

Marvin did not answer, forcing Horowitz to make his own decision.

Samuel Horowitz closed both his eyes. Then after a moment he opened his right eye and said, "Okay."

"Good!" Marvin was quite relieved. "Now I have to go. She has all the instructions, all the keys, she knows the stores you shop at."

Marvin was at the door when Horowitz called out, "One thing, Marvin."

Fearing a change of mind that would upset his plans, Marvin slowly turned to look the length of the living room toward his father. "Yes, Pa?"

"Bernadine," Horowitz said.

"What about Bernadine?"

"That's exactly what I want to know, what *about* Bernadine?" Horowitz demanded.

"I explained to her what you need now. She understood. I gave her four weeks' salary and let her go. I had to."

"Four weeks' salary?" Horowitz demanded. "A woman is with your mother eleven years, and with me three years after that and you gave her four weeks' salary? A woman her age, who won't be able to get another job easily, if at all? And you gave her four weeks' salary?"

"She'll have social security," Marvin countered.

"Social security you can put in your eye these days! I want that woman on a pension! You take it out of my money."

"Pa, you're not required . . ."

"Stop being a lawyer and become a human being for a change!" Horowitz exclaimed angrily. "Bernadine is to

46

have a pension. And if you don't want to arrange it, I will. So I'll leave a little less to my grandchildren, who are too damned rich anyhow!"

"Okay, okay, Pa," Marvin relented, "I'll arrange it."

"Thank you, Mr. Hammond, eminent counselor at law," Samuel Horowitz said to his son. "Now you can leave, congratulating yourself on having done a good day's work, badgering an old man into agreeing to something that he knows is going to wind up very, very badly. If you like, send me a bill for the excellent advice you have given me this fine day."

"Pa . . ." Marvin made one last effort to mollify him.

"One more 'Pa' and I'll change my mind!" Horowitz threatened.

Because he knew his father's propensity for sudden and perverse decisions, Marvin Hammond left at once.

Horowitz looked around the living room, dwelling on pieces of furniture, all of which Hannah had assembled so joyously in anticipation of long years of use.

He rolled himself to the large graceful breakfront of mellow wood and rubbed his fingers across it. Walnut, polished to a fine sheen. He stared at the sofa, of simple graceful line, covered in a brocade of gold and white, with comfortable down cushions that, when you sank into them, welcomed you. As did the velvet-covered pillows of the upholstered sidechairs.

In the corner, the hand-built bridge table, with its four gleaming wood-and-leather-upholstered armchairs, carved by an old Italian craftsman with a skill so rare these days. The gold-embossed red leather of the tabletop matched the leather of the chairs, adding a splash of bright contrasting color to the gold of the carpeting.

At that table, Horowitz and Phil Liebowitz had fought many a pinochle war in the old days. And when Liebowitz was away, or unavailable, Hannah and Horowitz had played pinochle there. Now, except for photographs of the grandchildren, taken when they were young, the table was abandoned, useless.

With great difficulty, Horowitz wheeled himself across the thick gold carpeting to the foyer, to refamiliarize himself with the rest of the old place. Actually, to him it seemed two places. The cozy comfortable apartment where he and Hannah had lived for so long. And the large empty place where he had lived alone these past three years.

He reached the bedroom and stared in, but only briefly, because that woman was in there, tidying up. He did not feel up to facing her. So he wheeled himself across the foyer and into the dining room. Across the polished floor he rolled and onto the rug. He stared about. Of all the rooms, this was, to him, the least familiar. He had not eaten a meal at this large, carved, polished, dark wood table since the week of Hannah's funeral.

He wheeled himself across the carpet back onto the exposed wood floor and to the door of the kitchen. There he had trouble propelling his chair over the doorsill. But once over it, he found the kitchen linoleum as easy to traverse as the hospital corridor had been.

The refrigerator was humming efficiently. The white Formica counters which Hannah had had installed were gleaming and clean as she herself always insisted on.

He thought warmly, Bernadine had been diligent in his long absence. Or was this the work of that woman, what was her name? In his stubborn hostility to accepting her, he had already obliterated her name. He preferred to credit Bernadine with the gleaming cleanliness of the kitchen floor, the gas range, the counters, and the small table at which he'd had his morning fruit juice and instant Sanka these past three years.

He wheeled himself back into the living room, thinking, Large, empty, lonely as it is, still it is at least home.

48

He stared out at the park, the playgrounds, the children, the joggers, the buildings across on Fifth Avenue and beyond. Everything seemed the same. Only it no longer felt the same.

For it was Samuel Horowitz who had changed. He stared at his damaged left hand, tried to make a fist and failed. As far as he could force it, it was now only a claw that mocked him.

He stared down at the playground just inside the park, saw mothers there with their preschool-age children at play. He thought, That is the beginning of life, easy, carefree. I wonder, do they know the end of it?

He became aware of the woman once more, as she bustled from his bedroom toward the foyer. He called to her.

"What's your name again?"

She called back, "Mrs. Washington."

"I know that," he declared impatiently. "I mean your full name."

"Harriet Washington."

"Well, Harriet, I will tell you how it's going to be."

"*Mrs. Washington*, if you don't mind," she reproved firmly.

"What's wrong with Harriet?" he demanded, irritated.

"If you wish to address a maid by her first name and she permits it, that may be all right. But I am a nurse and my professional dignity demands that I be called Mrs. Washington!"

"Not *Ms.* Washington?" Horowitz taunted.

"I was married to a fine man named Horace Washington. I don't intend to forget it. Nor do I want anyone else to forget it. So it's *Mrs.* Washington!"

"Well, if that's what you want, okay, *Mrs.* Washington!"

49

Chapter Four

Samuel Horowitz knew that for the time being he would have to make his peace with the obstinate woman. The only question was how. He decided it would be best if he did not have to look into her reproachful face when he did it. So he remained in place, using the window as a convenient diversion as he called out, "Mrs. Washington?"

Evidently she had not heard him, so he called more loudly, "Mrs. Washington!"

When she did not respond, he exploded, "Damn that woman! Where is she?"

He heard her soft firm voice in almost a whisper, "Right here."

He half-turned his head to find her behind him. He realized he had not detected her footsteps on the thickly carpeted living room floor.

"You don't have to go tiptoeing around here. Or sneaking up on me. I don't like surprises!" he declared.

"What do you want me to do, wear bells on my shoes?" she asked sarcastically.

Horowitz slowly turned his wheelchair around to face her. He took a long look at her. The first really good look he had of this woman whom he had determined to banish from his life at the first opportunity.

"Tell me, Mrs. Washington," he began with a superfluous degree of courtesy that was actually demeaning, "what do you know about bells on shoes?"

"Well, Mr. Horowitz, as I understand it, there was once a famous rabbi, a . . . I forget the word . . ."

"*Tzaddik*," Horowitz supplied.

"That's right, he was one of those," she agreed. "It seems . . ."

Horowitz interrupted, "If you don't mind, when you are referring to a *tzaddik*, you don't say, 'He was one of those.' A *tzaddik* is a very special human being. Not 'one of those,' like you would say of . . . of a . . ." He fumbled for another word since the first one that came to his mind would have created a fresh crisis. "Of, say, a Puerto Rican. Of them you can say, 'He was one of those.'"

She knew exactly the example that had first crossed Horowitz's mind. As she stared at him, he knew that she knew. So he hastily continued. "A *tzaddik* is an unusually righteous man. Not only a scholar and a philosopher, but a great human being. With an enormous love for all of God's creatures, even the smallest."

"And the blackest?" she asked provocatively.

Horowitz changed the subject abruptly. "I asked you what you knew about bells on shoes!"

"Well, the way I heard it, this . . . this . . ."

"*Tzaddik*," Horowitz supplied, impatient to get the story over with.

"Yes, he felt so responsible for all God's creatures that he did not want to kill even the lowliest ant. Consequently, he had small bells affixed to his shoes so

51

when he walked the ants would be warned and could scurry out of the way."

"Hmm," Horowitz remarked in surprise. "Very interesting."

"I thought it was. That's why I remembered it."

"I meant, it's very interesting that you would pick up such a bit of obscure information," Horowitz said. "Tell me, where did you come across it?"

"For a time, before I studied nursing, I worked for the Rosengartens."

"Which Rosengartens?"

"Charles Rosengarten."

"Charles . . . Rosengarten. . . . No, didn't know him," Horowitz said. "And they talked like that at home? About such things?"

"Mister was president of a *schul* on West Seventy-ninth Street. So we had the rabbi to dinner very often. One night, at dessert time, I was bringing in the cake when I heard the Rabbi tell that story."

"Hmm!" Horowitz remarked, then granted condescendingly, "Interesting. But why are you telling me this? Did I ask you where you worked before? Or are you trying to tell me that some of your best employers were Jewish, to make your presence here more acceptable?"

"I told you that because you accused me of sneaking up on you," Mrs. Washington recalled.

Reminded, Horowitz responded with an "I see" that was intended to close the matter. "In the future, when I am sitting looking out the window, with my back to the room, don't come in without announcing yourself. That isn't too much to request, is it?"

"No," she granted, then asked, "Do you intend to spend much time looking out the window?"

"I will send you a written memorandum as to what I intend to do in the future," Horowitz replied. "Now do something useful around here. Like go fix my lunch."

"It's ready," she said, taking him by surprise.

"How could it be ready? I didn't even tell you what I want," Horowitz said, eager to find fault with everything the woman said or did.

"What would you like?"

"What I would like is hummingbirds' wings on toast. But my doctor said I can't have toast," Horowitz replied sarcastically. "What would I like . . ." he reprised resentfully. "They put me on some damned diet there in the hospital. I lost my taste for food altogether. And their food! Served on plastic dishes, to be eaten with plastic knives and forks. No wonder the food tastes like plastic!"

"So what would you like?" the black woman insisted.

"What I would like . . ." Horowitz began, "What I would really like is for . . . for . . ." He turned his head away.

"Mr. Horowitz?" she asked, gently.

He did not reply, for if he had, he knew he would begin to weep. He was silent, and she respected it. In his time he would tell her. He did.

"What I would like is for Hannah to be here, in the kitchen, making me one of the dishes she made so well. She knew exactly what I liked, and the way I liked it. No one else could duplicate her recipes. People have been in this house and raved about her food. She would give them the recipes. But they could never make it taste the same. Never. She had a genius for cooking. And a genius for people. People loved her . . . loved her. Sometimes I think they tolerated me just to be near her."

He found himself sniffling. He brushed the moistness from his eyes, excused his tears by remarking, "Mrs. Washington, you will find as you get older that your eyes tear up for no good reason. The faucets, or I guess they call them valves."

"Ducts?" she suggested.

"Yes, the ducts, they get . . . loose. . . . That's it, loose ducts."

"What about your lunch?"

"I don't care about lunch."

"It's ready, you might as well eat it. You're going to need your strength."

"How much strength does a man need to sit in a wheelchair?" he asked, turning the chair about slowly to indicate that he was starting out of the room.

When he reached the foyer and started to swerve left toward his bedroom, she called out, "No. It's set up in the dining room."

"Dining room?" Horowitz challenged. "I haven't eaten in the dining room since Hannah."

"From now on you will eat in the dining room," Mrs. Washington said.

"That's a lot of trouble to go to for just one person," he protested. "Besides there's no television in the dining room."

"You don't have to watch television in order to eat," she pointed out with firm authority.

"Maybe President Carter will be having a press conference. He has one every Monday and Thursday. He's the mid-afternoon Johnny Carson. Except he's on more often."

"You don't like President Carter?"

"I haven't liked any President since Roosevelt. And if you want to know the truth I wasn't crazy about him either. Now, what's for lunch?" he asked, rolling himself toward the dining room.

He was trying to pull himself up to the table but the arms of the chair prevented it. "You see," he said. "It won't work. This is no place to eat. I'd be better off having my food in the bedroom. Maybe in bed. That's it! A tray in bed."

She did not reply, but loosened the clamps on the arms

54

of his wheelchair and slid them back. "Try it now."

He rolled himself up flush to the table. Then he cast a resentful glance at her. "Wise guy!"

He stared at the table, needing to find fault with anything. "Hannah's best china? For a measly little lunch? She would turn over in her grave."

"Then we won't tell her," Mrs. Washington replied.

He glared up at her. She smiled. She had a warm smile. Bright, sparkling ebony eyes set in a glistening black face, white even teeth, and skin so smooth it seemed to have been hand rubbed like fine mahogany. He could not resist her smile.

"So where's lunch? You said it was ready," he demanded.

"Have your tomato juice," she said as she started for the kitchen.

"I don't like tomato juice. It gives me heartburn."

"Drink it. It's good for you."

"I don't want to be told by you or anyone what's good for me!" he exploded. "I do not like tomato juice. I have never liked tomato juice! I will never drink tomato juice!" he exploded.

"Your son said your wife served it all the time," she replied.

"Oh, that," Horowitz said sheepishly. "Well, Hannah's tomato juice was different. She did something to it, added something. Nobody ever served tomato juice like Hannah's."

"I know," Mrs. Washington replied. Horowitz could not tell from the look in her eyes if she were agreeing with him or being sarcastic.

"Well," he reconsidered. "This one time I'll drink tomato juice! But never again! You hear?" he bellowed.

"Mr. Horowitz, everybody on the West Side could hear."

He glared at her, lifted the glass in his sound right

55

hand and took a sip, intending to hate it. He stopped, disbelieved his taste buds, then took another sip.

"You put something in here," he accused. "What?"

"A dash of lemon, a touch of anise."

"It's . . . it's not bad. In fact, it's . . ." he hated to make such a concession, "it's very much like Hannah's."

"It's exactly like Hannah's," Mrs. Washington corrected. "I found her recipe file when I was here yesterday."

"You were prowling around here yesterday?" he demanded indignantly.

"Don't worry, Bernadine was here to help me get acquainted with the place," she said, adding pointedly, "so you don't have to count the silverware."

Embarrassed by his earlier accusation, he demanded irritably, "Look, what's for lunch?"

Mrs. Washington went back to the kitchen and he heard her taking out plates and glasses.

"I thought you said lunch was ready!" he called out impatiently.

"And I thought you said you weren't hungry!" she called back with equal voice and combativeness.

"Well, as long as I'm here and there's no television, I might as well eat and get it over with!"

"In a moment," Mrs. Washington called back. "Oh, by the way, a man called this morning. Phil Liebowitz. Said he was a friend of yours. He wants to come by."

"So what did you say?" Horowitz asked defensively.

"That you would call back when you arrived."

"In the future, Mrs. Washington, if I am in need of a social secretary, I will hire one. Meantime, don't you go promising people I will call back! That's my business, I'll handle it!"

"Of course. Sorry," she replied from the kitchen.

"What do you think would happen if I called back?

Liebowitz would say, 'Come to the house for a little game of pinochle.' Because he likes to play pinochle? He's a lousy player. Always was. So why? Because he wants to see me this way. He wants to gloat. He's a vulture. A scavenger on other people's problems. His main enjoyment is going to funerals and making hospital visits. Next time he calls, don't answer!"

"Of course," Mrs. Washington said in such a way as to underscore his ridiculous command.

Self-conscious, he called back, "You said lunch would be ready in a moment. Some moment! A person could lose his appetite waiting so long!"

Finally the swinging door was pushed open. Mrs. Washington appeared carrying a large dish in one hand, a smaller, salad-size plate in the other. She set the large dish down before him. He glared at it, then raised his eyes to stare up at her. In a sarcastically sweet voice he asked, "*Mrs.* Washington, did someone tell you that I was a millionaire?"

"I never ask my employers for bank references," she replied. "Eat!"

"Steak?" he complained. "Steak for lunch? Am I made of money?"

As Horowitz had a habit of doing from time to time, he addressed the world at large. "The woman is crazy. Steak for lunch. Who ever heard of steak for lunch?"

He turned back to her, "*Mrs.* Washington, let me give you a little advice. If you are thinking to ingratiate yourself with me by such little tricks, you can forget it. I don't like you. I never will like you. The only reason I tolerate you here in my house is that if I didn't agree, my dear darling son, the eminent barrister Marvin Hammond, Esquire, and his equally renowned sister, the Purim Queen of San Diego, want to put me in an institution. Well, between a nursing home and you, you

57

are the lesser of two evils. But don't press your luck, as they say. Otherwise soon, a nursing home might look pretty good!"

She waited patiently through his entire tirade and then said simply, "Your steak is getting cold."

"No more steak! Do you hear me?"

"As clear as if you were right in this room," she remarked. "Now, eat!"

"And if I don't, what'll you do, call me honky?" he accused. But he did pick up his knife in his right hand and tried to pick up the fork in his left. He could not quite force his fingers to grip the fork securely. When he tried to pin down the steak, the fork slipped from his damaged hand and dropped to the carpeted floor.

"Sorry," he said.

She knelt down and retrieved the fork, wiping it carefully on her neat apron. She handed it back to him, seeking to place it in his left hand. Again, he could not grip it properly. He stared at his hand, at the fork, and then at her.

"I told you, Mrs. Washington, steak is not the right thing to serve at lunch. For lunch you serve something like canned salmon. Tuna fish. A sandwich, maybe. A simple dish that can be eaten without a knife and fork. A fork, maybe," he conceded, "but that's all. Something a man can do with one hand. So you can take this steak away and throw it out. Or, if you want, eat it yourself. Is that what you had in mind all along? I wouldn't be able to eat it, so I would give it to you? Is that it? Well, I'm on to your game. No, don't take it away! Leave it right here! You cut it! You feed it to me!"

She turned abruptly and went back to the kitchen.

"I said, cut it!" he called after her.

When she returned she carried a second fork. This one had a thick foam rubber pad wrapped around the handle, held in place with colorless Scotch tape.

"Try this," she said, holding out the fork to him.

Reluctantly, he reached out with his left hand. He slowly closed his fingers around the thick handle. This time he was able to grasp it firmly. He inserted it into the small filet on his plate. With the padded fork he was able to hold the steak securely in place while he cut it with the knife in his right hand.

He cut off a bite-size piece, basted it in the juice, and with his right hand brought it to his mouth and began to chew. He repeated the entire maneuver several times, each time a bit more easily than the time before. He did not speak until he was halfway through the small filet.

Needing something to criticize, he said, "I like my steak a little better done."

"I have to get used to your broiler," she explained.

"Don't bother. Steak is too expensive and too much trouble to eat," he said, proceeding to eat it bite by bite until he had consumed it all. "We won't have steak anymore!"

"Okay," she said simply. "Now eat your salad."

"I don't like salad," he said.

"Eat it anyhow. It's good for you."

He was about to protest, when she anticipated him. "From what I could find in Hannah's file, she served salad very often."

She cleared the steak plate and shoved his salad squarely before him. He would not eat it until she left the room. By the time she returned, he had finished it.

He still grasped the padded fork, but this time in his right hand.

"You did this on purpose," he accused.

"Did what?"

"Served me steak. So you could point out that I am a cripple! I don't need anyone to tell me that! I never want to see this fork again! Do you hear me? Never!"

He hurled the fork across the room. It hit the far wall

and dropped to the carpeted floor. He wheeled his chair about to confront her.

"I can see what's in your mind! You have a plan. To prove that I am a cripple. To prove that you are better than I am. Or do you want to prove that you are indispensable around here? Well, I don't need you! I don't need anyone! And most of all I don't need to be reminded that I . . . that I can't . . ."

He hesitated before he could admit, ". . . that I can't do the things I used to do. . . ."

Slowly he turned the chair in the direction of the door. He tried to readjust the arms to their usual length but could not. Despite that he rolled himself out of the room, trying to maintain an air of dignity.

He rolled himself to his bedroom, to the window that looked over the park. He brought his right hand to his face to cover his eyes, and he wept. He hoped desperately that that intrusive woman would not come in and find him that way. He had suffered enough indignities in her presence in the brief time he had known her.

He need not have worried about being caught crying, for Harriet Washington was in the kitchen on the phone.

"Dr. Tannenbaum?" she requested. "Mrs. Washington, Mr. Horowitz's nurse."

She waited briefly and soon the doctor came on the line.

"Yes, Mrs. Washington, how did it go?"

"He resisted every step of the way. Especially the steak. He does not want to be reminded that his left hand is damaged."

"How did he handle the padded fork?"

"Pretty well. But he resents it."

"Still, it was a good idea you had, to feed him only those dishes that require the use of both hands," the doctor said.

"It's worked before," Mrs. Washington said. "Tomorrow, lamb chops."

"Good!" Dr. Tannenbaum encouraged. "And his general attitude?"

"Hostile, resistant," she reported. "He doesn't want even his close friends to see him this way. He's a man with a great deal of pride."

"His son warned me," the doctor said. "Well, pride can be helpful only if it gives him the will to recover. If it doesn't, it can be crippling, even fatal."

"I've seen it happen," Mrs. Washington recalled from sad personal experience with Horace. "They either want to live just as they lived before. Or else they'd rather be dead."

"Let's hope that doesn't happen in this case," Tannenbaum tried to encourage her.

"Yes," she agreed but without much hope.

"It'll be up to you," the doctor said.

"I know. But he doesn't want anyone to like him and doesn't want to like anyone. I guess the last person he loved was his wife."

"Well, she can't help him now," the doctor warned.

Chapter Five

Mrs. Washington had served his dinner, cleared the table, done the dishes, and seen to it that he was safely in bed for the night.

She had been careful to point out, "If you have to get up during the night, put the light on. And be very careful with your quad cane. This carpet's a little too high-piled for absolute safety."

"Thank you, Mrs. Washington," Horowitz replied sarcastically. "This carpet was personally selected by Hannah. It was one of the last things she did. Redecorate this apartment. I am sure she would not pick out a carpet that was dangerous to my life."

Mrs. Washington shrugged, said a soft, "Good night, Mr. Horowitz," and departed, feeling quite tired after a day more enervating because of friction than the amount of work she had been called on to do. She wondered, Were the advantages the job offered sufficient to recompense her for its obvious difficulties?

Alone, in his own bed, for the first time since he had suffered the double indignity of the mugging and the insult to his brain, Samuel Horowitz settled down, determined to enjoy his privacy. With his right hand he reached for the remote-control instrument of his television set. One of Hannah's last extravagances, a remote-control TV set.

Secretly he resented it, believing that all the troubles of the human race could be traced to soft living. Kids these days, especially his own grandchildren, needed deprivation. A kid should know what it was to go hungry every once in a while. Should be forced to work, for money, before they were graduated from high school. Should learn to walk a little further than from the door to the driveway.

If kids had to do that they would not have time for drugs and sex and drinking and all the other things one read about.

If people did not appreciate a miracle like television enough to cross a room to turn it on or off or change the channels, then they did not deserve to have it. Civilization and the whole human race was going to hell out of sheer softness.

Nevertheless, he had to grant that for a sick man who had suffered a disabling injury, a remote-control television set was not only a convenience but a necessity. So he turned it on with a press of the button, blessing Hannah for having been so considerate as to anticipate his present condition.

The first program did not intrigue him. The police were in search of a killer. In the second program a killer was in search of someone to kill. The third channel offered a family comedy about a black family. He watched that for a while but only to mobilize his resentment against that fresh Mrs. Washington.

He wondered how many people in that studio audience who howled with laughter had been mugged and slashed by black hoodlums. They wouldn't laugh if they had been. He flicked to another channel. There was a basketball game. Two teams in which he had no interest, one in red uniforms, one in blue, were chasing a ball up and down the court. That, he decided as he flicked the dial, was not an occupation for grown-up men. Yet he read in the papers that they got paid hundreds of thousands of dollars a year to do it. And most of them were black. And still they kept protesting about lack of opportunity.

You can't do enough for them, he lamented silently, blacks are not only greedy but ravenous. Give them a finger, they want a hand. Give them a hand, and good-bye, Charlie.

Which reminded him, he had to find out what Marvin had agreed to pay that Mrs. Washington. Probably an arm and a leg.

Which, in turn, reminded him that it was because of his arm and his leg that she was here at all. Oh, for the old days of Bernadine! If he were able he would kick out that overbearing, obnoxious Mrs. Washington and restore Bernadine to her rightful place in the Horowitz household.

With that he switched from the basketball game and became involved in an educational program having to do with teenage pregnancy, a subject he had not thought about since Mona married Abraham Feldstein, who now calls himself Albert Fields. He remembered the night he and Hannah returned from the wedding at the St. Regis. A small but very expensive wedding. As he removed the studs from his dress shirt, he remembered thinking, up till tonight Mona's getting pregnant had been his worry; from now on he would worry if she didn't become pregnant. Let her be fruitful and multiply, as it said in the Bible, now that she was properly married. Although the Bible did not mention names like Bruce and Candy.

He must have drifted off, because he woke to a test pattern and an annoying hum. He clicked off the set and fell back asleep.

The next thing Horowitz knew, the sound of great activity caused him to open his eyes. It was morning. He listened to the bustle of energetic cleaning, of furniture being moved about, while a vacuum cleaner maintained a steady drone. His first reaction was one of relief. It sounded like Bernadine. Then he realized it couldn't be. It must be that Washington woman. Immediately he resented that she had wakened him with her noisy intrusive sounds. Surely, it was possible to clean without making such a racket so early.

His fury mounted until he glanced at the bedside clock. Nine twenty-two. He had not slept this late in years.

As he had been instructed in the hospital, he carefully rolled himself onto his side. Then he raised himself to a sitting position, trying to maintain his balance. It was a point the therapist in the hospital had made quite often. Balance on sitting, balance on standing. He had to work at those. He tried to raise himself from the bed, while at the same time reaching for his quad cane, that metal contraption that permitted him brief spans of walking.

For a moment he hung suspended between bed and quad, and then, thankfully, was able to grasp the handle of the cane. He breathed a sigh of relief. For he would hate being forced to cry out for help, not to that woman. Slowly, with halting steps, dragging his left foot in which the dorsiflex action had not been restored, he made his way from the bedroom to the bathroom. Fortunately, he thought, the bedroom and bath are closed off from the rest of the apartment so he could perform his private functions in private. A man had to retain his dignity. His self-respect. Especially with that woman who sought every opportunity to humiliate him.

His luck lasted only until he tried to shave himself. In the hospital there was a barber who made rounds every morning. Now Horowitz had to resume shaving on his own. He already had more than a day's growth of white bristly beard. He wet his face, squeezed some cream from the tube by pressing his right thumb against it, though they had instructed him to use his left hand for such functions whenever possible.

He overdid the pressure, sending a white unruly snake of shaving cream across the washbasin and onto the mirror. He had to wipe it all away, messily, and start again. More cautious this time, he pressed delicately and laid a decent amount onto the fingers of his left hand. Now he had the impossible job of rubbing it into his face. He would have been wiser, he realized, to have squeezed with his left thumb and applied the stuff with his right hand.

Awkwardly he borrowed some of the cream from his thickly coated left cheek and applied it to his right.

The first few strokes of the razor against his right cheek told him that the blade was old and dull. Why not? After all, he had not used it in over a month, and probably had used it a time or two before that. Fortunately, he had some fresh blades. Carefully he picked up the blade cartridge in his right hand and tried to pick up the razor in his left. But the handle of the razor was too thin to grasp, thinner even than the unpadded fork he had tried to handle yesterday. So he switched hands, taking up the razor with his right hand and the cartridge with his left. He managed, holding it by its broad flat bottom, but when he brought razor to cartridge, he discovered that he could not sufficiently control his left thumb to slide out a fresh blade.

He tried several times. But his left thumb stubbornly refused to follow the instructions of his brain. Finally in a burst of outrage and defeat he called angrily, "Mrs. Washington!"

66

From behind closed doors, and over the noise of the vacuum cleaner, she heard him. It was impossible not to, for it was the trumpeting outrage of a wounded elephant.

The door of the bathroom opened swiftly.

"What's wrong? Did you fall. . . .?" She was quite relieved when she realized that he was on his feet, though he held desperately to the edge of the washbasin to sustain his balance. Now, more quietly, she asked, "Is there something wrong, Mr. Horowitz?"

To cover his own insufficiency, and because staring at the scar on his face in the mirror had reawakened all his hostilities, he mocked bitterly, "'Is there something wrong, Mr. Horowitz?' Why, of course not. Look at me. A handsome figure of a man. All right, a little beard. But maybe that's good. To cover up the scar your fine young men put there. Look at it. Take a good look! See that? Twenty-two stitches!"

Mrs. Washington stared, not at his wound, but into his eyes. "I'm sorry," she said simply.

"That's a very convenient word. You wipe out everything with one 'sorry.' I'll have this for the rest of my life."

"If there were anything I could do . . ." she started to explain.

"Yes, there is something you can do! You can bring up your young savages to have respect for human life, for human dignity!" Horowitz raged. He faced away from her, raising his left hand to the wound, but not quite managing to reach it. "Look, I think that you and I are not going to get along. I think I should find someone else. Perhaps a white woman. You could find another job, I'm sure. You're a practical nurse, my Marvin said. Well, there's always a shortage of nurses. You wouldn't have any trouble. So, after today . . ." He made no effort to complete the thought, nor did he have to.

"I'd rather stay on," she said simply.

"Why? To do penance for what your savages did to

me? What are you, one of those born-again Christians? You're here to do good deeds? Like Jimmy Carter? He is determined to do good deeds even if he wrecks the country and the whole world. I'd rather you left."

"I can't," she said firmly.

"Why not? There must be other jobs."

"There are."

"So?" he demanded as if inevitable logic were on his side.

"This job has special inducements for me. And because it does, I am willing to do the work of a housemaid, a cook, a nurse, a physical therapist, and a whipping boy for a mean, nasty old man who is trying to blame everybody but himself for his present condition."

Having delivered herself of that, Harriet Washington stood staunchly staring at Samuel Horowitz.

"If that isn't the best reason in the world for quitting I don't know what is," Horowitz grumbled.

"I will explain it to you so you *will* know," Harriet Washington said deliberately but with a touch of impatience in her voice, for she never liked to discuss her private affairs with others. "I have a daughter. Who has two children. Very fine children, I might add, before you make any of your remarks. The boy is twelve, the girl eight. They are in the process of growing up, of going to school, of needing someone to look after them."

"So I am inviting you to go look after them," Horowitz pointed out.

"During the day my daughter looks after them. But in the evening she works as night supervisor of nurses in a hospital. Someone has to be with those children. To make sure they do their homework. To see that they are not out on the streets. To see that they grow up well. That they do not become 'savages,' Mr. Horowitz. Do I make myself clear?"

"So this job . . ." he began.

"Yes," she resumed command. "This job fits ideally

68

into that situation. It provides me with a living. And it permits me to be home before my daughter leaves for her work."

"Two grandchildren . . ." Horowitz mused. "You don't look old enough to be a grandmother."

"I'm old enough," she said sadly. "Old enough."

"How old?" he asked.

"Sixty-one."

"No!"

"Yes."

A new thought assailed Horowitz. "Tell me, in what you said about your daughter, there was no mention of any husband. Did she . . ."

"She's a widow!" Harriet Washington interrupted sharply.

"I see," Horowitz said, embarrassed that she had read his mind so accurately. "And her husband?"

"He was killed. Shot."

"Oh?" Horowitz said, not daring to give any further hint as to what he suspected.

"Killed by one of the 'savages.' He was answering a 911 to stop a holdup in a supermarket on Columbus Avenue."

"Oh, I'm sorry," Horowitz said.

"So I have taken this job because it fits our family's needs. And I don't intend to be driven out by anybody. Certainly not by you. Because you need me, as much as I need this job. Now you can make it uncomfortable for me. You can insult me, berate me, get angry, shout, yell, rant, and rave. But I am here for the duration! So get used to me!"

"You think you're a pretty tough cookie," Horowitz tried to mock.

"I *know* I'm a tough cookie," Harriet Washington corrected. "Now what did you want?"

"I didn't want anything!"

"What was that outcry before? Vocal exercises you do

every morning to get in shape for shouting the rest of the day?" she asked acerbically. "I haven't heard such an outcry since Bobby Thompson hit that home run off Branca to win the National League pennant."

"You follow baseball?" Horowitz asked, encouraged.

"Ever since Jackie Robinson, I follow baseball," she confessed. "I don't particularly like it, but I follow it."

"I know what you mean," Horowitz said. "I was a Giant fan all during the time they had Sid Gordon. He was the only Jew with a good batting average since Hank Greenberg. You ever heard of Hank Greenberg?"

"Detroit Tigers. First base."

"Right!" Then Horowitz asked, "You said you only became interested in baseball since Jackie Robinson."

"On weekends Mr. Rosengarten wouldn't eat lunch without listening to the ballgame on the radio."

"I see."

Now that they had found some community of interest, tenuous as it was, she felt free to ask gently, "You were calling . . . what was wrong?"

Much as it pained him to acknowledge needing help over such a simple matter, Horowitz admitted, "I . . . I need a fresh blade in my razor. Do you know how to do that?"

"Mr. Washington always used to use a blade razor," she said, as she inserted the fresh blade.

Before she handed the razor back to him, she asked, "Are you going to insist on shaving yourself this way?"

"Don't touch me!" he protested. "I have shaved myself for the past fifty-five years, and I can shave myself for the next fifty-five!" Then he reconsidered, "Well, maybe not fifty-five, but for the rest of my life. I have never been shaved by a woman and I don't want to start now, thank you!"

"That's not what I meant," she started to explain.

"So you will write me a letter and explain what you meant. Right now, I have to shave," he said, taking the razor in his right hand and about to make the first stroke across his face, which had by now become caked with the drying soap.

"There's another way," she suggested.

"Of course, I could grow a beard," he countered.

"Why can't you use the razor your son bought for you?"

"What razor?"

"When we were going over the things you would need, I suggested an electric razor. Most men in your condition use one. It's much easier."

"First, I am not in any 'condition.' Second, with the energy shortage I am not going to use an electric razor. And third, I don't like the idea of you telling my son what I should do. I will tell my son what I should do. Besides, shaving with an electric shaver is not shaving. It is getting a close massage. If you want to shave, you need a blade, a sharp blade. Now, do me the extreme honor and favor of getting out so I can do that."

"Okay," she said regretfully, resigned to his stubbornness.

She was gone, thanks God. He could now apply himself to the luxury of a slow, meticulous shave. He tried to draw the razor across his face but realized that in the old days his habit had been to hold his cheek taut with his left hand while applying the razor with his right. Now he could no longer use his left hand in that manner. At first he blamed his difficulty on the caked cream. So he washed his face clean and began again, a fresh squeeze of cream applied to his wet face. He used the razor again. When he was done, he examined his face in the mirror. He could still see patches of white stubble. It had not been his most successful shave.

As he thoughtfully rubbed his hand over his cheek, it felt even more quickly than it looked. He had to seriously consider his next move. He rinsed the razor under the faucet, tried, not too effectively, to dry it and replace it in its ancient case. Then he reached out to grasp his quad walker and slowly made his way out into the living room. By the time he arrived there he was breathless and perspiring. He had to admit the thick carpet did prove a hindrance to walking.

Mrs. Washington was in the living room, just finishing dusting the wood pieces there. She polished them with the same care that Hannah had always lavished on them on nights after company had gone. Mrs. Washington was either unaware of his presence or pretended that she was.

He had to initiate the conversation. It was not easy.

"Uh . . ." he began, "Mrs. Washington, do you know what conviction is?"

"You mean when someone is found guilty?" she asked, obviously puzzled at such a total non sequitur.

"That's a different kind. What I mean is when a man has conviction. When he believes in something very strongly. Like when Jimmy Carter believes that only people from Georgia are qualified to serve in the United States government. Or when, well, let me put it another way, Martin Luther King was a man with conviction."

"Yes," Mrs. Washington agreed, more puzzled now than ever.

"Well, the fact that a man has convictions does not mean he is stubborn or unreasonable. Understand?"

She did not, but she nodded as if she did.

"Good. And to prove to you the difference between conviction and stubbornness, I am going to demonstrate that I am a man of conviction but with an open mind. I know the proper way to shave is with a razor and a blade. But I am a fair-minded man and I am willing to be convinced. So I will risk experimenting with that electric razor."

That preamble enabled him to ask without sacrificing his dignity, "Where is it? I would like to try it."

"Of course," she said, careful not to look at him and embarrass him at a most delicate moment. For she knew

72

another difficult crisis would soon present itself when she had to plug the cord into the razor and the other end into the wall socket.

He watched as she did it. He accepted the razor from her hand and started it. Then he passed it over his cheek as he had seen done on television commercials, in short repetitive strokes. When he wanted to assess the results he found himself with an activated razor in his right hand and no proper place to put it down safely. So he stowed it, still buzzing away, in the pocket of his robe and felt the right side of his face with his right hand. It was smooth. Unbelievably smooth. He continued shaving.

He was done, had yanked the plug end of the cord out of the wall, and by holding the razor firm against the side of the washbasin with his left hand, he was able to free the cord with his right. Drawing the cord into a neatly folded bundle was a difficult exercise which he decided he would accomplish later, after breakfast.

He went out to the living room, but discovered Mrs. Washington was making the bed. He labored into the bedroom.

"Well?" she asked. "How did it go?"

"Not exactly a shave," he denied. "But a convenience. I guess in a water shortage or a drought it could come in very handy. I . . . I'll try it a few more days. I am not a hasty man. I am not given to snap judgments. But I guess you have already observed that."

"Yes," she lied. "Now how about some breakfast?"

"Good idea."

"And, later, since it's such a nice day, maybe we'll go out for a little fresh air and sunshine," she suggested.

Chapter Six

Horowitz had never been a man for baths. Hot baths, he used to pontificate, only exhaust you. To be peppy, a man needed a good night's sleep and a warm shower followed by a brisk cold one. With great care, he removed his robe, slipped off his pajama top, turned on the water in the stall shower and regulated it until his right hand told him it was the proper temperature. He tugged loose the tie string of his pajama bottoms and let them fall to the floor. He was ready.

But what had been a routine occurrence every day of his life had suddenly become a dangerous venture. He recalled something had been said about installing safety railings in the shower, like the ones they had in the hospital. But it had not been done yet. However, he was determined to proceed. With no small effort he lifted his left leg over the base of the stall shower. He followed with his right. Holding on to one faucet with his right hand he raised his face to the stream of hot water and gloried in the way it beat down on his face and his chest.

He felt fairly secure again, almost back to normal again.

Until he had to reach for the soap and begin the difficult task of lathering up his body. It was a slow laborious task. He managed to accomplish it, though several times he was terrified that he was losing his balance. The faucets offered him support and he survived the procedure.

Only when he turned off the water and reached to open the steamy door did he remember that he had not provided himself with a towel. It had always been his habit to put a fresh bath towel on the edge of the washbasin, a hand's reach from the shower. This time, concentrating on undressing himself, he had forgotten. He seemed to forget many routine things these days. Now he would have to trail a flood of water across the bathroom floor to get to one, and make sure not to slip.

But when he opened the shower door he found a fresh thick bath towel resting on the side of the washbasin exactly where he would have put it. And the bathroom door was slightly ajar. Just in case he had to call for help, he realized. At once he resented that she had had the effrontery to come into his bathroom when he was taking his shower. Certainly Bernadine would never have done it. If a man couldn't have a little privacy in his own home . . .

But he did use the towel and felt relieved, if not thankful, that he had not had to traverse the wet bathroom floor in his precarious condition.

Buttons. He never realized how damn many buttons there were in a man's clothing. On his undershorts. Then on his shirt. He resented the buttons most fiercely. Until he attempted to close the zipper of his pants and failed. He tried holding the bottom of the fly with his right hand while closing the zipper with his left. But the tab was too small to grasp. So he reversed the process, trying to zip with his right while holding down the fabric with his left. Each time it slipped out of his grasp, bunching up the zipper, making it impossible to close.

He was forced to face the most humiliating moment of his convalescence. He would have to call Mrs. Washington for assistance. Stubbornly he refused. He argued with himself, It makes no sense to go out. True, it's a sunny day, warm, pleasant. But what good would it do him to go out if he had to be wheeled out and back? Just to sit in the sun? To get a tan? What for? So he could be the healthiest-looking sick man in New York? To hell with going out, to hell with getting dressed, to hell with the whole damn world!

In the end, he closed his eyes and called sheepishly, "Mrs. Washington?"

"Yes, Mr. Horowitz?" she replied from the living room where she was dusting.

"Could you come in here for a moment?"

She came into the bedroom and took one long look at him. "You're not going out looking like that, are you?"

"Of course not, that's why I called for you." He opened his right eye and embarrassed as he was he tried to sound casual as he asked, "I . . . I want you should help me with . . . with my zipper, please?"

"We can do that. But that outfit," She shook her head sadly.

"What's wrong with my outfit?" he demanded indignantly.

"That is the oldest, baggiest pair of slacks I've ever seen. I bet they don't even make material like that anymore."

"What's wrong with this material?" he asked, welcoming the chance to be offended.

"You have nicer clothes than that. I've seen them in your closet."

"I will thank you to stay out of my closets!"

"I simply will not take you out looking like that," she said with finality.

"Where are we going? To a reception in the Rose Garden of the White House?"

"Sorry. That oufit just won't do."

"Look, just zip up my fly, that's all I called you in here for!" he said, his explosion a cross between anger and embarrassment.

She only stared at him.

"You want me to ruin a perfectly good pair of slacks sitting in a wheelchair? Well, I don't want to. In fact, I don't want to go out at all! There! Settled! So you don't have to zip me up. And you don't have to read me the latest fashion hints! Just leave me alone! Get out! Get out!'"

She did not move. She knew what was at work here. She had had it with other patients before Horowitz. Though his situation was unique to him, his reaction was far from unique. Consciously, or otherwise, he was contriving to avoid going out in that wheelchair. He could not abide being seen in the bright sunlight as the captive of a wheelchair. It was of a piece with his shabby outfit, his oldest slacks, a revolting combination of colors, all of which added up to a reflection of his own depreciated assessment of himself.

"Mr. Horowitz, we are going out in the park. But I am not going to be seen with you in that outfit. I cannot allow people to think that I permitted you to appear in public that way. It would be a reflection on me. And I have a reputation to maintain."

"So you can sit on another bench," he argued. "Make believe you don't know me. Which would suit me fine!"

"Get out of that shirt. Get out of those slacks," she ordered.

He glared at her defiantly. "Even Hannah never dared to talk to me like that!"

"I'll bet you never dressed this way when Hannah was alive!"

"Please call her Mrs. Horowitz," he said angrily.

"Okay. Mrs. Horowitz! I'll bet Mr. Horowitz never dressed like this when Mrs. Horowitz was alive."

"That's better," he approved.

"So get out of those clothes," she insisted. When he made a defiant face at her, she added, "Because if you don't, I'll take them off you and dress you!"

"You wouldn't dare!" he defied. But not so strongly that he did not admit to himself not only the possibility but the likelihood that she would dare. She glared at him. He began to grumble, "There's nothing wrong with this shirt and these slacks." But he struggled with the top button of his shirt and finally had it open.

Suddenly he looked up from his task to assail her. "Okay, I'm doing it! So you can go!"

But she did not move, staying to watch him complete the slow difficult procedure, for she was studying the difficulty he was having with the buttons while making mental notes of the exercises she would have to employ to overcome his deficiencies.

"And while you're at it, you might tie your shoelaces," she suggested firmly.

"I already tied my shoelaces!" he protested. But when he looked down he found them dangling. The puzzlement and frustration were so clear on his face that she felt obliged to explain gently.

"It happens, Mr. Horowitz. Left hemis—"

He interrupted, "*Left hemis?* What is a *left hemi*, half a Communist? I am not Communist."

"Left hemiplegics," she explained, "are people who have had strokes on the right side of the brain and thus have left-sided impairments. Left hemis tend to forget routine things like tying shoelaces, buttoning shirts or coats. Sometimes they even forget to put their left arms into the left sleeves. It will take a bit of thinking each time. But eventually you'll get the hang of it."

He nodded as if her explanation had satisfied him, but she could see how discouraged he was.

Sadly he said, "The last time someone had to tell me to tie my shoelaces, I was seven years old."

"A tie, too?" he rebelled, once he had changed into well-pressed slacks and a fresh white shirt.

"Yes, a tie, too!"

"Black Hitler," he muttered as he selected a tie from the rack on the closet door. He held one up in a mock effort to solicit her approval.

"You can do better than that," she said.

He grumbled but selected another tie, an expensive woven Macclesfield. Sarcastically he held it up. "The best Neiman-Marcus has to offer. From my darling daughter, Mona, last Christmas. Except she said it was for Chanukah. You know about Chanukah?"

"Yes, it's like the Catholics. You light candles."

"Some comparison," he scoffed, suspecting she had said it intentionally to annoy him. "We lit candles before there ever were Catholics!" He began the laborious procedure of tying the thick, rich cravat into a passable knot. As he made the effort, he grumbled, "Some people get the fanciest gifts from Neiman-Marcus. I get a tie. And such a tie. No wonder I never wore it before. It's impossible to tie! I'll bet even you couldn't tie this!" he challenged.

"You're right," she said, "I couldn't tie it, because you are going to tie it."

Impatiently, he took it apart and started over again. Slowly, fumblingly, he proceeded, step by step, wrapping the thick silk over, then around. But the fingers of his left hand were not quite up to accomplishing the task smoothly.

"Sorry. I can't," he confessed softly.

"You can if you try," she insisted.

"I tried. It didn't work. All right, Beau Brummel I'm not. So you'll be ashamed to be seen in public with me. I don't know why. Nobody is going to think we're married.

They won't blame you for the way I look."

"That's not the point, Mr. Horowitz. The question is how you are going to feel about being seen in public like this."

"Who gives a damn how I look!" he exploded. "Hannah, she used to care. She used to say I was the best-dressed man anywhere we went. Not fancy, not showy, but quality, taste! Now, who do I have to dress for?"

He glared at her angrily, but there was a moistness in his eyes that betrayed him.

"Look, if you're going to be so ashamed to be seen with me in public, maybe we shouldn't go out at all."

"We are going out. Now. It's going to be a warm day. And I want you in the sun before it gets too hot. So let's go!"

"Isn't it time for lunch?" he asked.

"It is time for going out to the park," Mrs. Washington said firmly.

"Idi Amin would be nicer to do business with," he muttered, but he seized his shiny metal quad cane and started to slowly make his way toward the foyer. "I don't have to go in the wheelchair. I can walk with this damned thing," he called back over his shoulder.

"Just keep your eyes on the carpet and don't try to talk at the same time," she ordered.

He shuffled out into the hallway, careful to observe where the bedroom carpet left off and the smooth floor began, where the foyer carpet started and left an edge that might serve to trap the four metal legs of the quad and trip him. By the time he reached the foyer and the wheelchair, he was forced to admit to himself that he was exhausted enough to welcome sitting down. Twenty-one steps he had taken, and he was sweating. Time was, in very recent months, when he would start away from the house and walk briskly to Columbus Circle before taking the subway to his business.

His place of business, he recalled sadly; Marvin had

said that Abe Gottshall was taking care of things and everything was fine. Abe was a nice man, an honest man, but no genius. As soon as they let him, Horowitz decided, he must go down to the office and see how things were going.

His thoughts were interrupted when the elevator door opened and there was Angelo, smiling brightly. "Good morning, Mr. Horowitz. Is nice to see you gettin' out on a day like this." Horowitz suspected his bright smile. True, Angelo usually smiled. But today, Horowitz thought he detected a bit of smug superiority in that smile. No doubt Angelo was gloating inwardly at his opportunity to feel superior to sick, old Mr. Horowitz. Horowitz rewarded his smile with a curt, "Morning, Angelo."

That ended all pleasantries. The door eased shut. The car started down. When they reached the street floor, Angelo worked meticulously to make sure that the car was exactly level with the floor so Horowitz would have no trouble getting his wheelchair out. It took several tries, during which Horowitz said to himself, The bastard is doing this on purpose. To point up that I am now helpless. But when Angelo was satisfied with the level of the car, Horowitz found it quite easy to roll the chair out.

He propelled himself along, until he arrived at the three steps that stood between him and the tall glass and iron front doors.

Those damn three steps, Horowitz said to himself, the architect who designed this building should rot in jail! Imagine putting steps where they could only be a nuisance. How many hundreds of times had he seen young mothers in the building trying to get their baby carriages up and down those steps when the doorman was unavailable for some reason. Some architect!

Now, in a sense, he was the infant. He and his carriage—call it a wheelchair, if you wish—would have to be assisted up those same damn steps. Juan, the doorman, was coming in to help, and Angelo, that sly

81

Puerto Rican, had silently followed them from the elevator car to assist. When Mrs. Washington tried to help, both men waved her off pleasantly and each seized a side of the chair and lifted it up the steps so it was clear to roll out the door and onto the street.

Horowitz made it through the door without touching either side. At least he had been able to carry that off without disgracing himself. He looked about. The street was lined with parked cars as always. The traffic raced by, emitting noxious fumes and making noises punctuated by an occasional protesting horn blown by an impatient driver irritated by an empty cab that had stopped short to pick up a fare.

The street was the same as it had always been. Even old lady Goldstein, who he had seen those mornings when he used to leave for the office a bit late, was in her place in the sun near the corner, wheeled there by her black companion.

In the past, their conversation had been confined to an exchange of casual greetings, as he started his morning walk down toward Columbus Circle. This time, he was no longer walking, but rolling along, slowly. It was obvious from the look on her face that she wished to exchange more than the usual "good mornings," which were merely empty phrases that served only to acknowledge each other's existence.

"Mr. Horowitz, I'm glad to see you again. I heard and I am terribly sorry."

"What did you hear?" he asked resentfully.

She stared at his face, at the red welt, the whitish marks where there had been sutures. "God, what they did to you! Never fight back," she advised. "That's one thing my grandson Sheldon told me. Did you know he's in the district attorney's office? And only two years out of law school? He said he's seen too many cases of people who got killed resisting muggers. After all, it's only money."

"Only money," Horowitz echoed. "What about consenting to let a crime be committed? If we're all going to lay down and let ourselves be robbed, crime will get worse and we'll be the prisoners, not them."

"A person could get killed," Mrs. Goldstein warned.

"There are worse things than getting killed," Horowitz said sadly. It was clear that he referred to the confinement to which he was now subjected.

"After a while you won't feel that way," the woman consoled. "Just think of your children and your grandchildren. You want to see them grow up and become something. You have grandchildren, don't you?"

"Oh, yes," Horowitz said sadly, "I have grandchildren. At Harvard."

"Harvard, that's nice." Then Mrs. Goldstein added, "I have a grandson in Cornell Medical School," to even the score.

"Well," Horowitz said, "got to be going." He tried to sound as jaunty as if he were taking off for his morning walk. Then he slowly rolled himself to the curb, where the city had thoughtfully hollowed out a declivity to afford bicycles, baby carriages, and wheelchairs easy access to the gutter. He turned the chair about, ready to cross the street as soon as the light changed. He was completely aware of the ubiquitous Mrs. Washington right behind him, though she had not said a word from the time they had entered the elevator.

The light changed. He started to propel himself across the street. A car approached from his right, and for an instant he feared it might not observe the red light and would crash into him. But he glared at the driver, who came to an easy stop right at the white line. On the park side of the street, Horowitz rolled along until he found a place clear of trees and open to the midday sun. He maneuvered the chair about so he could raise his face to the sun, remembering that Hannah had always said he looked especially handsome when he acquired a tan

83

down in Florida, or up in the country during the summer.

Mrs. Washington sat down on the bench close to him. She made no effort to engage him in conversation. The fewer points of friction in their young relationship the better.

After some silence, during which the street noises seemed unusually loud, he finally was moved to say, "She's a very gabby person."

"Who?"

"That Mrs. Goldstein. Talk, talk, talk!" he complained. "A man in my situation has got to stay away from widows. They're always scheming to get their hooks into you. First it's an invitation to dinner. Then, it's 'If you're not doing anything maybe you would like to go to a movie.' Or else, 'My son or my nephew happens to be in show business and he gave me two tickets to a show, would you like to go?' Believe me, the most dangerous thing in this world is a widow on the prowl."

"Yes, I know," the widowed Mrs. Washington agreed pointedly.

Censured, he added quickly, "Of course, present company excepted."

He paused. "After your husband died, you never wanted to marry again?"

"Not particularly," Mrs. Washington said.

"You're an exceptional woman."

"No, he was an exceptional man."

"It's nice you can feel that way," Horowitz said quite earnestly.

Another long silence followed, during which Horowitz sat, eyes closed, face raised to the warm sun. Suddenly a thought occurred to him, so he opened his right eye and asked, "Tell me something. Do black people get sunburned?"

"Yes."

"The same as white people?"

"Not really. We have a built-in sun shield. But we do get sunburned. Why?"

"I was just sitting here thinking. With white people, you can tell how well-to-do a man is by the amount of sunburn he shows in the winter. How do you tell about black people?"

"Cadillacs," Mrs. Washington responded.

.There was another silence.

"So your husband was a very nice man," Horowitz commented, impressed by her loyalty. "What did he do? For a living, I mean."

"In good times, he was a welder."

"Hmm," Horowitz responded, impressed.

"During the war he made out well. Steady work. Very good pay. Between wars, things were not so good. He went long stretches without any work at all. Twice he had to take jobs as a janitor in tenements up in Harlem. I couldn't stand to see him break his heart in menial work when he was so good at his own. That's why I decided to study practical nursing. So he wouldn't have to do that kind of work."

"Then what did he do?" Horowitz asked.

"Took care of the children, of the house. Did odd jobs."

"That's no way for a man to live out his life," Horowitz commented.

She did not answer. Horowitz opened his eyes only to discover a jogger in a sweat suit. The man approached them, plodded by, and Horowitz realized the man was not much younger than himself. Ah, if only he were able to jog. Or even walk again, free and unhindered. All the aids that were supposed to help him were only hindrances, encumbrances. He closed his eyes again.

"Your husband, how long has he been dead?"

"Nine years," she responded.

"Then he never lived to see his granddaughter," Horowitz realized. "Sad."

"Yes, sad," Mrs. Washington said. "It was right before Christmas. My daughter was expecting her second. Horace was lucky to get a job in a department store. He was planning what he would buy the new baby for a first Christmas gift and suddenly he was dead. No warning, nothing."

"Very sad," Horowitz said, truly compassionate.

"I don't know," she said strangely.

"A man dies without seeing one of his grandchildren get born and you don't know if it's sad?" he asked, turning to look at her.

"At least he was relieved of the struggle of trying to be something he could never be. The provider. He lay there in his casket with a peaceful look on his face, as if the struggle and the failure were over. I said to him, 'Don't worry, Horace, I always knew what you were, and what you could have been. You didn't have to justify yourself to anyone else in this world.'"

"You said that? To a dead man?"

"Didn't you say anything to Mrs. Horowitz?"

He did not respond at once, but after a while he admitted, "I didn't say. I just thought. While the rabbi was talking, saying such nice complimentary things about her, I was thinking, Hannah, darling, what can any stranger say about you that will come close to the truth? Sure, he was our rabbi, and he knew you. But no one knew you like I knew you. How tender and kind you were. How you could encourage a man with your words. Yet you had a golden gift of knowing when a man needed silence. When his feelings had been too hurt to talk about, or his troubles too big to share.

"It was always such an experience to wake up in the morning with you. You came awake with a smile. You looked forward to the day. And because *you* did, *I* did. So when I started out on my morning walk I was happy and bright and the whole world was a good place. Now that you're gone, nothing will ever be the same again.

The rabbi can pontificate about the Lord giving and the Lord taking away, I will never forgive Him for taking you, Hannah, never. Even if it is a sin to feel that way. That's what I thought," Horowitz admitted, for the first time to anyone.

Mrs. Washington nodded slightly. "For two sad people, we have both been very lucky."

"Yes," Horowitz agreed, "I just hope you've been as lucky as I was."

There was an explosion of sound down the block—loud, raucous shouts, laughter, threats, boasting of young teenagers free on their lunch hour. They were from the high school on Columbus Avenue. They came in groups, a tidal wave of black youngsters, boys and girls, many of the girls quite mature physically. They came with shouts that were obvious and obscene. With music, loud and rock, from many transistor radios.

At the sight of them approaching, Horowitz involuntarily drew back. Mrs. Washington noticed. He clutched the arms of his wheelchair until his right hand was white at the knuckles, and his left hand groped desperately to establish a grip. She noticed, but said nothing, aware that his reaction was the automatic response he would exhibit for a long time to the two young hoodlums who had attacked him.

The tide of black youngsters swept by them into the park. Once they were gone, Horowitz said grimly, "I think I've had enough sun for the day."

"I think so," Mrs. Washington agreed.

Chapter Seven

He had suffered the indignity of being carried down into the lobby again, smiled at by Angelo, and was relieved, finally, to achieve the privacy of his own bedroom. He waved Mrs. Washington out of the room. He wanted to be alone while he struggled to get out of the chair, grasp his quad and make his way to the bed that had once been his and Hannah's and was now only his.

He felt tired, more than tired, exhausted. He sank down on the side of the bed, lost his balance and slowly keeled over onto his weak left side. He lay still, recovering breath. Then he struggled to push himself further into the bed and draw up his good leg and arm. Thus, he fell alseep, a light sleep, brought on by physical and emotional exhaustion. Samuel Horowitz, who only six weeks ago had been able to walk a brisk twenty-five blocks from his house to Columbus Circle, was exhausted from having sat for an hour in the sun in Central Park.

She was gently waking him a short time later.

"Hmm? What?" He came to, startled. He looked up and saw her standing over him. "Oh, it's you," he acknowledged resentfully.

"Who did you expect? Zsa Zsa Gabor?"

"Hattie McDaniel," he shot back bitterly.

"Sorry. But then you're not Clark Gable either," she said. "Time for lunch."

"I don't want lunch."

"I didn't want to make lunch, but I did, so you'll eat it," she said firmly.

"When your kind takes over, they'll put you in charge of a concentration camp, for sure," he said. But he did not resist. He proceeded to exercise bed mobility. Slowly he rolled on his side, got himself up, sat in balance, and then raised himself to his feet. Not as good as he should by this time, she observed. Instead of determination, he still exhibited resistance. A few more weeks of such an attitude would doom any recovery.

"I would like a little privacy," he said brusquely.

"Why?"

"I want to get back into my pajamas and robe."

"Why?"

"Why not? What am I going to do, go dancing? Tell me, Mrs. Washington, would you like to go to Roseland with me and do the bustle?"

"You mean the hustle?" she corrected.

"Okay, the hustle. You might meet a nice rich man who would take you away from all this," he joked bitterly. Then added angrily, "I want to get into my pajamas and robe!"

"I don't think that's a good idea," she remonstrated, to ward off any incipient tendency toward invalidism.

"I didn't ask you what you thought. Just get out. And leave me free to do what I want to do!" he commanded. "Besides, there isn't any time."

"No time?" he scoffed. "Between now and the six o'clock news all I have is time!"

"Your blintzes will get cold."

"Blintzes?"

For the first time since he woke, his eyes lit up in anticipation. "Blintzes." But he refused to grant her the satisfaction of knowing how pleased he was. "I don't like frozen blintzes! I tried them once, after Hannah was gone. Like rubber. My Hannah's, there was a blintzeh!"

He interrupted his happy remembrance to explain, "You know, Mrs. Washington, people think the singular of blintzes is blintz. Nothing could be further from the truth. It goes this way. *Blintzeh*, singular, *blintzes*, plural. And the way blintzes are made, you beat up some eggs, you mix in some flour, add salt, and stir until it's smooth. No lumps. That's very important. Then the whole trick in making the pancake is to pour a dipper of the mixture into a hot frying pan, roll it around until it covers the pan, very thin, then quick pour the rest back into the bowl. When what's left in the pan is just done enough to be dry, you turn the pan over onto a nice clean kitchen towel, give it one little tap so it falls out. Presto, you have a perfectly lovely round thin pancake that is ready to be filled. Now, for the filling . . ."

She interrupted, "Your blintzes are getting cold."

"So you'll heat them up," he replied impatiently.

"They'll become dry. Like rubber."

He resented her throwing his own words back at him. "Okay!" he conceded angrily. He turned toward his wheelchair.

"You can walk," she said, indicating his quad cane.

"My frozen blintzes, which are already like rubber, will get dry and become even more like rubber!" he responded irritably.

"Walk," she insisted.

He reached for his quad and followed her out of the room. It was a slow, labored walk, made more so by the luxurious carpet, which he reminded himself had cost him twenty-six dollars a yard. Twenty-six dollars a yard for a booby trap, an obstacle course, he lamented, as he headed for the foyer.

As he reached the dining room, and despite the fact that Mrs. Washington had shut the swinging door to the kitchen, Horowitz could smell the warm and welcome fragrance of frying blintzes. His taste buds responded nostalgically to the memory of Hannah's blintzes. Each *bletle* she made was a magnificent crepe, thin, even, a perfect circle. And her fillings! She could take a pound of ordinary cottage cheese, a raw egg, some vanilla, a touch of sugar, add a bit of magic with lemon rind and some spice and turn that *bletle* into a golden delight to the nose and the palate. She would fold them and fry them to a delicate golden brown on both sides and they were ready for serving. Hot, fragrant, and just the right color.

Some people liked to add jam or syrup to blintzes, but with Hannah's, most people ate them plain, to savor the taste. Or with only a dab of sour cream to add a bit of tartness. The fragrance in the air had, for a moment, recaptured all that. Then Mrs. Washington swung open the door and entered, carrying a plate and a small dish of sour cream which she set before him.

Horowitz did not begin eating at once but stared down with a connoisseur's critical eye.

"This is blintzes?" he asked disparagingly.

"What's wrong?"

"For one thing, they're a little too brown. Fried too much."

"Taste them," she urged.

"For another thing, they're folded the wrong way."

"Taste them," she persisted.

91

He leaned forward to inhale their perfume, with the aloofness of a sommelier appraising the cork of a freshly opened bottle of wine.

"Different," he delivered his opinion. "They smell different from Hannah's."

"Try them!" Mrs. Washington persisted.

"What did you fry them in? Not butter," he accused.

"Your doctor doesn't want you to have too much butter," she explained. "Try them, before they get cold."

"What did you use, lard?" he asked accusingly. "You people are always using lard or bacon fat."

"Margarine. Low cholesterol margarine," she corrected. "Doctor's orders."

"That doctor doesn't know any more about making blintzes than you do," Horowitz accused.

"Try them!" she said impatiently.

"I guess one taste couldn't poison me."

He took up the fork in his right hand, cut into the lightly browned delicacy. The crepe was tender, the inside steamy white and tempting. He brought the first forkful to his mouth, inhaled deeply, then finally engulfed it with more anticipation than he had intended to betray. He chewed slowly, savoring it. Mrs. Washington awaited his judicial pronouncement. Instead, he said only, "One swallow doesn't make a summer, or a blintzeh. Let's not be hasty." He took a second forkful. Then a third.

Finally he was willing to grant, "Well, at least they're not the frozen kind. Not Hannah's exactly, but not bad."

He was attacking the last of the three when he asked, a bit casually, "That's all? I mean, Hannah always used to give me at least four. Sometimes five."

"The doctor said three, at the most."

He was down to the last forkful when he asked, "Who made these? That Mrs. Resnick on the third floor? After Hannah died she kept sending up food. A very persistent

92

widow, that one. If she couldn't entice me into her bed, she figured she would trap me in the kitchen."

He turned on Mrs. Washington suddenly. "Don't laugh. I am still a man, if you know what I mean!"

"I know what you mean," she agreed, to protect his vanity.

"Okay, now who made these?"

"*Eliyahu Ha'Nawvi*," she responded easily.

Slowly, more out of annoyance than physical inhibition, he turned to glare at her.

"I do not like wise-guy remarks. When I ask a question, I want a straight answer. Who made these?" he demanded.

"I did," she responded. "Who else was here to make them?"

"Okay, then that's what you should have said, 'I made them.' Not a fresh remark like *Eliyahu Ha'Nawvi*. Besides, what do you know about *Eliyahu Ha'Nawvi*?"

"When I worked for the Rosengartens, they had a big seder every Passover. And they would have me set aside a silver cup of wine for Elijah, the Prophet, in case he showed up. Of course, he never did. So later I would pour the wine back into the decanter. And I always thought, how like the Gospels."

Until the mention of that word, Horowitz had been an interested listener. "Mrs. Washington, there was a Passover before there was any Gospels! In fact, the Last Supper was really . . ."

She anticipated him, "A seder."

"Exactly! So don't ever make any comparison such as *Eliyahu Ha'Nawvi* is like the Gospels!" Having made the point forcibly, Horowitz relaxed enough to ask curiously, "So?"

"So what?"

"So how is *Eliyahu Ha'Nawvi* like the Gospels?" he asked, irritated.

"In the Gospels, Jesus says, I was hungry and you fed me, thirsty and you gave me to drink, a stranger and you took me in. And when they said to Him, we never did that for You, He answered, inasmuch as you have done it to the least of these my brethren you have done it unto me.

"So on Passover, when I set out the cup for Elijah, I would think, he won't show up either, but some poor people, some lonely people might. Mrs. Rosengarten would call her rabbi every Passover and ask if there were any strangers in town who might like to celebrate Passover with them. So it was really the same."

Horowitz was thoughtful for a moment before he said, "And I thought all you people ever did in church was clap your hands and sing 'Amen' or 'Hallelujah.' Which, by the way, is also from us Jews. It's in the Old Testament. Many times."

"Yes, I know," Mrs. Washington granted.

"You still didn't tell me."

"What?"

"Where you learned to make such blintzes?"

"From Mrs. Rosengarten."

"But the taste, exactly like Hannah's," he replied nostalgically. "A mere coincidence, I suppose?"

She did not respond to that, but said instead, "While you were napping your daughter called."

"Why didn't you tell me before?"

"And let your blintzes get cold?"

"A wise decision," he granted. "I have a daughter, Mona," he began to complain, "the Perle Mesta of San Diego. The hostess with the mostest in the land. She is a doer. And also a crier. When doing is required, she can *do*. When crying is required, she can *cry*. With the best of them. She is the perfect Jewish woman, wife, and mother. If they ever put up a Statue of Liberty, in Israel, my Mona will pose as the model. But as a daughter,

94

she leaves a little to be desired."

"She sounded very concerned, asked a lot of questions about how you are, how you're getting along," Mrs. Washington pointed out.

"Oh, sure," he scoffed.

"She really did. And I'd know if she was just pretending. She even asked if you would be better off out at her place."

"What did you tell her?" he asked, suddenly defensive.

"I said you needed familiar surroundings."

"Good, good," he said softly, then confessed. "I don't want her to see me this way. Later, when I'm better, maybe . . ." he speculated without promising. "No," he decided, "I wouldn't feel at home there. Never. Believe me, Mrs. Washington, if *Eliyahu Ha'Nawvi* showed up at Mona's house he couldn't even get into the circular driveway without a Rolls-Royce. Or at least a Mercedes. You ever notice, you can't tell if a doctor is Jewish unless he drives a Mercedes. Some world!" he lamented.

"She said, when you woke up to call her back."

"It costs too much to call California during the day," he evaded.

"She left an 800 number, it won't cost you anything."

Deprived of his last excuse, Horowitz finally surrendered. "Okay, I'll call her."

"I'll get your wheelchair," Mrs. Washington said.

"I can walk," he protested.

"You walked in here and it was too much for you," she pointed out gently.

"I don't wish to talk to my daughter from a wheelchair. Can you understand that, Mrs. Washington?" he asked softly.

"Yes," she responded in an equally gentle tone. "My Horace was the same. When our grandson was due to visit, he didn't want him to see him hobbling around on a cane. It was very hard for him, but he carried it off. And spent the whole next day in bed to make up for it. So, I understand."

"I will walk into the bedroom. I will sit in the big chair there. And I will call her."

She followed him at a respectful unintrusive distance as he struggled across the thick carpeting with his quad cane. When he was safely in the upholstered armchair in the bedroom, he reached out. She handed him the phone and plugged it into the wall jack.

The 800 number was direct to the offices of Albert Fields Associates. The operator there had orders that if a Mr. Horowitz called she was to put him through to Mr. Fields' home. Patiently Samuel Horowitz waited until Mona's home phone was answered. A Spanish-speaking maid responded and after some difficulty made it known to Horowitz that Mrs. Field was in a meeting with one of her ladies' committees and left orders to be interrupted just as soon as her father called.

Despite that, it took a long time before Mona came to the phone. Which caused Horowitz to apologize to Mrs. Washington, "My Mona is busy. In a meeting. My Mona is always busy. Hadassah. United Jewish Fund. Hebrew Home for the Aged. Israel bonds. My Mona has been a president more times than Roosevelt. Lucky for the Pope, she's not Catholic. Otherwise he would be out of a job!"

At that instant, Samuel Horowitz heard his daughter exclaim, "Dad!" And before he could even acknowledge the relationship, she began to cry. "Oh, Dad . . . Dad . . ."

"Mona, Mona, darling, I'm all right. There's no reason to cry. I'm fine. I'm sitting right here in the big blue chair in the bedroom. The sunlight is streaming in. I feel fine. I just had a good lunch. Blintzes! Delicious!"

"Blintzes?" Mona asked, horrified. "Do you know how much cholesterol there is in just one blintz?"

"No," Horowitz admitted.

"An outrageous amount. How many did you have?"

In order to avoid a national crisis, Horowitz admitted to only, "Two."

"Two blintzes!" she exclaimed, outraged. "Does your doctor know about this?"

"He wasn't here."

"Then I'll call him and ask him if blintzes are on your diet."

"Mona, please," Horowitz tried in vain to stem the tide of her indignation.

"A man who's had one stroke can have another. You've got to cut out cholesterol. You've got to keep your blood pressure down. You've got to live on a safe, moderate diet. No fats. No salt. No sugar. There's such a thing as senile diabetes, I think they call it. Older people get it."

"I'm not senile and I don't have diabetes," Horowitz protested. But to no avail.

"I'm calling Marvin as soon as I hang up. I want him to have a long talk with your doctor." Suddenly it occurred to her, "Oh, my God!"

"Mona, darling, what is it? What happened?" Horowitz asked, expecting news of some fresh catastrophe.

"Don't tell me you had sour cream with your blintzes!"

"Okay. I won't tell you."

"Tell me!"

"You just said not to tell you."

"I want the truth, did you or did you not have sour cream with your blintzes?"

For a moment, Horowitz debated telling her. It was not a simple decision, or without consequences. If he told her, God alone knew what steps she would take. She might forsake all her committee meetings and come rushing to New York to organize his life. As it was, she would badger his doctor, make life miserable for Marvin, and it might not end there. So he thought a judicious lie was in order.

"Mona, darling," he began in a tone sufficiently ponderous for delivering a Supreme Court decision, "there was no sour cream."

"Good!" she exulted, greatly relieved. "Do you know that sour cream has as much butter fat, and sometimes more, than sweet cream."

"I didn't know," Horowitz said, with what he thought was a proper degree of shock. "I'm glad you warned me."

"Forbidden, absolutely forbidden!" Mona pontificated.

Horowitz tried to terminate the conversation. "Mona, I don't want to keep you from your meeting. Besides, long distance during the day costs quite a bit of money."

"We're on Albert's 800 line and it doesn't cost a cent. And as for my meeting, the black people of this nation waited two hundred years for equality, school integration in San Diego can wait a few more minutes when my father's life is involved."

"Mona, darling, your father's life is not involved. Go take care of the black children. Please!"

"Not till I have your situation under control," Mona declared. "I want your doctor's name and phone number!"

"Mona, please, the black children are waiting!" Horowitz tried to interrupt.

"And I insist on talking to that woman! Is she there now?"

"Mona, please . . ." Horowitz made one last desperate plea.

"Is she there?"

"She's here," Horowitz admitted.

"Good! But, first, you will come out here as soon as you're able to travel. I've checked all the details. American has non-stop flights, New York to San Diego, twice a day. They have special accommodations for people in wheelchairs. In addition, Albert plays golf with one of the executives at American. So you'll go VIP all the way."

"VIP all the way," Horowitz repeated. "Sounds like I'm running for President."

"I'll find out from your doctor the moment you're able to fly," Mona declared, as if they had struck an agreement.

"Mona, darling . . ."

But she overrode any possible objection. "Now put that woman on! What's her name?"

"Mrs. Washington." His hand covering the mouthpiece, Horowitz said, "She wants to talk to you."

Harriet Washington hesitated, then took the instrument. "Hello. This is Mrs. Washington."

"Do I understand that you fed my father blintzes?"

"Yes," Harriet Washington admitted.

"Is that on his diet?" Mona asked, with the measured delivery of a prosecuting attorney.

"He doesn't have a diet. He is allowed to eat everything. In moderation," Harriet Washington informed.

"What kind of a doctor does he have?" the outraged Mona Fields demanded.

"A doctor who believes there's no point to torturing a patient who's in fairly good health. Your father's cholesterol count is within normal limits. He is not overweight. His medical condition is stable. I would say that the only thing wrong with him is his attitude. He is a nasty, irascible man. In fact, his main source of enjoyment these days is being nasty."

Horowitz glared up at her, but she ignored him.

"That's the only thing in which he does not exercise moderation," Mrs. Washington said.

"I'd like his doctor's name," Mona said.

"I don't think that's a good idea," Mrs. Washington tried to point out.

"I didn't ask what you think," Mona came back sharply. "He's my father and I have a right to know. In fact, if my father is not fit to travel out here, as soon as I can clear up some matters here I'm coming to New York! I'd come at once. But there are our black children to think about."

Mrs. Washington suspected that her own speech had indicated she was black and Mona was seeking to capitalize on that. She proved right. For Mona lowered her voice to a conspiratorial hush as she said, "Mrs. Washington, you have the 800 number, don't you?"

"Yes."

"Well, use it!"

"I don't understand."

"You take care of my father and I'll take care of the black children of San Diego," Mona promised.

"I still don't understand."

Irritated that her elliptical attempt at conspiracy had not succeeded, Mona ordered, "Call me several times a week! I want a detailed report on how my father is doing! We just won't let him know that we talk. Okay?"

"I don't like to make promises like that," Mrs. Washington demurred.

Mona lowered her voice even more, "I'll make it worth your while."

"I don't know any black children in San Diego," Mrs. Washington said.

"I mean, there'll be a little extra in it for you every week. Say, twenty-five dollars?" Mona proposed.

"I'm afraid I can't do that," Harriet Washington replied. "I report to the doctor. And I understand your brother talks to him several times a week."

"I see," Mona said, openly frustrated and quite annoyed. "Thank you!" she said curtly.

"Do you want to talk to your father again?"

"No, I'll handle this in my own way!" Mona declared.

Chapter Eight

Mrs. Washington had hung up.

Horowitz commented, "A living doll, no? If the Equal Rights Amendment passes, the next Hitler will be a woman."

"She said she's fighting for integrated education for the black children of San Diego."

"Why not? Her children are both in college in Boston. They ride to school in sports cars, not buses. That leaves my darling Mona free to tell everyone else how to educate their children. I can see it now," Horowitz said. "The buses are ready. The black children are being marched into them. But some black children don't want to go. They keep climbing out the windows. And there is my Mona throwing them back into the bus. There is no shortage of energy in this country, Mrs. Washington, only it's in the wrong places. You hitch my Mona to a truck and she would be able to pull it. Like those strong men you've seen who can pull a locomotive holding a rope in their teeth. Except with Mona, she could do that and talk at the same time."

He reached out his right hand to seal a bargain, "Mrs. Washington, we got to make an agreement. You are never going to tell Mona that I am well enough to travel. Okay?"

But she would not take his hand. "Mr. Horowitz, an agreement has to be two-sided. If *I* agree, *you* have to agree."

"I'm agreeing," he protested.

"I haven't even told you what it is I want," she pointed out.

"Okay. Name it! Anything. Just protect me from Mona."

"Mr. Horowitz, you are going to get well. Even if you don't want to. Not for your sake, but mine. I have a professional reputation to maintain."

"Get well?" Horowitz evaluated sadly. "What for? I have children I don't have anything in common with. Grandchildren I hardly know. What is the big value in living? In fact, Mrs. Washington, you want to know something? These days, old people are not afraid of dying. They are afraid of living. So what's the big *gedillah* to get well?" He started to explain, "*Gedillah* is a word that means . . ."

She anticipated him, "Joy. Great joy."

"How could you know?" he asked, then realized. "Don't tell me. Mrs. Rosengarten!"

"No," Mrs. Washington corrected.

"Then who?"

"Mr. Rosengarten," she informed, smiling.

"Okay, wise guy," Horowitz granted sourly. "But it doesn't change what I said. Life is no more a *gedillah*. But for your sake, I'll try. Now?" He extended his hand again.

"Not the right one, the left."

"For sixty-eight years I have shaken hands with my right."

"Starting now, you'll use your left whenever possible."

She extended her left hand to him. Reluctantly and with effort he reached up slowly to seize her left hand, which she deliberately held too high for him to reach easily. She exercised pressure on it, expecting he would try to respond in kind. When he did not, she reminded, "Press! Every chance you get, press. Hard as you can."

He made the effort but she could feel that he was far from having recovered enough of his strength.

"And now, we'll do our exercises," she announced.

"Exercises," he disparaged. "Torture, you mean!"

"One exercise you don't need is speech therapy," she commented wryly. "Now, let's begin."

"I did enough exercises in the hospital," Horowitz protested.

"You'll have to keep doing them until you're well again," she insisted. "So, let's begin. First exercise!"

"I don't remember," he deliberately denied.

"Lie on your back. . . ."

"I already know how to lie on my back."

"Lie on your back," she continued despite his attempt to interrupt, "and reach your left arm high above your head until your hand touches the wall behind you. Come now! Reach! Slowly! Up! All the way! Far as you can go! Try to touch that back wall!"

"I'm trying, I'm trying," he protested belligerently.

"You can do better than that. More! More!" She was aware that he was trying, but that the resistance of his own damaged nerves prevented him from approaching any closer than ten or twelve inches from the wall. It would take work, stretching, using his muscles, forcing his brain to cooperate.

When he had done that exercise ten times, she ordered, "Now, arm up and across the head, keeping your elbow

103

stiff. Like this." Though she pretended she was merely demonstrating, she actually knew she had to assist him or he would fail and become even more discouraged. She forced him to execute the maneuver ten times.

"Okay, now grab my hand. Hard. Like we're shaking hands but much harder."

He made a feeble effort, this time not from choice. She knew she would have to persist in hand exercises if he were ever to recover fine hand movements and control. A padded fork handle might do for the moment. But if he were allowed to rely on that he would never progress.

She felt compelled to drive him even harder, "Now, on your back, knees bent!"

Reluctantly he assumed the position.

"Raise your toes," she commanded.

He made a halfhearted attempt before he said, "Can't!"

"Can!" she insisted.

"Can't!" he fought back.

"Mr. Horowitz, you are going to raise the toes of your left foot!" When he made no effort, she seized his foot and pressed his toes upward in the direction of his leg.

"Ow! You hurt me!" he protested.

"Good! Where there's sensation there's the promise of increased motor ability," she explained calmly, deliberately repeating the move, this time exerting even more pressure.

"Okay, okay, I'll try by myself." And he did. Performing it several times, with a slight, but perceptible increase in flexibility.

"Five more times," she ordered. He complied, grudgingly, but nevertheless with some effectiveness.

"Now, leg straight up, far as it will go. Then let it down. Slowly," she commanded.

He struggled to raise his left leg stiffly, exerting effort from his hip, which had also been damaged by the stroke.

"Higher," she suggested, as she stood over him observing.

"Higher? What am I doing, getting ready for the Olympics?" he protested.

"Higher!" she insisted.

He tried, succeeded only modestly, and was out of breath. She allowed him to recover before going on with the regime in which she had been instructed by the young black therapist at the hospital.

She had put Horowitz through the entire series of exercises for the early afternoon. He was breathing hard, a film of perspiration shining on his brow and his sunken cheeks. She would have to put him through the ordeal once again before dinner, and still another time before she left for the night. She was not satisfied with his progress. He was not trying. Obeying, yes, only if forced to. But not trying enough on his own.

Perhaps if they could circumvent that wheelchair, bring him to the point where he could maneuver on his own for distances long enough to make it possible for him to go out to the park with the help of only his quad cane, it might restore his pride sufficiently to give him the will to go on. If not, he would simply deteriorate, waste away, and, likely, die.

The phone rang. Horowitz reached out to his left. But, though the phone was in its accustomed place on the night table, his hand was far from touching it. He was aware of his failure. It showed in his eyes as he reluctantly conceded her permission to answer.

"Mr. Horowitz's residence," she announced.

He braced himself for some intrusion. It could be a distant relative who heard he was home from the hospital and felt duty-bound to call. He had had his fill of such calls when Hannah died. People called, with only clichés to offer, and he found himself answering in kind. He felt it demeaned Hannah's memory, and her whole life, to

105

speak of her in clichés. Now, he did not feel able to contend with what amounted to his own eulogy.

"He wants to talk to you," Harriet Washington said, holding out the phone.

"Who?"

"Dr. Tannenbaum."

"Hello, doctor! I feel fine! I have never felt better in my whole life. In fact, I am thinking of marrying a nineteen-year-old girl and going on a honeymoon cruise to the South Seas," he defied, before the doctor had a chance to say a word.

"Mr. Horowitz, did you have a conversation with your daughter, Mrs. Fields?"

"Yes," he admitted warily.

"Well, she called me."

"So?"

"She does not like the way you sound."

"Frankly I don't like the way she sounds either," Horowitz complained, "but it's too late to do anything about it."

"She is very upset," Dr. Tannenbaum said.

"She was born upset," Horowitz reported. "With her first breath, she started talking, and she reorganized the whole delivery room."

"What did you say to her?"

"What did I say? Nothing. I was as sweet as I could be."

Mrs. Washington interjected, "That's not saying much."

"Well, whatever you said, she feels that you're not getting the right treatment and that if things continue that way, she wants to have you come out there," the doctor reported.

"I'd leave the country first!" Horowitz protested.

"She says otherwise she'll talk to your son and have you placed in a nursing home where you will get the proper treatment."

"Nobody is going to put me in any nursing home! You hear, nobody!"

Indignantly he tried to slam the phone down in its cradle, but was wide of the mark by half a foot. Without a word, and no look of reproach, Mrs. Washington took it from his hand and silently settled it into its proper place.

From his attitude of defiant belligerence, he was reduced suddenly to sad acknowledgment of his condition.

"I should have been able to do that, shouldn't I?" he asked softly.

"You will, in time. But only if you keep trying," she pointed out.

"I'll . . ." he began but faltered. "I'll tell you something," he was finally able to admit. "Earlier, when I was trying to get dressed, something happened. . . . I . . . I put my right arm into my right sleeve, and then my left arm into my left sleeve. Only when I started to try to button up I discovered that my left arm was never in my left sleeve."

"That happens," she said gently.

"But I thought it was, I thought . . ." He failed to complete what he had started to say and asked, "Do you think she could?"

"What?"

"Put me in a nursing home?"

"I don't think so. After all, there's your son . . ."

"Mona could convince anyone of anything. She convinced her husband he could succeed in real estate in San Diego. And she was right. She's always right. Even when she's wrong, she's right."

He shook his head gravely.

"Why not practice your walking, Mr. Horowitz," Mrs. Washington suggested to divert his mind.

"Good idea," he agreed unenthusiastically.

He raised himself from the bed, pointed toward his metal quad cane. When she did not push it closer, he glared at her. Finally he realized that she was making him do it on his own. He tried to balance himself and reach at the same time, lost balance and fell back onto the bed. Much as he hated to admit it, he had to ask, "Give me your hand?"

She reached out. He seized her hand with his right and pulled himself to his feet. This time she moved the quad cane closer. When its four metal feet were solidly planted on the thick carpet, he gripped it in his right hand and started to take the first step. She stood off, watching him move.

His gait was uneven. He tried to lift his left foot, but could not, and it threw him off stride. The ultimate aim of the therapy was equal strides between left foot and right. He was far from accomplishing that goal. Twice he failed to plant the legs of the cane properly and almost toppled forward. But he labored on toward the bathroom.

When he was in there too long, she eased the door open slightly and discovered him supporting himself against the washstand, leaning close up against the mirror to examine the scar on his cheek. At that moment his eyes strayed from the scar to catch sight of her through the crack in the slightly open door.

"You're spying on me!" he accused.

"I only wanted to make sure you're all right."

"Oh, I'm all right, give or take a few scars! Look at that! Look at it!" he demanded furiously, as he turned awkwardly, afraid to relax his desperate hold on the washstand. "They did that to me! Your nice, misunderstood, underprivileged hoodlums! I never hurt a black man in my whole life. For years I contributed to the NAACP. To the Negro College Fund! And this is what they did to me. So no need to come sneaking around. Come in, my dear Mrs. Washington. And take a good look!"

He was breathing hard, perspiring freely, as he thrust his face toward her defiantly.

He took up his quad cane and started slowly out of the bathroom, mumbling as he went, "They should have killed me. I'd have been better off. To come to my age and be dependent on other people. Not enough they try to cut my throat, they had to give me a stroke, too," he accused.

"That's not true," she corrected gently.

"What do you mean, it's not true?" he demanded irately.

Quietly Mrs. Washington explained, "There could be no connection between being mugged and your stroke. No physical connection, no emotional connection. You would have had the stroke anyhow."

"And what makes you such a professor of medicine, my dear *Mrs.* Washington?"

"I'm a practical nurse, have been for years, and I know certain things. That's one of them."

"You're only trying to defend them. All I know, I got my stroke while that doctor was stitching up this wound! There has to be a connection!" he insisted, bringing the argument to a close.

"There isn't," she said in a whisper.

He did not respond but only glared at her as he walked laboredly with the aid of his quad cane. He made his way slowly out to the foyer and into the living room where the bright light of a sunny summer afternoon flooded the room. He selected the easy chair near the window and sank into it, relieved but tired.

"Can I get you something?" she asked.

"*The New York Times,* did we get it today?" he asked formally, trying to maintain a distance between them.

"Yes."

"Then where is it?"

"In the kitchen."

"What's it doing in the kitchen when it should be in here?"

"I was reading it before you woke."

"From now on, I do not want anyone reading my *Times* before I read it," he declared.

"It isn't your *New York Times*," she said.

"When a paper is delivered to my door, it is my paper!" he began to shout.

"This wasn't delivered. I brought it in," she said.

"What do you mean it wasn't delivered? My *Times* is delivered every day! Except maybe if there's a blizzard or a strike," he shouted indignantly.

"Or if the service is cut off when you go to the hospital," she corrected.

"And nobody remembered to start it up again," he realized. "I'll call them right now. Get the phone, plug it in," he ordered, trying to sound crisp and businesslike to cover his embarrassment.

The delivery office agreed to restore service in the morning. But despite his protests that he had been a steady customer for twenty-eight years, and had suffered the unfortunate fate of being confined to a hospital for some weeks, they could do nothing for him about today's paper. He hung up irritated and depressed.

Mrs. Washington volunteered, "You could have mine. I'm through with it."

"No, thank you," he refused stubbornly.

"There are a lot of interesting articles in it today," she tempted.

"I can guess. Black articles written by black reporters saying how uneducated blacks should go to medical school while smart Jewish boys should be turned away," he grumbled.

"There's not a single article about that today," she assured.

"There must be. They sneak it in every chance they get. I wouldn't want to live in a world run by *The New York Times!*" he declared.

"Still you might want to read today's copy," she suggested.

"I said I don't want to read today's New York Times!" he announced with finality.

"Okay," she said.

She started out of the living room but he called to her, "Mrs. Washington, where are you going?"

"You can't just sit there," she said.

"Who said I can't just sit here? This is my house. My living room. My window. My park! If I want to sit here and look out at it, I will! At least here I won't get mugged!" he accused, as if she were responsible for his injury.

She did not stop to respond but continued on her way, thinking he's a stubborn man, and his own worst enemy. However little cooperation he exhibited in trying to overcome his hip, leg, and foot deficits, he was making no effort at all toward overcoming the equally important and far more difficult task of retraining his hand and arm in their fine motor skills.

They had warned her of this at the hospital Occupational Therapy Service, and had prescribed what she must do. Despite his irascibility, she was determined to do it.

She went into the kitchen and secured the objects she had bought and those she had found in the household during her day of preparation for his homecoming. She was also careful to fold her New York Times neatly and bring it with her.

Chapter Nine

When she returned Horowitz was staring out the window, longingly. He was aware of her presence as he sighed, "A day like this I used to walk home from business. Leave early and walk uptown through the park."

"You will again," she encouraged.

"Never."

On the permanent bridge table in the corner she set down the objects she had assembled. A deck of cards. A child's toy of plastic putty. A jar of marbles. And a small but heavy cardboard box.

"What's all that?" he asked.

"Open the deck and you'll see."

"I don't play cards," he said dogmatically. Then under her questioning gaze he admitted, "A little pinochle maybe. But I'm not really a card player. Hannah had a brother, Abe. There was a card player. I can't tell you how many times he came to see me in my place to beg for help. Always in debt, and always playing cards. Cards is for bums," he declared.

"Open that deck," she commanded. When he hesitated, she volunteered, "If you can't get the paper off the box I'll do it."

"I can do it!" he insisted. "If I want to. And now I want to!"

He took the box in his right hand and tried to tear off the paper with his left, but could not close the fingers tightly enough to do it. So he switched hands and was able to grasp the box in his left while removing the paper with his right.

"There!" he said, vindicated.

"Now open it," she said.

"Why?"

"You have to shuffle them," she said.

"I told you I don't want to play," he insisted, eyeing her *New York Times.*

"You're not going to play. You're just going to shuffle them."

"What for?"

"To use your hands. To get better."

"If my brother-in-law Abe had a stroke, he would be cured in one night if shuffling could do it," Horowitz grumbled. But he did pick up the box in his left hand, break the seal with his right, and finally get the cards out. He tried to shuffle the cards in the conventional manner. He did it very slowly and seemed able to accomplish it until some of the cards escaped his grasp and spewed across the living room carpet.

"I told you I'm not really a card player!"

Mrs. Washington said nothing, just gathered up the cards and presented them to him. He tried to shuffle them again. He did it more slowly but this time he managed to retain them all. He looked up at her. "Okay?"

"Do it again," she ordered.

113

He glared back at her but he did it again. Then again. And again.

"Now hold the halves on the table, flat," she ordered. "Press your thumbs down on them and shuffle them that way."

"I already shuffled them," he protested.

"Thumbs pressed down! Shuffle!"

"Anything you say, Mrs. Legree."

Samuel Horowitz proceeded to apply himself to the task, which proved far from easy.

After he had done it several times, and felt the strain and the pain in his left hand and arm, she ordered, "Now spread them out."

"But I just got them put together!" he protested.

"Spread them out. All around the table."

"What for?"

"So you can gather them up," she explained.

"That makes a lot of no sense," he said. But her firm stare made him comply. He spread the cards across the table and commenced to gather them up with his right hand.

"Left hand only!" she commanded.

"Jawohl, mein fuehrer," he responded sarcastically.

When he had gathered up each card, using only his left hand, and had restored them to the box, he exhaled in relief, and turned his gaze toward her *New York Times* again. But she shoved forward the plastic putty game. He stared at it hostilely.

"What's that?"

"Theraplasty."

"It looks like the Silly Putty I used to get for Marvin's children when they were little," he disputed.

"It may look like that, but it is therapy."

"I may be sixty-eight years old but I am not senile! Nobody, you hear me, nobody is going to make me play children's games!" he shouted.

114

She glared at him while he glared at the plastic putty. After a long interval of such stubborn silence, he looked up at her, "Well, go on."

"And what?" she asked.

"Hit me! It's what I expect. Or maybe you'd like to sneak up on me from behind with a razor?"

She ignored his jibe and ordered, "Dig into that plastic with your left hand. Roll it into a ball. Then flatten it. And then press each finger into it leaving a nice deep print."

"And if I do, will you take me out to the playground in the park and put me in the kiddies' swing? Or maybe the slide?" he countered sarcastically. "If you do, get someone to help you. After all, my dear Mrs. Washington, I wouldn't want you to strain yourself and get a hernia."

He had assumed a physical attitude of such intransigence that she did not press the matter. She pushed aside the box of putty and opened a jar of varicolored marbles. She poured them slowly from the jar, allowing them to spread across the table, while she guarded them from rolling off.

"Marbles?" Horowitz scoffed.

"Marbles," Mrs. Washington confirmed. "Now gather them up, one at a time, with your left hand and put them back into the jar."

"An idiot could do that," he resisted.

"An idiot with a good left hand," she corrected. "Start!"

Grumbling and mumbling to himself in protestations that ranged from her color to her personality, he nevertheless commenced the task. He was able to pick up the first two and drop them into the jar. But he did not quite secure the third, and it skidded from between his fingers and shot across the room like a projectile.

"Two out of three isn't bad," he defended, self-consciously.

115

"You've got fifty more to go," Mrs. Washington said as she went to recover the stray. She stood over him as he completed the exercise. He leaned back with the air of one who had completed his day's work, and he eyed the *Times*, which lay temptingly just out of his reach.

"I'm tired," he declared. "I would like to rest. And maybe do a little reading," he hinted.

"Two more exercises to go," she announced like a tyrannical schoolteacher.

"My hand is tired," he protested.

"Buttons!" she responded.

"What kind of an answer is buttons?"

She did not reply but opened the cardboard box and poured out an array of vari-sized buttons of all types—plastic, horn, metal, dull, shiny, round, square.

"Pick those up, one at a time, in your left hand and put them back in the box," she commanded.

"I'm not in the button business," he declared. "Paper and twine, I know. Not buttons."

"Start picking them up," she commanded, her black eyes quite intense.

"Buttons," he lamented. "A man my age should pick up buttons like a child of five."

"Mr. Horowitz," she began patiently, though underneath she was seething with impatience, "in a certain way, you *are* like a child. You have to reeducate certain of your muscles again to do things that you took for granted before. So start picking up those buttons!"

He glared at her, he glared at the buttons, but in a while he reached out his left hand, slowly and tentatively. He tried to engulf the largest of the buttons close to him. His fingers responded only partially, barely sufficiently to finally clamp his thumb and forefinger around the large, round, slippery horn button. He lifted it, transferred it to the box, and dropped it in.

116

"It's not such a big deal," he attempted to trivialize the difficult maneuver, but he proceeded to select only the largest buttons. When the large ones had been collected, he attempted one of the smaller ones, but it proved too difficult and, in the end, elusive. He could not grasp it. He sat there helpless and inept. Unable to look up at her, he stared straight ahead, feeling his failure so obviously that she felt quite sorry for him.

Before he could dwell on it too long, she said, "All right, now for the *Times*."

In great relief, he asked, "My reading glasses? I think I left them on the bedside table."

"The *Times* is not for reading, it's for exercising," she informed.

"Exercising?" Horowitz exclaimed impatiently. "We've had enough exercising for one day!"

Ignoring his protest, she explained, "What we do is take one whole sheet of the *Times*, and hold it out wide like this," she illustrated, spreading her hands as wide as they could go. "Then we crumple it in toward the center until it is one big ball of paper. In the process we use our hands, *both* of them, and our fingers, *all* of them."

"And when do 'we' get to read the damn thing? After all, I cannot read and crumple at the same time. Can you?"

"I don't have to."

"Well, I'll be damned if I will!" Horowitz declared and he assumed his intransigent pose once again. When she did not relent, he muttered, "You are an impossible woman, Mrs. Washington. I begin to see now what it was that killed your husband. He didn't die, he escaped."

Still she would not relent. Her face, which could be warm and pleasant in repose, was set as grimly as his. Meantime, Horowitz could not conceal his curiosity. There were two headlines that intrigued him and he was itching to know more. Finally his desire overcame his stubbornness. He closed his eyes. Then he opened his right eye stealthily.

"We . . . we could maybe discuss a normalization of relations," he suggested obliquely.

"Such as?"

"Well, for openers, Mrs. Washington, what good is a crumpled up newspaper?"

"Exercise!" she maintained firmly.

"Okay, so tell me something, how do you measure the exercise power in a sheet of newspaper? Hmm?"

"It's in the way you are forced to use your hands together. To crumple a newspaper into a ball takes two hands. That means it is good therapy."

"So who is arguing?" Horowitz asked, at his most ingratiating best. "Actually we are fighting to agree with one another. But . . ." and here he paused to give his words great significance, "tell me this, my dear Mrs. Washington. When you went to the hospital to learn all this, did anyone ever say to you, a newspaper that has been read first has lost its exercise power? Did they?" he asked, with the air of a Talmudic scholar.

"Nothing was said about reading it," she admitted.

"Therefore," he declared, as if they had overcome a negotiating barrier of considerable importance, "we must assume that merely reading the paper does not diminish its exercise potential. Correct?"

"Yes, I suppose so," she granted, though not too willingly, for it appeared she had reservations.

"Take my word for it. I've been in paper and twine over forty years. Well, it seems we are now in a position to achieve a compromise, as they say. So let me suggest the following. First, I will read your *New York Times*. And when I am done, I will, with both these hands, crumple every sheet until it forms a perfect ball. What do you think of that?"

118

"Well, this one time . . ." she granted.

"I'll need my reading glasses, Mrs. Washington."

"Of course, Mr. Horowitz. Right now would be a good time to get in a little walking. See if you can make it into the bedroom and back."

"A little thing like getting a man's reading glasses," he bemoaned, "is that too much to ask?"

"A little walk into the bedroom and back, is that too much to do?" she countered.

He knew she would not relent. In their comparatively brief relationship, he had already learned enough about her to know one thing: No matter how much he talked and how little she talked, somehow, in the end, he always wound up doing exactly what she wanted him to do. How could a woman be so stubborn, he protested silently to himself. But stubborn she was. As he had discovered that first day, a real tough cookie.

So now, having no choice, he reached out for his quad and lifted himself from the chair. As he labored along, step by dragging step, he began to mumble, ostensibly to himself, but with an occasional sly turn of the head to see if he was having any effect on her.

"My family never owned any slaves," he muttered. "In fact, when your family were slaves, we lived in Poland and had our own *tsores*. Cossacks! Drunken cossacks used to come riding into the town at night, killing, burning, raping! Do I blame you for that? So don't blame me. It wouldn't do any harm you should be a little more friendly. Stop thinking about me as whitey. Think of me as Horowitz. Samuel Horowitz, who never owned a single tenement in Harlem. I am not a honky. I am a nice, refined Jewish gentleman, who never harmed a fly. After all, I didn't attack those two black gorillas. They attacked me."

By that time he had made it out of the living room. When he returned, he was still muttering.

119

"And not only that, but do you know that we Jews were slaves long before your people? We go back thousands of years in this slavery thing. Egypt. Did you know about Egypt, Mrs. Washington? How we were slaves there and had to build the pyramids?"

Unmoved by his plaint, she observed, "Let my people go."

"Exactly," Horowitz said. "The first big freedom movement in the history of the world. And after Egypt, we were slaves in Babylon. And after Babylon, Rome. Hannah, bless her memory, she and I went to Rome one year. And there, overhead in one of the archways of the Coliseum, it is written in ancient Roman script that that huge stadium was built by Jews brought to Rome as slaves. So you see, Mrs. Washington, we have a lot in common. We should be allies, not enemies. It wouldn't do any harm if you were a little more friendly toward me. And not such a tyrant. After all, if I want to have my every minute run by someone, if I want to be dominated, I don't have to stay here. I could go to San Diego and let Mona do that, God forbid."

By that time he was back in his chair by the window, had his reading glasses on and was so immersed in the *Times* that no further talk was necessary. Mrs. Washington was free to go into the kitchen to begin preparing his dinner.

Even from the kitchen she could hear his bursts of outrage at some item or editorial he was reading. He seemed to carry on a perpetual war with the *Times*. Every so often the air was punctuated with a "Sonofabitch!" or "Insane, they are all insane at the *Times*!"

That was followed by a long silence and another outburst, "Crazy, that Tom Wicker is crazy!" Or else it was "Let the *Times* run this country, we'd be bankrupt in a week!"

There followed a longer silence, a total silence. She was curious and provoked enough to slip back into the living room. He was slumped in his chair. Her first impulse was to rush to his side. But she noticed that his breathing was regular, and that he was snoring just the faintest bit. He had fallen asleep. And no wonder, she thought, it had been a tiring day for him. She left the room quietly, without disturbing him, and went back to the kitchen.

When she returned, he was awake again and crumpling the large sheets of the Times into balls. He did not accomplish it easily, but at least he was trying. When he detected the look of satisfaction on her face, he felt called on to deny her her victory by remarking, "If more people crumpled the Times instead of reading it, this country would be better off!"

Then he announced, "I'm saving the editorial page and the Op-Ed page for last. Oh, will I give them a crumple!"

He had eaten his light dinner. Lamb chops that required considerable two-handed cutting, a baked potato, and a salad. With his Sanka she served him fresh peaches over a slice of plain cake.

During the meal he called to her, "Mrs. Washington?"

"Yes?" she responded from the kitchen.

"Could you come in here?"

"Something you need?"

"Yes."

"What?"

"You."

She appeared in the doorway, curious.

"Would you sit down, please?"

"Where?"

"There," he pointed.

Hesitant and puzzled, she sat in the chair opposite him. When he did not speak, she urged, "Well?"

121

"Well, what?"

"Anything else?" she asked.

"Just sit there," he said softly, before confessing, "When Hannah was alive we used to eat in here every night. Me here. She there. And it was fine. Fine. After she died I couldn't eat in here anymore, alone. I would make something and take it into the bedroom and eat off a little table while I was watching television.

"They say television is used as a babysitter for children. Even more for grown-ups. We try to fight our loneliness by knowing there is a big world out there. And people. We say, I am not alone. But we are alone. I know Walter Cronkite. But he doesn't know me. I could sit there watching and die, but he would never know it, or even care. We keep reaching out, but no one reaches back. It's a terrible thing to be lonely."

"I know," she said sympathetically.

"You don't know," he corrected. "You have a daughter and grandchildren to take care of."

"You have a son, a daughter, and four grandchildren," she reminded.

"Yes, but they don't need me. Hannah and I, when we sat down to dinner at this table, we were a family. Just the two of us, but still a family. She needed me, I needed her. We didn't have to say it, but we knew it."

As if he felt naked having exposed his feelings too freely, he applied himself industriously to his dessert. While appearing to be engrossed in that, he dared, "Mrs. Washington, could I ask you a favor?"

"Of course."

"Would you have dinner with me every evening? It would help to have someone sitting there on the other side of the table."

She did not answer at once. He took it to be a rejection so he hastened to argue his case. "After all, it doesn't take any more time to make four lamb chops than it does to

122

make two. Or to bake two potatoes than it does to bake one."

Still she did not respond.

"As for doing the dishes, you put them into the dishwasher anyhow. So you put in four dishes instead of two, and two cups and saucers instead of one," he pleaded his case. "So? What do you say, Mrs. Washington?"

"Mr. Horowitz, please understand . . ."

He shook his head sadly. "As soon as someone says, please understand, then the answer is no. I must have offended you. That's not my fault but yours. You take me too seriously. Do you think, do you really think, Mrs. Washington, that I blame you for this?" He pointed to the scar on his cheek.

"I don't blame you. All those things I say to you, they're not intended for you. It's because I can't say them to those two black cossacks," he explained. "So . . . so, don't think I hold anything against you. And reconsider what I asked."

"I would like to, but I can't," Mrs. Washington said.

"Why not? You're afraid of what people will say? That it shows a lack of respect? I don't need respect, Mrs. Washington. I need a person there, else I might as well have my meals in my bedroom and watch television and get ready to die."

"It hasn't to do with respect, or what people might say," she explained tenderly, "it's the children."

"You think my children would object to you sitting in Hannah's place?"

"We have a routine in my home. My daughter starts to cook dinner. I come home and complete it. Then my grandchildren and I have dinner together. Every night. It gives them a sense of family even though their father is not there and their mother is off working. They know grandma is there. It is time to say grace and eat, then

123

watch a bit of TV, and go off to bed. I can't upset that routine. It wouldn't be fair to them."

"No," he was forced to agree, "it wouldn't be fair." But he could not conceal his disappointment.

"Of course," she volunteered, "there's no reason why I can't just sit here while you're having your dinner every evening."

"That would be nice," he agreed. "And maybe have a cup of coffee? Would that be all right?"

"I think so."

"Then . . . then get yourself a cup now," he suggested. "In fact, if you like regular instead of Sanka, order some tomorrow."

"No, Sanka is fine with me."

"Good, good!"

She went out into the kitchen and returned with a steaming cup of Sanka. She sat down opposite him. He glanced at her over his own cup. And he smiled.

It was the first time Mrs. Washington had seen him smile.

PART
II

Chapter Ten

The fitter in the orthopedic appliance store addressed himself to Samuel Horowitz's problem with all the gravity of a surgeon about to perform cardiac surgery. He studied Dr. Tannenbaum's prescription, he studied Horowitz's shoe, he studied Horowitz.

"This the only kind of shoes you have?"

"This is a fine English-made shoe which I have been buying from Saks Fifth Avenue for the past thirty-five years. Treat them right, keep them on shoes trees, they can last a lifetime. What's wrong with this shoe?" Horowitz demanded indignantly.

"It won't do," the fitter said.

"Thirty-five years the same last, thirty-five years the only thing that has changed is the price. Always goes up. Now suddenly it won't do! You ever heard such nonsense?" He addressed his question to Mrs. Washington. "Seven pairs. Four black. Three brown. Different styles but the same last. And now it won't do."

"If you will give me a chance to explain," the man tried to interrupt.

"This is a shoe, from the first time you put it on it's comfortable. No breaking in, no blisters, no bunions."

"Please, Mr. Horowitz . . ."

"Okay," Horowitz acceded with enormous intolerance.

"In order to insert a short leg brace, it's better if the shoe is a blucher. It opens wider and is easier for a man like you to slip into."

"What do you mean, a man like me?" Horowitz shot back.

"Well," the man proceeded warily, "any man who's not used to wearing a leg brace is going to have a bit of trouble getting the shoe off and on. It's only natural. So what we suggest is a blucher that opens wider. And a Velcro closing that doesn't have to be laced."

"I know how to tie my laces. Ask her, she can tell you!"

"He can tie his laces, when he remembers," she said, warning the fitter by the look in her black eyes that he had better proceed cautiously.

He picked up his cue. "Well, there's no reason why you can't have laces. Frankly, it's a pleasure to deal with a man who can. We get so many of the other kind."

"Those bluchers," Horowitz said, "I don't like them. They're ugly. Broad-toed. Not graceful. A shoe like mine, a nice English wing tip, has class."

"A blucher would be better," the fitter kept suggesting.

Mrs. Washington decided to intervene. "Tell me, sir, after you build a brace into a shoe, when it comes time to take it out . . ." The man was about to explain that most patients had permanent need of such braces, but she overrode him, "What does it do to the shoe?"

"You mean, can the shoe be restored to what it was before we put in the brace?"

"Exactly," Mrs. Washington said.

"Once the brace is in, it's in. That shoe can't be used for any other purpose."

"Well," she considered a moment before pointing out, "it would be a shame to ruin such a fine pair of English shoes."

"It certainly would!" Horowitz agreed.

"Then a pair of bluchers would mean you didn't have to ruin these?" she asked, inviting the fitter's agreement.

"That's right."

"Well," Horowitz began to reconsider, "if it's only temporary, and if it saves my own shoes, okay, I'll take bluchers. Nine and a half B."

"Fine," the man said quickly. "I'll order up a pair and we'll attach the brace on the left one, exactly as Dr. Tannenbaum ordered."

"Tell me," Horowitz began to inquire, prompted by second thoughts, "that brace . . . it shows?"

"Your trouser leg will cover most of it."

"But it shows?" Horowitz persisted.

"Only slightly. On the side, below the trouser leg. Women have a much worse problem."

"Tell me," Horowitz said, "what color plastic is that damned thing made of?"

"White," the man said.

"Well, is there any law says you can't blacken the bottom of it. Where it sticks out from under the trouser leg? Any medical reason?" Horowitz asked, his left eye closed, his right open.

"No, I guess we could do that," the man agreed.

"Good! You do that!" Then he admitted reluctantly, "I don't like people staring at me."

From the moment she arrived the next morning, Mrs. Washington knew that Mr. Horowitz had experienced a difficult night. There was evidence that he had come out into the living room after she had made sure he was

129

safely in bed. That fact alone would not have disturbed her, for it could be a sign of resurgent independence. However, just in front of one of the easy chairs there was a rough swirl in the carpet betraying a struggle. He must have come out during the night on his quad cane, and when his impatience with it overruled his caution, he had obviously fallen.

She tiptoed to the door of the bedroom and listened. She heard no sounds of the radio, which he usually played when he was awake and awaiting her arrival. She eased the door open slightly and listened. He was breathing steadily, deeply, in sleep. Reassured, she decided to allow him to sleep until she had finished most of her housekeeping chores.

But when she entered the kitchen she found a shattered cup and a large, dried black stain spread untidily across the linoleum, obviously produced when a cup of Sanka dropped and shattered. She gathered up the pieces, got down on her knees and scrubbed at the black stain until she removed it. Then she felt forced to wash the entire floor, else the newly cleaned spot would make the rest of it look dowdy.

By the time she had finished it was long past his waking hour. She decided to disturb him. He woke angry. Which, to her, meant that he felt guilty. She mentioned nothing about the kitchen, nothing about the living room carpet. After his ablutions he presented himself for breakfast. She served him a simple meal, but made only one change in his equipment. She had reduced the padding on his fork to almost one half of what it had been. He had trouble handling it, but silently he applied himself and managed to use it well enough to feed himself without resorting to his right hand too frequently.

He had yet to say good morning. He ate and stared off into space. She watched, trying not to appear too inquisitive. Something had seriously disturbed him and he was refusing to talk about it.

Finally, she barked at him, "Good morning, Mr. Horowitz!"

"What's good about it?" he asked hostilely, but went on eating. Eventually he granted, "Good morning."

"That's better. Would you like your Sanka now?"

The word caused him to look up sheepishly. "You . . . you found that mess out in the kitchen?"

"Yes."

"Sorry."

"That's okay." Then having opened a channel of communication, as gently as she could, she asked, "You had a bad night?"

He did not reply. She did not press the issue. Either he would tell her in his own time, or never. He was one of the most stubborn patients she had ever encountered.

Later, he proved most uncooperative during his exercises, which she had to force on him. He muttered throughout, uncomplimentary epithets, ranging from Hitler to Idi Amin and Andrew Young.

As she worked with him, she observed, "If your arm and hand showed as much resistance as your mean temper, you'd be cured by now."

Thus, insulting each other, they gradually got through the first exercise session of the day. It was time for him to take his shower and get dressed. But he had still given no hint of what troubled him. She was growing more concerned, for in his present impatient mood if he fell in the shower, as he had obviously done last night in the living room, the consequences could be grave. Many stroke victims suffered broken bones and skull injuries as a result of such falls. In his case she knew it could prove fatal, if not from the physical trauma then from the defeat to his spirit.

So while he was in the shower, she lingered at the

bathroom door, peeking through to watch him. He moved carefully enough. He was cautious with the soap. When he was finally finished and pushed open the door of the shower, he groped for the towel. He could not reach it; she handed it to him. He took it easily enough, but a moment later it dawned on him that she was too conveniently near.

"You were watching me," he accused. She did not deny it. "You think that's nice? A grown woman spying on a naked man?"

"This may come as a shock to you, Mr. Horowitz, but you have nothing to show that I haven't seen before. Many times."

"Don't be fresh," he countered, continuing to dry himself, always careful to keep certain parts of himself covered.

"I'm not going to rape you," she said, commenting on his maidenly modesty.

"Why not? You people are experts at it!" he replied bitterly. He was sorry at once. "I . . . I didn't mean to say that," he apologized. "It just slipped out."

"But you did think it," she replied. "Else it couldn't have just 'slipped out.'"

He did not reply but groped for his robe on the hook on the bathroom door. When he failed to reach it the first time, she stood back and made him try again. He slipped his right arm into the sleeve, but his left missed the mark, not once but twice.

"Aren't you going to help me?"

"It's better if you do it for yourself."

Self-consciously, he worked at it until he had sufficient control and coordination to accomplish that simple feat. As he fumbled with the sash, he muttered, "You're angry because of what I said, so you won't help me anymore."

"The more you do for yourself the better," she an-

132

swered with a marked degree of professional coolness. "Now get dressed. We're going out to the park."

"I do not wish to go to the park today."

"It's a nice day. But hot. The earlier we go the better," she vetoed his objection. "So get dressed. Neatly," she added.

. "In what? Flared purple slacks and a big wide-brimmed hat?" he commented acidly on the uniform he had seen young blacks in the neighborhood adopt.

"You just get dressed in a shirt and slacks that won't disgrace me," she said firmly.

He struggled with his shirt and managed the buttons out of sheer stubbornness. He even managed to zip up his slacks almost all the way rather than give her the satisfaction of having to ask her help. When she came in to inspect him, she discovered his zipper was not completely closed and locked in place so she reached for it to complete the operation.

"It's okay," he resisted, drawing back.

Undeterred she finished the job. "There. You're safe. No one can rape you," she said. "Now, walk!"

"No wheelchair today?" he asked hopefully.

"Use your cane to the door. You need the exercise. You'll get into the chair there."

"You're going to drag me through that lobby again in that damned chair?" he accused. "You're trying to humiliate me. That Angelo on the elevator, and especially Juan at the door, they just wait to see me like this! I don't know why. Every year at Christmas, I give them a nice present. In fact, Hannah always used to say . . ."

But he broke off the remembrance abruptly. "All right, I'll walk to the door. I'll get in that damn chair. But if either of those two smile at me, I'll give them a what for!"

But when Angelo opened the elevator door, smiled and said, "Ah, good morning, Mr. Horowitz. You lookin' much better today," instead of resorting to the vitupera-tion he had threatened, Horowitz said, "Thank you."

At the front door when Juan helped the chair up the three steps, saying cheerily, "One day soon, Mr. Horwitz, you goin' to be walking up those steps by yourself," Horowitz responded with a pleasant smile, about which he was self-conscious because he noticed that Mrs. Washington's black eyes sparkled impishly.

They had been sitting in the sun for almost an hour. Nothing had been said between them. The sounds of traffic, more oppressive in the city during summer days, were all that could be heard. Occasionally from off in the playground behind them came the sound of children laughing, or the sudden anguished outcry of some child injured at play, or suffering the destruction of some fragile toy until a watchful mother hushed away the weeping with an embrace or a kiss. The sounds of life were comforting to hear, and yet distressing.

Horowitz spoke first. "I used to take her out to that playground when she was small."

"Mona?" Mrs. Washington asked.

"Even then she used to tell the other kids what to play, and how to play. Once she took a toy from another kid and wouldn't give it back. Not even when I promised her one like it. She kept that one. And I had to buy a new one for the other little girl. You think kids are born with all the characteristics they're going to have later?"

"Yes," Mrs. Washington agreed. "Conrad, he was like that from the day I first remember him. He would reach for a finger and hold on as if his life depended on it. And he's like that to this day. Tightfisted. He won't spend a penny if he can save it. He'll grow up to be the same. He'll be a success, Conrad will."

"Conrad?" Horowitz asked.

"Oh, here I'm talking about him as if you knew him. My grandson."

"Conrad . . . nice name," Horowitz said. "And evidently a nice boy."

"Oh, yes, and he's going far, far!" Mrs. Washington said with pride and determination. "He's already first in his grade in school. Mind you, not just first in his class. First in his whole grade."

"That's nice. One thing we Jews learned, the only way out of poverty is education," Horowitz said. "I have two grandchildren in Boston. Harvard."

"Mona's children," she recalled.

"Yes. And you want my honest opinion? The reason they picked Boston was to get as far away from their mother as possible." Then he added, "Nice kids, though."

He was silent for a long moment, until, "One day you'll see them for yourself. They'll come down and visit me," he insisted. "Of course, this summer they're taking special courses so it's hard for them to get away."

Her sensitivity to the emotional abandonment by his family forced her to remain silent. After a moment, Horowitz said, "Hmm! First not only in his class but in his whole grade. You must be very proud of Conrad."

"Of course," she admitted, straining to be modest.

"And the girl?"

"Louise," Mrs. Washington said.

"Louise," he savored the name. "Louise. Lovely name. Mrs. Washington, I hope you won't mind if I give you a little advice. Don't be so proud of Conrad that the girl feels . . . feels like second best. Find something in her to be proud about. She's pretty, maybe?"

"Yes."

"Good!"

"And very bright," Mrs. Washington hastened to add. "Her record in second grade was every bit as good as Conrad's."

Greatly relieved, Horowitz said, "Fine." Then he added, "You know, just because I don't get to see them

135

very often doesn't mean I'm not close to Bruce and Candy. So I know how sensitive grandchildren can be when you start comparing them. I'm very glad for your sake that Conrad and Louise are both so bright. In fact, one day soon, it might not be such a bad idea if . . . if . . ."

But a sense of futility prevented him from completing his thought.

The traffic noises and the sounds of children at play took over again until Mrs. Washington announced, "Time for lunch!"

She took her place behind the wheelchair and was about to assist him with it. This offered him the first chance he had to speak without risking her inquisitive, opinionated eyes.

"Mrs. Washington . . ."

She was about to move from behind the chair, but he stopped her. "Please, no. Just where you are. Listen for a moment."

"All right."

"You didn't say anything about the Sanka I spilled on the kitchen floor. That's because you are a very considerate woman. Well, I want to apologize."

"It happens," she said, seeking to make light of his accident.

"It made so much more work for you."

"The kitchen floor needed a scrubbing."

"You washed it only yesterday," he reminded.

"So what? It isn't going to shrink."

"Anyhow I want you to know that I appreciate that you didn't mention it."

"Thank you."

"And also, you must have guessed that I fell last night in the living room."

"Yes."

"Is that why you spied on me in the shower this

morning?" he asked. Before she could answer, he corrected himself, "I mean is that why you *observed* me in the shower this morning?"

"Yes."

"And that is exactly why I was so nasty with you. I didn't want anyone to know that I fell. You won't tell Marvin will you? Or Mona?"

"Not if you promise not to get yourself into such situations again."

"I . . . I couldn't help it. I couldn't sleep last night," he tried to explain.

"I didn't sleep so well last night myself."

"Why?" he asked, genuinely solicitous.

"I have nights. I stay awake and worry. What will happen to Conrad and Louise if something happens to me?"

"They have a mother," he pointed out.

"Yes, but when she's off working, and they're alone, who'll see to their supper and their homework, and what they do nights? Who'll hug them, kiss them, and put them to bed? That keeps me up nights." She invited his confession. "And you?"

"Ah," he said with a sweeping gesture of his right hand, dismissing the entire subject. "Lunch," he said, inviting her cooperation in getting safely across the street before the green light changed to red.

During lunch, which consisted of a broiled veal chop and some carrots, the chop requiring the use of his left hand to pin it down while his right did the cutting, she sat across from him as he had requested. She sipped her Sanka and watched, silently observing that he now used the less padded fork a little more easily than he had this morning. But he was still troubled by his secret burden. Perhaps during his finger exercises she would be able to worm it out of him. It was the way child psychiatrists

137

handled reluctant children. Engage their hands so it freed their minds and their tongues.

At the end of lunch, as they sat opposite each other sipping their Sanka, he observed softly, "Mrs. Washington, I don't want you to take this the wrong way. But my Hannah, when we had veal chops, she used to fry them, not broil them. Mind you, I'm not saying yours was not good. For a plain, dry veal chop it was pretty tasty. But if you want a *meichel*, you take a chop like that, dip it in a little egg, roll it in matzoh meal and fry it in chicken fat. Fantastic!"

Suddenly he remembered, "Oh, let me explain what *meichel* means."

"An especially tasty dish," she replied.

"Rosengarten?" he asked grudgingly.

"He used to like his veal chops that way, too."

"I see," he pouted, having been denied the privilege of adding to her education. Then he mused suddenly, without seeming motivation, "Hannah . . . Hannah . . ."

He said no more until Mrs. Washington had put him through his arm, foot, leg, and hip exercises. When they reached the dexterity exercises involving marbles and buttons, he was as uncooperative as ever.

"Those kids out in the park, that's for them. Not a sixty-eight-year-old man."

But he labored at them and finally managed to seize most of them. Though three marbles skittered out of his inefficient left-handed clutch and ended up across the room and under the couch. Mrs. Washington had to get down on her hands and knees to retrieve them, adding to his discomfort. To make amends, he offered, "You play gin rummy?"

"Yes."

"Would you care to indulge?" he invited.

"I have a better game," she countered.

"Pinochle?" he asked eagerly.

138

"No," she said, and left the room to secure a package she brought with her this morning. Before she could unwrap it, he had already decided to hate it, and asked suspiciously, "What's that?"

"A game," she said, continuing to unwrap it carefully.

"What kind of game?"

She held up a brightly illustrated flat cardboard box.

"Chinese checkers?" he exploded. "What kind of game is that for a grown man?"

"We'll try it and see."

"I don't play anything Chinese. Not checkers. Not Ping-Pong. Let Nixon and Kissinger be friends with the Chinese, not me!"

"It's a game invented by Americans, made by Americans. There's nothing Chinese about it."

"So why do they call it Chinese checkers?" he demanded defiantly.

She placed the game on the bridge table and proceeded to set up her side of the board, dropping each white marble into place where it belonged. When he refused to join, she urged, "Go on. Set up. At least try. You might like it."

"Why do I get the black marbles? Why not the white ones?"

"Okay, you get the white ones."

He proceeded to take advantage of his minor victory by attempting to turn the board around.

"Oh, no!" She intercepted his hand by placing her own strong black hand on the board. "You want the white ones, set them up yourself with your left hand!" She swept them out of their holes and across the board, forcing him to laboriously pick up each marble and place it in the hole.

"Some game," he muttered. "You start by taking advantage of me! While I'm concentrating on moving my marble with my left hand you're already thinking three

139

moves ahead! Next thing, you'll want to play me for money." He had finished setting up his part of the board. "How does this work?"

She demonstrated and they proceeded to play a game. During which he muttered disparagingly, "Pinochle, it's not."

"Play!" she commanded.

"And if I don't?" he defied. "What'll you do, hit me? It would be like you to strike a defenseless man," he accused. "That's what happened to Joe Abelson. He had a private nurse; a male nurse. Black. After Abelson died, the undertaker discovered bruises on his body. So go ahead, I expect the same!"

She ignored his insult, concentrated on the game and on the fact that despite his protests, competition had stimulated him to a little more use of his left hand.

After a while, as he studied his next move, he admitted, "Actually that was only a rumor about Abelson. I never did know for sure there were any bruises."

"And the nurse?" she asked skeptically.

"He wasn't exactly black," Horowitz had to admit.

"What does 'not exactly black' mean?" she asked.

"It means . . . it means white, I guess." To change the subject quickly he said, "I bet if you put your mind to it you could learn to play pinochle."

"Chinese checkers is a better game," she persisted.

"If I shuffled the cards every time, if I used my left hand a lot, would you learn pinochle?"

"I guess I could learn," she acceded.

Eagerly he pointed to the large walnut breakfront. "In there, in the top drawer you will find a couple of decks of pinochle cards. They've been there ever since Hannah . . ." He did not say the word.

"She put them there, and I never touched them since," he confessed. "Look for them. Please?"

Mrs. Washington found two decks of pinochle cards in

140

their boxes. One had been opened and used. The other was still sealed. She handed them to him and he grasped them as if they were holy artifacts. He felt them tenderly, even using his left hand to do so. As he became aware of his left-handed limitations he said, "I'm glad Hannah never saw me this way. It would have hurt her too much. Too much."

He took the cards from the opened box and began to shuffle them laboriously, as he proceeded to instruct, "In this deck there are not fifty-two cards but forty-eight. And only aces, kings, queens, jacks, tens, and nines. Two of each suit. So there are twelve each of spades, hearts, clubs, and diamonds. Making forty-eight. Now there are two ways you can make points in this game. You can win tricks. And you can meld."

"Meld?" Mrs. Washington asked.

"Lay down combinations, like in rummy," Horowitz explained. "But you can only meld after you win a trick. Now, what is meld? There are two kinds. There's runs, like a flush in trump, ace, king, queen, jack, ten. And there's a marriage."

"Marriage?" Mrs. Washington was puzzled at the anomalous term.

Impatiently, Horowitz explained, "Marriage! Marriage! A king and queen of the same suit. That's worth twenty points. But a royal marriage is worth forty."

"Royal marriage," Mrs. Washington remarked, unwilling to ask and incur his wrath again.

But he suspected, so he explained without being asked, "A royal marriage is a king and queen of trump."

"You never said anything about trump," she pointed out.

Bristling, he declared, "I'm getting to that. First, melds! Now, in addition to runs you can also meld combinations. Four aces, one of each suit, is worth a hundred. Four kings, eighty. Queens, sixty. Jacks, forty."

"I see, four each of different suits. Now, about trump . . ." she said.

"I'm not finished with melds yet," Horowitz reminded impatiently. "There is what's called a pinochle. A jack of diamonds and a queen of spades. That's worth forty points."

"Only forty? Why?"

"What do you mean, why?"

"Well, if that combination is the name of the game shouldn't it be worth more than any other combination?"

"Well, it isn't!" Horowitz declared. "Such questions! Look, just be silent and listen. I'll tell you everything you have to know."

"All right," she agreed reluctantly.

He glared at her and continued, "So we know about melds. Now, about tricks! Each trick you win gives you points, because each card has a point value. For instance, an ace is worth eleven. A king is worth four, a queen, three, a jack, two, and a ten is worth ten"

"Why?"

"What do you mean, why?" Horowitz exploded. "Because that's the rules of the game!"

Mrs. Washington shook her head, saying softly, "Strange game where a ten is worth more than a king and queen."

"Take my word for it!" Horowitz bellowed. He regained his composure and, assuming the air of a reasonable man, he continued. "Now, as I said, there are forty-eight cards. The dealer hands out three at a time, like this."

He proceeded to peel off three cards for Mrs. Washington. Then three cards for himself. He repeated the procedure four times.

"Now you have twelve and I have twelve, which adds up to twenty-four. And which means there are twenty-four still in the pack. Only we call it *stock*."

142

"Why?" Mrs. Washington asked, but quickly withdrew her question. "Never mind why. Just continue."

He glared at her, but proceeded to explain. "Now the top card of the stock we turn over like this. And this is now trump!" He slipped the ten of diamonds halfway under the stock. "Does that answer your question about trump?" he demanded.

"Yes, it's all very clear now," she agreed.

"Well, I'm not done!" he said. "Because there is yet another important rule about trump. If you are holding, or if you draw one of the nines of trump, you can exchange it for the trump card that is showing. Like, for instance, if you happen to have the nine of diamonds you can put it down and take this ten, which has a higher point value. You also get ten points for that. See?"

"I happen . . ." Mrs. Washington said.

"Happen what?" he asked, irritated.

". . . to have the nine of diamonds," she said.

He glared at her, then finally admitted, "Well, when you take a trick you can exchange the deece for the jack."

"Deece?" she asked.

"Deece, deece!" he shouted. "The nine of trump is called the deece!"

She was about to ask why, but the look in his eyes made her forego that bit of esoteric information.

"Okay, so now you know about trump, about melds, and about the deece. The rest is tricks. A higher card takes a lower card. A trump takes anything else. And after each card you play, you draw one from the stock. Until the stock is gone. Then we play out the hands and, at the end, we add up melds and tricks and whoever has the highest number of points is the winner. Understand?"

"Understand," she said, to avoid any further apoplectic outbursts.

"So let's play," he said, picking up his hand and

starting to arrange his cards in suits while she watched furtively to see how well he used his left hand in the process. Unconsciously, he favored his right hand, which distressed her. But she said nothing.

In the midst of the game, as he was reaching for a stock card with his right hand while clutching the rest in his left, he paused, his hand resting on the card he was about to draw.

"I would like to say something . . ." he began, but halted, hand still resting on the card.

"Yes?" she encouraged.

"I would like to say that I am very sorry about this morning."

"You woke up depressed. That will happen, Mr. Horowitz. From time to time you'll get discouraged. You'll resent your limitations. You'll feel you are not making progress. So you'll resent me and say things you don't mean. I understand."

"That's very kind of you, Mrs. Washington," he said, "but the truth is you don't understand. I mean, you can't understand. Why am I having so much trouble saying what I really mean?"

He withdrew his hand, laboriously put down his cards and looked into her face.

"Last night," he began, "after I fell asleep, I woke up suddenly. Something was bothering me. What, I didn't know. But I couldn't fall asleep again. I thought and I thought. What was it I wanted to do and didn't? It didn't have to do with Marvin, or with Mona, or with the grandchildren. Bernadine I already took care of. So what could it be?

"And then just when the first light was beginning to show through the shutters, it came to me. *Yahrzeit!* You know what means *yahrzeit*, Mrs. Washington?"

Now that he had started to reveal the source of his anguish, she did not wish to divert him so she shook her head slightly.

"You mean the Rosengartens never observed *yahrzeit*? What were they? Reformed?" he asked in a tone of disapproval. He proceeded to explain, "*Yahrzeit* means just what it says."

"I see," she replied, encouraging him to continue.

"*Yahr* means year. And *zeit* means time. Which together mean time of the year. Now what time of the year, you are asking? It is the time of the year for a most unhappy anniversary. The day on which a loved one died. A father, mother, a husband . . . or a wife. And that time of the year is not measured on the regular calendar but on the Jewish calendar. My Hannah, she should rest in peace, died on the tenth of June 1974. Which on the Jewish calendar was the twentieth day of the month of Sivan. This year the twentieth day of Sivan came out on the sixth of June.

"So why was I so troubled last night? Because Hannah's *yahrzeit* was while I was in the hospital. So Hannah's *yahrzeit* came and went and I did nothing. Nothing! Do you hear? I shamed her memory.

"Not I said *kaddish*, not Marvin said *kaddish*. We didn't light a *yahrzeit* candle the night before. We didn't go to *schul* the morning of the sixth of June. Of course, Marvin is too high-class to go to *schul*. He goes to temple. And then only for board meetings. He's a trustee. But God forbid you should ask him to come to synagogue early some morning to form a *minyan*, he has to go to court in Washington, or fly to Dallas or Chicago on business.

"And Mona, well, women do not go to *schul* on *yahrzeit*. So who is there left to remember Hannah, and to honor her memory? *Me*. And where was I on the twentieth day of Sivan, the sixth day of June? In the hospital. I must have been drugged. The whole thing went out of my mind. So no candle the night before, no *kaddish* at *yahrzeit*, nothing!"

He fell silent for a moment, then reproached himself,

"I should have remembered! Because in that bag of groceries I was carrying when I was mugged were two *yahrzeit* candles. I can even remember hearing the glass shatter when the bag hit the street and broke open. Still, once I was in the hospital, I . . . somehow I forgot . . . yes, I must have been drugged, to forget something like that. But whatever the reason, Hannah Horowitz was like she never lived. Nobody went before God and said, 'Remember this good woman. She was an angel. So, God, I praise You in my *yahrzeit* prayers so You will remember her and give her eternal peace. Maybe even make up to her for the nuisance I was during her lifetime and which she put up with.'"

He looked at Mrs. Washington and in all seriousness said, "Frankly, Mrs. Washington, I can tell you that I am sometimes very difficult to get along with."

"No," she said, attempting to portray surprise.

"Oh, yes," he insisted.

"Well, if you say so. . . ."

"So that was what woke me in the middle of the night, gnawing at me like an ulcer in the stomach. Hannah. And no *yahrzeit* this year. Of course, knowing Hannah, she forgave me. But how did it look before God? It woke me, it tortured me. And that's what made me so grumpy and insulting today. I hope now you understand."

"I do."

"You forgive me?

"I forgive you," Mrs. Washington said.

"Thank you," he said. He attempted to pick up his cards with his left hand but this time had too much difficulty and shoved them back. "I don't feel like playing anymore. In fact, I would like to go back to my room and lie down. I need to be alone for a while."

"You have your exercises first," she said. "We've only done them once today."

He rose, thoughtful, then said, "Couldn't I just be alone for a while?" he pleaded.

146

"For a while," she granted, for she sensed that if she persisted he might give way to tears. He was so deeply wounded and guilty about having passed over the anniversary of Hannah's death.

When she knocked on his door, he did not reply. Thinking he had fallen asleep, she opened the door gingerly and peeked in. The room was dark. He had closed the shutters before lying down. His eyes were shut. But he was not asleep. He said softly, "Yes, Mrs. Washington, I know. Exercise time."

She entered, was about to open the shutters and permit the bright light of the summer day to flood the room, when he interrupted, "I don't need any light to do my exercises! Besides it hurts my eyes."

It was not till she began working with him on the resistance exercises that she drew close enough to see his eyes were red from weeping.

"Mr. Horowitz, what you were saying before about *yahrzeit*?"

"Yes?" he replied as he tried to raise his left leg against pressure from her strong hand.

"Does it make such a difference what day it is?"

"Of course!" he insisted. "After all, *yahrzeit* is *yahrzeit*. It's not like Congress passes a law and says, this year Washington's birthday is on the twenty-eighth of February. Or next year Fourth of July is on the fifth of August. Nobody fools around with *yahrzeit*! Not Congress, not any peanut farmer, nobody!"

"I just thought . . ."

"Who asked you to think?" he demanded intolerantly. But when they were cooperating on the exercise which involved her helping to push his arm across his chest as far as it would go and she was poised over him, he looked up into her black eyes and asked, "So?"

"So what?" she asked, giving his arm an added push.

"So first, don't break my arm. And second, you start

147

saying what you just thought but you never finish. What were you just thinking?" he asked.

"I was thinking that *yahrzeit* is like Yom Kippur, isn't it?"

"Yom Kippur isn't till September and we are in the middle of July," he corrected with some degree of annoyance.

"I meant, way back when I worked for the Rosengartens, they never wanted me to work on Yom Kippur. It was a holy day."

"The holiest of the year," Horowitz pointed out.

"When I came in the next day there were these three burnt out candles in small glasses," Mrs. Washington explained. "And I would melt the wax out of them and we would use them for drinking glasses."

"Of course, so what does that have to do with anything?"

"That's the kind of candle you meant when you talked about Hannah and *yahrzeit* before, isn't it?"

"Yes."

"Well, what I was thinking . . ."

Impatiently he interrupted, "Get to the point already!"

"Well, some years the Rosengartens lit those candles as early as the twelfth of September and sometimes as late as the tenth of October," she recalled.

"Because that's the day Yom Kippur fell that particular year," he explained intolerantly, while trying to raise his foot to improve his dorsiflex action.

"So I said to myself if you can light a Yom Kippur candle sometimes in September and sometimes in October, God is not such a stickler for dates that He wouldn't overlook such a little thing. Especially for a man with a good excuse like yours. After all, if you said to Him, God, I was in the hospital. There were no candles and I couldn't go to *schul*, I'm sure He'd understand and make allowances."

148

"What are you suggesting?"

"That tomorrow is as good a day as any for going to schul and saying what you have to say," she said.

"Hmm!" he scoffed. "A whole Talmudic scholar. Mrs. Washington, there are no excuses before God! A man has a duty to perform, he should perform it. Without excuses!"

"Oh, I don't know," she differed.

"You don't know but I know!" Horowitz insisted.

"I remember one Yom Kippur when Mrs. Rosengarten was sick with the flu. The mister asked me to come in just to take care of her. And he said, even though she fasted every other year, that year, because she was sick, I was allowed to give her a little chicken soup."

"Well," Horowitz conceded, "for a sick person, to save a human life, one makes allowances."

"But you were sick," she pointed out.

"Look, don't be a Talmudic scholar on my time!" he said irascibly. And proceeded, out of anger and impatience, to increase his effort at raising and lowering his left leg and it responded more than previously.

They were completing the regime when he granted, in his grumbling voice, "However, it is possible that tomorrow morning they might need an extra man in schul to complete the minyan. Especially in the summertime, when so many people are away."

A moment later, he exploded, "Over a million Jews in this city but go find ten men for a minyan. Yes, I think tomorrow I will go and offer my services."

"What time tomorrow?" Mrs. Washington asked.

"Early. Seven thirty. So men who have yahrzeit can fulfill their duty and still get to work on time," he explained.

"I'll be here," she said.

"There's no need," he said. "I'll make it on my own."

"I'll be here," she insisted.

149

*   *   *

The next morning at seven twenty-five, Mrs. Washington wheeled Samuel Horowitz in through the double doors of Anshe Chesed synagogue. The sexton, a short, portly man with a small white goatee and wearing a black silk *yarmulke*, greeted them.

"Ah, Mr. Horowitz, I've missed you. What happened?" the sexton inquired, staring at the wheelchair in a way that made Horowitz feel most uncomfortable.

"I . . . I had a little stroke," Horowitz admitted self-consciously.

"A stroke," the sexton lamented. "At that, you're very lucky. Remember Mr. Cooper? Heart attack. Gone. And Mishkin? The lawyer? Also gone. Cancer. Every day it's someone else. You're one of the lucky ones."

"Thank you," Horowitz responded ascerbically.

Mrs. Washington wheeled him to the door of the sanctuary, where some nine or ten men were gathered in the first two rows before the ark. As she started to push the chair through the door, Horowitz raised his hand to forbid it. He raised himself from the chair, and using the back of each pew for support, he labored down the aisle to join the others. He selected a prayer shawl and book and took his place.

During the service, though it required great effort, he rose and sat at the appropriate times. Mrs. Washington suspected that the sexton, who conducted the service, deliberately slowed down matters to accommodate him.

At the end, when it came time to say the prayer in remembrance of the dead, Horowitz raised himself with considerable difficulty and spoke the prayer more loudly than the others who had *yahrzeit*. The other men departed, leaving Horowitz alone in his seat. Mrs. Washington wheeled the chair down the aisle and he was relieved to get into it, for the service had been most taxing.

She was wheeling him home when he admitted, "I

150

hope I didn't hurt your feelings in synagogue. It wasn't that I didn't want you there because you're not Jewish. It was because I didn't want Hannah to see me this way. Needing your help."

They had returned home. She had prepared and served his breakfast, which he ate with considerably more appetite than usual. The morning's prayer had obviously lifted a burden from his conscience. He was ready to leave the table.

As she cleared the table, Mrs. Washington asked, "Do you want to light it now?"

"Light what?"

"The *yahrzeit* candle," she informed.

"Who's got a *yahrzeit* candle?" he demanded. "That day they were broken, smashed, laying in the gutter, along with all my groceries," he recalled bitterly.

"We happen to have one," she suggested.

"We do?"

Rising with the help of his quad cane, he made his way into the kitchen. There, on the stainless steel drainboard, were two fresh, white *yahrzeit* candles in small jelly glasses alongside a box of kitchen matches.

Leaning against the sink to support himself, for his task required the use of both his hands, he struck a match and lit the tiny wick that protruded from the middle of the white paraffin base in one of the glasses.

It took the flame, and started to burn in a steady glow that flickered only when his breath disturbed it. He studied the flame for a moment, then set the glass down in the stainless steel sink.

"So it shouldn't start a fire," he explained. He struggled out of the kitchen, coming eye to eye with her at the door. "How come we happen to have them?" he asked.

"On my way home I just happened to be passing a supermarket."

151

"So you just happened to stop in and buy them?"
She nodded.

"And they just happened to have them," he concluded skeptically.

Again, she nodded.

"Tell me, Mrs. Washington, do many supermarkets up in Harlem carry *yahrzeit* lamps?"

"It happens."

"How many stores did you have to go to before it 'happened'?" he asked gently.

"One or two. Maybe three," she admitted.

"Four or five? Maybe six?" he asked.

"I don't remember."

He reached out and patted her cheek tenderly. "If only for your sake, I don't think God will mind that I was a little late this year."

He took several steps with his quad cane before he stopped and looked back.

"Next year," he said, "next year I would like to go there on my own. Walk down that aisle without holding on to the pews. Next year . . ."

But Mrs. Washington could tell that the words were hollow, the wish vain. For he had neither the resolve nor determination to survive until next year.

Chapter Eleven

In the physical therapy department of the hospital, Samuel Horowitz was going through his weekly evaluation. Mrs. Washington stood off in the corner watching the therapist, a brisk, bright, well-trained young woman, put Horowitz through the tests indicated by his chart. He complied with each of her commands with a bored lack of enthusiasm. He seemed constantly out of breath, not from exertion but from sighing to express his resistance and contempt for the entire procedure. But the young therapist persevered.

Horowitz's shoes stood by the exercise bed. One plain black one, and the other with its insulting brace sticking up in the air like a distress signal. He found it most embarrassing and he resented it.

He resented, too, the white shirt Mrs. Washington had made him wear, and the tie. It was altogether too fancy just to go to a hospital. But she had insisted, "When we go out where other people see you, you are going to look decent. My Horace never went looking for a job or to church or even to the Unemployment looking like a slob."

"I am not a slob!" Horowitz had protested.

"Look at you." She pointed to his baggy corduroy slacks and the garish, old, worn sport shirt. "What would you call that?"

"Casual," he replied, more in defiance than pride. "They can put a shirt and tie on me when they bury me and I have nothing to say about it."

"If I know you, you'll have something to say about it," she snapped back. "Now you'll put on a shirt and tie, or else I'll do it for you."

He had glared at her. If her black eyes had not revealed a high degree of determination, he would have resisted. But, damn that woman, she could and would put a shirt on him.

"Picking on a sick man," he mumbled as he slipped out of the sport shirt. "Harry Truman always wore shirts like this."

"When you get to be President you can wear them, too," she replied, not relenting one whit from her domineering attitude.

So here he was, dressed in a white shirt, with a nice neat tie, delivered into the hands of another tyrant called a physical therapist, who was putting him through his paces as if he were a trained animal. Stretch! Bend! Walk! Grip! Resist! Lift! Raise! Lower! He complied as well as he was able within the limits imposed on him by his brain, his body and his attitude.

When she had run through the checklist, she suggested, "Okay, now, pop, let's see if you can put your shoes back on."

"In the first place, I am not your pop. In the second place I can put my shoes on like I have been doing for sixty-eight years now!"

154

Whereupon he proceeded to demonstrate, a bit awkwardly. He fixed the short leg brace in place, lowered his trouser leg so the brace was hidden from view except from the side.

Slowly, and with great effort from his left hand, he tied the shoelace into a creditable knot. When he was done he presented himself defiantly for inspection.

"There! Okay?"

"You forgot to tie your other shoe," the therapist pointed out.

He glanced down. True, he had forgotten again. It seemed that no matter how many times Mrs. Washington had called him to account about it, he would forget to do some little thing such as tie both laces, or button his shirt, or slip both arms into his jacket.

"All right, pop, let's see you walk. To those parallel bars and back."

"I told you, I am not your pop," he protested, but he commenced walking.

The therapist watched critically. Too much drag. His dorsiflex action had not improved since last week. He was not making the progress he should. If that continued for another month or two he would remain at his present plateau for the rest of his life. She would have to call his doctor and report her findings. Meantime, she would turn him over to the occupational therapist.

The occupational therapy room was too small to permit Mrs. Washington access. So she waited outside, and eavesdropped to hear how the session progressed.

"Okay, Mr. Horowitz, let's see you gather up these cards," the O.T. suggested.

"I can do it," he protested. "What else?"

"Let me see you do it," she insisted.

"Okay."

Mrs. Washington could hear the sound of each card as it was slid across the smooth table top and gradually

155

lifted. It was a long laborious process. When it was done, the therapist said, "Now, shuffle them."

"Why? You want to play pinochle? Okay. Twenty-five cents a hand."

"Mr. Horowitz! Shuffle! All three ways. Regular. Thumbs down. And palm," the therapist ordered.

The sound of cards being shuffled reached Mrs. Washington's ears. He was doing it defiantly and not nearly so well as she had got him to do it at home. She grew fretful and was strongly tempted to burst in and say, he can do better, if you force him. But she waited patiently, and a bit sadly.

When the O.T. had finished putting Horowitz through a number of exercises and tests, she said, "Okay, Mr. Horowitz. That'll be all for this week. But wait outside."

They waited almost half an hour, Mr. Horowitz and Mrs. Washington. Then the door of the office of the department head opened and the O.T. and the P.T. both came out. The department head, a tall, blonde woman with the physique of an Amazon and golden braids wound Germanically about her head, beckoned toward the waiting couple. They started forward. But she said crisply, "Only the lady, please!"

Mrs. Washington entered. The department head closed the door, shutting out Mr. Horowitz.

The department head, identified by the plastic sign on her desk as Ms. Hilda Wolff, R.N., P.T., studied the two reports she held. She looked up at Mrs. Washington and said, "Not very good, you know. Little progress. Do I understand correctly that you're only a practical nurse?"

"A very good practical nurse," Mrs. Washington replied, resentful at having her profession demeaned.

"The trouble with nurses, even registered nurses, either they baby the patient because they feel sorry for him, or else they keep him inactive and sedated so he won't become a nuisance. Frankly, if I had my way, I

156

would never allow a nurse to take care of a patient like this."

"I don't baby him," Mrs. Washington protested, "and if you think he's sedated, just talk to him. He's bitter, resentful, sharp, and combative. He's anything but sedated."

"He's not making the progress we like to see in the first two months," Ms. Wolff said sharply. "You have to drive him more."

"He does better at home than he did here. He resents coming. He hates the whole idea of being less than he was."

"Well, he'll have to get used to it. Especially at the rate he's going. He is not improving. I will have to report that to his doctor," Ms. Wolff said. It was also by way of warning Mrs. Washington that her work had been judged and found wanting. "Do you understand?" she asked, if by any chance Mrs. Washington had not appreciated the warning.

"Yes, yes, I understand."

"What he needs is discipline, and also incentive. He seems not to have any incentive to improve."

"I'm afraid that's right," Mrs. Washington admitted.

"Well, a good part of that is your job. You've got to keep after him."

"I'll try, but it doesn't seem to help," Mrs. Washington explained. "He was greatly attached to his wife and since she's gone he doesn't care. He has decided, either he is going to be totally the man he was, or else give up and join her."

"Do you think he might benefit from psychiatric help?" the department head asked.

"He might," Mrs. Washington said, but not too hopefully.

"I'll discuss it with his doctor," Ms. Wolff said crisply, dismissing Mrs. Washington.

*   *   *

On the way home in the cab, they were both silent. But once inside the apartment, Horowitz asked, "So what did Brünhilde have to say?'

"Brünhilde?" Mrs. Washington responded, puzzled, for he had interrupted her fearful thoughts that she might lose this job which served her needs so well this summer.

"The lady giant," Horowitz explained. "With the blonde hair. You think that hair comes that way or does she have to do it up every morning? While taking an ice-cold shower."

"She doesn't like your attitude," Mrs. Washington said.

"I didn't like hers either," Horowitz replied.

"She thinks it's interfering with your rehabilitation. You're too negative. You're not making progress."

"I beat you in Chinese checkers three games out of four, isn't that progress?" he asked.

"Progress with your exercises," Mrs. Washington pointed out impatiently.

"Exercises? Soon I'll be ready for the Olympics!" he protested.

"Soon, you should be able to walk longer distances. And after that, you should be getting rid of that brace," Mrs. Washington said, hoping to give him some incentive to change his attitude.

"Ah, *buba meinses!*" he said bitterly. "You know what means *buba meinses*? Fairy tales! Once Kantrowitz had his stroke, he never got out of his wheelchair. That was it, lived that way, died that way. These things don't get better. They only keep you doing those exercises to fool you into thinking that they do."

"Someday, if you put your mind to it, you could walk without your quad. Maybe with just a simple cane. Or no cane at all."

"Someday," he scoffed. "The whole human race con-

158

sists of donkeys chasing a carrot called Someday. We live our whole lives looking forward to someday. When we'll do all the things we deny ourselves because we are saving for someday. But that day never comes. Life slips by. Hannah dies. I become like this. There is no someday. There is only now.

"And, frankly, what is now I don't like. What's to like? A man can't even go for a walk like a respectable human being. He has to be wheeled around. And carried up and down three small stairs! Three small stairs, and Samuel Horowitz has to be carried. You want me to like that?

"Don't you see, Mrs. Washington, for me there is no longer someday. There is only now. Well, I don't like now. And I can't help it."

He turned his head aside, ostensibly to look out the window, but actually to hide his tears.

"Mr. Horowitz . . ." she began to console him.

"Please, Mrs. Washington!" he forbade gruffly, but in so doing his voice broke. He could no longer conceal his soft weeping. In a while, he sniffled back to his usual crusty self. "You know," he said, making every effort to seem gruff again, "when you get older, your eyes tear. Especially in the sunshine. It's too bright out. I should wear sunglasses. Yes, once you get past sixty-five you'll find that out. Your eyes tear." Then he demanded, "So what's the matter, today is Yom Kippur? No lunch?"

He was just finishing lunch when the phone rang. Mrs. Washington came into the dining room.

"It's her."

"Mona," he said, resigned, "who else? Tell her I'm out jogging."

"You'd better talk to her. She sounds very upset."

"Okay," he resigned himself. He pushed the wheelchair back from the table, turned it about and started for the kitchen phone.

"Mona?" he asked into the phone, hoping the voice on the other end would dispute him.

"Yes, Dad, it's me," she said sternly.

"Calling on your 800 number," he concluded unhappily.

"Dad, an 800 number is only for incoming calls. It allows people to call us long distance without any charge."

"You mean, this call is costing? Long distance from San Diego. It must be very expensive, I better be quick. I'm fine and good-bye!"

"Dad! Just a moment!" Mona interdicted imperiously. "This call is not costing me anything."

"You're cheating the phone company? You can go to jail for that!" Horowitz protested.

"Dad, I'm calling on Albert's WATS line," she informed.

"Albert's who line?"

"WATS line. W-A-T-S. We can call New York all we want without any charge."

Just my luck, Horowitz thought. Aloud, he said, "Well, Mona, darling, so talk. All you want," preparing to submit to a KGB investigation.

"Dad! Now, what's this I hear?"

"Since you heard and I didn't, you tell me."

"I just got a call from Marvin. . . ."

"Oh, yes, Marvin Hammond, Esquire. Well, what did Esquire have to say?"

"Dad, this is no laughing matter."

"Mona, dear, if you think I'm laughing you are sadly mistaken. Now, what's the trouble?"

"Marvin got a call from Dr. Tannenbaum, who got a call from the physical therapist at the hospital. She says that you're not making progress. You should be getting better faster. Otherwise you limit your own improvement and the damage could be permanent."

160

"So?"

"So unless you show some improvement in your attitude, in your desire to get better, unless you do your exercises when you should and with the proper motivation, we'll have to take steps."

"You mean, if I don't soon take steps, you will take steps," Horowitz said.

"Dad, this is serious!"

"That's what I need, someone to tell me how serious my situation is," he said sadly.

"Now, Dad, it's come down to this. If there isn't a marked change in your attitude, and very soon, we'll have to insist that you see a psychiatrist," Mona issued her ultimatum.

"And who is 'we'?" Horowitz asked.

"Marvin and I. And Albert, who said if it's a matter of money, he'll pay for it."

"That's very kind of Albert," Horowitz said, "but frankly, Mona, there is an old Jewish saying. Not exactly from the Talmud, but it says, anyone who goes to a psychiatrist should have his head examined."

"Dad!" she exploded in exasperation.

"Okay, okay," he mollified.

"One other thing, Dad."

With Mona no conversation ever came to an end. There was always one other thing.

"Yes, Mona," he inquired with impatient patience. "What is the one other thing?"

Mona's voice dropped into a low, conspiratorial tone. "First, is *she* there?"

"Who?" Horowitz asked, puzzled.

"She. Your nurse. The *shvartzer*."

"She's on the extension," Horowitz said to irk his daughter.

"Dad!!" she screamed.

"Okay, so she's not. You want to talk to her?"

"I do not want to talk to her," Mona said haughtily. "I want to talk to you."

"So talk."

"The therapist said that nurses tend to baby their patients. They don't drive them enough. So she may have to go."

"Believe me," Horowitz defended, "she is a tyrant. If I owned a string of concentration camps I would put her in charge. She is the meanest, nastiest person I have ever met."

He noticed Mrs. Washington glaring at him, and explained, "I'm defending you, believe me." He turned his attention back to Mona. "You couldn't find anybody stricter or meaner than this woman. In fact, when I hang up I'm afraid she might beat me, she's so mean. So if they think she's too soft on me, nothing could be further from the truth. Now do you feel better?"

"Dad, this is nothing to joke about!"

"I'm not joking. If you were here I'd show you my bruises."

"Dad!" Mona said in that exasperated tone that made him fear he might have provoked her sufficiently to fly East.

"Okay, darling, I'm sorry. She is a nice, conscientious woman, who is doing her best."

"I hope so. Because if things don't change for the better, and soon, I'm going to have to come East and take charge," Mona said. "So try, please, Dad, try! You can do it if you decide to. One thing you never lacked was determination. All you have to do is *want* to," she stressed.

"Okay, Mona, darling, I'll *want* to," he promised, only to get off the phone.

"So work hard at your exercises all week. And next time you go back to the therapist, I want a good report. Understand?"

"Yes, dear, a good report. Otherwise, steps! Yours, not mine!" he said briskly, trying to give her the satisfaction of thinking she had had some beneficial effect.

He felt free to hang up. His hand still rested on the phone, as he realized how little time it had taken for that nosy therapist to call his doctor, his doctor to call Marvin, Marvin to call Mona, and Mona to call him. All the wonders of twentieth-century technology had been mobilized, messages had flashed instantaneously across three thousand miles and back, so the whole world would know that Samuel Horowitz had failed his test at the physical therapist's. If that's what the telephone has done for us, Horowitz decided, then to hell with it. He was tempted to rip the instrument out of the wall.

He felt like a criminal who had been hunted down and made to face his crime. Mona would have made an excellent prosecutor. Or a detective. She could even have her own television series, "Police Daughter." Why not? More ridiculous shows had appeared on TV.

For all his fantasied raging against Mona, he had to admit, she was right. He had made little progress. And there was nothing he could do about it. He felt empty and purposeless.

He wheeled himself back to the living room. Mrs. Washington followed, announcing, "Now, your exercises!"

"Okay, get out the pinochle cards," he said, resigned.

"Today, no pinochle cards. Today no games. Today straight fine-motor coordination exercises."

"Fine-motor coordination exercises," he mocked.

"First," she said firmly, "tie your shoelaces. Both shoes!"

He resisted with a look but her glaring gaze overruled him. So he bent down and tied his laces, as she watched with a critical eye. He fumbled a bit with his left hand, but he finally completed the job.

163

"Now back to the marbles and the buttons, and I don't want to hear any complaints!"

She turned over the box, spilling the buttons across the table.

"One at a time, pick up each button, put it into the box."

He resisted by staring away from her and out the window at the park.

"I know exactly what went on in that conversation with your daughter. I know how therapists feel about nurses. Well, you, Mr. Horowitz, are not going to be indulged. And you are not going to be neglected. And I am not going to lose this job, which I need for the sake of my grandchildren! Understood?"

"Understood," he said, but resisted nevertheless. She glared at him until he finally turned his attention to the buttons. Selecting the largest ones first, he began to pick them up with the reluctant fingers of his left hand.

As he worked he grumbled, "Mona! I knew she would start trouble. All her life she's been that way."

He turned his wrath on Mrs. Washington. "And you, you're no bargain either. The only way I'll be able to get rid of you is I'll get a message to Israel. And they'll send over a commando force and free me, like they did at Entebbe."

"Keep picking up buttons!" Mrs. Washington commanded. "And when you're finished with that, marbles! And then The New York Times, sheet by sheet!"

"You're even worse than I told Mona," he said, but he continued picking up buttons until the table top was cleared.

Chapter Twelve

Horowitz was shuffling the cards carefully, forcing his left hand to do most of the work. He was about to deal when he noticed Mrs. Washington's reproving look.

"Okay!" he conceded intolerantly. He placed two halves of the deck down on the table, pressed both his thumbs hard against them and shuffled them into a single pack again. "All right?" he asked testily. She did not respond. He knew what that meant. He had to repeat the operation nine more times. Then he dealt out two hands, holding the pack in his right hand and meticulously peeling off each card with his left. It was a laborious operation. But still, Mrs. Washington felt he was not making much progress.

He gathered up his cards, placed them into his right hand, using his left to arrange them into suits. By the time he was done, she seemed to still be in the process. It irked him, for he knew she did that deliberately not to make him feel inept or self-conscious.

"You should, maybe, do a little finger exercise yourself. It would improve your dextrose," he suggested
acidly.

"Dexterity," she corrected. "Play!"

But before he could, the phone rang.

"If that's Mona again, I'm not here!" he interjected at
once.

"What shall I tell her this time, you're out skateboard-
ing?" Mrs. Washington retorted. "She knows if I'm here,
you're here."

"Make up any excuse, I don't care what!" he protested.

"I'll tell her you're meditating and can't be disturbed."

"Good!" he agreed. "And tell her my mantra is
Hadassah."

Once Mrs. Washington went to the phone he strained
to overhear the conversation.

"Hello," Mrs. Washington began gingerly, fearing that
indeed it was Mona Fields. Then her voice changed,
becoming a bit more cautious. "Person to person? Yes,
this is Harriet Washington. Yes. The same Harriet Washington. What can I do for you? Oh, oh, I see. Well, if I can
remember, of course."

She listened for a while, replying only, "Uh-huh . . .
uh-huh . . . uh-huh . . ."

Bursting with curiosity, Horowitz called out, "One
more uh-huh and I'll have you arrested for practicing
medicine without a license!"

Ignoring his protest, she continued, "Uh-huh . . . uh-
huh . . . uh-huh . . ."

"That woman is trying to kill me with suspense!" he
muttered.

"Oh, no, *that's* where you went wrong," Mrs. Washington said suddenly.

"Wrong about what?" Horowitz called indignantly.

"No, Mrs. Goodman, you do not use a Cuisinart."

"Cuisinart? What the hell is a Cuisinart?" Horowitz demanded.

"Hand-chopped," Mrs. Washington said into the phone. "Otherwise, your ingredients are right. Equal parts of whitefish, pike and winter carp. Eggs. Right. Onions. Salt. Pepper. Of course, matzoh meal! Right. Right. And some sliced carrots. But the secret is hand-chopping. If the texture is wrong, you might as well buy the commercial kind in jars," she insisted.

Then in a moment she said, "That's perfectly all right, Mrs. Goodman. Think nothing of it. Glad to help. Any time."

She returned to the card table and silently resumed assembling her hand. Horowitz stared not at his cards but at her.

"Hanging by the thumbs is also physical therapy?" Horowitz accused.

"What are you talking about?"

"You use my telephone to get a long distance call. Take my time to speak. And you leave me hanging by the thumbs? You won't tell me what it was about?" he grumbled. "The woman has no heart! No sense of fairness!"

"It was a call from a Mrs. Goodman."

"That I was brilliant enough to figure out myself when you addressed her as Mrs. Goodman. But the rest? Carp, whitefish, pike? That's for gefilte fish."

"Of course."

"A Mrs. Goodman is calling you long distance for a recipe for gefilte fish?" he asked incredulously.

"She lives in Connecticut. And the women up there were having an argument about the best way to make gefilte fish. She remembered when she was a little girl having gefilte fish at . . ."

"Don't tell me," he interrupted in an anguished

167

moan, "at the Rosengartens."

"Yes. So she called Suzy Ross, who was once Stella Rosengarten, to ask for her mother's recipe. And Stella told her that her mother never made the fish. I did. So she called my home and my daughter told her I was here."

"You made all the gefilte fish for the Rosengartens?" he asked with new respect.

"It's really very simple. But the secret is texture. Hand-chopping."

"I know," he pontificated with his newly acquired expertise. "Never use a Cuisinart!"

"Right," she agreed heartily.

After a moment of studying his cards he asked, "What's a Cuisinart?"

"A machine that chops, cuts, dices, and does a hundred other things that women used to do," she explained. "Only it cuts too fine. Fish comes out so thin you could drink it."

"This machine, it runs on electricity?" he asked after taking a trick and while trying to pull the cards out of his hand to meld forty jacks.

"Naturally."

"That's what we need! More machinery that runs on electricity. So we can have a bigger energy shortage. So women can have more free time to go around campaigning against the energy shortage," Horowitz grumbled. "My Mona must have two Cuisinarts. She has so much free time to meddle in everybody else's business."

Suddenly he asked, "You really make such good gefilte fish?"

"Everyone seemed to love it. Sometimes guests wouldn't leave without my recipe," she admitted.

"Hannah also made excellent gefilte fish," he observed, while attempting to maintain a degree of modesty. "Occasionally I get lonesome for a really good piece of homemade fish."

When she did not volunteer, he studied his hand before observing, "I was reading in one of those booklets they give you when you go home from the hospital. It says in there that fish is a very high protein, low cholesterol food. Recommended for people who have heart attacks or strokes."

She did not reply, but instead took the next trick and melded a hundred aces. He considered that an act of treachery since she had given no indication, facial or otherwise, that she was holding them. A woman who would do that would not look with favor on his hint about gefilte fish, so he dropped the subject. He played the hand out grimly, and lost.

It was time for his exercises again and his prelunch visit to the park. Though it was only mid-morning, the humidity had already become oppressive. It warned of a heat wave of the kind that one encountered only in New York. Hot, oppressive, polluted air, made more so by the increase in humidity day by day, until one longed for that cataclysmic thunderstorm that would finally dispel it.

Mrs. Washington had allowed him to sit in the sun only briefly before making him wheel his chair into an area in the park shaded with wide-spreading leafy trees, where the temperature was at least fifteen degrees cooler. They passed the time in silence, listening to the sounds of traffic, to the cries and laughter of children, and the occasional sound of a bird presumptuous enough to make itself heard above the other noises.

"Hannah loved this park," he said. "That's why we lived here so long. Of course, in her last years I never let her go in here alone. Too dangerous. But it was nice just to be able to look out the window and see it.

"In winter everything was bare, the trees like skeletons. Except when it snowed. Then it was a fairyland. At night you could look out and the lights would make

169

everything sparkle. Came spring the park began to get green. And way over on the other side, east, there, near the Metropolitan Museum, there were magnificent trees with pink flowers. When a breeze made them drop their blossoms it was like standing in a pink rain. Then came summer and the green was so thick you couldn't see the paths or the cars or the people. But fall, fall Hannah loved best of all. The golden colors, and the red. The leaves under your feet—it was a shame to walk on them they were so beautiful.

"All that we enjoyed together, Hannah and me."

He was silent for a time before he asked, "Your husband and you, you must have had such pleasures, too."

"Yes," she said softly.

"So?" he coaxed.

"Eastertime," she recalled, "if he had a job, and it was his money we'd used to buy the children new clothes, he would stroll proudly up Lenox Avenue to the church. That was one of the best times. Or Christmas. If he'd been working and got paid well, we always made sure to have a good Christmas day, because we knew he would be laid off right after. Except during the war. During the war he worked steady. It's sad, isn't it, that people have to yearn for war because it means a decent job."

Horowitz felt free to stare at her for she was turned away from him. Hers was a strong face. But if one looked close one could find there the lines that a lifetime of care and worry had left. Her hair, which seemed so ebony, had silver strands running through it. Behind her spectacles, her black eyes were now neither so bright nor combative as they usually appeared. They were softer, and a bit moist.

"It'll get better," he tried to console. "Our generation was the one that had the struggle and the worry and the fear, so that our children would have it better. And they

170

do have it better. Don't they, Mrs. Washington? Don't they?" he asked, hoping to elicit her agreement and thus change her mood.

"The grandchildren, if they grow up right, they can have it better," she agreed.

"With a grandmother like you for an example, they'll grow up right," he assured.

"These days," she said wearily, "the schools they go to . . ." She shook her head.

"So you help them with their homework," he advised. "That's what Hannah and I did. It's the only way."

"It's the violence, the drugs. The things they're exposed to. Girls becoming pregnant at twelve and thirteen. Boys learning how to push, and deal, and steal. The money that's around. How do you keep them from being tempted?"

"It's a problem," he agreed, but could offer no solution.

"It's getting too hot out here. I better get you upstairs so you can be air-conditioned," she said to avoid the subject.

He turned his chair about and started to wheel himself toward the street.

The phone was ringing as she turned the key in the lock. Resignedly, Horowitz predicted, "Twelve o'clock New York time, nine o'clock San Diego time. Mona. Let it ring."

"It could be your son. Or one of your friends."

"My friends are either all dead or in Miami, which is the same thing. Mona. Let it ring," he repeated like a man dogged by an evil fate.

"Phil Liebowitz called again yesterday," she reminded. "But you wouldn't talk to him."

"He calls only because he wants to gloat. He'd like to see me in this damn chair. He'd like to see this scar on my face. I know that bastard like a book."

171

"His wife called, too."

"When?"

"While you were napping. She wanted to know if you were allowed to go out for dinner. At their place."

"So she too can see me this way?" Horowitz demanded angrily.

The insistent phone prevented Mrs. Washington from replying. She unlocked the door and raced to the phone, forcing Horowitz to maneuver his chair up and over the doorsill. By that time, Mrs. Washington was back in the foyer, and looking embarrassed.

"Mona?" he guessed.

"Mona," she confessed.

"I told you not to hurry," he grumbled. He wheeled himself to the kitchen, steering expertly so that he did not make contact with the sides of the doorframe.

"Hello, Mona?"

"Dad!" she responded. He knew she was about to rebuke him. "You haven't called."

"Why should I call if I have nothing to say?" he asked.

"I want to know how you are, that you're getting better. I want you to call every day!" she insisted.

"I don't get that much better in a day," he explained.

"It would be a comfort just to hear your voice, to know you're okay."

"I am okay. And I just said that in my own voice. Which is not exactly like Frank Sinatra, but if it makes you feel better, there you are."

"Dad, you're being difficult again," she chided.

"Sorry," he said, hoping she would hang up. Then he remembered, and asked, "Tell me, Mona, darling, do you own a Cuisinart?"

"Of course. Why?"

"Just one?"

"Yes. Why?"

"Never mind. Except I hope you don't make your

172

gefilte fish in it," he advised.

"Of course not."

"Good!" Horowitz said.

"We have a caterer out here who makes the most divine gefilte fish. For private parties, for the temple seder, and for the country club buffet every Sunday."

"That's nice," he agreed without much enthusiasm. "Your mother also made a fine gefilte fish. Delicious, tasty, a real machayah. But somehow we never called it divine."

"You're being difficult again, Dad," Mona said testily.

"Mona, do me a favor?"

"Of course. What?" she asked immediately.

"Just once, call me Papa instead of Dad?"

She paused, annoyed, then condescended, "Okay. Papa. There. How's that?"

Sadly he admitted, "Even Papa sounds different in San Diego." He hung up.

"When I was a boy, if you wanted the best gefilte fish you went to your grandmother's house. Nowadays, they have to go to the country club. Some world."

"Time to do your exercises," Mrs. Washington reminded, to change his mood.

"Yes, of course. Always time to do my exercises. What for?" he protested, but turned his chair about and started toward the bedroom.

While he went through the routine—lifting, stretching, turning, pressing against her resistance, resenting her aid—he kept up a steady muttered protest.

"She is not dragging me off to San Diego. Not Sam Horowitz. I will not be a charity case. Even in my daughter's house. Big as it is. A mansion. You never saw such a house. Like a Holiday Inn. But even a house that big is not big enough for me. I would feel like a prisoner. I'd rather stay here. On my own!"

Mrs. Washington did not respond or interrupt except

173

to count the number of times he performed each therapeutic task, and to tell him which one was next. But to herself, she thought, if he became a prisoner, it would not be through Mona, but because of his own lack of will, his sense of hopelessness.

His dinner was over. A simple meal. Roasted chicken. Green beans. A light custard and Sanka. This woman has a way, he was forced to concede. She makes simple food very tasty indeed. Not exactly like Hannah every time, but good. Very good he had to admit, as he sat before his television set and watched the evening news while he heard the comforting sound of her bustling about the kitchen cleaning up before leaving.

On the news, local version, the weather indicated no letup in the heat wave. The forecaster issued a judicious warning from Con Ed to keep power consumption at a minimum, especially during the early hours of evenings when people returning home from work were used to throwing their air conditioners on in high to insure a quick cool-off of their apartments.

Horowitz comforted himself with the fact that he never ran his machines on high. A nice even low, throughout the day, and in the bedroom at night he kept his machine on something called "slumber." Perhaps because the steady hum was supposed to be conducive to sleep. Whatever, he felt no guilt at his consumption of energy. He considered himself a reasonable man with modest needs.

Mrs. Washington was ready to leave. He invited her to sit a while and cool off in front of the machine before she braved the heat outside. But she begged off, saying it was late and that she had better get home because her daughter had to leave and she did not want the children to be alone. This was especially important in the summertime.

174

"On a night like this," she said, "they'll be bound to want to be out. It gets pretty hot in that little apartment."

"I can imagine," Horowitz said. "When we were kids and lived in Brooklyn, a night like this Mama would put out blankets and we kids would sleep on the fire escape all night long. Sometimes, in the middle of the night, would come up a sudden storm. We would get drenched and have to come inside and get dried off like after a bath. Then we would listen to the rain beat against the windows, and know that in the morning the city would be clean. The air would be fresh and there would be a breeze in Brooklyn. So I know," he recalled ruefully, "I know."

It was the middle of the night. He woke with a start, as if someone had nudged him. He was suddenly lost, and puzzled. He listened. He realized it was the absence of sound which awakened him. His air conditioner, which he had carefully set on "slumber," had stopped, disturbing his slumber. He reached for the switch on the bedside lamp. No response. He clicked it again, then again. Nothing.

For a moment, he was terrorized. A sudden spurt of sweat covered his body. He was undecided whether to lie still and listen, or get up and investigate. Had some burglar made his way into the apartment and cut off all lights to render him defenseless? He listened but heard nothing. On the West Side it was not unusual for cat burglars to make their way into an apartment, work in total darkness, taking all valuables they could lay their hands on, then disappearing without a sound or trace.

Even after his eyes became adjusted to the darkness he saw nothing. It was then that he became aware that there was no light coming from the outside either. With considerable effort he raised himself from the bed, and, like a man suddenly blind, made his way cautiously

175

toward the window. He peeked through the slats of the window shutter, down at the park.

There was not a light to be seen down there. The city was in total darkness. As if it had died in a single moment. He was puzzled at first, then not so fearful any longer. For he recalled the early evening warnings from Con Edison about power shortages. He groped about the room trying to remember where he had last used the battery radio that Marvin had brought him in the hospital.

He groped across the night table. It was not there. He reached about until he found his quad cane and started the slow, careful process of making his way across the thickly piled carpet. He collided with the chest of drawers. The sudden contact caused him to totter and almost fall. But he pressed down on his cane and regained his balance. He reached the doorway, cautiously lifted the cane so it did not strike against the raised doorsill. He paused, trying to remember whether he had left that damned radio in his bathroom.

He found it, finally, on the chairside table in the living room. He flipped on the switch, and was heartened by the fact that this, at least, was working. His suspicions were confirmed. The news announcer was talking about a city-wide blackout.

He felt much relieved. For he remembered the last blackout ten or twelve years ago when he had been working late and had to walk home. That night there had been a bright moon, which lent a holiday atmosphere to what could have been a disaster. But people took it kindly, helping each other, cheerfully walking uptown in groups, making jokes. For all that visitors accused them of, the people of New York were good people, warm, friendly, and they had proved it that night. By the time he had got home, Hannah was terribly worried, but he had kissed away her fears and finally had her laughing

176

over some of the jokes he remembered from the long march home.

This time, he thought to himself, this may be exactly what the city needs. There had been so much talk about the city becoming bankrupt, deteriorating, and going to hell, maybe just such an emergency would bring everyone together in a friendly, cooperative, cheerful spirit.

He recalled, too, that, as if by magic, Hannah had produced candles that night, using her Friday night candles and the ones she loved to decorate the table with when she gave small dinner parties. So there had been sufficient light in the apartment that night and they did not have to grope about like blind beggars.

But for three years now there had been no dinner parties, no Friday night candles. He was forced to sit alone in the darkness.

Until he recalled. There was a candle. That second *yahrzeit* candle Mrs. Washington had brought. He must find it. He made his way most carefully toward the kitchen. He counted each step, and made sure to avoid the doorsill between the dining room and the kitchen. He tried to recall where Mrs. Washington had stored it. He finally found it in the cabinet over the sink. Alongside the box of safety matches.

He struck a match and held it to the wick of the *yahrzeit* candle until it took flame.

"You see, Hannah," he said silently, "you have provided me with a candle this time, too."

He wrapped his left hand around the glowing glass, and with a secure right-hand grip on his quad cane, he made his way back to the living room.

The radio was still on. But now the announcer's voice adopted a quite different tone and attitude. He talked more rapidly, and could not keep the astonishment from his voice as he read what turned out to be the first of a series of news bulletins announcing an outbreak of looting and rioting in Harlem.

Men and boys, even women and young girls, had come streaming out of their tenements and were shattering store windows, breaking down barriers and metal grills, even driving cars through store barricades, to loot any kind of merchandise that could be carried off. Television sets, hi-fi's, air conditioners, washing machines, clothing, watches, jewelry, liquor, groceries.

"The police," Horowitz kept muttering, "where are the police?"

But it became apparent from ensuing news reports that the police had been given orders not to intervene lest they create a race riot. The looting continued throughout the night. After a time, radio newsmen were doing their reporting from the scenes of the pillage. Television film was promised as soon as power was restored. Now fires had been added to looting.

Samuel Horowitz sat in his chair near the window, staring out at the darkness, listening, as the city which he loved and was determined not to abandon was being destroyed. He heard the sound of endless police sirens racing past beneath his window. And the sound of fire trucks heading off in whatever direction the emergency existed. A city had gone mad.

He was terrified. Not for himself. But for his city. His only consolation was that Hannah had not lived to see this. He sat in his chair listening until he drifted off to sleep. When he woke it was dawn. The sounds of the night of terror had diminished. There seemed to be the normal orderly hum of traffic on the street below, punctuated only by an occasional distant siren. He lifted himself from his chair, looked down. Central Park West was carrying its usual slow stream of early morning traffic. In the park, through the leafy green trees, he could make out the flow of cars southbound into the heart of

178

Manhattan. It was as if last night's lawless outbreak had been a bad dream.

His phone began ringing. Very insistently. He forced himself to get out of the chair. He made his way across the living room toward the bedroom. He was hot and sweaty, the air in the apartment was heavy and dank. Obviously power had not yet been restored. By the time he reached the phone it had stopped ringing. He lifted it, and heard only a dial tone. He hung up and waited. No ring.

He settled himself in bed, anticipating Mrs. Washington's arrival. The phone rang again. This time he moved quickly enough to interrupt the second ring.

"Yes? Hello?"

"Dad?" It was Marvin calling from Washington. "Are you okay?"

"I'm fine, yes, why?"

"When I heard the news this morning, I was worried," Marvin said, "and when you didn't answer before, I was really upset."

"It took me a long time to get to the phone," Horowitz explained.

"Mrs. Washington, why didn't she answer?"

"Because she isn't here yet."

"Not yet? Dad, it's already nine fifteen."

"It is?" Horowitz asked. Then he realized, of course, the bedside clock would be wrong. The power was off. Nine fifteen and Mrs. Washington was not here yet.

"Maybe she had trouble getting downtown. Things must be a mess in New York this morning. But as long as you're all right," Marvin said, relieved. "Call me if you need anything. I'll be in the office all day."

"Of course, yes, if I need anything," Horowitz echoed, his mind on other possibilities.

Horowitz hung up the phone, reluctant to draw his

hand away, hoping that at any moment it would ring and reassure him about Mrs. Washington. Things could have happened to her. Terrible things. Perhaps the looting was not limited to stores alone. Perhaps they were breaking into apartments. Especially one like Mrs. Washington's. Where her daughter had a steady job and she did, too, looters would suspect there were things of value to be stolen. Knowing Mrs. Washington, a tough lady, she might berate him for resisting, but she was of exactly the same stuff as he. Willing to work hard, but equally determined to defend what was hers.

Of course she would have resisted. And when she did some big black sonofabitch would have hit her across the head, splitting her skull open, killing her. Poor woman, he conceded, for all her bossy ways she was a good person, a kind person. And so concerned about bringing up her two grandchildren. It was not her fault, his having been mugged, and slashed. He must apologize to her when she arrived. *If* she arrived. And from now on he must be nicer to her, more cooperative and pleasant when she drove him to do his exercises so many times every day. Even those damned marbles and buttons! She did it for his own good and he must let her know that he appreciated that.

Now, he had better try to get his own breakfast. Though he had to admit his fears about Mrs. Washington had destroyed his appetite. He was functioning out of sheer habit. In the morning one had breakfast, hungry or not.

He had risen from the bed when the phone rang again. He answered at once, "Yes? Hello?"

"Mr. Horowitz?" It was her voice, thanks God.

"Are you all right?"

"Yes, yes, I'm all right." Yet there was something in her voice that was far from reassuring. "I'm sorry I'm late, but I'll be there within the hour."

"As long as you're all right," he said.

"I'm sorry," she reiterated. "I'll be there as soon as I can."

"That's okay, don't worry about me. I'm fine, fine," he insisted. He hung up.

Chapter Thirteen

When a child is late coming home, or missing for a time, having wandered off without word or explanation, parents, in their concern, conjure up all sorts of punishments and recriminations for the moment the wanderer returns. But at the sight of the errant child, all punishments are forgotten and parents are relieved to clutch him to their bosoms and cover him with kisses.

With Horowitz it was quite the reverse. As concerned as he had been about Mrs. Washington's safety until he had heard from her, by the time she arrived, he was critical and disapproving. When he heard her key in the door, he summoned his anger and was ready for her. He greeted her sarcastically, 'Ah, good morning, Mrs. Washington."

"Good morning," she said grimly. Then quite businesslike she asked, "Had your breakfast yet?"

"Yes, I had my breakfast. Freshly squeezed papaya juice. Eggs Florentine. Sturgeon at twenty-six dollars a pound. And croissants flown over from France just for me. Flaky and delicious," he responded.

She rewarded him with an impatient look and proceeded to the kitchen where she cleaned up the mess he had made. She returned to force him to do his first set of exercises for the day. He did not resist, but cooperated with obvious impatience.

He was in the middle of his dorsiflex exercises when he took the opportunity to remark acerbically, " Some show last night. You people can be very proud of yourselves."

Mrs. Washington did not answer but continued counting the number of times he raised his left foot to strengthen it, so he might eventually walk without noticeable leg drag.

He taunted once more, "Animals! Not human beings but animals! A man works all his life to build up a business. Everything he has in the world is invested in one little store and they break in and destroy him in one night. Some world!"

Still she did not respond, but only consulted the list the hospital had given her to make sure she did not let him skip a single important exercise.

"All right now, I'll put pressure against your foot and you try to raise it."

"That one never works," he complained.

"Do it!" she ordered in a low, firm tone.

He tried, and this time he was able to move it with some small degree of success. He suspected her guilt had prevented her from applying the maximum amount of resistance.

"When one man is attacked like I was, the police say, 'Mister, you're not the only one. We get hundreds like this every day. And there's nothing we can do. We can't get identifications. And when we do, the judges put them out on the street before the cop gets back to the station house.'

183

"That's the way it starts. We let them get away with attacking men like me and next thing you know they are looting whole blocks up there. Something has to be done. Else we are living in a jungle. Last night was only the beginning. It'll get worse. Mark my words, it'll get worse."

She did not respond but kept at him to complete his exercises. Her silence irked him. He became more resistant about complying with his routine. But she made him finish it nevertheless. Which only served to increase his anger and his need to inflict punishment on her, as if she bore some personal guilt for the terrible events of the night before.

"The trouble with you people," he began anew, "you don't bring up your children to be decent. You teach them to hate whitey. To think that everything we have, we stole from you. You never had anything to begin with, how could we steal from you?"

She did not respond, except to remind him that he might want to take a shower after his long hot night.

"Okay, a shower," he acquiesced gloomily. Then, quite acerbically, he added, "And, later, maybe we will *dare* to go out in the park. Hmm?"

"Not today," she said quietly.

"Why not? Are the animals finished up in Harlem? Are they planning to come down here and do a little plain and fancy looting?"

"We cannot go to the park today because the elevators are not running. The power hasn't been restored yet."

"But you came up," he began to protest, until it dawned on him. "You mean . . . Mrs. Washington, did you?"

"Did I what?"

"Walk up all ten flights?"

She did not answer, but silently turned and left the room.

*　　*　　*

184

It was almost an hour later. They had not spoken to each other. Horowitz sat alone in his bedroom chair looking down at the park. The playground was empty. The mothers and children were obviously prisoners of stalled elevators, like himself.

Suddenly there was a comforting sound. His air conditioner came on, softly, on "slumber." The air in the room began to stir. He reached for the bedside lamp. It came on. The power was flowing again.

"Mrs. Washington," he called, "the power is on! It's on!"

She did not respond at once. But after a time she came to the door.

"If you'd like, there's still time to go out to the park before lunch," she suggested.

"I would like," he said.

In the elevator, out of respect for Mrs. Washington's presence, Angelo made no reference to the grim events of last night. But at the door, Juan said, "Sad. Very sad about last night. I was afraid to come to work today. Afraid it spread down here, too. Anybody wanted, they could break the glass on these front doors and come right in. Nobody to stop them," he lamented. "Sad."

Neither Horowitz nor Mrs. Washington responded.

They were both silent during the time they sat in the park. Though their stay was shorter than usual, it seemed far longer. They heard the occasional sounds of far-off police sirens, of fire trucks racing to the scene of some emergency uptown. North of the park, it was as if a war were still raging.

It was late afternoon when he thought to turn on the television set. Regular programming had been suspended in favor of special news coverage. On-the-scene footage, taken the night before, of break-ins and pillaging kept being repeated. There were marauders, mostly black,

185

bursting into stores and carrying off anything that was portable. Where an object was too big or too heavy, two and three men or women helped. Furniture, bedding, electric appliances of all kinds were being carried away through the shattered, jagged glass of what had once been storefronts.

Horowitz watched, shaking his head. "Look at them, look at them," he mumbled. Until he could not contain himself and called out, "Mrs. Washington! Come in here and look! See for yourself! Animals!"

When she did not appear, he called out again, "You have to see it to believe it! Come and look!"

When she could no longer ignore him, she came to the bedroom door and stared in. She watched the screen, witnessed the events of the night before, heard Horowitz's running commentary.

"My city! The biggest city in the world! Would you believe such a thing could be happening? At least they're arresting some of them. But what will happen? Some nice, stupid judge will let them all go. You'll see. They are opening up the zoo and letting the animals out. Animals!"

At that, Mrs. Washington turned and left the room at once.

Horowitz called after her, "There's no law anymore. A black man can commit murder and they don't dare convict him!" He summoned up his full voice and sent a resounding cry through the apartment, "Animals!"

As if he had issued a challenge and expected her to defend against it, he sat immobile, waiting. But a time went by, a long time, and he heard nothing. There was not even the familiar sound of the vacuum cleaner, which, he had noticed, was usually her defense against listening to his unflattering opinions. After a suspiciously long silence, he decided to confront her. With the support of his quad, he slowly dragged himself into

186

the foyer. She was not in the living room. Nor in the dining room. There was no light on in the kitchen.

For an instant he feared that she had deserted him. Perhaps he had been too harsh. But sometimes, he justified himself, the truth itself was harsh and he was not to blame for that. The kitchen door was closed, but he thought he could hear the sound of sobbing. He pressed his ear against the door. There was no doubt now. The woman was weeping. He had surely been too harsh. He must make amends somehow. But apologizing had never been his forte. He could relent, he could grumble, he could circumvent sensitive issues, but apologizing was an art at which he had little practice. Even Hannah used to rebuke him for that.

But this was an emergency and he must improvise some way to express his regret. He balanced himself on his sturdy quad, pressed against the swinging door cautiously, until he could peek into the kitchen. Mrs. Washington sat at the small table, her elbows resting on it, in her hands a damp handkerchief, which she held to her eyes while she sobbed so that her whole body shook.

"Mrs. Washington . . ." he ventured. She did not respond. "Mrs. Washington," he said more boldly. "I'm sorry about what I said. Even if it's the truth, I shouldn't have said it."

His well-intentioned but awkward apology had no effect on her. She continued to weep, using the already saturated handkerchief in a vain effort to dry her eyes. She kept whispering a forlorn, "Oh, God, oh, God."

"I said I was sorry," he reiterated, as if that alone could heal her anguish. When it failed, he pleaded, "Mrs. Washington, what more can I say?"

She did not respond until he flicked on the light switch. She called out, "No, don't! I'd rather it was dark!"

Out of respect for her feelings he snapped off the light,

187

returning the room to the shadows of late afternoon.

"Mrs. Washington, please, if it would make you feel better to holler at me, holler. I'll understand." He had run out of ways to apologize. So he stood there, waiting, like a recalcitrant little boy who had offended his mother to the point of tears and was hoping for punishment to absolve his guilt.

She began to sniffle, the first sign that her intense weeping was over. She caught her breath in short gasps. Finally she was able to say, "It's not you."

"Then what?"

She shook her head. Whatever it was, it was too painful to talk about.

"You can tell me," he coaxed. "I swear whatever it is, I won't say anything. Not anything nasty, that is."

She sniffled again, used the damp handkerchief to wipe her eyes.

"So you were a little late today. So what? Who's blaming you? A day like today a little late is understandable. And climbing up ten floors, that could take a little time also," he pardoned.

"It wasn't the stairs."

"What difference? Did I say anything about docking you? You would have been paid if you were five hours late. It's an emergency. Never in all my years in business did I ever dock an employee because of a storm, or a subway tie-up, or something that was not his fault. I could stand the loss better than they could. Fair is fair. So don't cry. And don't worry. Please?"

She shook her head and resumed crying again.

"Mrs. Washington, be reasonable," he pleaded. "Don't cry."

"I'm sorry," she said, but it only occasioned more tears.

"I'm not asking you to be sorry, I'm only asking, don't cry!" he insisted.

188

"I'm trying to tell you something," she said, "and I don't know how."

"Tell me. You know I'm an understanding man," he urged, giving every appearance of reasonableness.

"I don't know how," she said, still not daring to face him.

"There's nothing so bad that you can't tell me. After all, we are not exactly strangers. You have seen me in some very intimate moments. I would like to think that we have at least a little feeling for each other. What's so bad that you can't tell me?"

"The reason I was late today . . ." she began, then faltered.

"The reason you were late today . . ." he coaxed, "is . . .?"

"I had to go to court this morning."

"Court?"

"Yes," she admitted in a whisper.

"What was in court this morning?" he asked, sensitive to her feelings. Gently, he urged, "Mrs. Washington?"

"Last night . . . once the blackout started . . . there was all that noise outside. Like I always thought a tidal wave would sound. Except it was voices, human voices. They rose up from the street like a great big wave. But it didn't pass. It kept growing, building. We looked out and saw them. The street was full of them. They were shouting, laughing, cheering, shattering windows, looting."

"Yes. So?" Horowitz asked.

"Conrad . . ." she began but could not continue.

"Your grandson?"

She nodded.

"What about him?"

"He watched, he listened, then suddenly said, 'I'm going to get ours!' He started out of the apartment. I went after him, I held onto him. But he pushed me away. He . . . he hit me. And he was gone. I ran after him. I lost him

189

in the darkness in the street. I found my way back. But he never got home last night."

"They arrested him?" Horowitz ventured.

She nodded.

"Ho-ho-ho!" Horowitz consoled.

"I had to go down and find him today. There he was, in with hundreds of them, thousands. This boy, who until last night was a fine boy, a good student, the son of a policeman. A boy who had been brought up to be better than the others. A religious boy. And in one night he had become one of them," she said, beginning to weep again.

"You were able to get him out?"

"One of the officers there had worked with his father. Had been one of his pallbearers. He helped."

"Thanks God," Horowitz said.

"He'll have to go back for a hearing."

"I'll call Marvin right away. Someone in his New York office will handle the case. Without a fee!" Horowitz promised.

"Thank you."

"Now, will you stop crying?"

But his request only occasioned more tears.

"What now?" the distraught Horowitz pleaded.

"It was my fault," she accused herself.

"How could it be your fault? You tried to stop him," Horowitz became her advocate.

"For days now, with this heat wave, I kept complaining how hot it was. How difficult to sleep. How much better it would be if we had an air conditioner."

"The heat spell was your fault?" Horowitz asked.

"Complaining about it was."

"Everybody complains about the heat."

"When they caught him, he was trying to steal an air conditioner. For me," she admitted, dissolving in tears again.

"I see," Horowitz said sadly. "Yes, I see."

He shuffled closer to her, reached out, patted her on the head. "I promise you, he'll get the best legal advice. We'll make sure the judge knows why he did it. Nothing bad will happen to him."

"It's already happened," she said sadly. "It's what I've always been afraid of. I kept saying to my daughter, we've got to move away. To some place on Long Island. There are nice communities, black communities there. But always her answer was the same. We have to be close to our work. And we can't afford to put down a payment on a house. So we stayed.

"And it's a disease. Just living there is a disease. A child is exposed and can catch it. Like last night. It was an epidemic. A fever. And he caught it. I don't think that boy ever thought to steal for one minute in his life before last night. All the years of bringing up, gone in one night. One night," she said, and fell to weeping again.

"Mrs. Washington, when the whole world goes crazy, you expect one small boy to remain sane?" Horowitz asked. He hobbled to the kitchen phone, dialed a number he knew well. He asked for Marvin Hammond. When the operator challenged him, he said, "Tell Mr. Hammond his father, Mr. Horowitz, is calling!"

Since they had spoken only a few hours earlier, Marvin came on the line greatly concerned, "Dad! Something wrong? What happened? Mrs. Washington never showed?"

"Mrs. Washington is here. And I'm fine. Now, Marvin, you listen to me! There is a boy. His name is Conrad . . ." He put his hand over the mouthpiece. "What's the boy's full name?"

"Bruton. Conrad Bruton," Mrs. Washington informed.

"His name is Conrad Bruton," Horowitz informed his son. "He was arrested last night."

"What for?"

Already undertaking the boy's defense, Horowitz said,

191

"They claim . . . mind you, they only *claim*, that he was stealing an air conditioner."

"Stealing an air conditioner?" Marvin exploded. "Dad! How would you have contact with someone who steals air conditioners?"

"In the first place, it's not air conditioners. Just *one* air conditioner. In the second place, we are not conceding he was stealing it. In the third place, he is the grandson of a very good friend of mine and I want to see him defended. And in the fourth place, not only defended, but I want to see that he gets off! Scot-free! He is a good boy. And I don't want his record ruined. So do something about it!"

"Dad! We do not practice criminal law," Marvin declared self-righteously.

"What about those corporate clients of yours? Those conspiracy cases, those price-fixing cases I read about in the *Times*?"

"That's different," Marvin protested.

"So consider this boy different, too," Horowitz insisted.

"Dad! You don't seem to understand!"

"Marvin! Do it!" Horowitz ordered. "Unless you want me to go to court myself and be a character witness for the boy!"

Marvin finally conceded, "I'll see what I can do."

"Don't *see*. Just *do!*" Horowitz commanded. "And if there is a bill, if you want to charge your own father, who put you through Harvard Law School, okay by me!" Horowitz declared, and hung up.

He turned to Mrs. Washington, "There! Done! Don't worry anymore!"

"Thank you, Mr. Horowitz," she said.

"What kind of thanks?" he minimized. "It's little enough to do for a friend."

192

"Now, we'd better get on with your exercises," she declared.

"Even today?" he pleaded. "A day of such upsets? I have to do exercises?"

"Even today!" she insisted, shoving her damp hand-kerchief into her apron pocket.

"You certainly have a strange way to show appreciation," he complained.

To divert her mind from the troubles of the night, Horowitz proved more difficult than usual during his exercises. Mrs. Washington was forced to insist more, exert more resistance, force his arms and his legs higher, further over than usual. She labored over him until, despite the cool air in the room, she was in a sweat. She seemed to be pouring all her frustrations about her grandson into making sure he performed his exercises with an extra measure of devotion this afternoon.

Secretly, Horowitz enjoyed the experience. She was no longer weeping. She no longer felt that she had failed. Self-pity was gone. She was the tough Mrs. Washington he was used to. He felt better, much better.

Chapter Fourteen

It was some days later. They made their usual visit to the park. This time, however, instead of sitting on a bench near the playground, Mrs. Washington suggested moving down to Eighty-first Street to the small shallow lake above which rose the skeletal structure of the Shakespeare-in-the-Park theater. She arranged his wheelchair so that they caught the sun, which had risen almost to its zenith. That angle had him facing the lake and the open-air theater.

"You ever been in there?" Horowitz asked.

"No," Mrs. Washington said.

"Must be interesting to see theater at night under the stars," he said. "Hannah and me, we often talked about going. But who wants to stand in line for hours to get tickets, even if they're free?"

They were silent for a time. Then he asked, "Would you like to?"

"What?"

"Go to the Shakespeare?"

"At night? I couldn't."

"Of course, the *kinder*," he realized.

"Yes, the children," she commented sadly, sighing.

He hesitated before asking, "When does his case come up?"

"Tomorrow."

"It'll be all right," he promised, trying to appear confident. "Did he say how he likes the young lawyer Marvin sent up?"

"He likes him. But they say the judges have been given orders to be very tough on looters," she said grimly.

"With a good lawyer even a tough judge is putty in the hand." After a pause, he asked, "If it was possible, I mean, if it could be arranged that someone was with the children, one night, you think we could go?" he asked.

"Where?"

"The Shakespeare," he explained impatiently.

"We might," she said, evading, not promising.

"Try. For once I would like to go. Always it was Hannah wanted to go and I didn't. Now I would like to go, so when I meet her again I can tell her how it was."

"You're not going to meet her for a long time," Mrs. Washington said.

"How do you know?" he replied, offended. After all, he had a right to his own fantasies.

"When the Angel of Death comes for you, you'll be too damn stubborn. He's going to show you how to die and you won't even pay attention."

"That's not a nice thing to say, Mrs. Washington. I'm as reasonable as the next man. When the time comes to go, I'll go. With or without instructions," he insisted. But he could tell that he had had no success diverting her mind from what was troubling her. Not Shakespeare, nor talk of Hannah, or even of death could draw her mind from what was going to happen today in some courtroom in one of those buildings downtown that he had always shunned, except when he was summoned to jury duty.

He was wheeling himself along the paved path that led by the theater, when he said suddenly, "Mrs. Washington, go in and ask if they would make a special case for a man who had a stroke. Maybe we wouldn't have to wait in line like all the rest. And ask if they have a ramp for wheelchairs. Try, please?"

She left the path and made her way along the railings that led to the box office, where a young girl was preparing for the night's audience. She was blonde, long-haired, tanned, plump, and very pretty. She was, mainly and most of all, young.

"Miss," Harriet Washington called to attract her attention.

She turned, with a bright smile, a patient smile. "Yes?"

"Do you have special provision for an invalid? Not really an invalid. But a man temporarily confined to a wheelchair."

"Yes. It could be arranged. For what night?"

"We don't know yet, but I had to ask," Mrs. Washington said.

"Any time your husband wants to come, just let us know a few hours ahead," the young girl suggested. Then looking beyond Mrs. Washington she spied, sitting in his wheelchair, Mr. Samuel Horowitz. Much against her own youthful and tolerant attitude, she instinctively reacted in surprise and disapproval.

"A patient, my dear," Mrs. Washington explained.

"Well, whoever he is, you bring him any night and we'll see he gets in without any trouble. And, yes, we do have a chair ramp," she volunteered.

The phone was ringing when Mrs. Washington inserted the key in the lock. She opened the door, did not attempt to assist his chair into the apartment but raced to the kitchen. Horowitz maneuvered himself over the doorsill and wheeled himself toward the kitchen just in time to hear the end of the conversation.

"Yes, darling, now go home. Straight home. Do you hear me?" Mrs. Washington was saying. "And I'll call you there in half an hour. If you're not there, you'll catch it when I come home!" she said sternly.

She hung up, turned away, and found Horowitz sitting in the doorway.

"Well?"

"The judge let him off with a warning. Because of his school record and what two of his teachers wrote about him."

"Good!" Horowitz said. "I must call Marvin and tell him they have at least one bright young lawyer in his firm."

He turned about and wheeled himself toward the bedroom.

She was putting him through his therapy and being unusually insistent with him.

"You know, Mrs. Washington, what occurred to me?"

"Save your breath for your exercises," she cautioned.

"No, I have a terrific idea!" he enthused.

"All right." She was resigned to listening even though it would interrupt his rhythm.

"Conrad and Louise, they ever been to see Shakespeare?"

"No. Why?"

"Then what would be so terrible, you should bring them down here. We all have dinner together. There's a few nice restaurants on Columbus Avenue. And then we all go to the Shakespeare. That's not impossible, is it?" he asked.

She did not respond at once.

"Conrad is free. That's an occasion to celebrate, no?"

197

"Yes, I guess . . ."

"So when you have something to celebrate, I say celebrate!"

She would only promise, "I'll think about it."

"Mrs. Washington, we're getting too old to think about things," he said. "When Hannah used to suggest going to some new place, or doing some new thing, like the Shakespeare, I would say, 'I'll think about it.' But somehow we never went to those places, like we never went to the Shakespeare. So no thinking. I want your word. Now! We'll go! Right?"

Because he had never shown such determination and optimism before, Mrs. Washington said, "Right!"

"Good!" he said, then gloated in anticipation. "And the next day I'll call Mona. On Albert's 800 number. And I'll just casually toss off, 'Last night I went to see Shakespeare.' That should keep her from coming here and trying to organize me!"

Horowitz laughed, and Mrs. Washington joined him.

On the appointed day of their visit to the theater in the park, Samuel Horowitz seemed unduly busy. Leaning on his quad for support he rooted through the drawers of his chest searching for something. For most of the day he did not seem to find it. When Mrs. Washington inquired if she could help, he ignored her, muttering that he had to learn to do things for himself. Each time she interrupted him for his exercises, or his walk about the apartment, or his lunch, he performed the required duty in haste, so intent was he on resuming his search. But by mid-afternoon, his anxiety seemed to have subsided. After his nap, he rose, took his shower, unassisted. He began to assemble his wardrobe for the evening. He selected a pair of lightweight navy slacks, explaining, "We bought these the year we went to Florida, just before Hannah died. And this, this was her favorite shirt," he explained as he

198

laid out a long neglected, brightly colored sport shirt.

Then across the slacks he laid the shirt to make absolutely sure of a harmonious combination. He looked up at Mrs. Washington, "You think a sports jacket, too?"

"It could get cool after the sun goes down," Mrs. Washington reminded.

"Yes, it could."

He shuffled across the carpet to the closet, rummaged among his clothes until he found a cotton jacket of a blue and white check. He added it to the slacks and shirt on the bed. "Not bad," he concluded after a long appraisal. "What do you think?"

"Not bad," she agreed.

"Then that's settled," he said with finality. "Now, Mrs. Washington, you ever heard of Bon Vivant?"

"Bon Vivant?" she echoed, confused.

"It's a little French-style restaurant just around on Columbus Avenue. Juan, the doorman, tells me the other tenants say it's nice. And French-style, what could be bad?" Horowitz asked.

Though he was confined to his wheelchair, Horowitz insisted on acting the host with all the officiousness of which he was capable. He ordered the waiter about. He insisted Conrad and Louise be brought their milk. He held forth over the menu, suggesting one dish after another, hoping to tempt them into expressing a choice. He was far more animated and enthusiastic than Mrs. Washington had ever seen him.

Once he made sure the children had everything they desired he ordered his own dinner. From the first trip he and Hannah had ever made abroad, he knew when you were in a French restaurant, and confused by the dishes on the menu, always order quenelles. French for gefilte fish, though not nearly so delicious, it was a dish easy to eat, and generally safe.

He ordered them, and made every pretense at eating them. But mainly he studied the children. Conrad was a lean boy, tall for his age, with bright active black eyes, his grandmother's eyes. He deported himself well. A polite boy and respectful. And when he spoke you could understand him. Most black boys, Horowitz grumbled to himself, you couldn't understand half of what they said. Except when they said, "Hand over your money or I'll kill you." Then there was no misunderstanding them.

This young boy was well spoken, ate correctly, and showed every sign of having been very well brought up. And, no wonder, Horowitz said to himself, with such a tyrant for a grandmother.

Louise, two years younger than Conrad, was a slight child of eight. Pretty, despite her glasses, one could already see that she, too, would grow up tall and graceful. She carried herself well for a child so young. She handled her utensils very nicely. Better, Horowitz realized sadly, than he was able to do in his present condition. Though it was one of the added advantages of quenelles that they would be eaten with only a fork and thus did not tax his left hand.

When the main course was finished, Horowitz summoned the waiter. "Garçon, I want you should bring a tray of absolutely the richest, fanciest desserts you have!" When Mrs. Washington tried to intervene, he swept aside all protest. "The richest, and the best. After all, we are celebrating!"

The waiter presented a tray of delicacies abounding in chocolate and whipped cream. There were eclairs rich with custard, puff pastries overrunning with whipped cream, large slices of chocolate layer cake festooned with dark red cherries.

When Conrad was faced with a final crucial dilemma between two pastries, Horowitz insisted, "Have them both! As long as you have an extra glass of milk!"

Mrs. Washington said only, "Conrad!" with a rising inflection. The boy chose the simpler dessert. Louise had no problem. She made her choice. They were all silent as Horowitz watched with pride and enjoyment while the youngsters consumed their dessert. He glanced across the table at Mrs. Washington and nodded warmly, giving his approval to her bringing up of the children.

The play was one of Shakespeare's Kings. It was loud, and theatrical, filled with swordplay and finally death. The miracle of it, Horowitz realized when it was over, the street sounds, so close, had been blotted out by the voices and the action on the stage. Even a distant storm, which filled the night with flashes of lightning and rumbles of thunder, did not intrude. The audience filed out quickly, making their way east toward Fifth Avenue or flowing out onto Central Park West. But Horowitz's little company waited until last so that he could make his way in his wheelchair, with the unasked for assistance of young Conrad, who was very helpful while trying to appear casual so as not to offend the old man's pride.

They had reached Horowitz's building. The night doorman, who had not seen Horowitz since his return from the hospital, was shocked to find him in a wheelchair. But he retained his outward calm, saluting Horowitz as ever, with a touch of the fingers to the peak of his cap.

"Good evening, Mr. Horowitz. I hear you're coming along fine," he enthused. With the help of Conrad, he eased the chair down the three steps into the lobby.

Once inside the door of his apartment, Mrs. Washington said, "I'll get you ready for bed. It's late and the children have been up past their time," she apologized for her haste.

"No, something else first," Horowitz insisted.

"It really is late, and the subways don't run often at this hour of night."

"It won't take long. Besides, you will take a taxi home," he insisted. "It'll be my treat."

"Taxis don't like to go uptown this late at night," she explained.

"The doorman will get you one," Horowitz said. "So instead of wasting time arguing, come!"

He rolled himself into the living room and to the bridge table near the window where he reached out to a ruby red cut glass box. His hand resting on it, he turned to the children.

"Conrad . . . Louise . . ." he began, "I want you both to remember this night. Not because you had a delicious meal. Believe me, your grandmother cooks better. Not because we saw a big show by Shakespeare, with costumes and music and actors. You will see other shows in your life. And not because you made an old man feel a little less lonely. That was very nice of you.

"But I want you to remember it because this world has changed. It's changing right this minute while we talk. Things you can achieve, your grandfather couldn't. Even your father couldn't. You have opportunity they didn't have. Just like I had opportunities here that my grandfather and my father didn't have."

He reached out to place a gentle hold on Conrad's arm. "But, my boy, you do not take advantage of opportunity by rushing out into the night and saying, 'I'm going to get mine!' and then taking what belongs to another man.

"Conrad, don't think I don't know that feeling of impatience. You want to show the world. You want to make things easier for your mother and your grandmother. When I was a boy I used to watch my mother working hard at home, and helping my father in the little grocery we had. All hours, from darkness in the morning until darkness at night. I knew the times she was too tired to move, but moved. Too tired to wash the clothes, but she washed. Too tired to cook, but she cooked. And I felt, it is my fault. She's doing so much for me, and I can't do anything for her. I would be angry with myself, and angry with the world. I wanted to do something bold, and desperate. If only to show her how much I resented what the world had done to her.

"But that's not the way. Fight the world, it will crush you. Outsmart the world, it will reward you. You will have time, plenty of time, to do good things for your mother and your grandmother. But do it right. Do it honorably. So you can look them in the eye. More important, so you can look your own children in the eye and not feel you have to apologize to them."

He shook his head gravely, admitting, "That's a lot of talking for an old man to do. And a lot of listening for a young boy and girl to do. But so that you'll remember at least part of it, I have a little gift for each of you. I think they call it a momento, or maybe it's a memento. Whichever, I want you to think of tonight when you look at these gifts."

He opened the ruby cut glass box and took out a small coin. He handled it like a touchstone, gently rubbing his thumb and forefinger over it. It was worn, but shiny. He reached for Conrad's hand, held it palm up and he carefully placed the coin in the boy's outstretched hand. Horowitz cast a glance at Mrs. Washington, "You will notice, my dear Mrs. Washington, I did that with my left hand," he taunted.

"My boy, this is a five-dollar gold piece. If you can still make out the date you will see it says 1901. It was given to me by my father when I was bar mitzvahed. That means thirteen years old. Not much different than you are now. And he said, 'This is only a promise of what you can have if you work hard.' So I say the same to you.

Every time you get angry with the world, or with yourself for not doing more or being more, look at this coin and remember the answer is hard work."

He closed the boy's hand into a tight fist. "Keep it. Always. Until the time comes to give it to your son."

Horowitz turned to the young girl. "And for you, my dear Louise, I also have something."

He reached back into the ruby red box and brought out a small pin of old gold encrusted with tiny seed pearls, which had, in its time, been handwrought by some local jeweler. He gazed at it fondly, with the air of one about to say farewell to an old friend for the last time.

"This pin," he began, "this was the first gift I bought for my mother when I could afford it. It cost twelve and a half dollars when that was a whole lot of money. And there was no sales tax, even. I was working for a Mr. Riordan in his paper and twine business. As an office boy, errand boy, delivery boy, shipping clerk, for the big wages of sixteen dollars a week. He was a tough man, Riordan. He would order me around like I was his slave. Always, 'Sammy.' 'Sammy do this.' 'Sammy do that.' 'Sammy run out to the delicatessen and get me a ham on rye for lunch.' Because he knew that I hated to go into an unkosher place, especially for a ham on rye!

"But the second year I worked for him, he called me in the day before Christmas. And he said, 'Samuel, I am going to do you a big favor. I am going to fire you.' I was frightened, very frightened. I had come to depend on that job. My family had come to depend on it. The grocery business was bad that year. I started to plead with him, asking what I had done wrong, or if I hadn't done everything I was expected to.

"Riordan smiled. A big genuine smile. Not a customer-type smile. He said, 'Samuel, I am firing you as errand boy, office boy, delivery boy, and shipping clerk. You're too smart for that. And you know the business now. So I am hiring you as a salesman, an outside salesman. I think you will do very well at it. And to prove it, I am going to raise you to twenty dollars a week and throw in a little commission. Hay makes the horse go, as they say. So in this week's envelope you will find twenty dollars instead of sixteen. And a little bonus besides.'

"He shook my hand, which he had never done before, and he wished me Merry Christmas. I didn't open that envelope until I was in the toilet in the back of the loft. I counted the money. Twenty dollars. Plus another ten! Thirty dollars. Not I, not anyone in my family had ever had thirty dollars of our own all in one lump sum. So I said to myself, I have got to make up to Mama for everything she has ever done for me, for my father, for all of us, and which we took for granted as the duty of a mother and never even thanked her for.

"On the way home, I passed this little jeweler's shop. I saw this pin. Gold. Real gold. With little pearls." He picked it up and held it to the light. "If you look hard you will see that a few of the pearls have fallen out. But when you hold it out like this, you can't tell."

Then he admitted sheepishly, "Well, at least without reading glasses, you can't tell. But it is pretty. And it's what's behind it that counts. Remember that people are always a little better than you think. And life can be a little kinder than you think. I never forgot old man Riordan. When it came time for me to raise a worker, I always made sure to add a little something he didn't expect. Just like Riordan. I can almost hear him say, 'That's the way to do it, Sammy.'

"So you take this. Wear it. For special occasions. But look at it often and remember this night."

He closed her hand over the gift, as he had done with her brother. He held her fist in his hand as he said sadly, "I often say to myself, I wish my grandchildren had less, so they would appreciate little things more. I used to

205

think of giving these to them, but it wouldn't have mattered . . . wouldn't have mattered."

Though Mrs. Washington insisted on helping him get ready for bed, he would not hear of it, but pressed ten dollars into her hand and hustled them off, calling after them, "Make sure the doorman gets you a cab!"

Alone in the apartment, he latched the door, locked the two locks which had been installed for added security, labored to turn his wheelchair about, and rolled his way slowly into the bedroom.

He was in bed, in the dark, listening to the late night news. In a while, feeling content, he drifted off to sleep.

Chapter Fifteen

Samuel Horowitz had just finished reading his *New York Times* as Mrs. Washington completed vacuuming the rug in the foyer.

"Thanks God!" he called out from the living room. "A person can't think, no less read a newspaper with all that racket."

She came into the archway. "You're not going to leave the paper that way, are you?" she challenged.

"I am!" he insisted. "You want me to crumple the pages, get me another paper!"

"Another paper will be the same," she responded.

"Yes, but I want to save this one. I want to leave it with my will. For the world to know when this country and this world began to come apart."

"What is it this time?" she asked resignedly, accustomed to his ranting about what he found in the *Times*.

"The Russians are building up their army, navy, and

missiles, and the *Times* is yelling for détente. Do you know what détente is, Mrs. Washington? It is a French word for what they don't dare say in English. Surrender! Imagine, this was once the greatest country in the world! Now we are making détente with the Russians, who are building up their missiles and their navy so they can destroy us. And the *Times* is all for it. But then the *Times* has been wrong so often, what can you expect?"

She did not answer his rhetorical question, but separated the paper into its sections and handed the first one to him to take apart page by page and crumple into tight balls. He did not react, preferring to continue his tirade.

"Accommodation, Kissinger used to call it. The Russians are getting ready to kill us while we are providing them with grain, computers, and whole factories! How much more accommodating can we be?"

"Crumple!" Mrs. Washington commanded. He glared at her. "I can't stand here all day and supervise you as if you were a child. I have work to do."

"Work!" he scoffed. "You're worse than Bernadine! I used to say to Hannah, 'That woman will wear out the rugs and the furniture with all her vacuuming and dusting.' Enough is enough. How clean can you get?" he grumbled.

"Crumple!" she persisted.

"Crumple," he grumbled. "Where should I start? The financial page? The economy is crumpled enough. Any more would be considered cruel and unusual punishment. The sports pages? It's the only place in the *Times* where you can expect at least a little honesty, a little common sense. The entertainment section? Where a fat little Englishman is telling all Americans what's good for them to see and not to see. Or the news section? Where those reporters don't give you the news but their own opinions. Or maybe the cooking section?

"*The New York Times*, the great *New York Times*, is

suddenly specializing in cooking! If I want cooking I will read the *Ladies' Home Journal.* So I think I will start to crumple with the cooking section. And do you know what is in the cooking section today? How to make a cold fruit soup!

"When I was a boy, my mother made cold fruit soup. But she didn't need any *New York Times* to tell her how. She learned it from her mother, who learned it from her mother. Now, with all the education and all the learning we have, a woman has to read *The New York Times* to find out how to make a simple thing like cold fruit soup.

"I can assure you, my Mona, with her whole damn college education, cannot make a good cold fruit soup. But she doesn't have to. She has a cook. Or a caterer, who already knows how to make cold fruit soup. Mona would have to read *The New York Times!* Some America! *The New York Times* is now a cookbook."

"Crumple," Mrs. Washington repeated.

"Why not pinochle? Twenty-five cents a hand," he counterproposed. "It's more fun than crumpling."

"You already owe me twelve dollars and seventy-five cents," she reminded.

"So we'll play double or nothing."

"Crumple! Then the marbles. After that, buttons! Then if there's time left before lunch, a little pinochle. First, crumple!"

"It's the only word she knows. Crumple! It doesn't even sound medical! Crumple!" He sat at the table in a resistant posture, beating his fist on the newspaper until he declared, "I know! I'll start with Editorial first. Then Tom Wicker, then Anthony Lewis!"

The mere thought gave him great satisfaction.

"I don't care where you start, just start!" Mrs. Washington glowered.

"Go ahead, hit me!" he defied. "It won't be the first time a nurse has abused a patient. The courts are crowded with such cases!" When she glared at him, he modified his extravagant statement by admitting, "I read about one once."

When she exhaled impatiently, he surrendered, "Okay! I'll crumple!"

As he began, he continued muttering, "Today, affirmative action. Both of them. The editorial and Wicker. You think that's merely a coincidence? Not on your life. Somebody in the *Times* decided they should go all out for affirmative action and Wicker, a cagey sonofabitch, wants to be in good with his boss so he decides he too will write a column in favor of affirmative action. Freedom of the press!" he exploded, as he crumpled the editorial page with unusual vigor.

He held up the next page. "You see that, Mrs. Washington? They call this the Op-Ed page of the *Times*. A very clever trick. Because to most people it means it is a page reserved for articles that oppose the editorials in *The New York Times*. A lie! A big fat lie! Who is on the Op-Ed page most of the time? Wicker, Lewis, Reston. Who all work for the *Times*. So where is the Op? And today is even worse! Because today the biggest article on the Op-Ed page is by a black college professor, also in favor of affirmative action! Some Op, no?

"Lies. We are living in an age of lies. Affirmative action! That's a nice little lie! With a very attractive label. Because it is not affirmative. It is negative. You take a not-smart black boy, with so-so grades, and he can get into medical school. You take a smart Jewish boy with good grades and he *can't* get into medical school. Is that affirmative or negative?"

"Crumple, it's getting late," she reminded.

"It's later than you think! The world is coming apart!" he declared. "When we came over to this country, nobody gave us any affirmative action. We didn't even speak the language. But nobody gave us any bilingual

210

education. Another pet of *The New York Times*. A kid can't speak English but he can speak Spanish. So what do these geniuses figure out we should do? We should teach them Spanish, which they already know and which is creating the problem in the first place.

"I'll never forget, Mrs. Washington, the first day I went to school. Seven years old. And didn't speak a word of English. But my mother knew one thing. I had to go to school. I had to learn. That is the first thing every Jewish child knows. Learning is the important thing. So the first day, my mother took one of my father's books. She put a drop of honey on the first page. She said, *"Ess, mein kind."* Eat! Because a child must know that learning is sweet. Then she took me by the hand and walked me to school.

"She didn't speak English either. But somehow, from friends and relatives she had studied enough words to make the school understand. She was bringing her son to them to be educated. She left me with the principal. I was frightened. A boy of seven. In a strange place. Strange people. Speaking a strange language. I wanted to turn and run. And they put me in a class with a Miss McLanahan. In those days most of the teachers were Irish. The whole system was Irish. Why not? After all, insurance companies and big offices wouldn't hire Catholics. So they became teachers. Anyhow this Miss McLanahan was the tallest woman I have ever seen. A giant. She never smiled. And no kid in her class ever smiled either. They sat stiff, their hands clasped, pressed down on the desk. Until she asked for volunteers to answer a question. Then a few hands shot up. But everyone else, stiff, hands clasped, on the desk."

Horowitz illustrated, trying desperately to make his left hand obey, but not quite succeeding. His right fingers gripping his left, he sat with both hands before him on the table as he continued.

211

"A day went by. Another day. I didn't understand what she was saying. So I never raised my hand. Then I began to feel, Why shouldn't I be as good as the other kids. Why not raise my hand? After all, if six kids raised their hands she could only call on one. So my chances were pretty good she wouldn't call on me. I could take the chance, and not look like a dummy who never raised his hand.

"So she asked a question. When I was sure there were five other hands up, I raised mine. But instead of her calling on one of the first five, she called on me. I sat there feeling dumb and stupid. I didn't even understand what the question was, how could I know the answer? She stared at me. She waited. She said some things which must have been insulting. I could tell by the way she looked and the way the other kids laughed at me. And then I . . . Mrs. Washington, I started to cry."

"I don't blame you," Mrs. Washington said sympathetically.

"When the class was over, she pointed to me. She went like this." He made a gesture with his right hand, summoning someone to approach him.

"Try that with your left hand," Mrs. Washington suggested.

"She did it with her right hand," Horowitz protested.

"You try it with your left," she insisted.

"I can do it, I can do it." He proceeded to try, giving his left hand some much needed activity. "There!" He beckoned, in imitation of Miss McLanahan. "So I went up. She tried to talk to me. Very slowly. But in English. The more she talked, the more I cried. Until she realized that I didn't understand her at all. She took me by the hand. We went down the hall. It was the longest hall I have ever been down.

"Until we came to a small office where a tiny dark-haired woman sat. She was very thin, with small features, like a bird. There followed a long conversation between Miss McLanahan and this woman. Then Miss McLanahan left. There I was, this strange woman and me. She reached out, drew me close and spoke in the softest, friendliest voice I think I have ever heard, *'Fashstest Yiddish, mein kind?'*

"I began to cry again. This time, out of relief. Here was someone who understood. Someone I could talk to. It turned out she was an assistant principal named Mrs. Levenstein. I talked to her. I talked a lot. She talked to me. And it was wonderful. She said that every day after school, for one hour, she would go over with me in Yiddish what the other children had learned that morning. Until I was able to understand.

"It didn't take but three or four weeks and I didn't need any more help. I could raise my hand and answer the questions. And when I got my papers back from Miss McLanahan I always passed. Some days I even got a hundred. By the end of the term I could speak as well as any of them!" he concluded proudly. "Without government programs, without money wasted, without all that other nonsense."

"And mainly without any bilingual education," Mrs. Washington said pointedly.

He realized that, far from making his point, he had defeated it, so self-consciously he said, "It was something people did by themselves. You didn't need laws and bureaus and a whole *megillah!*"

Mrs. Washington glared at him, calling his attention to the task at hand. He resumed crumpling the sheets of the *Times*, fashioning them into balls which he then proceeded to toss across the room with his right arm.

"I wouldn't mind picking them up, if you would throw that far with your left arm," she said.

"Even when I was in school I was a right-handed pitcher," he countered. "But for you, my dear Mrs.

Washington, considering how sweet you have been today, I will throw left-handed."

He fashioned another paper ball, using his fingers as nimbly as he could. He tried to throw it across the room with his left hand but it slid awkwardly out of his unsteady grasp and fell to the carpet only a few feet away and in a direction other than he intended. His defeat silenced him. He shoved aside the paper refusing to crumple any more pages.

She urged more gently, "Try again. But this time, think about it more."

"Thinking does not throw balls."

"For people with left-sided trouble, thinking helps," she suggested. "Try! Go on!"

Reluctantly, he selected another sheet of the *Times*, carefully crumpled it into a ball, paused, seemed to arrange in his brain the functions now required. Then he tossed the ball. It went not nearly so far as it had gone right-handed, but it was in the direction he had intended and further than his previous effort. Encouraged, he concentrated on crumpling and throwing paper balls.

While he was so engrossed, Mrs. Washington continued to dust, but at the same time to voice her own opinions. Not directly to him, but in an at-large manner that was aimed at informing, but not irritating him.

"Some people are forgetting that for hundreds of years in this country it was against the law to teach a black person to read or write. Anyone doing so could be sent to prison. No wonder we are so far behind and need help. Or do we just say to young people, because your great-grandfather, and your great-great-grandfather were slaves you are going to start off behind everyone else and stay there? Is that what you want me to say to Conrad? And to Louise?"

"They happen to be very nice, very bright children," Horowitz conceded. "I'm talking about the others."

"What others?" Mrs. Washington asked, dropping her

dust cloth onto the nearest table and turning to confront him.

"The ones who are not so bright, not so nice," Horowitz countered. "Twenty-five years ago they couldn't read, now they all want to be college professors! And they want us to pay for it!"

"When there is something wrong, it is the government's job to set it right," Mrs. Washington said. "And the people's job to pay for it."

"You mean any black person can come to me and say, 'Mr. Horowitz, two hundred years ago my great-grandfather was a slave so you owe me a college education'?" Horowitz fought back, "I never owned a slave in my life. My family wasn't even in this country two hundred years ago. How is it my responsibility?"

Horowitz was now crumpling sheets of newspaper out of anger, not as therapy. Mrs. Washington did not attempt to respond but resumed her cleaning. Until the phone rang.

"If that's Mona, I won't talk to her!" he said at once.

"You always do," she reminded him.

"Well, today I won't. You talk to her. You two agree on almost everything anyhow," he grumbled.

The phone continued to ring.

"Don't answer it. She'll think we're in the park," he urged. Despite that, Mrs. Washington started to the phone, while Horowitz lamented, "With that damn 800 number she expects me to call every day like I lived right around the corner. And if not, she calls. On that damn WATS line. Between 800 numbers and WATS lines a man has no privacy anymore! It's like a do-it-yourself FBI! Maybe the phone company should invent a 900 number. For people who don't want to get calls from people who have WATS lines. As soon as someone with a WATS line called, the 900 number would cut in and make a busy signal!"

He was fully expecting Mrs. Washington to call out,

"It's your daughter," and he would be forced to take quad cane in hand and hobble into the bedroom to get on the extension. But Mrs. Washington did not call out. Instead, a strange unsettling quiet engulfed the kitchen.

In a moment, Mrs. Washington appeared, eyes fixed and staring. But when she blinked, tears started down her cheeks.

"Oh, Mr. Horowitz, Mr. Horowitz . . ." was all she could say as she slumped to the floor.

He reached for his cane, hobbled quickly to her side, tried to lift her but could not and damned his inept left arm.

"Mrs. Washington . . . Mrs. Washington," he pleaded.

Finally she came to, unaware for the instant what had caused her to faint. Then she remembered and began weeping and talking at the same time.

"Conrad . . ." she began. "Conrad was in a street fight. Got stabbed."

"Stabbed? Good God!" Horowitz said, daring to ask, "Is he . . . is he still alive?"

"Yes, but . . ." She could not continue.

"But *what?*" Horowitz asked, frantically. "What? Speak! Tell me!"

"If they can't stop the bleeding . . ." Mrs. Washington started to say, but gave way to tears.

"Where is he?"

"Harlem Hospital."

"Then you go! Don't stop to change clothes! Just go! Here . . ." He reached into his pocket, took out a fistful of bills. "Take a cab! Tell Juan to get you one! But go!"

"What about you?"

"Don't worry about me! I'll get along! You just go!" he insisted. "But call me as soon as you know anything!"

She was gone. As to his own situation, he assured himself that he could manage. He would find something

216

for lunch in the refrigerator. And it would do no harm for him to prepare it. Carefully, of course, as Mrs. Washington kept insisting. First, think out clearly what he wanted to do, then do it, slowly, using both hands. In fact, this would be a chance to prove to her that he was neither impulsive nor erratic.

Gradually, distressed by fear of what Mrs. Washington might find at the hospital, Horowitz began accusing the boy. His mother works hard to get him an education, his grandmother works hard to look after him because there is no longer any father. And that boy goes around getting into fights. Getting himself stabbed. Maybe even killed. It's true what they say about Negroes. In Horowitz's mind they were not niggers, but neither were they blacks. They had always been and would always be Negroes. But they all had razors. Or big switchblade knives. Like that bastard who jumped him and slashed his face.

Good God, he thought suddenly, Conrad could have been trying to rob somebody when he got into that fight! After everything Horowitz had said to him, trying to point out the right way, did that damned kid go and do something like that? Well, if he did, then better he should die now than grow up to mug and kill other people! His fury against the boy continued to grow.

He made his way to the kitchen phone, found and dialed the number of Harlem Hospital. But the hospital switchboard would give him no information.

He had waited almost an hour. Still no call from Mrs. Washington. Of course, he tried to console himself, at a time like this he was the last person Mrs. Washington should be thinking of. Or worse, suppose by the time she got there, the boy was already dead. She would be in no condition to call.

That damn boy, to bring such grief to a woman as fine as his grandmother. Children, Horowitz lamented, should be a source of joy, but how often they became a cause of sorrow and regret. He consoled himself only a little by saying, with all the faults I have to find with Mona, at least she did not disgrace me. A nuisance, yes, an overactive busybody, definitely, but, at least, not a disgrace. He must try to think more kindly of Mona from now on. And of his grandchildren, too.

Even tragedy yields some dividends, he decided.

Mrs. Washington's promptness had instilled in Horowitz the habit of expecting a decent lunch at twelve-thirty. It was now past one. He would have to forage about in the refrigerator. He found some raw chicken, which she undoubtedly had planned to serve him for dinner. There was an almost empty container of cottage cheese. Some margarine. And eggs. Since he had not had eggs for breakfast, he decided he could risk the cholesterol for lunch.

But how to make them? Fried, scrambled, boiled? He had to assess the hand operations involved in each process. He decided on two soft-boiled eggs.

Diligently, obediently, he tried to use both hands equally in selecting a pan, filling it with water, taking two eggs from the refrigerator and placing them in the pan. In actuality he used his right hand and only made a pretense with his left.

The water had come to a low boil. He could not remember how many minutes he liked his eggs, three or four, and decided that today it didn't matter. He took the pan to the sink and displaced the boiling water with cold so that the eggs would not be too hot to manage. He chose one, brought it to the counter opposite the stove and realized that he had not prepared a dish into which to break it. This simple task was proving more involved and difficult for him than he had expected.

But now he was ready. He lifted the egg in his right hand only to discover he could not properly grasp the spoon in his left. By the time he had made several tries at

218

it, the egg began to burn his right hand so he put it down and decided to reverse the procedure. Hold the larger object, the egg, in his left hand and use his right to grasp the spoon.

He picked up the egg in his left hand, was carefully picking up the spoon with his right hand when his unsteady left hand betrayed him. The egg fell to the floor and burst, causing the viscous egg white and the soft broken yolk to form a spreading yellow and white blob across the kitchen linoleum.

For a moment he stood still, until he felt a trembling overtake him. He reached out to the kitchen counter to hold on. The tremor passed. He took the sponge from the kitchen sink, slowly lowered himself to the floor and began to gather up the mess of broken shell and runny yellow and white. Eight times he had to do it, unsteady all eight times, cursing himself for his ineptitude, cursing that boy, Conrad, who had thrust this difficulty on him.

Chapter Sixteen

After he had shaved and washed up, he went into the bedroom. He stood before the closet carefully perusing his entire wardrobe until he selected a plain dark suit, of summer weight, which he had bought some six years ago for the express purpose of attending funerals, which had begun to occur with increasing regularity. He had never expected to, but it was the suit he had also worn the day of Hannah's burial. And to which the rabbi had pinned a bit of dark cloth, which he then cut, so that Horowitz would fulfill the biblical custom of rending one's garment in time of mourning.

Today, Samuel Horowitz selected that same suit. Not only because he had a premonition of the boy's death, but out of respect for Mrs. Washington's feelings. If he were to appear at the hospital dressed in a way that might reflect on her she would be embarrassed and distressed. He did not wish to add to her troubles on this particular day.

He selected a clean white shirt and a plain blue tie with a small red figure. Slowly, laboriously, he dressed himself, making sure to slip his left arm into the sleeve of the shirt, as if to prove to her that he remembered her every suggestion and command. He buttoned each button with meticulous care, using the fingers of both hands.

He had a good deal more difficulty with the tie than he had anticipated, and gave up twice until through sheer determination he was able to fashion a not particularly tidy but acceptable knot. He slipped on the lightweight jacket, buttoned the middle button, which, because of its larger size, proved less of a challenge than the shirt buttons had.

He examined himself in the long mirror on the closet door. He seemed a fair semblance of the Samuel Horowitz of some months ago. Even the scar on his cheek had diminished in its ugly redness, sufficiently so that it did not anger him as much as it had. He made faces in the mirror, alternately grimacing, smiling, twisting his mouth first to the left side then to the right to see if what that doctor had said was so, that the slash coming close to the natural crease in his thin cheek might eventually obscure itself. The doctor was either a bad doctor or a bad liar. For the scar would never become obscure by itself. He recalled the doctor had also said that plastic surgery might help.

Stubbornly, Horowitz had resisted the idea then, and did again now. I am not an actor, people do not expect me to be handsome. Besides, I want the world to know what those bastards have done to me. He made one final grimace to make sure the scar would remain noticeable. That seemed to give him a perverse kind of satisfaction.

But it also reminded him that he had better take some insurance with him. It was a city dweller's game, to decide how much cash to take along each day when he left the house. The sum must not be so great as to involve a substantial loss. Yet it must be enough to satisfy the mugger, lest disappointed, angered, he'd resort to malicious, spiteful violence.

Twenty dollars should do it, Horowitz decided. He selected two tens for the mugger. And two fives for himself for cab fare. He was ready to venture out into the streets of the world's greatest city. This time, he reminded himself, when the bastard is holding a knife to your throat give him the goddamn money!

So armed, and with his four-footed cane for support, Samuel Horowitz set out on the longest solo expedition he had undertaken since he suffered his stroke.

There was a certain pride involved in entering the elevator on his own two feet and seeing the surprise in Angelo's eyes that he was no longer in the wheelchair.

"Hey, Mr. Horowitz, we makin' progress," Angelo exclaimed, smiling.

Though he felt unsteady and tense, Horowitz managed a casual smile in turn. "Every day a little better. That's what life is all about."

He did not anticipate that traversing the lobby would prove to be so taxing. His days of practice with the quad had limited him to the length of the living room and the foyer. Twenty-three strides in all, slow, halting steps, with the inevitable drag of his left foot. But the lobby was a far longer distance than that. More than forty of his small, measured steps. He was forced to stop and rest, to catch his breath while using the wall for support. When Juan, the doorman, came to assist him, Horowitz brushed his hand aside saying, "I can do it. Don't worry about me."

But at the three steps up to the street level, he did require assistance, since he could not get a firm enough grasp on the rail with his left hand. He was finally out in the street. It was a warm day. The sun was bright and hot, unrelieved by any clouds or even the city's usual haze. It added to the perspiration he was experiencing from his unusual exertions.

When an empty cab approached, he attempted a jaunty wave of his left hand to flag him down. But he could not raise his arm swiftly enough nor high enough. The cab passed him by. Juan went out into the street to signal another cab. He opened the door for Horowitz, who fully intended to enter on his own. But the quad cane proved a greater hindrance than he had anticipated. Juan gently assisted him in and then put the cane in with him.

"Where to, mister?" the cabbie asked.

"Harlem Hospital."

"Harlem Hospital?" the cabbie repeated dubiously. "Are you sure?"

"Do I look like a man who wouldn't be sure?" Horowitz demanded angrily. "Harlem Hospital!"

"Okay, mister," the cabbie agreed reluctantly.

The cab proved not to be air-conditioned. The breeze created by its speed was hot, and also dusty with the pollution of the city air. Horowitz could feel particles of soot sting his cheeks. Once he thought he had caught a speck in his eye, but he managed to blink it out, though it left his eye moist and tearing.

He hated the cab, hated the day, hated this journey he felt forced to make. Most of all he hated that damn boy whom he had tried so hard to befriend and encourage and who had turned out to be another black street bum. Who knows, Horowitz asked, perhaps the little sonofabitch had been badly injured in what the newspapers and the television newscasters always called "a drug related crime."

Drug related, hell! Horowitz ranted. That nice-looking, intelligent-appearing boy is probably a shrewd, conniving little bastard, probably one of those juvenile drug dealers one reads about. Who actually make thousands of dollars a week and ride around in big, expensive cars

223

even though they are too young to get a driver's license. He must have had himself a good laugh all through that long lecture Horowitz had delivered about life, hard work, success. His sweet benign face as he listened must have been a very skillful act, a bit of expert fakery put on to fool an old Jew. All those black kids are brought up to hate Jews, to call them slumlords, to accuse them of milking ghetto people.

That night of the blackout was not the first time that kid was in trouble. He must be one of those who commit fifty crimes, sixty, a hundred, and get off scot-free every time because they are still juveniles.

Well, street justice had evidently caught up with the little black gangster. Good! And, if it were not that it would visit such suffering on a nice woman like Mrs. Washington, Horowitz was angry enough to wish the boy an untimely death. The length and the expense society goes to to save the lives of kids like him is a waste. Once they go bad they stay bad. Well, better they should kill each other off than be permitted to murder innocent people.

The cab stopped at the entrance of Harlem Hospital. Horowitz stared into the front of the cab. The meter read two dollars and eighty-five cents. He decided that a fifteen cent tip would be enough for this surly driver, making the total an even three dollars. He had completed that transaction. Now he began the difficult task of extricating himself from the cab. He opened the door with his right hand, pushing it outward but not far enough for the catch to hold it open. It slammed shut. He tried again, this time pushing it open with his quad until it remained fixed in an open position. He wriggled to the edge of the seat, set his quad onto the pavement, intending to use it as a lever to lift himself to a standing posture. But he had overreached himself. The cane slipped from his grasp leaving him half out of the cab with nothing to support him. The cabbie bounded out of the front seat, around the cab, and retrieved the cane. He supported Horowitz until he regained command of himself and the cane again.

"Thank you," Horowitz said, while reproaching himself for having given the man only a fifteen cent tip.

Now before him stood the Harlem Hospital. He looked toward the entrance to gauge the difficulties it presented, the size and weight of the door. He noticed, gathered outside the door, small groups of black people. The groups that contained one or two women did not alarm him. But there were several groups composed solely of black men, mostly young black men. With the Pavlovian reflex instilled by a dozen years of recent city history, Horowitz reacted in fear and suspicion. One black was dangerous enough, more than one meant a band of muggers. They wouldn't dare in broad daylight. Yet hadn't he been attacked in broad daylight before. But on such a busy street? On any street. Especially on any Harlem street.

Nevertheless, determined, he started on his labored walk toward the doors of the hospital. He had his twenty-dollar insurance policy in his pocket, carefully separated from his return cab fare. He could risk it. However, no one molested him. They all seemed too involved in their own private concerns even to notice him. Except for an old man near the door who held it open for him.

"Thank you," Horowitz said.

"Welcome," the old man said.

Horowitz sized him up in a hasty glance. The white-haired man seemed seventy-five, maybe more. Who could tell with black people? But surely he was older than Horowitz, yet he seemed perfectly healthy. Horowitz envied him, but only for a moment, for he felt compelled to resume his war against Conrad. He still had accusations he had not used against him. The closer he

225

came to confronting him, the more angry he grew. He dredged up every bit of news he had read in recent years, not sparing the boy a single indictment or condemnation.

He was building up to a peak of rage when he was confronted by a young black woman at the information desk. She looked up at him and at his four-legged cane.

"The outpatient department is around to the side," she volunteered.

"And who asked you about the outpatient department?" Horowitz shot back. "I am here to see a patient. A young hoodlum, who got hurt in a street fight or a battle with the police while he was trying to rob some innocent person. Where is he?" Horowitz demanded.

"Probably in Emergency. How long ago was he brought in?"

"Couple of hours," Horowitz said, his fingers tapping impatiently on the handle of his quad. "His name is Conrad."

"Conrad," the nurse repeated, picking up the phone. She dialed a three-digit number. "Emergency? Have you admitted a patient named Conrad in the last few hours. Hurt in a scuffle."

"Knifed!" Horowitz pointed out vindictively.

"Knife wound case," the nurse transmitted to Emergency. "No Conrad, you're sure?" Then she looked up at Horowitz, "What's his first name?"

"That's his first name," Horowitz replied intolerantly, "Conrad! His last name is Bruton!"

"Yes, of course," the nurse replied to avoid a confrontation. She repeated the information into the phone. She looked up again, "How old is the patient?"

"He is about twelve, maybe thirteen. Black, of course," he replied pointedly.

"Boy about thirteen," was all the nurse relayed. "Yes? Yes, I see. And where is he now? I see," she said, hanging up. "The boy is up in Surgical Intensive Care. Second floor." She pointed out the nearest bank of elevators.

"About his condition, what did they say?" Horowitz asked.

"Guarded," the nurse replied.

"He should be guarded! He's a hoodlum, a criminal!"

"That's not what they mean," the nurse corrected.

"Well, it's what *I* mean! Hoodlum! Mugger! And it isn't only what he did to some poor person out there, or even to himself, it's what he did to his poor grandmother! A fine woman, works hard, does a day's work cleaning, cooking, taking care of a sick gentleman, and then has to go home and cook and clean and take care of two grandchildren. And he does this to her. You should have seen that woman's face when that phone call came in! That little bastard, I'll give him a lesson to remember!"

By that time, people who had been passing by stopped to hear Horowitz's tirade. He became self-conscious. "Intensive Care, you said? Thank you." He hobbled toward the elevators, his left leg dragging a bit more than it had before, since he was trying to hurry. Realizing this, he deliberately tried to slow himself, remembering what Mrs. Washington had said about left hemis.

Well, Horowitz reminded himself, at least left hemis do not lose their power of speech! I will give that young bum a tongue-lashing he will never forget. Guarded condition, Horowitz fumed, guarded condition is nothing to the way I'll leave him. If I were myself, if I had my old strength, I would give him a whipping he would remember all his life. That's what that boy needs, a father who could give him a big hand across the behind a few times. It's sad, Horowitz conceded grudgingly, that his father was killed when the boy was young. But that didn't excuse the kind of thing he had done now.

The elevator door opened to interrupt his silent tirade. He was almost toppled by the outpouring of visitors, nurses, and staff doctors. He moved back shakily, and but for the quick act of one of the doctors, a black man in a white lab coat, he would have fallen.

"Thank you," Horowitz said, a bit resentful to be beholden.

"Watch it, pop," the young doctor said. "You're not too steady on that thing yet."

"I can manage!" Horowitz replied indignantly, more bold now that he was no longer in danger.

He stepped into the car, taking a place at the front and forcing all the other passengers to move around him. Then he pressed the button for the second floor in such a way that it became an act of aggression. At the second floor, he exited. He looked about. He saw a sign down the corridor that announced: Quiet please. Intensive Care.

His goal now in sight, he started down the hall, leaning more heavily on his cane, dragging his left foot more noticeably than before, fuming that he lacked his full physical powers so he could not be as effective as the situation demanded. He reached the door of I.C.U., stared in through the glass insert. There were six cubicles sectioned off by glass partitions. Three beds were empty. Two others were occupied by patients who, though assisted by oxygen tubes and intravenouses, were conscious and alert. Neither of them was the boy, Conrad.

Horowitz glanced at the cubicle with drawn curtains. Conrad must be in that one. He stared down below the curtains. He noticed the legs of a chair and a pair of feet shod in sturdy, plain white shoes. He recognized them. Mrs. Washington's! He knew all he had to!

He tried the I.C.U. door, which proved too heavy for him to manage. So he was forced to wait until a nurse came along. He suffered the indignity of having to ask her assistance. She held the door open until he hobbled in. He made his way across the smooth, polished asphalt tile floor, cane in hand, his left foot faltering, refusing to respond as he would have it. Finally he arrived at the curtained cubicle. His right hand occupied with the cane, he raised his left to push aside the curtain so he could peek in.

There Conrad lay, eyes closed. He had an oxygen tube in his nose, and his chest was heavily bandaged. He looked so benign and pitiful that Horowitz accused, The faker! He is trying to look like an angel, but he is really a thief, a bum, a mugger, an animal. His grandmother sat by the side of the bed, weeping silently.

Cry, Mrs. Washington, cry aloud. You have good reason. All your work, all your hopes, all your dreams end up here. And this is only the beginning. Wait till the police get through with him. Of course, these days, Horowitz scoffed, some judge'll send him home with a medal.

"So?" Horowitz demanded in a voice so strong it reverberated throughout the I.C.U.

Startled, Mrs. Washington turned and leaped to her feet. "Mr. Horowitz! What are you doing here?"

"What am I doing here? Better to ask, what is he doing here?" Horowitz demanded, not lowering his voice one bit.

At that, the boy's eyes opened and stared up, unable to believe it was Mr. Horowitz glowering down at him. Then he closed his eyes again, out of fatigue and weakness.

"That's right, close your eyes. I don't blame you. You can't look me in the face! You can't look your grandmother in the face!"

"Mr. Horowitz, please!" Mrs. Washington begged. "Quiet!"

"This is no time for soft speaking. This is a time for truth-telling. Young man, can you hear me?"

The boy nodded his head a single time, and even that seemed to take great effort.

"Then listen real good. If I had my strength back, I would get you out of that bed and give you the licking of your life! What kind of animal are you? You want to destroy your own life, go ahead! But to do this to your grandmother, a fine woman, a lovely woman, hard-working, industrious. Sometimes I wonder how she puts up with someone like me. But there's only one reason she does it, for your sake. For your sister's sake."

"Mr. Horowitz, no!" Mrs. Washington said.

"He needs a man now; not a mother or a grandmother to spoil him," Horowitz argued, his voice rising even more.

From a cubicle on the other side of the room, a voice called out, "Someone get that maniac out of here!"

Horowitz turned in the direction of the voice, "I'll give you a maniac! Buttinsky!" He turned his attention back to the boy, "After your grandmother and your mother work so hard, is this the way you reward them? Knife fights? You are a disgrace to them. A disgrace to your dead father! You should be ashamed of yourself!

"Well, let me tell you, this time no fancy lawyer goes to court to plead for you! This time you're on your own! They should lock you up with all the other animals! That's where you belong! In a cage! You rotten . . . vicious . . . there are no words to describe what you have done to this fine woman. I hope you get what's coming to you!"

"Get that crazy man to shut up!" the voice across the room called out.

"You be quiet!" Horowitz responded to his unseen accuser.

He turned on Mrs. Washington. "But you, I know what you'll do! You'll go before the judge. You'll cry. You'll plead, 'Give my boy another chance.' He had his chance! After the blackout! And look where he winds up. I'm surprised they don't have him handcuffed to the bed!"

230

"Mr. Horowitz, no ... Mr. Horowitz ..." But she began to sob. All he could make out was, "... don't understand ... don't ..."

"I don't understand?" he attacked again. "What do you call this on the side of my face? A beauty mark? Embroidery? Plastic surgery to make me look young again? Twenty-two stitches! Because of someone like him!"

At the crest of his outburst, the door to I.C.U. was flung open and a nurse entered demanding angrily, "Who is sitting on that buzzer?"

"I am!" the voice answered from across the room. "There's a crazy man in here. Get him out!"

"I'll give you a crazy man!" Horowitz turned, ready for combat.

"That's him!" the voice identified.

The nurse crossed swiftly to the curtained cubicle. She thrust her head into the guarded area and demanded, "Who are you? What are you doing here?"

"I am Samuel Horowitz!" he replied. "And I am here to help this woman! To protect her. From herself! From her own weakness!"

"I don't know what you're talking about," the black nurse said, "but you'll have to get out. Right now!"

"I don't go unless this woman goes!" Horowitz defied, taking as stern a stance as his infirmity permitted.

"Mr. Horowitz, please," Mrs. Washington begged. He could tell she was about to begin weeping again.

He relented only enough to say, "Don't destroy yourself over this ... this momser. He doesn't deserve it! I'll wait for you downstairs."

"I'm not leaving," she said firmly enough to convince him.

"Well, I ... I only tried to do what was best for you," he said, as gently as an angry man could. He turned to go.

As he did, Mrs. Washington said, "Wait. Just one

231

moment." He looked back at her, trying to balance himself at the same time. "Before you go, there's something you should see."

"I've seen enough," Horowitz said grimly.

Mrs. Washington spoke softly to the boy, "Conrad? Can you hear me?"

Without opening his eyes he nodded.

"Show him," was all Mrs. Washington said.

The boy did not turn his head to look up, but extended his closed fist. Then he opened it.

Horowitz looked down. There in the boy's pink palm lay a worn shiny coin. Horowitz recognized the gold piece he had given him nights ago. Horowitz raised his questioning eyes to Mrs. Washington.

"He was so proud of it he took it with him every day. Two boys tried to steal it from him. He fought back. They knifed him."

"He . . . he fought back . . ." Horowitz said. "Yes, I know how that happens."

"He wouldn't give it up, it meant too much to him," she said softly, closing the boy's hand to secure the coin.

"He . . . he . . ." Horowitz tried to say, but sniffled a bit. "Old age," he explained to the nurse, "the teary eyes of age."

"You have to leave," the nurse insisted.

"Okay, okay, I'll go," he replied meekly. "But a moment, please." She granted permission with an impatient nod. "Conrad, my boy, can you hear me? I'm very sorry for what I said. And let me tell you, for an old man who is hardly ever sorry, that's a lot of sorry. Get better. Get strong. And remember what I said that night. Because that's the truth. This, what I said today, was anger talking. Was hatred talking. Was people making bad assumptions about black kids talking."

He turned to Mrs. Washington, "Will I see you?"

"My daughter's home with the little girl, trying to

232

reassure her, trying to get her to stop crying. So I'll stay here."

"I meant, will I ever see you again, after what I said here today?" Horowitz asked softly.

"Yes, yes, of course. Tomorrow."

"Good, good, tomorrow. I'll get along somehow today," he said.

As he started to go the nurse reached out to assist him, but he brushed her hand aside. "I don't need any help. I can go on my own!"

He shuffled to the door where he paused long enough to call out to the other side of the room, "And you, whoever you are."

"Will you be quiet!" the nurse ordered.

"I will not!" Horowitz replied, calling out again, "That's no way to talk to an old man, calling him a maniac, and crazy! *You* are crazy. *I* am only indignant!"

With that he would have liked to make a dramatic exit. But unfortunately the heavy door was too much for him and he had to ask humbly, "Please? The door?"

The nurse opened it, holding it long enough for him to depart.

PART III

Chapter Seventeen

How was I to know? Horowitz kept repeating to himself as the cab made its way down the hot sun-baked avenue. A black kid gets knifed, naturally he has to have been in a fight. And what kind of fight would a black kid get into? Either he's trying to rob somebody or else he is fighting over the profits from drugs. How could he know the boy was only trying to defend what was rightfully his?

Mrs. Washington would surely hate him now, for having given the boy the coin that was the cause of it all. He couldn't blame her. After all, her world is built around that boy and his sister. If only more black people were like her. If they realized that to make progress there has to be sacrifice. One generation has to forego its own desires and ambitions to build for the next.

But no, they want the government to do all the sacrificing, which means the taxpayers, which means Samuel Horowitz. Some days when he was particularly bitter, he hoped that he would die broke so the government would not get its one last bite. When he figured out how much he had paid the United States government in the last forty-nine years he was shocked. They had far more to show for his labors than he did.

But when he contemplated his chrome quad cane and realized that no amount of money could take the place of two good, sound legs he felt less bitter than sad. He found solace in only one thought, that Hannah had not lived to see him in this condition. God, in His infinite mercy, had spared her that. She had always been so proud of him, and so confident. As other women they knew lost their husbands to one fatal disease or another, Hannah felt sure that he would never fall ill. She was used to thinking of him as being strong, reliable, always there to care for her.

Even at the very end, in Mt. Sinai Hospital, she died holding his hand and feeling secure. If she could see him now, an old man, a crippled old man, and alone. Marvin in Washington, Mona in San Diego, strangers. But maybe a good thing. He did not want their pity. Or their charity. He did not want to live out his life as a boarder in someone else's house. Or a burden. He did not want Marvin or Mona apologizing for him when they had to introduce him to their friends.

He had never had the educational advantages he had provided for them. He knew his speech was a bit rough and not quite correct. On occasion, he slipped into the Yiddish expressions that still hung over from his youth. Noel Coward, he wasn't. Nor did he ever pretend to be. But he had lived a decent life, made Hannah a happy woman, and produced two children who had succeeded in their own manner. He had nothing to apologize for.

Then why was he justifying and apologizing? he asked himself as the cab rolled up to the house.

Mrs. Washington, he realized.

The involved process of getting out of the cab, paying

238

the driver and making his way into the house now occupied all his concentration.

Juan came racing out to the cab. He opened the door briskly. "Ah, Mr. Horwitz! Wait, I help you."

"I can manage," Horowitz said with great dignity and assurance. But it proved too difficult. Finally he had to surrender his cane to Juan, who set the sturdy instrument down on its legs while he helped Horowitz gently out of the cab.

Damn cabs, Horowitz thought, too small for a normal-sized man to get out of. There ought to be a law. No cab allowed on the streets unless a man six feet tall could get in and out without banging his head. Or having to sit with his knees pressed against his chest.

Once he was out of the cab, he rested a moment on his cane, then dug into his pocket for the fare. He found the five-dollar bill, waited for change, tipped the driver only enough to avoid being insulted by him. As the cab drove off, Horowitz started for the entrance with Juan at his side, hands extended to help, but not quite touching him.

"I'm all right!" Horowitz protested. "You don't have to worry about me!" Awkwardly he waved Juan aside with his damaged left hand. Juan dropped back a bit, but stayed within range so that if Horowitz tottered he could catch him before he fell. At the door, Horowitz looked back at Juan, who was just over his left shoulder. "I said I'm all right!"

"Okay, Mr. Horwitz, okay," Juan said, backing away but still keeping a watchful eye.

When Horowitz reached the three steps down into the lobby, he wondered if he had not been too belligerent toward Juan. For he was confronted with a situation he was forced to cope with for the first time. Suddenly he realized that, with the cane in his right hand, he was on the wrong side of the steps. He would have to move to the left and use the left wall for support. If he did, would his left hand in its present condition offer enough support? And there was the problem of his foot dragging, even with the aid of the plastic brace. Whether he stepped down with his right foot first, or his left, there had to be a moment when he rested on his left alone. He considered now whether to step down with the left first, and follow with the right, or right first and follow with the left. He decided to support his left hand against the wall, set the cane down one step and follow with his right foot first.

All the while, Juan stood by watching, though pretending not to.

Damned Puerto Rican, Horowitz thought, spying on me, just waiting for me to fall so he can come and help. Well, to hell with him. I will make it by myself!

He took the steps one at a time as he had planned. Though he wavered a bit on the second step and was glad his left hand held firm when it had to. He made it to the elevator where Angelo greeted him, smiling, "Walkin' by yourself, Mr. Horowitz, tha's very good!"

Big deal, Horowitz grouched, walking by myself. One of the insults of old age, that a man should be complimented for doing what he had been doing since he was a year old.

Safely back in the apartment, he was relieved to lie down in the unmade bed, fully clothed, and catch his breath. He sighed, sorrowfully, that such a simple outing should have left him so exhausted. That Samuel Horowitz, who had briskly walked the streets of New York, Miami, London, and Paris, the boardwalks of Atlantic City and Rockaway Beach, should be reduced to this condition by walking a mere fifty paces and three small steps. Down, yet.

He fell asleep, thinking to himself, Not to wake up wouldn't be the worst thing in the world.

But he did wake. The persistent ringing of the phone rudely summoned him. He groped for it with his left hand because turning on his side was not easy or swift. He seized the phone, dropped it, had to turn and pull it up by its cord before he could answer. When he did he heard Mona's frantic, "Dad? Are you all right? Dad, answer me!"

"I'm answering, I'm answering," he said, annoyed that she had caught him in such an embarrassing and revealing moment.

"Dad! What happened?" she asked evidencing great concern.

"What happened was you woke me up, I reached for the phone in my sleep and dropped it. That's what happened."

"I mean all day. You weren't home. I called and called, and no answer. Where were you?"

He resisted telling her. But you could more easily keep a secret from the CIA. So he told her where he had been, what had happened to the boy, Conrad. And how valiantly he had fought to protect the gold piece Horowitz had given him.

Mona's only response was, "You mean Mrs. Washington isn't there to take care of you?"

"I mean she is where she ought to be. With her grandson," Horowitz said.

"I think I should come to New York!" Mona declared.

Oh, God, not that! Horowitz thought. She'll come here and she'll organize me. She had organized Albert and made him a millionaire in real estate. A miserable, unhappy husband, but well organized. She never gave Albert a moment's peace. Between business, charities, and civic activities, the poor man never had a chance to sit around the house in a pair of old pants and a sport shirt. She had him constantly on the go.

"Dad, did you hear me? I said, I think I should come to

New York," Mona persisted.

Diplomatically, he said, "There's nothing to be concerned about. I'm fine! In fact, Mrs. Washington being away for the day was the best thing that could have happened! It gave me a chance to get along on my own. And I'm fine. Fine!"

"Well," Mona equivocated, "that's a relief. I had all sorts of fears. I thought you'd had another stroke. That they took you to the hospital again. I even called Sinai."

"Naturally, with a WATS line," Horowitz commented, but it escaped her attention as she talked on.

"I couldn't get anywhere with Hospital Information so I called Doug Isaacson. He's on the board at Sinai. He called back. And I was relieved to discover you were not there."

I'll bet Mt. Sinai was relieved, too, Horowitz thought.

"Doug is a close friend of Albert's, and very active in Federation."

"I would hope so," Horowitz agreed.

"Now, Dad, what's going to happen?" Mona asked, businesslike and direct.

"What is going to happen, I will have a nice dinner, I will watch TV, then I will go to bed," Horowitz said simply.

"But how are you going to get dinner? Who's going to make it?"

"Very simple. I will call Fine and Schapiro and have them send up some chicken soup with matzoh balls, and some boiled chicken."

"Good!" Mona agreed. "But tell them to skim the fat off the soup. And take the skin off the chicken. That's where all the cholesterol is!" she pointed out expertly.

"The skin off the chicken, and the fat off the soup," he repeated as if committing her instructions to memory.

"Right! And no sour pickles! Too much salt and spices."

"Sour pickles?" Horowitz repeated, feigning as much revulsion as he could muster.

"I know how you love sour pickles."

"I wouldn't dream," Horowitz assured her.

"Good!" Mona said, concluding an agreement. "I'll call again tomorrow and see if Mrs. Washington's come back. If not, we'll have to do something."

"Of course," Horowitz agreed, glancing at his watch to see that it was already ten past seven and Walter Cronkite had covered the most important news stories of the night. He wished Mona would get off the phone and at least let him catch the rest of the news.

Finally she hung up. He snapped on the TV with his remote control, using his right hand, though Mrs. Washington always insisted he use his left. He reached for the phone, called Information, asked for the number he wanted, and dialed it.

It rang twice before a man greeted, "Fine and Schapiro!"

"Irving?" Horowitz asked.

"Yes."

"Sam Horowitz."

"Well, hello, Mr. Horowitz! Where have you been? Up in the country? Weeks since we heard from you. What can I do for you?"

"Irving, tell you what I would like. A nice, thick corned beef sandwich. Heavy on the meat, thin on the bread."

"One special corned beef," Irving repeated as he wrote down the order.

"You know how I like it," Horowitz reminded.

"I know, I know. Lean in the middle but don't trim the fat off the edges."

"Right!" Horowitz said. "A nice, new dill pickle, a big one."

"Dill pickle, large," Irving repeated.

"Some potato salad, some cole slaw, and a cold bottle of beer!"

"Any special brand?"

"Yes," Horowitz said righteously. "A beer that doesn't have any cholesterol in it."

"There's no cholesterol in beer, Mr. Horowitz."

"Perfect! Now get it up here as soon as you can!"

Horowitz hung up, leaned back to give his entire attention to Walter Cronkite and at the same time luxuriate in anticipation of the delicacies yet to come.

When the doorbell rang announcing his dinner had arrived, eagerly he called out to alert the elevator man that he was on the way. With the aid of his quad cane, twice almost tripping on the carpet in his haste, he reached the door. He tipped the night elevator man, took his cherished package, and made his way into the kitchen. There he opened the bag with all the excited expectation of a child opening a holiday gift.

Ah, the aroma! The warm pungent aroma of kosher corned beef! He opened the foil wrapping that protected his sandwich and kept the meat almost as hot as it had been when it was sliced. He lifted the top slice of rye bread and peered down with a connoisseur's eye. There they lay, slices of red beef with a thin border of fat, just enough to keep the meat from being too dry. He dabbed on some mustard from the container that Irving had thoughtfully sent along. Horowitz had tasted many kinds of mustard in his life, costly French, very hot English, several kinds of American. But, cheap as it was, none exceeded in taste, plain old kosher-delicatessen mustard, which they threw in for free. In his nostalgic exuberance he dabbed on an extra smear.

He opened his containers of cole slaw and potato salad, and, with no small effort, held and sliced in half, lengthwise, the large newly dilled pickle. His feast was

244

ready! He sat down at the small kitchen table and indulged in a repast he had dreamt of ever since he had become incapacitated and made a virtual prisoner of hospitals, nurses, carefully supervised diets, and plastic utensils.

He bit into the warm sandwich. It satisfied his every anticipation. The thin rye bread, the fragrant warm beef, the tang of the mustard. And, of course, the taste that little fringe of fat added to his enjoyment. If this is cholesterol, he thought, and I was a young man again, I would go into business and put a new flavor on the market called *Cholesterol* and clean up a fortune!

Hot corned beef, cold beer, creamy cole slaw, pickle that tickles the palate. Heaven! And also potato salad. Simply because with delicatessen one had to have potato salad. It was the finest meal he had had in months. Years! To add to the enjoyment there was the clandestine air that surrounded it. He had outwitted Mona. And his doctor. To say nothing of Mrs. Washington.

Ah, yes, Mrs. Washington, he remembered. He had better call her when dinner was done. Sandwich finished, he spent some time over the cole slaw and potato salad, finished the last, long, pale green and white slice of pickle and finished off the beer. A satisfied belch, and dinner was over.

Mona, he thought, with all your money you couldn't buy such corned beef in the whole city of San Diego. Not even in the whole state of California! And you want me to come out there and live. Not on your life. Certainly, not on mine!

The resolve to phone Mrs. Washington and inquire about Conrad's condition was not equal to the embarrassment involved. After having made such a fool of himself in the afternoon, what could he say? I'm sorry? Those two words could not excuse what he had done. And the look

245

on that boy's face when he opened his hand and revealed that gold piece. There is something about the look of a child when he feels he is the victim of injustice that is worse than facing a judge or a jury. If they would only accuse, or declare you guilty, or shout. But it is their silent recriminations that cause the most pain.

Four times Horowitz reached for the phone, four times hesitated. He could not think how to begin. He could say, "Good evening, Mrs. Washington, how are you?" But how should the poor woman be? Her only grandson lying in a hospital bed, stabbed in the chest. Then perhaps, "Hello, Mrs. Washington, how is the boy?" And if the boy was worse and she began to cry, then what? What good would he have done her or himself by such an opening?

Finally, out of indecision, he abandoned the idea of calling. Having done so, he picked up the phone and dialed, and when someone answered, he blurted out, "Mrs. Washington! I want to apologize! I made a fool of myself today. And of you. Did they make any trouble for you in the hospital? If so, I will go back tomorrow and explain it was my fault. But I'm sorry, very, very sorry and I wanted you to know!"

He blurted it out on a single burst, so when it was done he was exhausted and had to pause to regain his breath. As he did, he heard a voice that was not Mrs. Washington.

"Mr. Horowitz?"

"Yes."

"This is Mrs. Washington's daughter."

"Oh?" Horowitz hesitated. "Tell me, how is the boy?"

"The boy is doing . . . all right. The doctors said if he doesn't get any worse during the night he should be out of danger by morning."

"I'm glad. I'm very . . . relieved," Horowitz said. "I feel so guilty. It's my fault. If I didn't give him that coin . . .

but did I have any way of knowing?"

"I understand, Mr. Horowitz," the young woman said. "We're not blaming you."

"Thank you."

"Do you want to talk to my mother?"

"If you don't mind," Horowitz said meekly. Before she could put down the phone, he added, "And forgive me for calling. I should have known better."

"What do you mean?" she asked.

"The way you answered the phone, I can see now that you thought it was the hospital. With bad news. Right?" he asked gently.

"Right," she conceded wearily. "So, thank God, it was you." She turned her head from the phone and called out, "Mama! It's him."

Him? Horowitz protested. Is that what they call me, him? Not Mr. Horowitz, but a little three-letter pronoun. Him? Well, he argued their case, after what I did today maybe they'll always call me him, the crazy one. What did that patient in the hospital call me, maniac? He said, "Get that maniac out of here." I'll give him a maniac!

Mrs. Washington came on the phone. "Mr. Horowitz?"

He was tempted to say, No, it's him. Instead, more solicitously, he inquired, "Conrad is all right? Getting along? Recovering?"

"So far, so good," the gentle woman said.

"I'm glad, glad for him, glad for you, glad for little Louise. This must have been terrible for her, to see such a thing happening to her brother."

"She can't stop crying," Mrs. Washington said. "She's terrified."

"Can you blame her? Listen, I would like to send her a little something. Maybe a doll. A toy. Something. You know what she would like. Pick it out. Give it to her. Say it's from me. Let me know what it costs. And don't be stingy. Get her something nice, something she'll like.

247

There must be something she's dreamed about, or asked for . . ." He had run out of words.

"What she would like," Mrs. Washington said softly, "is for her father to come back. When she gets frightened, she calls for her daddy."

"Ah, yes," Horowitz said, "even Mona used to do that. And for this poor child there is no daddy. Some world, some world," he lamented. "Get her something anyhow. It may not do much good, but it certainly can't do any harm. Please, get her something."

"All right, I'll try."

"And tomorrow, don't bother to come in. You got too much on your mind to take care of a foolish old man. I'm sorry about today in the hospital. You should have thrown me out. I wouldn't blame you. In fact, I wouldn't blame you if you never came back. After the things I said."

"I planned to come in tomorrow," Mrs. Washington said.

"You don't have to, I'll get along," he protested. "Who's going to visit Conrad? Who'll stay with Louise? They need you more than I do."

"My sister is coming in from Long Island to stay for a few days. My daughter will be with Conrad during the day. I'll go in the evening. And my sister will care for Louise. So I'll be in."

"You don't have to do it for my sake," he protested. "I got along today, didn't I?"

"I'm not doing it for you. I'm doing it for me," she explained.

"I'll pay you as if you were here!" he argued.

"You don't understand," she said firmly. "When things go wrong, in time of trouble, the best medicine is to do what you are obligated to do. So I will be there."

"I will be . . . glad . . . to see you, Mrs. Washington." Before he could hang up he had to ask again, "You

248

forgive me about this afternoon?"

"I forgive you," she said gently.

He hung up with a sense of great relief. A remarkable woman, Mrs. Washington, strong, yet very sensitive. Hannah had that same quality. But somehow between Hannah and Mona something had got lost. Mona, too, was strong. But she had never inherited her mother's sensitivity. Mona could run a revolution, but never take time to feel a moment of sorrow for the victims.

He turned to the refuge of the twentieth century, his television set. Talk to me, he said silently, show me pictures, amuse me, fill up my time. Displace my thoughts. Wipe out my feelings. Between Valium and television, human beings no longer had to suffer the pain or inconvenience of feeling.

He tuned into a show that had been on for half an hour. The characters were strangers, the plot was confusing, but still he watched. As long as his eyes were engaged, his mind was exempt from functioning. At the moment, the only feeling he had was a slight heartburn from the pickle. Well, he consoled, it was worth it. Besides, a little garlic couldn't hurt. Some people considered garlic a medicine. When he was a child, during the flu epidemic of the First World War, his mother, like all other mothers, had sewn a clove of garlic into a little sack which she hung around his neck to ward off the killer disease. So garlic was good for you, and worth a little heartburn.

His flagging interest in the television drama was suddenly revived when a commercial came on. Another dog food commercial. With millions of children the world over going to bed hungry every night, America spends hundred of millions of dollars to advertise pet food. And billions to buy pet food. Cats dance, talk, sing, to sell cat food. In his day, when he was a boy, and had finally badgered his mother into letting him get a dog, the dog was fed scraps from the table or from the butcher. No butcher worth his salt would refuse to throw in a bit of liver and a bone for your dog. And it was food, real, genuine, honest-to-god food, not something out of a can or a plastic bag. Dogs seemed to survive and grow healthy in those days. Without vitamins, without special itsy-bitsy chunks that were not meat but only imitations.

The dog food commercial was over. The drama came back on. Horowitz watched, as mystified and disinterested as he had been before. Finally he started flicking the remote-control device, going from channel to channel, seeking something that might engage him. He settled for a night baseball game at Yankee Stadium. The Yankees were ahead. A matter of no special comfort. Horowitz had not accepted there were any legitimate Yankees since Babe Ruth and Lou Gehrig. And never forget, he would say, before Gehrig was Wally Pipp, and Jumping Joe Dugan, Tony Lazzeri, and Bob Meusel. Those were Yankees!

Today what do you have? Hired hands. At very fancy salaries. They're not playing for the team, they're playing for the dollars. Where's the spirit? Where's the old pride?

He watched a parade of batters come to the plate. Many of them were black. And when you watched basketball it was even worse. Most of them were black.

Strange thing about these black people, when it comes to sports, where they are so good, they say let every man be judged by his ability. But when it comes to medical schools, or law schools, or colleges, where they are not so good, they say, don't let ability count. That's *chutzpah!*

What would happen if an NAAJP, a National Association for the Advancement of Jewish People, went to the major leagues or to the National Basketball Association and said, "We have here several Jewish boys, five feet eight, weighing a hundred and forty pounds, with bad eyesight. We insist you put them on the Yankees." Or the

Knicks. Or the Nets. The teams would say they're not good enough. So the NAAJP would say, "It's exactly bacause they are not good enough that we insist you give them a chance."

Some chance! The NAAJP would get thrown out on its ear.

But with blacks . . . Conrad, he remembered, Conrad. You could no more make general rules about blacks than you could about Jews. The black hitter at the plate seemed to rebuke Horowitz so he switched channels.

On channel thirteen there was an English historical drama. He watched it briefly until he fell asleep, the set still on.

When he woke the screen was blank and only a loud hum could be heard. It was dark. He knew it must be late. But the garlic from that pickle now burned even more. He knew he would have to take something for it. He lay in bed, on his back, rubbing his stomach with his good right hand. He pondered, perhaps it is more than the garlic. I've never had a heart attack, but they say sometimes it starts like an ordinary heartburn. Could he be having a heart attack? And if he were, what should he do? People say for any kind of trouble call 911. And if he did call 911? How would they get in? The door was double bolted, and with an extra lock besides. They might have to break it down. If it turned out not to be a heart attack he would have made a terrible fool of himself twice in one day.

He decided to settle for a simpler course of action. In the medicine chest there should be some Alka-Seltzer. A box of foil-wrapped tablets, the kind that stay fresh a long time. They must be there. If not, there was always bicarbonate of soda. Back in the old days people knew only bicarbonate of soda for stomach distress. No fancy boxes or aluminum foil wrapping. A plain five-cent box of baking soda lasted for months, and never went flat

251

because it didn't fizz in the first place. And somehow, nobody died of a heartburn in those days.

Those days, those old days. The days of Arm & Hammer baking soda in a yellow box, without television commercials or big ads in the newspapers and the magazines. He could remember so vividly his father drinking down baking soda in a glass of cloudy water to quench the fire that his mother's fried onions had ignited.

If there were no Alka-Seltzer, Horowitz would use baking soda. If he knew where the baking soda was. He was a stranger in his own kitchen. Hannah always knew. So he didn't have to. Even after she was gone, he had barely learned from one of the helpful widows in the building how to load and start the dishwasher. And he considered that a major achievement.

So there had better be some Alka-Seltzer, else he was doomed to a night of heartburn and remorse. Next time, he vowed penitently, corned beef, but no pickle.

He carefully rolled himself over on his side and rose to a sitting position. He groped for his quad, found it and raised himself to his feet. He stood there, poised and making sure of his balance before he dared to take even the first step. He made his way around the bed, using its side and then its foot as a guide. Once he left it, he regretted at once that he had not turned on the light.

He proceeded slowly, in the dark, his bare left foot dragging, his right hand firmly gripping the head of his quad cane. He made his way to the bathroom, flicked on the light, searched the medicine cabinet. No Alka-Seltzer. He could remember quite clearly having bought some recently. Still, there was no familiar blue and white box. Bicarbonate soda it would have to be. Arm and Hammer, where are you?

He headed for the kitchen, slowly dragging his way, concentrating on his left foot so it would clear the foyer carpet with as little hindrance as possible. It was dark out here. The only light had to be turned on at the front door, which was at the other end of the foyer. In the dark, he felt his way, paying more attention to his left leg than to his quad cane with its four shiny steel feet. Until one metal foot became entangled in the thick pile of the foyer carpet. Suddenly the cane was trapped enough to throw him off stride.

He knew he was falling. He cried out and reached frantically for the doorknob to support him. But his left hand did not respond quickly enough.

He pitched forward, his head striking the door. By the time he slid to the floor he was unconscious.

Chapter Eighteen

At eight o'clock, Mrs. Washington stepped off the elevator, went to the door of apartment 10C, was surprised to find The New York Times still on the doormat. Mr. Horowitz must have overslept. Of course. Undoubtedly he had a restless night, to judge from how upset he seemed when he called. Poor man, she thought. But then, he had no right to assume that all black kids are thieves and knifers, she said to herself as she bent to pick up the paper. She unlocked the door, started to push it open but discovered that something blocked her way. She pushed a bit harder, but still met with resistance.

She peeked in through the narrow opening. There she saw him. Horowitz lay on the foyer floor. Dead, she assumed, for he was inert and seemed lifeless. For a moment she almost gave way to panic and was about to scream. But she regained control, knelt down, inserted her thin, strong, wiry hand into the opening, gradually edged his body away from the door, opening it wider, reaching into it further, until she was able to slip into the apartment.

She dropped beside his body, instinctively reaching for a pulse in his wrist, then in his throat. She was finally able to locate it. It was slow, but palpable. She turned him over and saw that he had sustained a large bruise on his forehead; the broken skin created slight bleeding which had already started to crust.

"Mr. Horowitz," she whispered, "Mr. Horowitz?"

He came to slowly, as if in response to a far-off call. He moaned, then coughed slightly, and finally opened his eyes.

"So where's the Alka-Seltzer?" he asked, indignantly.

"What Alka-Seltzer?"

"The Alka-Seltzer! I just got up to get some Alka-Alka . . ." He broke off, looked about and became aware of the daylight. "It's morning?"

"Morning."

"So what happened to last night?" he asked.

"The question is what happened to you?" Mrs. Washington replied, a bit more dictatorial now that she was sure he was alive and well.

"Nothing happened to me," he said evasively, then changed the subject. "So tell me, how's Conrad this morning? What do the doctors say?"

"He's much better. Out of danger."

"Good!"

"So?" Mrs. Washington persisted, in a manner she had adopted from Horowitz.

"So what?" he avoided.

"What happened to you last night?"

Reluctantly, he explained about last night, without mentioning the real cause of his heartburn. He was fine, it was all the fault of the carpet. Mrs. Washington took a close look at the wound on his forehead.

"Hmm!" she uttered.

255

"Hmm?" he asked.

"We'll have to call the doctor," she said.

"Doctor?" Horowitz protested. "Who needs a doctor? I'm fine! In fact, Mrs. Washington, I have discovered a sure cure for heartburn. You get up in the middle of the night. You trip and fall. And by morning, behold, no more heartburn! I have never felt better in my life!"

"Just to make sure," she insisted. "I'll call Dr. Tannenbaum."

"You better not," he warned.

"Why not?"

"Just you better not, that's all."

"It's my duty as a nurse to report any significant change in the patient's condition."

"And when he asks you where you were all day yesterday, when he wants to know why you weren't here? Hmm?" Horowitz asked, seeking to strike a bargain with her. "You don't call Tannenbaum, I won't tell him you weren't here."

"No deal."

"You're a very unreasonable woman, Mrs. Washington," he pouted.

"Sorry. I have to call," she said firmly.

She helped him to his feet, picked up his quad cane for him, and started toward the kitchen and the phone.

"I know why you're doing this!" he accused. "You're getting even with me because of all those nasty things I said about Conrad. I apologized, didn't I? What more do you want? Blood?"

She dismissed his accusation with an appropriate stare of impatience. Having failed to move her by accusations, Horowitz softened and pleaded, "Mrs. Washington, don't make that call?"

She came out of the kitchen, and asked gently, "Mr. Horowitz, nothing else happened last night, did it? You didn't have any pains you're not telling me about, did you? No chest pains, like in a heart attack?"

"No, I swear. Just a little heartburn. And that's gone," he insisted.

"Do you feel any new weakness in your hand or your arm?" she probed.

"Nothing. Not a thing. I'm fine."

"Then what harm can it do to have Dr. Tannenbaum look you over?" she asked.

"It . . ." he began grudgingly. "It isn't Tannenbaum. But he'll call Marvin. Marvin'll call the Golda Meir of San Diego and next thing you know she'll be insisting I come out there and live. And I don't want to do that. I don't want to be a burden or a prisoner. I want to be me, in my own house, living my own life, what there is left of it. So don't call Tannenbaum, please?"

"Mr. Horowitz, I know how you feel. But I'm obligated to call the doctor on the case."

"Then tell him . . . no, when he gets here, I'll tell him," Horowitz finally said, accepting her decision.

Mrs. Washington had discovered the empty delicatessen bag in the waste can when she went out to set out the garbage. She promptly marched into the living room where she had set Horowitz to work on his marbles and buttons.

"What's the meaning of this?" she demanded, brandishing the bag that had emblazoned on it in big blue letters: Fine and Schapiro. Kosher Delicatessen. We Deliver.

"I ordered a little something for supper last night," he evaded, applying himself overdiligently to his marbles, picking one up with his left hand and examining it as if it were a gem, instead of a bit of blue glass.

"What?" she asked. "A little chicken soup and matzoh balls?"

"You guessed!" he exclaimed.

"Really?" she asked dubiously.

"What kind of question is 'really'?" he demanded, indignantly ready to defend his honor.

"Because when Fine and Schapiro sends chicken soup and matzoh balls, they send it in a jar. There is no jar in that kitchen or in the garbage can."

"How do you come to know so much about Fine and Schapiro?" he demanded, hoping that outrage would disguise his guilt.

"Because . . ."

Before she got beyond that one word, Horowitz exclaimed, "Don't tell me! The Rosengartens! They used to take from Fine and Schapiro too!"

"Exactly."

"My luck!" he complained. "I should have known. You know how you see on some English products, 'By appointment to the Queen.' On their bags, Fine and Schapiro should have 'By appointment to the Rosengartens' so a person would know. All right, so it wasn't chicken soup!" he granted angrily.

"So what was it?" she asked, drumming her fingers impatiently on the wrinkled bag.

"What it was . . . was nothing. A sandwich, that's all." Her demanding stare forced him to continue, "And possibly a little potato salad. After all, what's a sandwich without a little potato salad?" Her stare did not relent. "Also a bit of cole slaw," he admitted. Still that stare.

Finally, looking down at his hated marbles, he confessed, "Corned beef. Mustard," and, belatedly, he admitted, "and a piece or two of sour pickle." He added, "It's not a crime to eat a little corned beef."

"So you got a heartburn and had to get up and . . ." She did not bother to finish the sequence of events he had set in motion.

"You want to know why I did it?"

258

"It doesn't matter," Mrs. Washington said. "Just don't do it again!"

"Even a convicted criminal is given a chance to explain before sentencing. You've seen that in the movies and on television, haven't you?"

"Okay, Perry Mason, speak your piece," she permitted intolerantly.

"Mona," he said, with an air that indicated that one word explained it all.

"Mona?" she asked, completely baffled at the relationship between Mona and corned beef.

"She called. She insisted I order chicken soup, skimmed. And boiled chicken, naked. The skin is the best part. Well, I said, I'll teach her to run my life!"

"So you ordered . . ." Mrs. Washington could see it all clearly now. She was about to give vent to her anger when the doorbell rang.

"Tannenbaum!" Horowitz said, identifying the enemy.

Dr. Tannenbaum, a tall, thin man, with a flowing mustache and thick glasses, was putting Horowitz through the routine examination. He had Horowitz cough and breathe, deeply and shallowly. All the while the reluctant old man kept asking himself, how is it possible in the middle of the summer for a stethoscope to be so cold? Do they keep them in a freezer all day?

Finished with that part of his examination, Tannenbaum appraised Horowitz's reflexes, then performed some resistance tests on him. He looked into his eyes, using a flashlight. He spent considerable time examining and pressing that wound on his head. Mrs. Washington had washed away the crust with alcohol, so all Tannenbaum saw was a slight swelling and the thin red line where the break had occurred in the skin.

All the while Mrs. Washington stood in the doorway

259

awaiting the doctor's verdict. After a series of "uh-huh's" of no particular informative value, Tannenbaum rendered his verdict.

"So far everything seems fine."

Horowitz half turned to Mrs. Washington and made a defiant facial grimace, just short of sticking out his tongue at her.

"However . . ." Tannenbaum said.

"Ho-ho-ho, the howevers," Horowitz lamented. "The howevers could kill you. So what's however?"

"However, I'll have to stop by tomorrow and maybe the day after, just to make sure nothing develops."

"Nothing will develop!" Horowitz protested. "I was always a quick developer. When I ran into someone with a cold it didn't take me three days to catch it. If I was going to catch it I had it that same night. So if I don't have anything now I am not going to have it tomorrow. Or the day after. You don't have to bother."

"I'll come by," Tannenbaum said firmly.

"I won't be here!" Horowitz threatened.

Tannenbaum looked at him through his thick-lensed glasses. "Where will you be? Playing second base for the Mets?"

Defeated, Horowitz had no resource but to ask softly, "Look, you want to come, that's okay. Though it wouldn't do any harm first you should warm up your stethoscope a little. Just do me one favor?"

"Yes?"

"Don't tell Marvin?"

"You suffered a serious fall, Mr. Horowitz. I can't withhold that from your son. After all, it may be necessary to have a night nurse. I'd have to discuss that with him. I feel it's my duty," Tannenbaum explained gently, for he was not insensitive to the old man's pride.

"Duty . . . duty . . ." Horowitz complained. "Everybody has a duty to everybody, except to me."

"It's for your own good," Tannenbaum consoled.

"Tell me, doctor, at what age does a man lose his right to decide what's for his own good? Is there some law? Something written in the Bible? In the Constitution? Something that says everybody can tell me what's for my own good?" Horowitz asked earnestly.

"Just take my word for it," Tannenbaum said, because he could think of nothing else to say.

"Take your word?" Horowitz echoed, shaking his head sadly. "We took Jimmy Carter's word that he knew how to run the country and look what happened. Believe me, whatever General Sherman did to Georgia, we are now even! We don't owe the South anything. Not even an apology!"

He was restless and fretful for the remainder of the day. He was impatient throughout their hour in the sun. He did finish his lunch. He applied himself during his four exercise sessions, stretching, straining, resisting, lifting, as Mrs. Washington ordered. But she realized that, though he made progress, he took no joy in it. He was worried, far too worried. He was too concerned about what would happen if Dr. Tannenbaum called Marvin.

Before she left for the evening, Mrs. Washington called Dr. Tannenbaum to ask him not to call Marvin. But she discovered that Tannenbaum had already done so.

She did not tell Mr. Horowitz, thinking it would do no good to increase his anxiety. Instead she prepared his bed for the night. She placed a glass of fresh water on the night table. As a precaution she set out the small vial of Valium that Tannenbaum had prescribed for him.

Horowitz was sitting out in the living room, staring down at the crush of home-going traffic. It was one of those days when Central Park was closed to automobiles.

261

So the streets had to absorb the heavy flow of cars. He became aware of Mrs. Washington standing in the archway.

"Evenings like this, a person could make better time walking than riding," he observed. "Times like this, I used to walk home. Even after a full day at the business. Now nobody walks. Either they ride or they run. All day, from early morning till late at night they're running. You notice, Mrs. Washington?"

"Yes, I notice."

"In those funny suits, with those funny shoes, they're running," he observed. "Everybody. Old men, young men, old women, young girls. Running." Then he admitted sadly, "I wish I could."

"Mr. Horowitz, tonight, if you must get out of bed, put the light on first. Each room you go into, put the light on!"

"Okay, big deal! So I'll put the light on. Or maybe you want to give me instructions in how to turn on a light?" he demanded impatiently.

"Last night if you had put the light on it might not have happened," she suggested.

He nodded, accepting the fact.

"I left some Valium on the night table with your water. Just in case you can't fall asleep. Or you get up in the middle of the night."

"I don't like pills!" he protested. "That's the trouble with this whole country. We have a drugstore philosophy! No matter what's wrong, there's a remedy for it in the drugstore."

"Just in case you can't fall asleep," she urged gently.

"And what makes you think I won't fall asleep? I am an instant sleeper. Ask Hannah, she could tell you! I could fall asleep standing up if I had to!"

Having gotten that impatient protest off his chest, he softened considerably as he said, "Mrs. Washington, I want to thank you for being so considerate. And I want to apologize for being so silent and surly all day. I know you had to call Tannenbaum. I know he will have to call Marvin. But I also know what will happen if my daughter finds out."

"You may be anticipating too much," she comforted. "After all, you're all right. Dr. Tannenbaum said so. Unless something develops and there's no sign that it will."

"Mrs. Washington, you know your business and I know mine. And mine is being Mona's father. I know exactly what she'll do before she does it. And I don't like it," he observed in his singsong warning.

"Personally, I think you're exaggerating," Mrs. Washington replied.

"Exaggerating? How could I? Mona herself is an exaggeration," he complained. "But she's my headache. Meantime, did you do what I said?"

"What?"

"The present! For Louise! Did you get her something nice?"

"I told you, no gift is necessary."

"Who said anything about necessary? I want that child to have a gift. And if you don't get one for her, I will!"

"All right, I'll get one," she placated him. "Just you get a good night's sleep."

"And when you stop at the hospital, tell Conrad . . . well, just tell him I was asking about him. Please?"

"Of course."

Chapter Nineteen

Mrs. Washington preceded his wheelchair to the door and had inserted the first of the two keys into one of the locks when the phone began to ring. She hastened to unlock the second lock, though Horowitz cautioned, "Take it easy. Don't rush. It's only Mona."

"How can you tell?"

"If you know Mona, you know her ring," Horowitz said.

"That's ridiculous."

"Ridiculous or not, I'll bet it's Mona," Horowitz said. "Say the four fifty you owe me for pinochle?"

"You owe me four fifty," she corrected.

"Okay, so we'll bet that four fifty," Horowitz agreed affably.

By now she had the door open. Without pausing to help his chair over the doorsill, she raced to the kitchen. But when she picked up the phone there was only a dial tone to reward her. Meantime, with special effort, Horo-

264

witz forced the chair over the sill and was into the foyer. He swung the chair about to confront her victoriously, "Well? Mona! No?"

"Dial tone," she informed.

"That's Mona!"

"You know her dial tone too?" Mrs. Washington asked, not a little exasperated.

"Even when she was a child, she was always in a hurry. If she didn't get what she wanted right away, she would stop asking. Until she thought of another way to ask. But she always got what she wanted. The first time she saw Albert, she said, 'I'm going to marry him. I can make something out of him.' And she did. The world may need women like that. Only *I* don't need women like that." Horowitz said a bit sadly.

The phone rang again. This time Mrs. Washington picked it up on the first ring.

"Hello?"

"Is my father there?" a stern female voice asked.

Mrs. Washington hesitated before answering, "Yes, he is." She handed the phone to Horowitz. "Mona," she admitted.

"Four fifty, please," he replied, taking the phone. "Hello, Mona, darling. And how are you today?"

"I was fine. Until I heard from Marvin. What's this about a fall and hurting your head? What happened?"

"Well," Horowitz began, "you saw that new dance they're doing on TV, the hustle? Well, I was teaching Mrs. Hess, the widow from the third floor, how to do the hustle, when somehow our feet got tangled up and I accidentally fell."

"Dad, this is serious!" Mona said impatiently.

"Serious? With Mrs. Hess? Don't be silly. She's a terrible cook."

"You know what I mean! Now, Dad, exactly what happened?" she demanded.

Horowitz glared at Mrs. Washington, held his hand over the mouthpiece and muttered, "You had to call Dr. Tannenbaum. Now I'll get it!" Into the phone, he said, "It was really nothing. I got up in the middle of the night to get an Alka-Seltzer and I fell. That's all there was to it."

"Why did you need an Alka-Seltzer?" Mona demanded.

"I don't know," he avoided. "Unless suddenly I have an allergy to chicken soup. I have read that people who have been eating something all their lives can suddenly become allergic."

"Nobody, absolutely nobody, has ever had a heartburn from chicken soup," Mona declared.

"Then maybe it was the chicken," Horowitz offered to compromise.

"I have never heard of anyone getting heartburn from a little boiled chicken."

"Well, like they say on the television news, you heard it here first. An exclusive!" Horowitz said.

"Now, Dad, I heard you fell so hard that you suffered a gash on your head? And you were unconscious for hours?"

"No gash. A little cut. Not even enough to put iodine on. The doctor could hardly see it. And I was not unconscious. But since I had fallen, and the foyer carpet is so soft and thick, I decided instead of getting up, it was the middle of the night anyhow, I would sleep there. That's all that happened."

"Dad," she remonstrated impatiently.

"I must have been comfortable," he argued, "because when Mrs. Washington came in she had to wake me. Anyhow, it's over and I'm fine. I had a good breakfast, a nice little airing in the park. It's a nice day, temperature about eighty-two. The sun is out, and the air is clear. And what else can I say, except it was nice of you to call. Now don't worry. Just give my love to Albert and take care of yourself. And good-bye," he concluded in one long breath.

"Dad!" she interdicted, with as much force and effect as if she had reached across three thousand miles and seized his hand to prevent him from hanging up the phone.

He glared at Mrs. Washington, as he said resignedly, "Yes, Mona, darling?"

"Dad, it is quite obvious to me that you're not getting the kind of attention you need," Mona declared.

"How can it be obvious to you since you are so far away and don't know what's going on?" he asked testily.

"A man in your condition should not be left alone in the middle of the night!"

"I'm not going to be saddled with nurses all night long! It's enough I put up with Mrs. Washington during the day," he declared, making a gesture to her to indicate that he was only arguing his case, not stating the truth of things.

"What you need is a household where there is full-time staff. Albert and I have a couple. A sleep-in couple. If you were here, and something happened in the middle of the night, all you would have to do is buzz."

"I'm not such a good buzzer," Horowitz argued.

"You wouldn't have to get out of bed and go prowling around in the dark, falling and hurting yourself. Why . . . why you could have hit your head on a piece of furniture and . . . and died!" she said, and began to weep.

Horowitz whispered angrily to Mrs. Washington, "You see what you did? Now she's crying. I warned you about her. Strong as she is, crying is what she does best. It's how she got Albert to move to San Diego. She cried four straight days. About how terrible New York was becoming. She cried that man right into a fortune. And now she's trying to cry me into an elegant prison called San Diego. I'll die there, and it'll be your fault. All because you had to blab to Dr. Tannenbaum."

Into the phone he consoled, "Mona, darling, there's nothing to cry about. I'm fine. I'm getting better every day. You know, for example, that as I am talking to you I am holding this phone in my left hand? Yes, my left hand! And to prove to you how well I can do that, without any assistance from my right hand, I am going to hang up this phone. When you hear the click, you'll know that I was able to do it with my left hand!"

Whereupon he hung up promptly, cutting off her desperate, "Dad, no!" from three thousand miles away.

"You see, Mrs. Washington, what you have done? You almost sent an innocent man to his death! You will have that on your conscience for the rest of your life."

"Don't go dramatic on me, Mr. Horowitz."

"Dramatic? You call that dramatic? They take a poor, defenseless man and put him in prison. That's what it would be out there. A prison. Who would I have to talk to? Nobody. Who would there be to play pinochle with? Nobody! I would shrivel up and die from loneliness. There's no Central Park in San Diego. There's no Fine and Schapiro!"

"And no heartburn!" Mrs. Washington reminded.

"Heartburn?" he seized on the word. "I understand that the air out there is so thick with smog, you get heartburn just from breathing! And that's what you wanted to do to me! How could you?" he exclaimed tragically.

"But do I harbor any hatred against you? No, Mrs. Washington, I say to myself, the poor woman has a right to revenge. After all, I did make those accusations against her grandson. So what difference does it make to her, if, one day a few weeks after I have gone to San Diego, someone calls her and says, 'Did you know Samuel Horowitz?'

"That's the tipoff, Mrs. Washington. Somebody calls

you—and they say, 'Did you know?' not 'Do you know?' You can be dead only a few minutes and right away you are past tense. That's what's going to happen. Someone will call you and ask, 'Did you know Samuel Horowitz?' It will haunt you the rest of your life. Down through the ages that call will come to you, 'Did you know Samuel Horowitz?'

"I don't envy you, Mrs. Washington, to carry that burden on your conscience through eternity!"

Completely ignoring his diatribe, Mrs. Washington said, simply, "It's time for your exercises."

He pouted, "I don't think I want to exercise today."

The phone rang again. "Don't answer it!" he commanded.

"It must be your daughter calling back."

"You see?" he pointed out. "Already you're able to recognize her ring. So answer it and say wrong number!"

"She'll recognize my voice."

"So say I'm out," he suggested.

The phone continued to ring.

"Mr. Horowitz, you have to answer!" Mrs. Washington said, her black eyes peering at him through her silver-framed glasses.

"It's on your head!" he replied. "Whatever happens, it's on your head!" He picked up the phone and said sweetly, "Hello, darling!"

"Dad! Dad I don't ever want you to do that again!"

"What did I do?"

"You hung up on me!" she accused.

"I thought we were finished. What more is there to say?"

"I am coming East!" she declared.

"What for? I'm fine."

"I am coming East!" she repeated. "And I am taking you back with me. So make plans to close the apartment, pick out the things you want to take with you, and we'll

269

sell the rest. There are brokers who deal in furniture, housewares, silver, and such. I'll have someone in Albert's office find such a person!"

"When are you coming?" he asked with great concern.

"I've called a friend of ours who has his own Lear jet. He promised to put it at my disposal a week from Monday. I'll fly in, spend a day or two taking care of details, and we can be back here by Wednesday evening. So get ready."

"Mona . . ." he tried to interrupt.

"Dad, I can't let you continue on your own. It's too dangerous. Mother would never forgive me." She began to weep again. "She always said to me, 'If I go first, take care of your father.' That's what she always said."

"Take care of your father," he echoed sadly. "Mona, I am fine. I don't need any more taking care of than I am getting from Mrs. Washington. And I like it here. This is my home. I want to live here until I die."

At the word *die* he was greeted with a fresh torrent of tears.

"Mona, please, don't cry . . . Mona?" He glared at Mrs. Washington, but into the phone he said, "Okay, so I won't die. I'll live forever. All right? Mona? Mona?" he pleaded. "In San Diego, when they cry it's like a tropical rainstorm."

"Dad, I'll see you a week from Monday," she said once she had regained her voice.

"But Mona . . ."

"A week from Monday, Dad!" This time it was Mona who hung up.

Horowitz was left with the dead phone in his hand. He stared at it, then said, "You see, Mrs. Washington, what your sense of duty has done to an innocent man?"

All through lunch, though she had tried to tempt him with fresh blintzes, which were golden, tender, and just a bit crisp at the edges, he ate morosely. He finished one, had barely cut into the second when he pushed back his plate, saying, "We've got to do something! We've got to keep her from coming here!"

"How?"

"Maybe we can call the San Diego airport and say we are Puerto Rican freedom fighters and we put a bomb on board that Lear jet," he suggested.

"We don't even know whose jet it is," Mrs. Washington pointed out.

"True," he granted. "Besides, even if there really was a bomb and it went off, to Mona it would just be a minor interruption. She would go right on managing and talking."

"Finish your lunch," Mrs. Washington suggested.

"I don't want any more," he said petulantly.

"After I spent all that time making those blintzes?" she asked, obviously hurt.

"Now you're sounding like a wife, not a nurse," he replied testily. Then his face lit up in a big smile. "I *have* it!" he exulted. "I *have* it!"

"What?"

"Mrs. Washington, would you do me the honor to marry me? And also at the same time to save my life!"

"That's ridiculous! Besides how would that save your life?"

"Don't you see?" he argued. "We get married . . ."

"Hmm!" Mrs. Washington interrupted to scoff belligerently.

"Hear me out!" he insisted.

"Ridiculous!" she insisted. "No Baptist like me is going to marry any Jewish man like you."

"What's the matter, I'm not good enough?" he asked indignantly.

"It's not a matter of good enough or not good enough. But how would it look? Me Baptist, you Jewish. Me

271

black, you white. Who would we even find to marry us? I'm not getting married by any rabbi. And you certainly are not planning to get married by any Baptist preacher. Or are you?" she asked, beginning to take him seriously now.

"If you would stop being hysterical for a minute and listen to me, I'll explain. It doesn't matter who marries us."

"It does to me!" she insisted.

"All right, all right, so I go to some Baptist preacher!" he conceded.

"I haven't yet said I'd marry you," she pointed out.

"You have to!" he insisted. "After all, it was your call to Dr. Tannenbaum that got me into this situation. You have to help me get out! Now, this is what I have in mind. We get married . . ."

"I don't like the whole idea," she kept insisting.

"Just suppose!" he pleaded in a loud argumentative voice. "You can't lose anything by supposing, can you?" She rewarded him with a slight contemplative nod of her head, indicating she was at least willing to listen. "Okay. Suppose we get married. Before Mona arrives. She arrives, wants to take me back to San Diego and I say, 'My darling Mona, you no longer have any rights over me. I have a wife and she is the one to decide. You two fight it out.'"

"I don't want anything to do with your daughter. Especially if she's the kind of bitch you say she is." At once Mrs. Washington apologized, "I'm sorry I didn't mean to use that word about your daughter, Mr. Horowitz."

"Why not? I have to bite my tongue so I don't use it," he said.

"Anyhow, if she's like you say, I couldn't win any argument with her, no sir," Mrs. Washington concluded.

"Now wait! This is like pinochle! Whoever is holding

the most trump wins. And you, Mrs. Washington, are holding all the trump."

"I am?" she asked gingerly, suspicious of his next words.

"Mona overcomes you, outargues you, outinsists you. All of which she will certainly do. So you say, 'If that's what you think best for Mr. Horowitz!' . . . No, you better make that, 'If that's what you think best for Samuel.' After all, if we are going to be married we can't go around calling each other Mr. Horowitz and Mrs. Washington. In fact, you won't be Mrs. Washington anymore. You would be Mrs. Horowitz. So we better practice calling each other Samuel and Harriet. You go first."

Mrs. Washington shook her head. "This is crazy! We are not going to get married!"

"What harm can come from saying Samuel?" he demanded impatiently. "Just try it. You couldn't die from it. Samuel! Samuel! There, I said it. I'm still alive and breathing!"

She exhaled with great impatience and finally, in answer to his entreating look, she said, "Samuel . . ."

"Tell me, did it hurt? Did it stick to your tongue like a fishhook? Of course not. It is a very ordinary name. Samuel. Just like that. Now it's my turn. Harriet. Harriet. Harriet." He seemed to find great and growing delight in repeating the name. "Very good."

"Now, how is that going to help anything?" Mrs. Washington asked.

"Very simple, my dear Harriet. See how easily I can say your name. When Mona wins out in the argument, you say to her, 'I can see your point of view. It would be best for Samuel if we moved to your home in San Diego.' Understand?"

She nodded intolerantly, starting to say, "We are not getting married . . ." but he interrupted.

"Say the words, just like I said, 'It would be best for

Samuel if we moved to your home in San Diego,'" he urged.

"What for?"

"Just say it!" he exhaled in great exasperation.

Quickly, to put an end to his suggestion, she rattled off, "'ItwouldbebestforSamuelifwemovedtoyourhomeinSan-Diego.' Okay?"

"Wait, wait, wait," Horowitz overruled. "Slowly, like an actress would say the line. With the proper emphasis on the right words."

To humor him and yet express her own disapproval of the whole ridiculous plan, she said, "'It . . . would . . . be . . . best . . . for . . . Samuel . . . if . . . we . . . moved . . . to San . . . Diego.' Slow enough?"

"Frankly, I am not the theater critic for *The New York Times* but I would say a touch *too* slow. But that's not the main trouble. Emphasis! Emphasis, Mrs. Washington . . . I mean, Harriet. The word to emphasize is *we*. Just say, *we!*"

"All right," she agreed impatiently, *"we."*

"More!" he directed.

"What do you mean, more?"

"There has got to be more conviction, my dear. More . . . more warmth . . . more *schmalz*. You know what schmalz means?"

"Chicken fat. Mr. Rosengarten always liked a little dab of schmalz on the chopped liver I made."

"Well, put a little dab on the word *we*," Horowitz coaxed.

"I'll try," she agreed. "'It would be best for Samuel if *we* moved to San Diego.' How's that?"

"Perfect!" Horowitz sang out in great glee. "When my Mona hears that her father is moving to San Diego with a black wife, she will be so stunned she will forget to cry. She will simply drop dead and be glad to go back to San Diego alone. She will not even call me on her WATS line.

Fantastic, no?" he asked smiling broadly.

But the look on Mrs. Washington's face, the tears that welled up behind her silver-rimmed glasses, banished his sense of victory.

"Harriet?" he asked tenderly.

She sniffled, brushed the corner of her eye with her fingertips.

"Harriet?" he asked, more concerned now. "What's the matter? What's wrong?"

She shook her head and turned away to hide her tears.

"My dear, what is it?"

"I think it's very cruel of you," she finally managed.

"Nothing I could possibly do to Mona is cruel."

"And what about what you've done to me?" she asked simply.

"Do? What did I do?" he asked in all innocence.

"You made me the butt of this ridiculous game. You used me."

"I never meant . . ." he started to protest.

"You never meant, but you did it just the same. Used me, used my blackness, as a threat against your daughter. I am not a threat, Mr. Horowitz. I am a human being with feelings. I do not like to be reminded that your daughter would not think me fit to live in her house. And that rather than acknowledge me as your wife, she would prefer never to see you again."

"You don't understand. . . ." he tried to plead.

"Oh, but I do. The word we. With schmalz on it. That one little word would protect you from her. Why? Because I am black. Well, I have my own kind of pride. And it does not permit such cruel jokes."

She started out of the room before she broke down in tears.

Almost an hour later, after he had spent the time brooding in the living room alone, he made his way to the kitchen, where she sat at the small table. Her lunch was set before her but remained untouched. He stood in the doorway hoping to be noticed. But her face was hidden in a handkerchief.

"Harriet . . . Mrs. Washington . . ." he tried to open the conversation. She did not respond, not by word or gesture. "I'm sorry. Very sorry. I have just spent the last hour thinking about what you said. It *was* cruel. The only excuse I can give, is that I am a desperate man fighting to retain his last ounce of freedom and self-respect. I want to be on my own in my last days. I think I have earned that much out of life. But she won't let me. So I had to think of some way . . . some way . . ."

He smiled and admitted, "While I was thinking, I thought if I were eight instead of sixty-eight, I would run away from home. But how would it look, a sixty-eight-year-old man running away from home?"

He had hoped to entice her into joining in his joke but she did not. He was about to turn away, when he asked, "Mrs. Washington, suppose, just suppose, that I had asked you to marry me, not for that reason, but because I have grown genuinely fond of you, what would you have said?"

Slowly she turned to face him. "I would have felt greatly honored. But the answer would still have been no."

He nodded sadly, turned and started to hobble toward the bedroom.

Chapter Twenty

When she arrived the next morning, Mrs. Washington discovered the living room, which she had left so neat and clean the evening before, was now in disarray. Her first thought was that the place had been burglarized. Her first fear was that Mr. Horowitz had suffered injury or even death while resisting.

"Mr. Horowitz!" she cried out. There was no answer, which confirmed her fear. She raced toward the bedroom, expecting to discover a sight of blood and turmoil. "Mr. Horowitz!" she called out quite desperately, for the room was indeed in turmoil.

After a pause, his muffled voice came from inside the bedroom closet. Expecting to find him beaten and trussed up like a burglary victim, she flung open the closet. There stood Horowitz in his pajamas, leaning on his quad with one hand while trying to reach the shelf that ran the length of the closet just over the clothes rod. Since he had to reach so high with his left hand, he was not successful. But that did not prevent him from trying.

"What's going on here?" Mrs. Washington demanded, doubly annoyed. Annoyed at herself for fearing some harm to him, and at him for having obviously made such a mess of the apartment.

"I am getting ready," he declared dramatically.

"Ready for what?" she asked, ordering him out of the closet with a commanding forefinger.

For a moment he resisted, glaring at her. Then he surrendered and came out, dragging his left foot, leaning on his cane.

"How did you ever manage to turn this apartment into such a mess? Have you been up all night?"

"Mrs. Washington, please don't holler on me. I want our last days together to be pleasant and friendly. I want to remember you with warm feelings. And I would like you to feel likewise."

"Have you been up all night?" she reiterated.

"Not all night. But mostly," he admitted.

"You have a pill on your night table, and a glass of water. If you can't sleep, Dr. Tannenbaum said it's all right to take it."

"And sleep away my few remaining days of freedom?" he asked in martyrlike anguish.

"Mr. Horowitz," she intoned, warning that she had had enough of his dramatics.

"It's not going to work," he warned. "I am not going quietly. I am not going into slavery without a word of protest. Remember what Booker T. Washington said. 'Give me liberty or give me death!'"

"Booker T. Washington never said that," Mrs. Washington replied.

"Your own relative, and you don't know what he said?" Horowitz taunted. "No wonder they need classes in black studies."

"In the first place, he was not related to me. And in the

.278

second place, Patrick Henry said it," she pointed out.

"Well, Washington *could* have said it," Horowitz protested.

"Now, what is this mess?" Mrs. Washington demanded, pointing at all the items of attire, bric-a-brac, and personal memorabilia scattered across his bed, on the table and even on the top of the television set. "It'll take a month to get this place in order again," she complained.

"A month?" he lamented. "My time is measured in days. Hours!" Dramatically, he extended his left hand to point out the vistas of time that stretched before him. "A man lives sixty-eight years and suddenly all he has left are a few hours. Some men, in the goodness of a merciful God, are struck down without expecting it. They die suddenly, without even a warning. But me, I am doomed to know that a week from Monday comes Mona, and on that Monday good-bye freedom!

"The Hebrew Home for the Aged! That's where she'll put me!"

"Whatever gave you that idea?"

"I remember when she was helping to raise money for it!" Horowitz replied. "She said they would make it the best, most up-to-date home in this country! That's what she has in mind for me! An old folks home! A prison for senior citizens! I do not wish to be confined with a lot of aged people. I am not aged. I am not even old. I am, at the most, a man with a little trouble with his left foot and his left hand. So maybe occasionally I forget to tie my shoelaces or button my shirt or even put my left arm into my sleeve. Does that make me aged?

"Hebrew, I am. But aged, I am definitely not!" he ended up dramatically, using his right hand as well and letting go of his quad cane. For a moment he wavered, then as he was about to fall, he cried out, "Mrs. Washington!"

279

She reached out to embrace him and keep him on his feet. Once she restored his cane to him, he regained his dignity, and with it his belligerence.

"I don't need any help," he said disdainfully. "Now, where's my breakfast?" he demanded.

"Can I trust you not to make more of a mess of this place than it already is? If so, I will go prepare your breakfast," she offered.

"Mess?" he inquired painfully. "You call this a mess? The evidence of a lifetime, a mess? Mrs. Washington, how could you?"

"Mr. Horowitz," she warned.

"I know, I know," he conceded. "Don't get dramatic." Then he softened, and like a small boy, he said, "If I don't do that, I might be tempted to cry. Mrs. Washington, what you see strewn about is my life. Things Hannah and I brought back from trips we made. Little things. Of no value to anyone but us.

"When I couldn't sleep last night I tried to make a list in my mind of people who might like to have a bit of something to remember Hannah and Samuel Horowitz. I couldn't. There is no one. Hannah's jewelry, the really valuable pieces, they're already gone. To Mona, to Candy. To Marvin's wife and his daughter. What is left are little bits and pieces. A pin with the clasp broken, and it was too late to repair it. A chain that was never real gold to begin with. A few little earrings, inexpensive.

"Of my possessions, not much more. I was never one for jewelry. No rings. No expensive watches. Just some cuff links. And one set of gold links and studs to wear with a tuxedo. But I haven't worn a tuxedo in years so I gave those to Bruce when he was *bar mitzvahed*. To wear when he grew up. For the rest, nothing. A collection of odd coins that piled up in my pockets on trips to Europe. A few Israeli coins for sentimental value."

He stirred the coins that lay in an indentation in the coverlet on his bed.

"The life of Samuel Horowitz, and it couldn't even fill up your hand. But even that, they won't let me have."

"You could take them with you," Mrs. Washington suggested compassionately.

"What for?" he asked. "To amuse the other Hebrews in the Home for the Hebrew Aged. To tell them of my exploits, of my life that would prove very uninteresting and dull to anyone but Hannah. No, it's better if I give it away, all of it. The furniture. The dishes. The silver."

He turned to her, "You see anything you want, take it! The silver is solid sterling. Worth a lot of money these days. Take it. And the dishes. That's real Rosenthal, the good set. The other set is Japanese, for every day. And the Passover dishes are Lenox. Take, take whatever you want!"

"First I'll make your breakfast," she said, to change the subject.

"Yes," he surrendered, "first, must be breakfast."

"Don't do anything foolish, while I'm in the kitchen," she warned.

"Oh, then you suspected," he accused.

"Suspected?" she replied. "What?"

"Masada!" he cried out, as if it were a battle cry.

"Masada?" she repeated, puzzled.

"There, out in the desert, on the edge of the Dead Sea, there rises up out of the sand a mountain. And on the top of that mountain palaces, and storehouses, and homes. Two thousand years ago, Jews lived up there. The last free Jews when the Romans took over. So the Romans surrounded the place, with thousands of troops!"

He looked at Mrs. Washington to see if she appreciated the desperate straits of those ancient Jews. "Did you hear me? A few hundred Jews against thousands of Romans! Every morning those Jews stared down into the desert. And all they could see was Romans, Romans, and more Romans. Waiting to starve them out and force them to surrender. But those Jews would not surrender. So the

Roman soldiers started to build a ramp up to the top of that mountain. Day by day, more ramp. Considering it was a government project, it went very quickly. And before you knew it, there it was, right almost to the top!

"Now what did those Jews do? They held a meeting. And for one time in history a group of Jews all agreed on the same thing. Rather than surrender, and live as slaves, they decided that all of them—men, women and children—would commit mass suicide. So when the Romans finally broke in there what did they find? Hundreds of dead Jews. But *free* Jews!

"That's what I was thinking last night. When Mona comes through that door a week from Monday, I will be standing there with a knife in my hand, crying out defiantly, 'Mona, remember Masada!'"

Mrs. Washington shook her head in stolid disapproval.

Deflated, Mr. Horowitz asked meekly, "You think that's *too* dramatic?"

"No," Mrs. Washington said, "but we'll have to practice it right after your breakfast."

"Practice? No Jew needs practice in being a martyr!" Horowitz proclaimed. "We're born that way."

"Well," Mrs. Washington said, as she enacted his defiant stance. "In which hand are you going to hold the knife? Your left? A knife with a built-up handle? How would that look? And if you hold it in your right hand, what about your quad. Suppose you lose your balance and fall? That will surely convince her that you can't be on your own."

The practicalities of his situation overwhelmed him. "Yes, I suppose it wouldn't do any harm to practice it a few times."

"Right after breakfast."

"Instead of the damned buttons and marbles," he conceded.

"*After* the damned buttons and marbles," she corrected.

"What good are marbles and buttons to a dead man?" he grumbled.

"Breakfast!" she announced, putting an end to all discussion. "By the time your orange juice is on the table I want you in there! That's an order!"

As she was leaving the room, he called after her, "That kind of attitude may win you civil rights, but it won't win you any friends!"

He was in his place at the table when she entered with his freshly squeezed orange juice.

As she set down his glass, he asked, "So?"

"So what?"

"So are you going to make me guess what happened yesterday?"

She was taken by surprise. "Yesterday?"

"Yesterday! Yesterday!" he repeated impatiently. "A boy is in the hospital. Wounded. Thanks God, he recovers. And yesterday he is due to come home. So! *Did* he come home? A person has a right to know!"

"Yes, he's home. And he's fine!"

"Good!" Horowitz said. "And?"

"And what?"

"What did the doctor say?" he demanded anxiously.

"Aside from a scar on his chest, he'll be good as new, the doctor said."

"*That's* what I wanted to hear!" Horowitz said, relieved. Then dared, "He . . . he said anything about me?"

"The doctor?" Mrs. Washington asked, puzzled.

"No! The boy! The boy!"

"Oh. Oh, yes. He said thanks very much for the chemistry set."

"What chemistry set?" It was Horowitz's turn to be puzzled.

"I kept asking Louise what she wanted as a gift, and she said a chemistry set. I thought it was strange. But it turns out that Conrad always wanted one and this was her way of getting it for him as a welcome home."

"Now, that's what I call a sweet, considerate sister. And such a sister deserves a gift of her own. So you will . . ."

Mrs. Washington interposed firmly, "No!"

"What do you mean no?" Horowitz demanded, pouting.

"I mean, you've done enough," she said, and put an end to the discussion by leaving the room.

He finished his breakfast in silence. Without any orders or suggestions, he left the table and labored out into the living room to begin his appointed fine-hand movement exercises. With his left hand he picked up marbles and inserted them in the proper holes. He selected buttons and put them into the jar. Finally, he grew rebellious and threw a button against the wall with such fury that it brought Mrs. Washington out of the kitchen.

"What happened?" she demanded.

"What happened was I squeezed a button too hard and it got away," he explained. Her impatient glare told him she did not believe him.

"I suppose I might as well go and pack," he said, hoping to evoke some protest from her. But she only stared at him. He raised himself from the chair, leaned on his cane, and started to shuffle out of the room, muttering as he went. "If you had consented to marry me instead of being insulted, we wouldn't have this problem. What shall I pack? What do people wear in San Diego? Is it summer all year round there?"

"I don't know," she replied, not relenting one bit.

"They say people play golf there all year. I don't play golf. Never did. When you run a small wholesale business like mine you must be everywhere all the time. You can't trust anyone. So who had time to play golf? Now I have time but I don't know how to play. Besides, you

284

have to hold those clubs with two hands. I won't even be able to play golf in a place where all they do is play golf."

Dramatically, he raised his eyes to the heavens, "What did I ever do that You would inflict this fate on me? What did I ever do that You would deliver me into the hands of the enemy?"

"Time to go out in the park," Mrs. Washington insisted. "Get dressed!"

"Time to go out in the park," he echoed bitterly. "How many more times will we be able to do that, Mrs. Washington? Ten more times. One for each finger on your hands. And then no more Central Park. I wonder, will you remember those good times we had in the park? Watching the cars go by? And the number ten buses? All marked air-conditioned. But all with their windows open because the air conditioning never works. Ah, those were the days!" he exclaimed nostalgically.

"And to think," he continued, "we could have gone on doing that if only you took seriously my proposal of marriage."

"Mr. Horowitz, time!" she reminded. "Get dressed!"

When she came back to check on his progress she found him attired in a pair of pink linen slacks and a garish sport shirt, of which the basic color was purple.

"What do you call that?" she asked.

"I'm getting ready for the golf course!" he defied.

"I don't think there's any golf course at the Hebrew Home for the Aged," she said, "so change into something that won't disgrace me."

"That's it!" he accused. "You're not interested in me, or how I will be disgraced. You're only thinking of yourself! And whether you will be disgraced!"

"Get out of that outfit and into something more presentable," she said, "or I'll undress you and dress you myself!"

"Go ahead! Hit me!" he defied. "I wouldn't put it past you, a woman so cruel!"

But he did not resist, instead, carefully, and with great effort, he began to unbutton his shirt.

They said very little while in the park. The day was warm and dusty. The fumes from the cars seemed unusually oppressive. But they did not remark on it. Instead Mrs. Washington indicated he should wheel himself deeper into the park and away from the traffic. He started, but had some difficulty making it up the incline. She pushed slightly and he was able to manage the rest of the way. He wheeled toward the playground and through the iron gate into the round open area which contained a sandbox on one side and several small swings and a slide to the other. Around the inside perimeter, weather-beaten green benches filled every available space.

The children in the sandbox were hardly more than infants. They played with sand toys, which they took from one another, causing occasional tears and outcries. In the swings, small children, none older than four or five, were being kept in continuous motion by their mothers who gossiped throughout, so that propelling the swings became automatic and talking seemed to be the main occupation.

The more assertive children were climbing the slide and coming down, each making an accompanying sound of either enjoyment or fear.

Together the sounds of the playground blended into a happy orchestration of children at play, free from adult concerns, more carefree than they would ever be again as long as they lived.

Horowitz moved slowly to one of the farthest benches, within the shade cast by a large oak tree. He mopped his face dry, feeling a bit more than usual the pain of his face wound.

"It's going to rain," he observed. The first words he had spoken since they came out. "When my wound hurts, it means rain. I noticed that lately."

"The nerves are still healing," she informed professionally.

"Listen," he began apologetically, "if I hurt your feelings, I'm sorry."

"Hurt my feelings?" she asked, surprised.

"I don't really think you would hit me. I just said that to irritate you. I'm sorry. You didn't take it serious."

"I didn't."

"So why haven't you talked to me?"

"Why haven't *you* talked to *me*?" she countered.

"I guess maybe we haven't talked to each other, hmm?"

"I guess."

"I'm sorry it will cost you your job," he said. "I want you to know that's one reason I don't want to leave. I admire what you are doing for your grandchildren. And I would like to feel I am helping."

"Thank you."

"If it wasn't for your grandchildren," he confessed, "I would ask you to come to San Diego with me." Then he quickly amended, "As a nurse, of course."

"If there were no grandchildren I wouldn't need this particular job," she pointed out.

"You're very lucky in a way. I mean to have grandchildren so close to you. They say that's the best time in life, to be a grandparent. You have few of the day-to-day headaches but all the *naches*. You know what means *naches*?"

"Rosengarten," she responded.

"Then you know," he concluded. "I wish my grandchildren didn't live so far away when they were growing up. And now they're all away in different schools. All I can do is wonder what they look like, what they talk like, who they are. Sometimes Mona or Marvin's wife sends me a few pictures of them. But what can you tell from a picture? Except Mona's girl, Candy, she seems to resemble Hannah. The boy is tall, like his father. On the other hand, Marvin's Douglas is not exactly what I would call distinguished looking. But he must be smart. He's at California Institute of Technology. His grandfather on his mother's side was named David, from which comes Douglas.

"What's wrong with the name David? Did Michelangelo ever do a statue of Douglas? Never. So why is Douglas a better name than David? One reason I'm glad I'm still alive, if Mona or Marvin had another child and they wanted to name him after me what would they change Samuel into? Stewart? That's a name, Stewart? A name for a cafeteria maybe, not for a nice Jewish boy!"

Suddenly he remarked, "I'm talking too much. And when I talk too much it's because I have nothing of value to say. Like when Hannah was sick. I knew what she had. Maybe even she knew what she had. But we didn't want to say the word, or what it would mean. So I talked a mile a minute. About everything, and anything. Talk, talk, talk, only don't say anything.

"And every once in a while she would try to smile at me and she would say, 'Samuel, enough already,' and she would reach out her hand. I would take it, and be silent the rest of the time. It was such a relief to be able not to talk. That's the way she died, with me holding her hand and not saying a word. As if, in the silence, she was allowed to go. She didn't have to listen anymore, she didn't have to answer, or even try to smile. She was relieved of all obligations, finally. She was at peace."

He was silent, staring across the playground at the children at play. Mothers were beginning to gather up those youngsters who would be carted off to lunch at home. Other mothers began to unpack lunches they had brought with them. Some children wept at being separated from their playmates by mothers who tried to seduce them with promises of returning. One mother, at the end of her patience, resorted to threats, increasing her child's weeping, which had now become loud and painful to hear.

"Mrs. Washington, did you ever stop to think, little children cry as if their hearts were breaking. But in a while, sometimes only minutes, it's over and forgotten, like it never happened. But with grown-ups . . . ah, with grown-ups, when our hearts are really breaking we hardly ever dare to cry. But we never forget." He paused before asking circumspectly, "How was it with your Horace?"

"Very quick. It was just before Christmas. He had a job in a department store, for the holiday rush. Unpacking cases in the receiving department. Since it was before the holiday and they needed the time, and he needed the extra money, he worked overtime every night for twelve straight nights. He was not a strong man by that time, big but not too strong. Worry and loss of pride had taken the strength from him. And the pneumonia the year before when he made some money shoveling snow. He went off to work that morning, with a lunch I packed for him. The next thing I heard they were calling me from the hospital asking me if I was Mrs. Washington, and somehow I knew. I raced over there and found his body. Somebody had put his bag of lunch with his clothes, as if it was part of his possessions and I would want it back," she said sadly.

"Too bad," Horowitz said. "Too bad. A man to live his whole life and never have a steady job at work he liked to do. I wish I had known him. I would have given him a job. I didn't employ many men, nine sometimes, seven mostly. But I would have found a place for him if I knew him."

"Who knows?" she replied. "Maybe you did know

289

him. Maybe he came to you for a job and you turned him away."

"I would never do that to Horace," he protested at once, then acquiesced. "Maybe. God knows how many worthy men, black men, have come to me for jobs and I said no. If I were starting out now . . ." He knew the futility of following through on that supposition.

They were silent again for a time, and across the playground the children who were having lunch had been silenced by their food. Except for an occasional impatient automobile horn and the hum of traffic, all was quiet. It seemed an appropriate time for Horowitz to speak softly.

"Mrs. Washington, I am going to miss you. Very much."

She did not respond.

"I want you to know that I appreciate everything you have done for me. And, even more, the things you tried to do and I wouldn't cooperate. I am a stubborn old man. I know that. But then I have always been stubborn. The only thing that has changed is that I am now old too, which makes me worse.

"So I want to apologize for all the nasty things I said. All those things about black Hitler and concentration camps. If you hadn't been so firm with me I wouldn't even be able to do what I do now. So if there's anything I can do for you, some token of how I feel about you, something you've always wanted. A gift you never felt free to buy for yourself. I don't care how much it costs, just name it."

She did not reply.

"There must be something," he urged.

"No, I'm fine. I have everything I need or want," she said.

"Except a job that will let you take care of the grandchildren when your daughter is off at work," he reminded.

"I'll find a job, the right job," she insisted. But he could tell she was not nearly so sure as she pretended.

"That Mona," he complained. "If she knew what she was doing to you maybe she wouldn't be so stubborn. But then her mother always said she got that from my side of the family. Oh, that Mona!"

In desperation he suddenly suggested, "Listen! I got a great idea! What if you moved out to San Diego. I mean your whole family. Your daughter, the children. They say it's a nice place to bring up kids."

Before she could refuse, he realized, "No, that wouldn't work. Your life is here. Your daughter's work is here. You belong here. And so do I, if she would only let me."

"That damned pickle!" he exploded in frustration and despair. "If not for that damned pickle and the Alka-Seltzer I would never have fallen and this whole thing would never have happened. To think, a man's life, his freedom are taken away from him over one lousy pickle!"

"That reminds me," Mrs. Washington said, "time for your lunch."

"I don't feel like lunch," he protested.

"I didn't ask you to feel it, just eat it," she said, rising and getting behind his wheelchair, which was her way of saying that if he did not wheel himself out of the park, she would. Reluctantly, he began to wheel.

She prepared his lunch while he exercised by shuffling cards, picking up marbles and buttons, pressing his finger into the theraplasty with unusual and deliberate hostility. Each sharp stab of his finger into the substance was an act of resistance to Mona. By the time Mrs. Washington came in to summon him to lunch, he was angry enough to explode, "She can't make me leave if I don't want to leave! I'll go to court. I have some money! I can support myself! I am not dependent on her!"

"Time for lunch," Mrs. Washington announced, quelling his incipient rebellion.

"Time for lunch," he grumbled. "A sick man's day does not consist of hours. Only, time for breakfast, time for lunch, time for dinner."

He rose, grasping his shiny metal cane and raising himself from the bridge table. He started across the living room carpet with great determination, but without the agility to match. Mumbling all the way, he made it to the foyer. He stopped to regain his breath, taking the opportunity to give vent to his thoughts, "Like being in prison. A high-class, luxurious prison. Like the ones those Watergate fellows went to. But still a prison. Who wants to be a bird in a gilded cage in San Diego? With a Jacuzzi next to the swimming pool. Who needs a swimming pool? Who needs a Jacuzzi?" he defied.

"It could be very helpful for a man in your condition," she suggested, trying to defuse his growing wrath.

"I don't like to be called, 'a man in my condition.' I am not in any condition. I have a few little weaknesses, that's all! That is not a condition!"

He turned to face her, "What are you, on her side? You want to see me go? Well, I won't! I am declaring right now, on the fourteenth of August 1977 that I am a free man in a free country! Mona Fields, I defy you!"

With that he lifted his quad as if it were a weapon and thrust it forth, only to unbalance himself and totter. But for Mrs. Washington's proximity and swift assistance he would have pitched forward onto the carpet.

Fear and exertion caused him to breathe in short desperate gasps. When he was able to, he said, "Thank you, Mrs. Washington, thank you very much."

Gently she said, "Now you see why you should go with Mona. You do need care."

"What about you?" he asked in genuine concern.

"I'll find another job."

"Like this one?" he asked.

292

"Your lunch is getting cold."

He was toying with his Jell-O, when he called out to her, "Mrs. Washington, come in here!"

From the kitchen she called back, "I'm having my lunch. What do you want?"

"Bring your lunch in here!" he commanded. "We'll eat together!"

"I thought we agreed we'd have coffee together at dinner time," she protested as she came in bringing with her a plate of scrambled eggs and toast. She set it down opposite him. "Yes?" she asked intolerantly, angered by being ordered about in such a way.

He did not answer at once, but stared longingly at her plate.

"Those eggs look good," he said enviously.

"You've already had two eggs this week," she reminded.

"I know," he conceded. "Next time, you want to have something really delicious, throw in a little smoked salmon. Terrific."

"No onions?" she asked.

"I know, I know, Mr. Rosengarten liked browned onions with his scrambled eggs and lox. Right?"

"They taste better that way," Mrs. Washington said.

"Only if you like heartburn," Horowitz conceded. "I used to have that dish every Sunday morning and I would still be tasting it on Friday. By the time the heartburn cleared up, it was Sunday again."

"Is that what you called me in here to tell me?" she asked, still resentful.

Horowitz leaned back from the table to take one of his dramatic pauses. Mrs. Washington was prepared for almost anything now.

"Mrs. Washington," he intoned, about to embark on a long speech, "Mrs. Washington, what I am about to say cannot be said in mere words. It needs music!"

"Music?" the startled Mrs. Washington asked, for of all the forms of outburst she had expected, music was definitely the last.

"Yes, music!" he declared dramatically. "Mrs. Washington, name this tune and you will win an extra week's salary!"

"Is this a quiz show on television?" she asked, pushing back her plate and giving him her full attention, for she was now seriously concerned about the state of his mind.

"Listen! Listen carefully!" he commanded. When he thought he had her rapt attention, he began to chant a wordless atonal tune, *"Dydle di di deedee di deedeldo! Deedeldo. Deedeldo!"* He waited expectantly.

When she did not respond, he asked impatiently, "What's the matter, you don't have an ear for music?" He repeated the phrase, trying this time to emphasize the rhythm so she would guess. "Still don't know? Well, I will give you a clue. You people sing it all the time. In church. On television. Now listen carefully, *Dydle di di deedee di deedeldo! Deedeldo! Deedeldo!"*

In disgust he said, "It's a good thing we're not on television. You would just have lost ten thousand dollars. Maybe more! I'm afraid I will have to give you the answer."

Whereupon he sang, "'Joshua fit the battle of Jericho. Jericho. Jericho!' Now do you get it, Mrs. Washington?"

"Yes, I get it," she responded, keeping to herself her low opinion of Mr. Horowitz's ability to carry a tune *a cappella.* "Is that what you called me in here for?"

"It's the significance!" Horowitz pointed out impatiently. "I am sitting here thinking what can I do? What can this Hebrew do to escape the Hebrew Home for the Aged? And I am remembering some other aged Hebrews. There was Abraham, Isaac, Jacob. No great escapes there. No great victories.

"Moses? Was a talker. You ask me, he was the first great Jewish lawyer. He talked a whole people out of Egypt. Sure, a little courtroom hocus-pocus like a few miracles. But mainly a talker. Like Sam Liebowitz and the Scottsboro boys. But the first big hero to win the first big battle against great odds? One man! Joshua! So I said, What did he do that I couldn't do? Hmm? Tell me that, Mrs. Washington!"

"Well, for one thing, Mr. Horowitz, he walked around that Jericho so many times that the walls fell down," Mrs. Washington said because she could think of nothing else to say.

"Bingo!" Horowitz called out. "You hit it right on the nose, Mrs. Washington!"

"Hit what on the nose?" she asked.

"You're not eating," he chided, as she used to chide him in the early days. "While you eat, I will tell you what I have decided." Once she began to nibble at her eggs, he proceeded to expound. "When I was in business and things were not going too well, I would always sit down and ask myself what is the problem, and then set out to solve that problem. Well, what is the problem now?

"Merely because I fell down one night, Mona is sure that I need to be confined in captivity either in her palace or else in the Hebrew Home for the Aged. So what is the solution? To prove to Mona that I can walk perfectly well without falling down. That I can do everything I need to do without any help at all! Once I prove that to her, she hasn't got a leg to stand on."

"At the minute," Mrs. Washington reminded, "you barely have one good leg to stand on. How are you going to prove it to her?"

"How?" he asked, indignant that she would think he had presented her with an ill-prepared plan. "By doing just what I said. By walking without help. By eating

295

without help. By doing everything I am expected to do. *Without help!"*

"That *would* be a miracle," she agreed gently, knowing that his ambition exceeded his possibilities.

"And you, Mrs. Washington, are going to help me! My exercises instead of four times a day, I will do eight times a day. Cards? No more pinochle! Just exercise! Buttons, marbles, everything I am supposed to do , you will make me do double, three times as much, even. And when I do my exercises on the bed, you will force me to stretch more than I have ever stretched before!

"Together, we will outsmart her. She will come. She will be forced to admit I can get along on my own. And she will go back to San Diego. In that private jet. But without me! Your job will be safe. And I will have my freedom! Freedom!" he shouted and then broke into song again, "Joshua fit the battle of Jericho, Jericho, Jericho!"

When he finished he asked, "Deal?"

"We only have ten days," she reminded.

"So what? God created a whole world in six days! Horowitz should be able to accomplish a little thing like this in ten days. Mrs. Washington, please, say you'll help. Say it!"

"I'll do my best," she promised.

PART
IV

Chapter Twenty-one

"Streeeeetch," Mrs. Washington said as she applied extra effort to force Horowitz's arm up and over his head. He forced himself to extend his arm further and higher than he ever had before. Finally after six tries, on the seventh, eighth, ninth, and tenth he succeeded and then breathed a sigh of great accomplishment.

"Ho-ho-ho," he exclaimed. "Not bad, Mrs. Washington, not bad. Next!"

"Sit up!" she commanded. "Roll on your side and sit up!"

He rolled onto his left side, slid his bent right leg across his left, then maneuvered himself into a sitting position. It was a slow labored move.

"Try it again!" she commanded.

"I did it, didn't I?" he resisted.

"Do it again. But faster, with more zip!" she insisted.

"Zip?" he repeated sarcastically. "What am I training, to fight for the heavyweight championship? I'm the great white hope?"

"Mona!" she threatened.

"Okay, okay," he agreed quickly. No more threats were required.

He tried rolling on his side, sliding up his leg, getting up into sitting position.

"Again!" she said.

"I only have to do that once."

"Again!" she commanded. "Just suppose she came in here when you were taking your nap and you had to do this in front of her. Do it, and do it, and do it again. Until it seems so easy and natural that she would never suspect."

"Okay, I'll do it," he grumbled. "But Rome wasn't built in a day."

"She'll be here in a week," Mrs. Washington said.

He tried it again, and then again. Finally she was satisfied. "Now, dorsiflex!"

"Dorsiflex, dorsiflex," he muttered as he raised his left foot slowly, lowered it slowly, raised it again and again and again.

"Eight, nine, ten," she counted as she watched. "Now over again. Ten more times."

He glared at her, but he was determined. "Ten more times," he said but he was only able to complete six more. He looked up at her sadly. "Couldn't," he said.

"Tomorrow, then," she encouraged gently.

"Yes, tomorrow," he agreed, but he sounded hopeless. "Maybe . . . maybe Mona won't ask me to dorsiflex. After all, what does she know about dorsiflex?"

"But she'll notice if you drag your foot when you walk."

"Mrs. Washington," he asked hesitantly, "you think I'll ever be able to walk without dragging? Honestly?"

"It's possible," she said.

"Possible," he repeated, nodding his head skeptically.

300

"Possible."

She had put him through the rest of his routine of exercises. Then she prepared his breakfast. She sat at the table and served as a critic while he ate. She had deliberately served him a poached egg on toast so that he would have to use both knife and fork. She had gradually cut down on the padding on his fork handle during the past four weeks. But today he stared down at it and saw that there was no padding at all. He hesitated to try to pick it up, for fear of failing. She watched, cautiously. Finally he made an effort. The fork slipped from his hand, fell to the rug, bouncing onto the exposed floor with a clatter of sound that made him look up apologetically.

"Maybe we're going too fast," he said.

She did not reply but pulled a fresh fork out of her apron pocket. She set it down on the table.

"Again," she said.

This time he was even more hesitant. But under her insistent glare he tried. The result was the same, except that the fork hit the table first.

"We'll have to try again tomorrow," he said.

"We'll try again now," she said, producing another fork from her pocket.

"I can't . . ." he began to protest.

"When you're on the plane headed for San Diego and they give you your lunch, you'll probably be able to manage it," she said sarcastically. "Once more!"

He tried again, failed again, she produced a fresh fork again.

On the eighth try he was able to retain his hold on the fork handle. He held it, stared down at it, admired his grip and commenced to eat, pinning the toast with his fork and cutting it deftly with his knife.

"Eight times," he said when he had finished eating. "It

301

took eight times. How did you happen to have so many forks handy?"

She reached into her pocket and brought out four more.

"You thought it would take me twelve times?" he asked, then added a bit proudly, "and I did it in eight! Goes to show!"

She had made him walk the length of the living room twice before she ordered him to sit down at the table and do his occupational therapy exercises. While he shuffled cards, picked up marbles, and buttons, he asked, "What did they used to call this in the hospital?"

"P.N.F.," she said.

"No, the whole thing," he insisted.

"Proprialceptive neuromuscular facilitation," she informed.

"That's some big name for picking up marbles, isn't it?" he asked. "When I was a kid living in Brooklyn we had a big backyard. We would go out there and find a flat place where there was no grass. We would dig a hole in the ground with our heel, like this."

Unaware, he proceeded to simulate the action with his left heel.

"Then we would draw a line like this." He simulated the action with the side of his left shoe, leaving a mark in the texture of the carpet. "We had to stand back of that line and shoot for the hole. If you got in you won. And if you knocked the other boy's marble in you also won that. I was very good in those days, Mrs. Washington, very good. In fact . . ."

He seized several marbles with his left hand, let himself down from the chair and sprawled on the carpet on one knee, fixed the marble in his right hand between the forefinger and the thumb and shot it halfway across the room. Then he proceeded to shoot another marble in an effort to hit the first. He failed. He tried again and

302

failed. He tried once more. Then another time. On the fifth try he managed to hit one marble with the other.

"I was better when I was a boy," he said sadly. "But I wonder what those kids would have said if I called upstairs, 'Hey, Abie, how about a little game of proprialceptive neuromuscular facilitation?' They would have run me off the block!"

He laughed, then tried to pick himself up off the floor. He struggled and finally extended his hand seeking help. She reached out, gently eased him to his feet. She pointed to his quad cane, indicating that she would not assist him to that. He would have to make it on his own. He moved unsteadily, but just as he was beginning to waver and lose his balance he was able to seize it. He leaned on it for a moment to regain his security.

Sure again, he drummed his fingers on the shiny chrome handle, as he remained thoughtful for a moment.

"Mrs. Washington!" he declared. "Today, we are going downtown!"

"Downtown? What for?"

"It is time for me to get rid of this four-footed animal," he said indicating the quad cane.

"You'll need something," she warned.

"Yes," he agreed, "but this damn thing looks like a hospital. Looks like a sick man. If Mona sees this, she'll be sure I need help. So, after we come back from the park and do the exercises again, we are going downtown."

"This morning the radio said it's going to be very hot," she reminded.

"Hot it could be, but that will not stop Horowitz," he declared. "We are going to buy a cane. A nice, gentleman-type cane."

"There's an orthopedic supply store over on Lexington and Eightieth Street. We don't have to go all the way downtown," she tried to bargain.

"I do not want an orthopedic-type cane, I want something that will impress Mona," he said. "We are going downtown."

"Okay," she finally acceded. "Right after lunch."

"Right *before* lunch," he corrected. "We are eating out today, Mrs. Washington!"

He had remembered a small restaurant on one of the side streets in the fifties, where he would occasionally meet Marvin when his son still had his law offices in New York.

Mrs. Washington watched with furtive trepidation as he set about eating his roasted chicken, using an unfamiliar fork and knife. He caught her when he looked up suddenly, after having cut his chicken nicely. He smiled. With great aplomb he raised the chicken to his lips. But before he engulfed it, he reproved, casually as he could, "You're not eating, Mrs. Washington."

She knew it was safe to begin her own lunch.

When they had finished their main course, he leaned across the table and asked confidentially, "I want you to do me a favor, Mrs. Washington?"

"Yes?" she responded, puzzled.

"Every time one of the waiters wheels that dessert cart down the aisle, I notice there is a big, beautiful chocolate eclair on it. The chocolate is shiny. The custard is oozing out of it. And I am dying for a bite of it. But knowing what a tyrant you are, you won't let me have one. Too much cholesterol. So would you order one and give me just one bite? Just one?" he pleaded.

"Mr. Horowitz . . ." she began to protest.

"Was I a good pupil today? Am I working hard, extra hard, to save your job for you? Then do this for me? Please?"

She finally nodded. Horowitz turned and snapped his fingers briskly, the fingers of his right hand, of course.

304

"Garçon, Mrs. Washington would like some dessert with her coffee!"

"The first bite or the last?" she asked as her fork was poised over the chocolate-coated pastry.

"When I was a kid, we had a French bakery on the corner. Actually it was run by a man named Schmidt. But Germans were not in style then. It was right after World War One. And his wife made the most delicious chocolate eclairs. But the ends were always crusty. The juiciest part was in the middle. So when you get to the middle, that's my bite."

He admired her as she ate. She was a neat person, and very proper. In that way she was like Hannah. He became so engrossed in watching her eat, and admiring her regular, strong features that she took him by surprise when she announced, *"Now!"*

He realized she was exactly at the geometric center of the choice delicacy. He reached for her fork; she passed it to him in such a manner that he had to grasp it with his left hand. He hesitated, then said, "What the hell!" He reached, took it, a bit unsure, then fought against those imaginary rubber bands that still exercised a restraining hold on him. He fastened his hand on it. He cut into the soft, flaky pastry, watching the rich golden custard ooze out. He dabbed his bite of pastry in the custard, soaking up as much as he could manage, and brought it to his mouth. He chewed it slowly, savoring every morsel. He enjoyed the fragrance and the taste of the rich dark chocolate. He savored the soft, sweet creamy custard with every tastebud of his mouth.

When it was gone, he breathed a connoisseur's sigh of approval. "Not exactly Schmidt's, but not bad. Not bad," he said, still retaining his hold on the fork.

The look of longing on his face overcame her. She suggested, "Maybe one more bite wouldn't be too much.

You're having broiled fish and a baked potato for dinner."

He managed the second bite and seemed to have discovered even more delight in it than the first. He chewed it slowly, recalling the fragrance of Schmidt's French Pastry Shop. For a moment he was a boy again.

"Done," he whispered. "Mrs. Washington, you are a woman of great understanding, fine character. That was a *machayah*. Do you know what a *machayah* is?" he asked, prepared to explain.

"It was what Mr. Rosengarten used to say when he had my potted brisket and kasha."

A look of new admiration and surprise came over Horowitz's lined, scarred face. His blue eyes lit up in anticipation. "You . . . you can make kasha?"

"It's not that difficult," she said modestly.

"Not that difficult?" he argued. "You should see some of the kasha I've had in some kosher restaurants. Kernels hard as bullets. You could shoot them better than eat them. Tell me, how does yours come out? Each brown kernel soft, and yet separate? Some women, they make it soft, but it's like mush. I like a kasha should be soft to the tongue, yet you should feel each grain. Better than caviar! Of course, just as important as the kasha is the gravy. It should be a rich brown, with golden fat floating on top, and some browned onions in it. And the beef itself should have a little fat around the edges. . . ."

He could see her eyes staring through those silver-rimmed glasses.

"I know," he admitted like a boy whose illicit daydream had suddenly been exposed, "too much cholesterol in the meat and the gravy. But kasha without gravy is like . . . like . . ."

As he groped for a comparison, she suggested, "Like gefilte fish without horseradish?"

"Exactly!" he said. "Mrs. Washington, you not only

306

have the soul of a gourmet, but the words of a poet." He could not relinquish the thought, "So you can make kasha. My, my."

He had paid the check, and they were out on Fifty-Third Street. "And now," he announced, "Saks Fifth Avenue!"

The clerk was a young man who evidently had not had much experience selling canes. He took his cue from Horowitz's quad and produced an aluminum cane first. Horowitz banished it with a look of complete disdain.

"A cane like that should be part of a set. Cane, cup, and a few pencils. I wish something to use on informal occasions, yet shouldn't look out of place in the evening if a person is going to the theater."

"The aluminum one might be safer," Mrs. Washington whispered.

"You may be looking for safe. I am looking for sporty," Horowitz replied with great aplomb.

The clerk took three more canes out of the rack. One with a shiny bone handle, a second of fine light-colored malacca, the third with a padded leather handle. Horowitz leaned on each, and each one seemed to please him, though to Mrs. Washington he seemed to be a bit unsteady on them. But he was so determined, she had not the heart to contradict him.

He had narrowed it down to the malacca and the one with the leather handle, when he suddenly spied a gnarled Irish cane in the corner of the case.

"Let me see that one!" he commanded suddenly.

"That's more a shillelagh than a cane," the clerk protested.

"Let me see it!" Horowitz demanded. Once the clerk handed it to him, he fondled it, held it off to admire it. He leaned on it, while staring at himself in the mirror. "Sir Harry Lauder," he exclaimed.

307

Both Mrs. Washington and the clerk were baffled.

"Harry Lauder," Horowitz exclaimed. "I saw him when he made his twelfth farewell appearance in New York. He used a cane like this."

Horowitz began to sing, "Didi di di didi," while he attempted to imitate Sir Harry Lauder's jig until he almost lost his balance and needed assistance from both the clerk and Mrs. Washington. When he had regained his balance, to draw attention away from his near disaster he asked, "You didn't recognize that song? That was 'Roamin' in the Gloamin.'" He began again to chant, "Didi di di didi." Until he realized that other customers had gathered to observe him.

Briskly he said to the clerk, "I'll take this one!" as he brandished the gnarled old cane.

"Charge and send?" the clerk asked.

"What's the matter, cash has gone out of style? How much?" Horowitz demanded. "And I will take it with me. I have a little . . . a little practicing to do!"

That evening, after Mrs. Washington had left, Samuel Horowitz used his quad cane to shuffle out to the foyer where his new acquisition rested in the carved antique umbrella stand, which had been one of Hannah's prize possessions. He lifted the gnarled-headed cane and stared at it admiringly.

It had exactly the jaunty look that he would like to affect when Mona arrived. It would add just the right informal touch to convince her that he was a man capable of being on his own. A man who really had no great need for a cane but affected one because it added a touch of jauntiness, more for appearance than necessity.

But to carry it off, he would need to be able to handle it properly, easily, with an accustomed air. Since he now had only a few days left to accomplish that feat he had better begin at once.

He shuffled back to the bedroom to test himself before the full-length mirror there. Still leaning on the quad for support he gripped the gnarled top in his left hand. It would have been easier, he realized, if it had a handle like the leather-covered one. Perhaps he had made a mistake about that. But nevertheless he could grip it, and he fixed it firmly on the carpet and pretended to rest his weight on it.

He liked the look of it. It brought back more memories of the florid, robust little Scotsman, in his kilt and that funny brush he wore in front. Sir Harry Lauder. Sir Samuel Horowitz, he said to himself, as he grew bolder and waggled the cane a bit to present a more relaxed image.

Then he decided, why not? He pushed his quad aside, shifted the cane from his left hand to his right, took a firm grip on it, and rested his full weight on it. By God, he could stand without that four-footed ally! He could indeed!

Exultation led him to become a bit careless for he began to lose balance, and when he reached desperately for his quad, he realized he had shoved it aside too far.

He fell forward, narrowly missing the sharp corner of the chest of drawers and landing face down on the thick buffer of bedroom carpet. He lay there a moment, then dared to reach up to feel his face. His hand came away dry. Thanks God, no blood. He struggled to sit up, then he clung to the chest of drawers and lifted himself carefully to his feet. He barely reached the quad from there. Once he had resurrected himself, he stared down at the gnarled old cane on the carpet, and wondered, when the time came, would he be able to manage it, or would he have to greet Mona with that damned quad?

He surrendered himself to his bed with great relief. He did not even attempt to watch television. He was far too tired from what had been the most taxing day he had had since he returned from the hospital.

The doubled regime of exercises, the trip downtown, his near brush with disaster, had left him exhausted.

He fell asleep repeating to himself, I am a Hebrew but I am not aged.

Well, at least, not that aged, he protested before he finally went off.

Chapter Twenty-two

"Try it once more," Mrs. Washington said. She watched critically as Mr. Horowitz started across the foyer carpet leaning on his gnarled Irish cane. He walked with a labored gait, not so shuffling as he did a week ago, but there was still that inevitable drag of his left foot on the costly high-pile carpet. Mrs. Washington shook her head sadly.

"No?" Horowitz asked.

"I'm afraid not," she had to admit.

"I'll try again."

"I think that's the trouble, you're trying too hard and too much. You're overtired," she said. "Rest a while. And then we'll see."

Dejected, Samuel Horowitz relaxed and had an even more difficult time making it from the foyer into the living room, where he sank into a soft easy chair. He sat with his two hands resting atop the knob of the old cane, on his face a look of defeat. He nodded his head sadly.

Because she felt sorry for him, Mrs. Washington refrained from commiserating with him. He feels sorry enough for himself, she thought. I had better do something to give him a lift.

"Mrs. Washington," Horowitz suddenly began, "sit down!" She hesitated. "Why is it, in this house, you hardly ever sit down?" he demanded angrily. "What am I, Simon Legree? I'm going to bite your head off if you sit down? We are two human beings with a problem. We should discuss it. People discuss better sitting down than standing up. So sit!"

Still Mrs. Washington waited. He realized that in his defeated state he had been issuing brusk orders. He moderated his tone. "Mrs. Washington, would you care to sit down?"

"Thank you, Mr. Horowitz." She took a chair opposite him. "Now . . ." she opened the discussion.

"Mrs. Washington, I will make a confession to you," he began uneasily. "Underneath this reasonable exterior I am a very stubborn man."

"No!" she declared, trying to affect surprise.

"Oh, yes," he insisted. "In fact, even Hannah used to say, 'Sam Horowitz, you are one of the stubbornest men I ever knew.'"

"Hannah said that? I wonder why."

"But . . ." and he paused for dramatic effect, "but, I repeat, there comes a time when a man has to ask himself, Am I being too stubborn? So that is the question. And I want a frank answer from you, Mrs. Washington. Am I being too stubborn about this? Too . . ." he paused before he used the word, "proud? Tell me the truth, am I?"

She knew how much it cost him to ask this question, so she thought carefully before she responded. He mistook her silence for an answer.

"I know, you don't want to hurt my feelings. You don't

312

want to discourage me. But admit it, you think this whole thing with Mona is just a stubborn old man fighting off the inevitability of old age. I can't do it, is that what you are afraid to say? You think I'll be angry with you. You think I should just pack it in, give up this place, this city, my home for all these years, go west with Mona. And get ready to die."

"No, Mr. Horowitz," Mrs. Washington said. "I don't think so."

"You're only saying that to make me feel better."

"No, I mean it," she insisted.

"Then, tell me, why can't I do it? Why can't I feel right with this cane? Why can't I make this damned leg and this foot do what I want? Why do I have this terrible picture in my mind that the doorbell will ring, I know it will be Mona, I will try to go to the door and then right in the middle of the foyer I will trip and fall. And she will find me, her father, who she depended on through much of her life, a helpless . . . cripple . . . lying on the floor. Do you know what that would do to her?" he asked.

Then in a softer, but more pained voice, he continued, "Do you know what it would do to me?"

"Yes, I know," Mrs. Washington admitted.

"Then what would you suggest? I give it up? I forget it? I surrender and become one of the aged Hebrews?"

"No."

He studied her, trying to see whether pity had forced her to resort to deception. Her black eyes were firm and honest behind her silver-rimmed glasses.

"I think," she began, "I think you are tired from trying too hard. You must rest more. Resting is as much preparation as exercising."

"We only have three more days," he pointed out.

"You are better now than you were seven days ago," she argued. "Much better. The padding on your fork is gone and you can handle it."

313

"It's not easy," he disputed in his singsong. "Not because you can't do it, but because you don't think! Think before you do! Remember how in the early days you would forget to put your left arm through your left sleeve?"

"And forget to tie my laces," he added.

"Because you didn't think. Like most left hemis you rush to do things without thinking. If you think first, I believe you can make it."

"Mrs. Washington, if you believe I can do it, then I will think and I will try. Let's rehearse again!"

"No, let's just sit quietly and rest for a while."

"Will you sit here with me and rest, too?"

"If you wish."

"I wish," he replied, admitting, "Except for exercises and a little pinochle, most of the time you're off there somewhere doing something—cleaning, cooking. As if you're avoiding me. I need company, Mrs. Washington. I am actually," he hesitated to confess, "a lonely man. It was one thing when I was able to get about on my own. I could go out and feel the city. I could walk in the park, see children at play, go to the zoo, watch the animals. Watch the children watching the animals. I wasn't part of their lives, but I was part of life. Now, in my condition, it's no longer the same. And if they take me away from my city, to some strange place where I know no one, it will be even worse."

There was a moment of silence, a silence so deep that from far below they could hear the traffic of midday, and an occasional automobile horn impatiently insisting on the right of way or protesting someone else's right.

"Mr. Horowitz, if I may . . ." she began.

"May, may!" he granted anxiously.

"You've made *yourself* a lonely man these past weeks."

"I?" he defended. "I did this to my face? I got myself

314

mugged? I went looking to have a stroke?"

"Liebowitz has called. Six times. Mrs. Braun on the fourth floor called to ask if she could come up and say hello. That Mrs. Clevenger stopped by one day when we were in the park to ask you to come to dinner. You refused."

Mrs. Washington had tried to be as gentle as she could be. She hoped she made her point without arousing in him his defensive anger. When he replied it was in a soft voice that pleaded for understanding.

"Mrs. Washington, it's very hard for a person who has not been through this. Six months ago I would not have understood it myself. But I can't face these people. Liebowitz, a man I have known for forty-four years. We played pinochle together a thousand times. Walked together. Went to *schul* together. Visited each other's homes. Our wives were friends. *But* he has never seen me like this.

"I don't want him staring at the scar on my face when he should be looking at his cards. I don't want him to see me try to pick up a card with my left hand and not be able to do it the first time or two. Don't you understand, I refuse to be pitied.

"As soon as a Jew begins to pity himself, the battle is lost. A Jew must be strong, firm, proud! Unless a Jew feels he is better than anyone, the world will treat him as if he is worse than anyone. We have seen it too many times, too many times," he said sadly.

"Do you mind *my* seeing you this way?" she asked.

"With you it's different," Horowitz admitted. "You understand. When I'm with you I don't feel that you're staring at my face, at my scar. And also, Mrs. Washington, one other thing . . . you have never seen me any other way. This is the Horowitz you know and so accept. But those others . . . those others . . ."

"Mainly Mona?" Mrs. Washington asked.

315

He nodded, a bit reluctant to admit, "I think the trouble is, I want to prove something to her. But I'm afraid to face her. How can I show her, if inside there is only fear? Can you understand?"

"Yes."

"So what do you think?"

"I think we have rested enough and it is time to exercise again," she said resolutely.

He glared at her, then smiled, "Mrs. Washington, you are a tyrant. But a very smart tyrant. Yes, I think it's time."

He rose from the chair with the aid of his gnarled cane. Self-consciously, he asked, "You think, maybe I *was* pitying myself a little there?"

"A little," she said.

He glanced at her bright, black eyes, but said nothing.

Samuel Horowitz crossed off another day on his calendar. Two days, only forty-eight hours, before Mona arrived. He evaluated his chances. Certain things he did better, considerably better. The days of doubled exercise had yielded results. If he paused to think, he managed his table utensils very well. And the cards, the buttons, the marbles. But walking on that cane still presented a problem.

Dorsiflex, dorsiflex, he kept repeating silently. If his foot would only respond as it should.

He stared at his face in the mirror as he shaved with the electric razor. His daily time in the sun each day had done much to give him a nice even tan, which served to diminish that scar somewhat. But it remained reddish and pale compared to the rest of his cheek.

He smiled. The scar fell in with the crease in his lean cheek. But he could not sit there and smile like an idiot throughout the time Mona was here. She would surely notice the scar. But, he argued, you can't force a man to move to San Diego just because of a scar. It would all be decided by his walking, his eating, and the total sense that he was still a man on his own after a stroke that had passed.

He was ready for his daily foray into the park. He came out of the bedroom and found his wheelchair waiting near the door. In a single capricious instant, he made a resolve. Damn it, he said to himself, today no more chair for going out!

"Mrs. Washington!"

From the kitchen she called back, "Just as soon as I start the dishwasher, I'll be ready."

By the time she came to the door he was standing with his right hand on the cane and his left on the doorknob. The look of surprise on her face made him explain with a smile, "No more chair!"

"It's quite a distance," she pointed out. "To the elevator, across the lobby, to the corner, across the street, into the park."

"You are talking to a man who only six months ago used to walk four miles every day. Sometimes even in the rain."

"If you think you can, then fine!" she agreed, though inwardly she was a bit apprehensive.

Angelo was startled when he opened the elevator door. His surprise gave way to a big smile. "Ah, Mr. Horowitz, no more chair! *Bueno, bueno!*"

With dignity, Horowitz slowly entered the car and attempted to appear quite casual as he rested on his Irish cane. But he took advantage of the comforting support of the back wall of the elevator. He made his way slowly across the lobby, with Mrs. Washington at his side. When he came to the three steps up to the street level, he paused. For now he had to reconsider, should he seize the railing with his left hand and retain the cane in his right? Or was he stronger if he shifted the cane and reversed the procedure? He decided to grasp the rail with his left hand.

He raised his right leg, while he felt his left tremble a bit. Then he raised his left leg to the first step. Two more times he repeated the procedure. Juan, the doorman, watched with great apprehension, ready to leap to assist if necessary. To himself, Horowitz said, I won't give the sonofabitch the chance!

He made it to the street level. Then, relaxing after his accomplishment, in his momentary euphoria, he forgot the raised white marble doorsill, and his left foot did not clear it, causing him to totter. Juan was there to catch him.

"Thank you, but I'm fine," Horowitz said, fending off all aid once Juan had saved him from falling.

His journey to the corner was slow and more thoughtful, chastened by the near catastrophe at the door. When the traffic light changed, Horowitz and Mrs. Washington started across the street. He made his way slowly. She hovered protectively to fend off any anxious motorist who might try to move once the light turned against them. Though Horowitz did not make it on a single green light, the cars respected his difficulty and waited patiently.

Once on the park side of the street, Horowitz paused to catch his breath and look back at the distance he had traversed. It could not have been more than fifty paces. It felt like a mile.

They found a bench in the sun. He raised his face, seeking to earn as healthy-looking a tan as possible for his big test on Monday.

"Did you decide on the menu?" he asked suddenly.

"For dinner you're going to have a small steak with broccoli . . ."

He interrupted, "I was thinking about lunch with Mona."

"Oh, that menu."

"It has to be correct. By correct I mean, healthy or not, it has to look and taste like it's healthy," Horowitz said. "She is a fanatic!"

"What would you suggest?" Mrs. Washington asked. "Chicken? White meat of turkey? They're very low in cholesterol. Unless you want fish. Fresh broiled fish with just a touch of margarine has practically no cholesterol at all."

"And no taste either," Horowitz complained.

"If you want to make an impression on her," Mrs. Washington urged.

"Chicken, she'll insist it be naked. White meat turkey, without a little gravy or Russian dressing, what is turkey? And fish, broiled with a little margarine, oy," he assessed. "I can remember years ago when Hannah used to serve fish every Friday night. She would get flounder, big slices, with the bone still in. She would bread it and fry it in sweet butter. It was so delicious that I couldn't wait till the next day to have it cold for lunch. They don't make fish like that anymore, Mrs. Washington. Now, it's a piece of broiled fish with a touch of margarine. Some days you wonder why people fight to stay alive."

His long harangue over, he came to a sad conclusion, "Okay, some plain fish. What else?"

"Cottage cheese. Low-fat cottage cheese," she suggested. "On a bed of lettuce."

"Low-fat cottage cheese you should serve on a bed of pain," he grumbled. "What first?"

"Fresh fruit salad?" she asked. "I can do a very nice strawberry and orange salad."

"With a little sugar and cream?" he asked. Then corrected himself, "No, Mona sees white sugar and cream, she would get a court order to make me go to California. Just plain strawberries and orange slices. Then dry fish, dry toast, dry cottage cheese and dry

319

lettuce. What's for dessert?"

"Angel food cake. Very low in calories and cholesterol," Mrs. Washington said. "It's made from the white of egg."

"I thought it was made from glue," he said. "But it tastes just bad enough to look healthy. Okay, angel food cake. With Sanka. And skimmed milk, of course."

"Of course," Mrs. Washington agreed.

"Settled!" he proclaimed. But in a moment, he suffered an afterthought. "Mrs. Washington, dry fish, low-fat cottage cheese, there must be some way to . . . look, with the dry toast, what if you served a little butter. Just to help the rest of the food go down."

"Butter?" she questioned critically. "What would Mona say?"

"Well, this could be a little tricky," he explained, "but we can do it. Suppose, just suppose, we take a stick of butter and let it get soft. Then we take an empty little tub, the kind that margarine comes in. When the butter is soft enough you simply put it into the tub, flatten it out. Who's to know it's butter and not margarine? Hmm?"

Mrs. Washington resisted such deception.

"Please, Mrs. Washington, after all, I'm eating all that other stuff that's supposed to be good for me," he argued.

"I'll see," she finally promised.

The sun had become too strong. Mrs. Washington decided that they had better cut short their stay in the park. He made it to the corner. They waited for the light to change. Horowitz shuffled across the street, slowly, but with determination, for he could see Juan standing under the canopy watching him. I won't give the sonofabitch the satisfaction of seeing me stumble this time, Horowitz urged himself on. They had reached the canopy. Juan was smiling.

320

"*Terrifico!*" he cheered.

"Not bad," Horowitz admitted with a proper degree of modesty.

"Can I . . ." Juan began to offer.

But Horowitz said, "I can make it!"

Still Juan lingered close just in case. But slowly, thoughtfully, Horowitz managed the three stairs and was safely down in the lobby. There, it was his misfortune to confront Mrs. Fine, the widow on the third floor, whom he had not seen since the day his difficulties began.

"Mr. Horowitz!" she exclaimed. "My God, you look like you just came back from Florida. Such a color! And I heard you weren't doing so well. Just goes to show. You can't believe anybody."

"I'm doing fine, Mrs. Fine!" he said staunchly and proceeded to march, straight and proud, toward the elevator.

His preoccupation with Mrs. Fine and the fact that the relief elevator man had not precisely leveled the car caused Horowitz to trip as he entered the elevator. He lunged forward and only the quick action of Mrs. Washington saved him from a fall that could have been very injurious.

Once he righted himself, with great dignity he instructed the elevator man, "Tenth floor!"

They were safely back in the apartment. As soon as the door closed, he leaned against the wall and breathed a deep sigh of relief.

"Did it," he said. "Not exactly perfect, but I did it."

"Very good for a first time," Mrs. Washington encouraged.

"Mrs. Washington, you think, maybe after lunch Monday I should say casual-like, 'Mona, my dear, let's go out in the park for a little fresh air?'"

Mrs. Washington did not answer.

"I know," he said sadly. "I shouldn't take such a chance."

"It wouldn't be wise, Mr. Horowitz."

"No, it wouldn't," he agreed.

Chapter Twenty-three

Sunday was a bright morning. Samuel Horowitz rose early, not so much from a desire to greet the new day as from anxiety. It would be an hour before Mrs. Washington arrived. But he was too concerned about tomorrow to lose himself in the Sunday *Times*. He could delay that apoplectic hobby until later. So he lay abed, reaching out to the radio to switch on the early morning news.

The news ran true to form. They were still trying to find exactly what had caused the blackout, which had led to all of Conrad's troubles as well. Con Ed had by now issued three versions. The Public Utilities Commission, not having been instructed by Con Ed on what to say, remained deliberately vague. The governor and the mayor promised all sorts of investigations.

Horowitz thought angrily, Why is it every crisis ends up in an investigation which goes on so long that it is eclipsed by the next crisis and eventually forgotten? And from Washington, the President was still acting like he was running for office. Someone should sit him down and say, "Jimmy-boy, the rehearsals are over, this is the show. Do something!"

Oh Nixon, Nixon, Horowitz lamented, the worst thing you did to us was not Watergate but Carter. You made people hate and distrust government so much that they believed the first outsider who came along.

The news, aside from the Yankees winning again, was all bad. So, Horowitz thought, with the trouble I have to face tomorrow, who needs to hear the news? He turned it off. He lay on his back, staring up at the white ceiling and watching the play of the sunlight as it filtered through the shutters which Hannah had preferred to drapes. Every so often, sunlight reflecting off the bright work of a passing car lent a ripple of added sunlight and shadow.

Mona, he kept thinking, Mona. Tomorrow is Monday.

He tried to assess his chances. He was already used to his condition and made allowances for it. As did Mrs. Washington. And Angelo on the elevator, and Juan at the door. They could smile and cheer when he went out for the first time without his chair. But to Mona, who had never seen him in a chair or leaning on his metallic quad, walking fairly well with the aid of a thick gnarled cane would not seem so great an accomplishment. Mona would view it as a sign of weakness not progress. And she would have that damned jet standing by at LaGuardia to whisk him off to San Diego. Where, God knows, you probably could not get a decent water bagel. Or a nice tender slice of corned beef with just the right amount of fat around the edges. Or the freedom to walk in the park. Or pick up The New York Times at your front door and get a heart attack by just scanning the editorial page. What other city offered such delights?

Mona. Her very name was a threat.

Horowitz even considered legal remedies. Perhaps he should call some lawyer. But then, since Marvin's firm had always handled what little legal problems he had, he knew no other lawyer. Or maybe he could say he was being kidnapped and make it a criminal case. Then the district attorney would have to get involved. For a brief and wild moment he fantasized struggling while being carried out to that damned jet and screaming, "Kidnapped! I am being kidnapped! Help! Somebody help!"

But, of course, he would never do that. It was too undignified. If Mona insisted, he realized that he would go quietly, resigned to spending his last remaining days in isolation and virtual imprisonment.

One last resolve he clung to. He would not permit them to put him in the Hebrew Home for the Aged. Never! But even that resolve began to weaken when he realized that in a strange city he would have no resources with which to resist.

He came to the sad conclusion that his fate would rest solely on how well he could impress Mona tomorrow. He had better not leave that to chance. He eagerly awaited Mrs. Washington.

He heard her keys in the front door, heard the two locks open with their distinct sounds. He called out, "Mrs. Washington!"

Alarmed, fearing that he had fallen during the night and hurt himself, she came racing into the bedroom. "Mr. Horowitz? Mr. Horowitz?" She discovered him lying peacefully in bed, his hands under his head, as if he had not a care in the world. Irritated at her own emotional response, she asked coolly, "You called, Mr. Horowitz?"

"Yes, I called."

"Something wrong?"

"Today is the day," he announced.

"Tomorrow is the day," she corrected. "Today is only Sunday."

"Today is the *crucial* day. Or shall we say, today is the critical day? Or even the critic's day? Hmm?" he demanded in his rising Talmudic inflection.

She came further into the room, closer to his bed to stare down at him and see if he was quite himself. He stared up at her, out of his right eye, the left closed tight.

"What's the matter, Mrs. Washington, puzzled?" he asked, hoping to provoke her curiosity.

Deliberately, she said, "No, of course not."

"You are and you won't admit it. Just to upset me!" he pouted. "When I make a statement like that the least you can do is ask what did I mean?"

"Okay," she replied, giving every evidence of being bored and intolerantly so. "What did you mean?"

"Today, my dear Mrs. Washington, you are going to be a critic. And I am going to be an actor," he announced. "We are going to have a dress rehearsal!"

"A dress rehearsal of what?" she asked, totally baffled.

"A dress rehearsal of a play titled *Hello, Mona!*"

"Not *Hello, Dolly?*"

He turned on his side to face her. "Mrs. Washington, when it comes to matters of life, death, and freedom, we do not joke!"

"Who's joking?"

"*Hello, Dolly?* You call that being serious in the face of what Walter Cronkite would call an impending crisis?" he demanded. "In twenty-six hours she will arrive. I want to be sure that every detail is perfect. That I am perfect. So today we will, in addition to our other duties, have a complete dress rehearsal. For example, there are many serious questions we have not asked, or answered."

"To wit?"

"To wit," he repeated, "who goes to the door when Mona rings? You? Or me? And if it is you, where am I? And if it is I, where are you? That's a first impression and very, very important. Think about that."

"Let's discuss it at breakfast, or else we'll be so far

326

behind schedule, we won't be able to have any rehearsal," she commanded. "Up, wash, brush your teeth, and get in there!"

"Mrs. Washington, you could make moving to San Diego a pleasure!" he shot back. But compliantly he rolled onto his side and carefully got out of bed.

At the breakfast table, he spent more time holding forth on strategy than he did eating the simple meal she had prepared. While she sat at the other end of the table having a cup of coffee, real coffee, he dabbed at his margarined toast with a bit of sugar-free marmalade. Using his knife as a pointer, almost as a weapon, he held forth.

"Details!" he exclaimed. "In a situation like this, every detail counts! For example, if you go to the door, she is going to ask herself, Why didn't he come to greet me himself? He must be too weak. Also if you answer the door, where am I? Sitting at the window looking out? Or reading? All those are things for invalids to do. A man who has not seen his dearly beloved daughter for almost a year should rush to the door to greet her, *if* he is healthy enough."

"You? You are going to *rush* to the door?" Mrs. Washington asked skeptically.

"It's not impossible!" he shot back.

"Not if you can also change water into wine and do tricks with loaves and fishes," she commented.

"Mrs. Washington, your reference to the New Testament does not escape me. And I might remind you that the fellow who did that, at the time he was doing that, was also Jewish. Later on, what happened, that's another matter. So we are old hands at miracles. In this case, it calls for a relatively simple miracle. There is down at the front door a worthy Puerto Rican citizen of the United States named Juan. If he calls up here to say that Mona is on the way, I can make it to the door without rushing. I will be there before she is there. She rings. I slowly count, one, two, three, four, then I open the door! She wants to think it's a miracle, I can't stop her!"

Mrs. Washington glared at him with the look of a reproving schoolteacher.

A bit self-consciously, he replied, "Mrs. Washington, nobody, but nobody, should have a greater respect for human freedom than a black person. And that's all I'm fighting for. So whatever we have to do, we do."

"So what else?" she asked, unconsciously adopting his intonation.

"Well, there is the matter of lunch. We have gone over the menu. But I could stand a little practice with the equipment. I want you to watch and see if I handle my cup and saucer all right. I mean it would add a little touch of class if, when I have my Sanka, I pick up the saucer with the cup."

"Can you?" she asked.

He turned a bit sheepish and guilt-ridden as he admitted, "Yesterday when I was alone, I practiced. You will notice, there are now three less cups and three less saucers. Not the good china, the everyday kind."

"Could you do it now?" she challenged.

"I could try. You be the critic. How does this look to you?"

He lifted the saucer in his right hand, then tried to lift the cup in his left. But his hand trembled and he could not clear the cup from the saucer.

"Not very good," she said.

"You think maybe I shouldn't try it?" he asked, like an uncertain child seeking parental advice.

"It's risky," she advised.

He nodded his head sadly. To cover his regret at having to forego that ambition, he changed the subject.

"But the knife, the fork, using both hands at the same

time?" he asked. He demonstrated by applying an additional layer of marmalade to a piece of toast. His left hand was a bit unsteady, and she had to caution, "Not so fast. Take your time. It makes you look more confident. More at ease."

He tried again, this time, preparing himself in mind as well as body. Once he had the action under control, he threw in a bit of dialogue as well. "And what is the latest you heard from Bruce?" he asked.

Stunned, Mrs. Washington asked, "Bruce? Who's Bruce?"

"My grandson, of course," Horowitz said impatiently. "I want to be able to talk and do things at the same time. It will make a better impression."

They went through the entire lunch they had planned. Horowitz simulated eating his strawberries and orange slices, his broiled fish and cottage cheese on a bed of lettuce. With the fish, he used both his knife and his fork. On the cottage cheese salad only his fork. He practiced applying margarine to his toast. He did well with the fork on his imaginary angel food cake. When he reached the Sanka, he tried once more to manage the saucer as well as the cup, but gave it up. It was too much, demanding more skill from his left hand than he could muster.

Once the breakfast dishes had been cleared, and his regime of exercises was over, he suggested, "Time to raise the curtain!"

Used to his dramatic announcements, Mrs. Washington anticipated, "You mean from the moment that Juan calls from the front door?"

"Exactly!" he said. He looked around, choosing the spot where he might likely be at the time of Mona's arrival. "Let's see! We have come back from the park. Done the second set of exercises. Worked with those damned cards, marbles, and buttons!" Suddenly he decided, "I don't want her to see the buttons or the marbles. Cards, okay. But we will hide the buttons and the marbles."

Then back to his reconstruction of the scene, he said, "Where will I be? I will most likely be sitting near the window, reading the *Times*. Actually I will just hold it. Because if I start to read it, by the time she gets here I will be so furious I'll forget everything we practiced. So . . ." he said, taking his chair near the window, "I am sitting here. The buzzer rings from downstairs. And I . . ." He was about to rise, when he interrupted himself, "Wait! Wait one little minute!"

"What's wrong?" she asked.

"You go downstairs!"

"Why?"

"So we can time it. I want to know exactly how long it takes for a woman to come from the downstairs switchboard up here!"

"Mr. Horowitz . . ." she tried to interrupt.

"Go! Ring! Take the elevator up! I want to see!"

Shaking her head, she nevertheless complied with his order. She was gone. He sat in his chair, newspaper in hand, and waited. Several minutes later he could hear the buzzer out in the kitchen. He put aside his paper, took up his gnarled-head cane, rose and started across the living room carpet. He felt himself hurrying; he deliberately slowed down. By the time he reached the foyer, though he was breathing hard, he had hit a good smooth stride, his left foot barely skimming across the carpet nap. He was at the door and had almost regained his breath when the doorbell rang. He shifted the cane from his right hand to left, counted to four, and opened the door with enthusiasm.

"Mona, my darling!" he exclaimed, to the surprise and astonishment of two neighbors who were waiting for the elevator to come down again. With a look of defiance to them, Horowitz slammed the door shut. "Well?" he asked. "How did I do?"

"Perfect!" Mrs. Washington cried. "Especially the way you said, 'Mona, my darling!' Sidney Poitier couldn't have done better."

Irritated at her twitting, he said, "I meant the timing! I got there in time. But was I breathing hard? Did you notice?"

"You were breathing fine, fine," she encouraged.

"Okay, good. So much for that," he said. "Now, Mona comes in, she kisses me. Maybe she throws her arms around me. That could be a problem. Because my Mona is, to say the least, a little exuberant. I mean, when she says hello, it is no small hello. . . . And when she throws her arms around you, believe me, an octopus could take lessons.

"So," he continued, "you will go outside. I will open the door. I will say, 'Mona, my darling!' and you will throw your arms around me."

"I . . ." she asked, "will throw my arms around you?"

"Nothing personal! It's only a rehearsal!" he argued. "So go, and throw. Okay?"

"I'll do my best," she said, with an air of propriety that indicated her disapproval of the entire procedure.

She went outside, she rang, Horowitz counted to four, and flung open the door. "Mona, my darling!" This time, beyond Mrs. Washington, he could see Mrs. Turtletaub, the widow from 10A. Still, Mrs. Washington threw her arms about Horowitz and exclaimed, "Oh, Dad!"

Fortunately the elevator door opened and Mrs. Turtletaub disappeared into it, but not without looking back twice.

Under the double impact of Mrs. Washington's embrace and Mrs. Turteltaub's amazed glare, Horowitz reeled a bit and needed all the support his rugged cane could provide. But he weathered the storm and remained on his feet.

"Well," Mrs. Washington asked, "was that a Mona greeting? Or should I be even more exuberant?"

"It wouldn't do any harm to do it once more. Only this time, if you want to be a real Mona, kiss me. Right here, on the cheek!" he instructed. She glared at him. "I won't enjoy it any more than you!" he said. "Make believe you're in the movies or TV. It's part of the day's work."

"I'll try," she said, far from enthusiastic.

"All right. Outside. Ring the bell. Let's go!" he urged.

Mrs. Washington was outside. Horowitz set himself at the door awaiting her ring. When it came, he counted off a slow one, two, three, four. He threw open the door and exclaimed, "Mona, my darling!" As he did, the elevator door opened. Mrs. Turteltaub had evidently returned to confirm her suspicions, for she emerged from the elevator just as Mrs. Washington threw her arms around Mr. Horowitz and kissed him. With that Horowitz could hear a muffled, "Oh, my God! A *shvartzer* yet!" as Mrs. Turteltaub retreated back into the elevator.

He closed the door. "Good, excellent, Mrs. Washington! So much for greetings. Now she is in the apartment and I say to her, 'Come, Mona, darling, let me see you in the light.'" He began to lead the way from the foyer into the brighter light of the living room.

"Turn around, let me see. It's been so long," he said, and gestured for her to turn. Mrs. Washigton complied, twirling like a dancer.

"Good, good! Better than Mona!" Horowitz exclaimed, then hurried on. "Okay, we are now sitting and talking, Mona is asking about my stroke, and so forth. I am answering, making light of the whole thing. Then you come in and announce lunch. Now lunch rehearsal we have already been through. Except one thing. How would it look if I should offer her a cocktail? In those fancy

332

country clubs, they're always having a cocktail before lunch."

Mrs. Washington shook her head disapprovingly.

"No?"

"She knows you don't serve cocktails with lunch. So don't overdo."

"Okay, I won't overdo," he agreed. "Then lunch is over. Now I suggest to her, how about a little cards?"

"Mona plays pinochle?" Mrs. Washington asked, more than a little surprised.

"Of course not. But I could suggest poker. . . ."

Mrs. Washington shook her head.

"Two-handed bridge?" he asked.

"She probably plays bridge," Mrs. Washington agreed.

"Good!" But then Horowitz was forced to realize, "But I don't play bridge. Still, I would like her to see how well I can shuffle cards. Maybe a little casino? Or else, what if while we're talking, I just take the cards out of the box, nonchalantly, of course, shuffle them and play a little solitaire, like it is something I do every day."

"Much better," Mrs. Washington agreed.

"Okay! Solitaire! Meantime she is talking a blue streak. She is telling me about San Diego and why I should go back with her. And I am making believe I'm listening. But all the while I am saying under my breath, 'Mona. you should live so long.' After a while, I tell her, very nicely, but very clearly, that I am fine the way I am. It was nice of her to come and see for herself how well I am getting along but I am not going with her. She'll protest. But I'll kiss her and say, 'Go back home, Mona, to your husband. He needs you. I'm fine the way I am. Me and Mrs. Washington, we can do anything! We don't need anyone else!' Right?"

"Right," Mrs. Washington agreed.

"Okay!" Samuel Horowitz said with great determination.

For a moment Mrs. Washington felt quite sad. Because she felt sorry for him. She hoped things would go as he had planned. He was like a small boy with a daydream. Except that small boys change dreams from day to day and time takes care of all of them. But men as far along in years as Mr. Horowitz were not permitted many dreams, and each was precious.

Chapter Twenty-four

He had been restless all night. Despite the windows being shut against the muggy summer air, despite the steady muffling drone of the air conditioner, he was aware of every street noise, every taxi screech, every distant automobile horn. He had taken his sedative, but it had not worked. Stubbornly, he refused to take another. He lay on his back, hands under his head, mobilizing all the determination he fantasied he would need tomorrow when Mona began to insist he return. She had a way with her, had had since early childhood, of being quietly persistent. Then, if she did not get her way, she could become outwardly firm and dictatorial. Where she derived that trait Horowitz never discovered, surely not from Hannah. Hannah could be firm, but never domineering. Hannah had been soft, gentle. Yet she could be persuasive when she deemed it important. But Mona, oh that Mona.

Well, tomorrow would be a match of wills and skills.

He would not give her the slightest basis for insisting. She would go away knowing, or at least thinking, that he was perfectly capable on his own. At the most, he conceded, he might promise he would come out to visit in San Diego during the holidays. The ten days from Rosh Hashonah through Yom Kippur would not be too long. And it would be a family occasion. So he might indulge her to that extent. But not one day more!

To reinforce his determination he began to do his hand exercises, simulating the movements it had to perform to hold the fork, to shuffle the cards.

He drifted off to sleep finally.

He woke. He lay still, tired from his foreshortened night's sleep. Until he became aware of another presence in the apartment. He listened cautiously, not daring to breathe while making sure of what he heard. Yes, there was someone. An intruder, no doubt. He had heard and read stories recently of a cat burglar in the neighborhood, a person who stole in during the hour just before dawn and ransacked apartments, while the occupants slept through it all.

One victim had wakened, and the cat burglar had strangled her, an elderly woman, seventy-eight, who lived in the block between Central Park West and Columbus. Horowitz wondered if the same fate awaited him. A fine thing to confront Mona on her arrival, her father dead at the hands of a ruthless burglar.

He dared to move his head so that he could hear better. The rustle of the bedclothes sounded like thunder. He lay still. He listened. Yes, there was someone here. Whoever he was, he was moving things about in the living room. Searching, no doubt. For valuables small enough to carry away, expensive enough to be worth his time and his risk. No doubt to buy him a fix for the day, Horowitz thought. That's what they all did, those black bastards, stole to get money for heroin, killed if need be.

Suddenly it dawned on Horowitz, there was nothing of value in the living room, not of the kind that burglars took. In the chest in the dining room there was all that expensive sterling, but in the living room, nothing. Except a few silver ashtrays and a candy dish or two. The whole thing could not bring the bastard more than fifteen dollars, twenty possibly.

A good, experienced burglar should be able to see that without upsetting the place. Horowitz could remember hearing stories about burglars who, incensed by not finding anything of value, vandalized a place out of spite. That's what he must be doing, and Mona coming today. Surely it would prove her case. Living in New York was too dangerous for him. He would be safer, better off out West. He could never talk her out of it now.

Horowitz lay still, sweating freely, wondering what the burglar would do next. Finally the noises from the living room abated. There was a silence, a long silence, followed by other sounds which he could not interpret. A rustling sound, or was it really crackling? Something was being handled for which he could not account. Now there was the sound of a metal object being moved. Aha, a silver ashtray, Horowitz identified. He has decided to take the ashtrays and the candy dishes after all. Thanks God, he was no longer empty-handed and angry, Horowitz thought.

But now he could hear the presence stealthily approach his bedroom door. Horowitz lay still, not daring to breathe. He closed his eyes, hoping that if the burglar thought he was asleep he would not attack him. He had heard that advice many times, over the radio and TV. If a burglar is in the house, pretend you are asleep. Let him take what he wants. No possession is worth your life. So close your eyes, breathe evenly, and make believe you are deep in sleep.

Eyes closed, breath as near to regular as he could manage, Horowitz lay stiff, on his back, like a statue or a corpse. But the perspiration had reached such torrents that it rolled down his forehead, creating a damp halo on the pillow. Still the footsteps came closer. Now they paused at the door. He is watching me, Horowitz knew, he is watching to see if I am really asleep. Do not move, do not cough, do not sneeze. Just breathe slowly in, hold, out, in, hold, out.

Now the steps started into the room. Across the carpet, cautiously they came, so as not to disturb him. The suspense was becoming too intense, too much to bear. He wanted to cry out, Okay, kill me, only don't torture me! What do I care? What do I have to live for anyway? Go ahead, take my life! Only get it over with.

The presence was almost at his bed. He could feel a drop of sweat run down his nose, onto his cheek, and finally lose itself in the pillow. The presence was at the bed, leaning over him. He could feel it staring down at him.

Go ahead, what are you waiting for—kill! he wanted to call out. Instead, he barely opened his right eye, the one he used in tense situations. He could make out the figure, and now the face staring down at him, a black face. Black eyes peering at him through silver-rimmed glasses.

In an anger commensurate with his fear, he cried out, "Damnit, Mrs. Washington! What are you trying to do? Scare me to death?"

"I just came in to see if you were still asleep," she said, startled by his hostile outburst.

"What did you think, I died of a heart attack during the night?" he demanded. "If I die of a heart attack, it will be because you are prowling around this apartment in the middle of the night behind my back!" he accused.

"I wasn't prowling. And it isn't the middle of the night," she corrected. "It's past nine o'clock. You must have overslept."

"I did not overslept! I underslept! I didn't close an eye all night. Not a wink."

"I know how you feel," she commiserated.

"How could you know? You don't have a Mona," he said grimly.

"You have to stop talking about her as if she were some disease," Mrs. Washington admonished.

"I didn't say she was a disease."

"You said, 'You don't have a Mona.' It sounds like 'You don't have a cold, or a hernia, or a sacroiliac.'"

"Do I have a choice?" Horowitz asked. "Because there are two of those I would rather have."

"You don't feel that way at all," Mrs. Washington said.

"I do feel that way at all," he grumbled, then recalling he asked, "What did you mean before, you know how I feel?"

"I didn't sleep all night either. That's why I came in especially early this morning," she said.

"You couldn't sleep either?" he asked, genuinely solicitous.

"Tossed and turned."

"Me, too."

"Thinking about today."

"Me, also," he commiserated.

"So I had an idea."

"Aha! We run away from home together, right?"

"Wrong!"

"Naturally. Have I ever won an argument with you?" he complained. "Tell me, honestly, did Horace ever win an argument with you in his whole life?"

"We're not talking about Horace. We are talking about you. And Mona."

"So what was this genius idea you had in the middle of the night?"

"Get washed, have your breakfast, and I'll show you," she said.

"Okay, Gauleiter, I will follow orders. Meantime, what

339

was all that noise out there? Were you ransacking the place?"

"Wash! Breakfast!" she commanded.

He glared at her. "Just because you now have roots does not mean you own the world, Mrs. Washington!" Nevertheless he obeyed and started to get out of bed.

He had finished his breakfast and called to her, "Now, Mrs. Washington?"

She came out of the kitchen, wiping her hands on her apron, for she had been preparing the lunch she would serve when Mona arrived.

"Now?" he asked. "Your big terrific idea?"

"Come with me."

"We're going someplace?"

"Just into the living room," she said.

Seizing his gnarled cane, he lifted himself to his feet and made his way to the archway of the living room. There he stopped, stared, and let out a shriek, "What have you done? Hannah's living room! She redecorated it only six years ago! And you have destroyed it!"

Calmly, and a bit weary of his hyperboles and histrionics, Mrs. Washington said, "I just moved the furniture around a bit."

"Is that what I heard when I thought someone was ransacking the place?" he asked.

"I thought you were asleep. I tried to be quiet. Well, what do you think?"

"What I think is, Hannah should see this, she would turn over in her grave," Horowitz said.

"The chances of her seeing it are very small," Mrs. Washington pointed out.

Horowitz glared at her. "So this is your big idea?" he disparaged. "Some idea. Overnight she becomes an interior decorator."

"Try it," she suggested.

"Try what?"

340

"Try coming into this room."

"I have come into this room maybe five million times in the last twenty-eight years, what's to try?" he demanded, exasperated.

"Try it."

"No wonder the South Africans are against black majority rule. You people are impossible."

Slowly, using his gnarled cane to good effect, thinking carefully, so he did not allow his left foot to drop, he made his way into the room. His attitude was one of impatient intolerance as he cast disapproving glances at her.

Until, so determined to display his disapproval of her, he began to concentrate less on his walking. His foot dropped and caught and for an instant he was terrified that he would lose his balance and fall. Instinctively, his hand went out seeking support and rested assuringly on the wing chair that now seemed so conveniently close. He held on, regained both balance and confidence and continued.

Once he did, and was alert to his situation again, he began to realize that the furniture had been cleverly rearranged so that there was always a convenient piece to grasp, hold on to or lean against if he faltered. He walked to the window, touching each piece as he went, not for support, but to make sure it would be in the right place if needed.

When he reached the window, instead of staring out at the daylight and the park, he turned to face Mrs. Washington. A bit embarrassed, he admitted, "Not bad, not bad." It was the utmost in praise from Samuel Horowitz. He demonstrated his genuine admiration by going back to the archway again and retracing his steps. The second time he moved a bit more quickly, for he felt more secure. The third time he was even more relaxed and graceful.

He looked about the room, admitting, "And it doesn't

look bad either. In fact, it looks very good. Maybe you should have been an interior decorator! An interior decorator with insomnia!" he decided.

She accepted his praise with no smile, but made another suggestion, "Pick up that silver dish."

He stared down at the coffee table. The silver dish that he could never decide was an ashtray or a candy dish was filled with thin, dark chocolate after-dinner mints.

"Candy? After breakfast?" he tried to argue.

"Pick it up!" she ordered.

He was suddenly confronted by the fact that, standing, his right hand occupied with the cane, to pick up the dish would require a precise movement of his left hand. He hesitated, then slipped his fingers around the edge of the dish but could not quite achieve a secure grip.

"Under," she coaxed gently.

Sliding his fingers under the dish made it possible for him to get a thick enough portion of the dish in his grasp. Now he could hold it quite firmly.

"Now, offer it," Mrs. Washington said, indicating the wing chair where Mona might be sitting.

"Mona, my dear, a mint?" he proffered a bit more graciously than he felt.

"Very good," she enthused.

"Very good?" he countered. "Perfect!" So encouraged was Horowitz that he offered once more, "A mint, Mona, darling?" Delighted, he rewarded Mrs. Washington with one, saying, "Go on, you earned it." When she took one, he took one. "After all, I earned it, too," he declared self-righteously and with a pretense at modesty.

It had been more than an hour since Horowitz executed his rehearsal with the new furniture arrangement. He had done his exercises, worked with his buttons and marbles, shuffled the cards until he felt he had worn them out. He was staring at his watch. He had even tuned in the radio to hear any late news flashes of a private jet that might have gone down on route from San Diego to New York. There were no news flashes. Mona was on her way and nothing could stop her. Horowitz's nerves began to show the strain.

Mrs. Washington was aware of it as she went about her duties in the dining room and the kitchen. She had set the table with the finest linen mats, the Rosenthal china, the solid silver service. She had prepared everything in the kitchen so that cooking and serving lunch would take only half an hour. The fish filets, the purchase of which she had carefully supervised at the fish market on Columbus Avenue, were lying in long white strips on the oven tray awaiting their ordeal by fire, with only a touch of margarine to mitigate the dryness. The fruit, fresh and colorful, was ready in frosted coupes. The angel food cake was resting on a colorful Doulton serving plate which Hannah Horowitz had bought on a trip to England.

As the moment approached, Mrs. Washington found herself becoming as tense as Mr. Horowitz. When it was slightly past the appointed time, realizing how anxious he was, she came into the living room. She found him at the open window looking down, scanning every passing cab, wondering whether it would stop at his canopy.

To distract him, she suggested, "How about a hand or two of pinochle?"

"Pinochle?" he replied vaguely, as if the word were strange to him.

"You still owe me nine dollars and fifty cents," she reminded.

"Nine dollars and fifty cents," he roared. "We played double or nothing the last time!"

"And you lost," she reminded.

"Oh, oh, yeah. I remember now." He took one last glance below and could see no cab pulling up. "All right, one hand, double or nothing."

She watched as he dealt out the cards in approved fashion, holding the pack in his right hand, passing out each card with his left. Aside from a trace of nervousness, he did it well. If she were not aware of his history she would not have noticed any hesitation or defect. When he concentrated, he was rather proficient. If he could remember to concentrate and think before he acted, instead of being impulsive, he should be able to weather the confrontation with Mona.

He had assembled his hand, tapped the stock and invited, "Well, Mrs. Washington?"

She took the first trick and melded one hundred aces. As she neatly laid down the four aces, heart, club, diamond, and spade, he glared at her, "You're doing this to upset me!" he accused.

She played a card. He played one to take the trick. He picked a card from the stock. She picked a card. She took the next trick and laid down a jack of diamonds and a queen of spades for another forty points. He murmured, "Maybe I didn't shuffle the cards enough. Next time . . ." but he did not follow through on what he planned to do next time, for she had just taken the next trick, too.

They played the hand down, and though he had melded fewer points than she had, she pretended to make an error in playing that led to his winning the hand. That seemed to mollify him until he went back, turned the cards face up, replayed the last six tricks and realized what she had done.

"Ho-ho-ho, Mrs. Washington . . ." he reproved in his singsong rebuke.

Caught, she could only smile.

"Doesn't count," Horowitz said. "I still owe you nine dollars and fifty cents. But I appreciate what you tried to do." He confessed, "Yes, I need every little bit of confidence. Every little bit."

"Don't worry," she consoled. "Just get by the first few moments with her and everything else will be fine. But remember, don't be impulsive. *Think.*"

"Think," he repeated, like a scholar learning his lessons for the hundreth time. "There's only one trouble. I keep thinking, the way they name hurricanes after women, there should be a hurricane Mona. She will sweep in here like a tidal wave. She will organize, give orders, pack my things. All before I can even say hello."

"Do you want to run through the living room exercise again?" she asked, only to keep him occupied for he kept staring at his wristwatch.

"No," he replied, trying to give every pretense at being calm. "Like they say, I am ready for the race!"

Rising up from his chair, leaning on his shillelaghlike cane, he defied, "Come, Mona, my darling! I am ready for you! No matter what test you submit me to, I can do it! You want to see a man walk with confidence? I am your man. You want to see a man eat with an unpadded knife and fork, call on Samuel Horowitz! You want to see me shave, shower, and dress with ease, you are looking at him! I defy you Mona Fields! I . . ."

Suddenly, he paused. "Dress!" he exclaimed. "I wanted to be all dressed for her! My best shirt, my newest tie, my blue suit! My God, in all the excitement about the rearrangement of the furniture I forgot!"

He started for the bedroom, a bit too hasty in his determination and had to reach out and steady himself against one of the large chairs.

"Think," he reminded himself. "Think!"

He made his way to the bedroom with Mrs. Washington close behind.

"A white shirt," he ordered, "from the top shirt drawer. White broadcloth. So expensive I never wear them. I am going to leave behind me a fortune of things so good that I bought them and never wore them."

345

He turned to the tie rack on the closet door. "And for a tie . . ." He studied the selection carefully and selected a blue and red foulard, knowing it would be easier to tie than a heavier Macclesfield.

"And this suit," he said, as he selected a blue suit he had not worn in months.

Because it was too heavy for him to manage in his haste, Mrs. Washington picked it off the rack and laid it out on the bed. "Nice suit," she commented.

"My fall funeral suit," he said. "I have buried more friends in that suit than you can count. The suit is still here, but the friends are gone," he commented sadly. "And now, Mrs. Washington, you will leave me alone."

"Right now you may need help more than modesty."

"It isn't a matter of modesty, my dear Mrs. Washington, but I want to do this alone, all alone. Button every shirt button, tie the tie, zip up the trousers, tie the shoelaces. Everything! I not only want *her* to know, but I *myself* have to know that I did it. Confidence, Mrs. Washington. Confidence."

Finally, Samuel Horowitz presented himself for inspection. Mrs. Washington studied him quite critically, making him turn about several times.

"Well?" he asked. "Perfect?"

"Not quite perfect," she declared with a connoisseur's air of disturbance.

"What's not perfect?" he demanded, since she had deflated him slightly.

"I think it would look better if you had a handkerchief in your breast pocket. Horace never went to a funeral without a white handkerchief in his breast pocket."

"Horace was also a big man for funerals?" Horowitz asked.

"He was an Elk," she informed, as if that explained it all.

"An Elk," Horowitz repeated, more confused now than before.

"A member of the Elks. Horace was on the funeral committee. And whenever a member died, he always went to say a few words about how good a member the deceased had been. He went looking like a pallbearer should look, dark suit, white handkerchief."

"I am not going to any funeral," Horowitz declared.

"I still think a breast-pocket handkerchief would look nice," she insisted.

"You and Hannah," he admitted. "Okay, a handkerchief."

Mrs. Washington had just opened the drawer of the chest where his handkerchiefs were contained when they heard the house buzzer ringing insistently in the kitchen.

"Oh, my God!" Horowitz exclaimed. "That's Juan at the front door! She's here! Mona is here!"

In his excitement, he turned too quickly, dropped his cane and was about to fall when Mrs. Washington caught and sustained him.

"Now, remember, *slowly, carefully, think first!*"

"Okay, okay," he said, trying to calm himself as he started for the foyer and the door.

Chapter Twenty-five

Samuel Horowitz was planted at the front door, his cane in a tight grip, his left hand resting on the fat doorknob which he should be able to master with little difficulty.

Come, Mona! I dare you. Do your worst, you will not prevail today! he was thinking.

He heard the heavy elevator door slide back. He heard Mona's sharp heels on the tiled hallway floor. He heard the doorbell. As he had rehearsed, he turned his head away from the door to give the illusion of being in another part of the apartment as he called out in a faint voice, "Coming, coming!"

He took a long slow count of four, readied himself, and opened the door, trying to seem surprised as he exclaimed, "Mona, darling!" while steeling himself for her catapulting embrace.

Instead Mona stared at him. No move, no embrace. Nothing but that stare.

"Mona?" he asked, as if this woman were not his

348

daughter but a stranger masquerading. "Mona!"

Eyes fixed on his face, she broke down. "Oh, Dad, Dad!" she moaned between great gushes of tears.

"Mona, what is it?"

"Your face, what they did to your face!" she exclaimed.

"You mean the scar? It's nothing. Nothing. Mona, please, Mona," he implored. But he could not quench the flow of her tears. "Mrs. Washington!" he called out desperately.

Mrs. Washington came rushing from the kitchen where she had just placed the fish under a low flame in the broiler. "What's the trouble, what is it?" she called, alarmed that Horowitz had been knocked to the floor by the loving onslaught of his overexuberant daughter. Instead she found Mona, her face covered with her hands, and Horowitz shrugging to Mrs. Washington over this unexpected turn of events.

"Well, don't stand there," Mrs. Washington said, pointing to his breast pocket.

"Oh, of course," Horowitz said, reaching for his fresh white handkerchief. "Here, Mona, darling, dry your tears. Meantime, Mrs. Washington, a hand towel wouldn't do any harm either. I believe I mentioned once, my daughter can become very emotional."

Mrs. Washington glared at him to behave.

"Now, Mona, darling, come into the living room, sit down, relax, you'll get used to seeing me like this and it won't bother you. Come, darling."

He led the way, hoping that she would give up crying long enough to admire the skillful adept way in which he traversed the distance from the foyer through that obstacle course of a living room to the parkside windows. Like O.J. Simpson moving through an opposing line, he prided himself, as he made the trip smoothly. And when he turned around to find a glow of assent on Mona's face,

349

he saw that she was only wiping away her tears.

She looked about the room. "It isn't the same," she commented in disapproval.

"We rearranged the furniture a little," he admitted.

"I don't think Mother would have liked it this way," Mona said. Then came a fresh outburst of tears.

"Mona, darling, what is it this time?"

"Mother," she explained, crying more loudly now.

A hand towel won't be enough, Horowitz thought, a bath towel might be necessary. He waited through her second outburst. When she had tapered off to a simper, Horowitz asked, "So how was the trip?" because he could think of nothing else to say.

"The trip was fine. There's nothing like flying in a private jet! You'll love it."

Though tempted to inform her of his decision, Horowitz knew it would be unwise to do so before completing his entire rehearsed demonstration. So he allowed her comment to pass.

"I'm sorry I upset you," he began. "I'm so used to the scar I forget other people have never seen it. Is it really that bad? I mean, when I shave, I hardly seem to notice anymore. It folds into the crease in my cheek. Certainly nothing to cry about. As it was, I consider myself lucky. A few inches below, the doctor said, and it could have been my jugular vein. And that would have meant . . ."

The mention of that dire possibility started Mona weeping again.

"Mona," he pleaded, but in vain, for she had tears as yet unshed and no one could prevent them. Finally, when the flood abated, Horowitz dared to venture, "Darling, you can't take everything to heart so. This is life and things happen and we have to accept them and live with them."

"I know," she assented, sniffling down to a more quiet state. "Dr. Drees says the same thing. He's my psycho-analyst. He says I understand things intellectually. But emotionally it's quite a different matter. Don't you think that intellectually I knew what went through my mind the moment I saw you? I knew about your scar. Marvin had told me. Yet when I saw it, suddenly my security figure was destroyed. Damaged only a little, still to me, it meant it was destroyed. Dr. Drees says I have always looked on my father as a father figure."

"That's fantastic. Your Dr. Drees must be a genius."

"And when my father figure is threatened, well, I just go to pieces. Dr. Drees says that I tend to become too emotionally involved. Not that that's always bad. He says that one of the reasons I am so effective in working for causes and raising money for UJF, Hadassah, and the Hebrew Home for the Aged is that I get emotionally involved. Really involved."

"You must cry a lot these days," Horowitz commented.

"Dr. Drees says that there is a point when emotional involvement results in diminishing returns. That one gives too much of one's self. Like the times I go to visit at the Hebrew Home for the Aged."

To himself Horowitz commented, she has mentioned that place again. I am no Dr. Drees but I can see what is uppermost in her mind.

Unaware of his suspicions, she continued, "I don't believe that just raising money is enough. If you care, really care, about those old folks, you want to get to know them, spend time with them. Make special visits on holidays. This year I went to the first night's seder. Since Bruce and Candy are away at college, we don't do Passover at home anymore."

"You don't *do* Passover," Horowitz commented.

"So I went to the seder at the Home. I mean *the* Home. It's a magnificent new building. In the last report on homes for the aged, ours was judged the newest, best-equipped in the entire country, Jewish or non-Jewish. You'll see!"

Horowitz thought, Mona, my darling, my fondest wish

351

for you is that you should live so long.

"But care isn't just buildings, beds, and television sets. It's involvement, genuine involvement. So I went to their first night's seder this Passover. It would have warmed your heart to see those old folks around that long, long table. Those faces! Right out of the Bible! Such character! Such richness of age! Faces no artist could dream up. And to make the occasion, *really* make it, I arranged for one of the boys from our Sunday school to come in and ask the Four Questions. Well, they just loved it. They just sat there and their eyes brimmed over with tears. I couldn't help myself, I cried too. Oh, it was touching, very touching." It seemed the memory of it would cause another flood. But Mona managed to remain in control.

"Mona, darling," Horowitz ventured, "did it ever occur to you that maybe the tears in their eyes did not have to do with that drafted little boy? Maybe there were tears because they were thinking of where their own grandchildren or great-grandchildren might be, and how much better it would have been to celebrate with their own, instead of with a little stranger?"

Before Mona could answer, Mrs. Washington returned and announced, "Luncheon is ready!"

To himself Horowitz observed, every day till now it was lunch, today suddenly it's luncheon. That Mrs. Washington is full of surprises.

"Come, darling," he invited, rising slowly and with a full awareness of the test that lay ahead of him. He must perform well at the table, be deliberate, be careful. *Think*, he said to himself. *Think!*

The fruit cup was quite tasty. Not nearly so tasty, Horowitz complained silently, as it would have been with a touch of sugar and a dab of sour cream.

The fish was sufficiently dry to impress Mona with its healthful qualities. To Horowitz it tasted like uncrumpled sheets of the Sunday *Times* steamed in brackish water. With great aplomb he reached for the butter in the margarine cup and dabbed some on the fish to lubricate it.

"Try some, darling," he invited.

Mona added a bit to her own fish, watched it melt and ooze through the white flakes, turning it a rich golden color. She tasted it and was delighted. "Marvelous!" she exclaimed. "What brand of margarine is this?"

"It's not exactly margarine. It's an imitation margarine."

"Marvelous. So tasty. I must ask Mrs. Washington what brand it is."

"I think it's local. It's only sold in New York," Horowitz said. "In this neighborhood."

"Too bad. I've got Albert on this low cholesterol diet and he's always complaining about the taste of things. He'd love this!"

"I'm sure he would," Horowitz said.

With considerable flair, and with more obviousness than was required, Horowitz proceeded to choose a slice of toast from within the folds of the napkin in the silver bread tray. He broke off a piece. Holding the sliver of bread in his left hand, he buttered it lavishly with the knife he held in his right hand. He examined the buttered toast, and then with a sense of daring and a flourish he dabbed on a few more licks of butter. Without changing hands, he brought the morsel to his mouth and engulfed it.

"Hmm," he appreciated with delight, remarking matter-of-factly, "And to think a month ago I couldn't have done that. It goes to show. Remarkable woman, that Mrs. Washington. She made it possible."

As if to conceal it from earshot of the kitchen, he leaned toward Mona and whispered, "A tyrant. A strict disciplinarian. Tough? Don't ask! But worth her weight

353

in gold. When she first came here I was a sick man in a wheelchair. Couldn't dress myself. Couldn't shave. Could hardly get around. Now, we go for strolls in the park. I have no trouble at all. She's terrific! Only one thing. Her first name is Harriet, but we are not allowed to call her that. Always Mrs. Washington. But she is a miracle-worker. As you can see."

He ended on a note that he hoped would evoke some enthusiasm or at least implied agreement from Mona. But his daughter kept eating with a determination that revealed that she had not been swayed.

When she had finished her fish and cottage cheese on lettuce, Horowitz asked, "A little dessert, Mona, darling? A little coffee? Of course, not coffee coffee but Sanka coffee."

He reached for the silver bell that had not been used in this household since Hannah gave her last dinner party before she died. Mrs. Washington had deliberately placed it to his left so it became a handy and casual bit of proof of how he had relearned his left-hand skills. He rang the bell once, then as if to drive home the point, he rang again. Mrs. Washington answered promptly, and quite formally, "Yes, Mr. Horowitz?"

"Mrs. Washington, an excellent meal. The fish was very tasty, and so healthy. The cottage cheese on lettuce was just right. And now we are ready for dessert, which I hope," he said in a kindly but pointed manner, "is not one of those rich dishes full of sugar and cholesterol. I mean, just because we have company is no reason to change our usual style of eating."

"I think you'll find it quite satisfactory, sir," she said.

She had served the white slices of angel food cake and the Sanka with pale white skimmed milk in the small china pitcher, which looked a robust cream color alongside its watery contents. Mona watched with undisguised approval. She ate her angel food cake, sipped her almost black Sanka but continued in silence.

Meantime, trying to disengage the pasty angel food cake from his upper palate, Horowitz attempted to keep up a steady flow of conversation.

"This cake . . . made from egg whites, did you know that? Egg whites and just a little pinch of sugar. Not enough to be harmful. Just enough to add to the taste. Very healthy. In the Heart Association booklet on diet, this cake is highly recommended."

He took a gulp of Sanka to try to dislodge the lump from his palate. "Yes, very, very healthy," he commented.

Lunch had gone off without a hitch. Mona had found nothing to criticize or disapprove. But neither had she said anything encouraging. Horowitz could recognize that determined attitude with which he was familiar from her early years. When she was most silent, she was most determined. She had never been one of those girls who suffered pangs or pains or headaches with approaching examinations. She merely retired to her room, shut her door, and you never heard from her till the next morning when she went off to school and returned with a perfect exam paper. Mona was a doer. Always had been.

She was also what he and her mother used to refer to as *fahrbissen*. Determined, dogged, unswerving to the point of being beyond all reason.

She has that *fahrbissen* look, Horowitz warned himself. He was sure of it when they were seated out in the living room and she began, "Dad, we have to have a talk. A very serious talk."

Since he had deliberately seated himself at the card table near the window, and Mrs. Washington had made sure to set out the deck of cards in their original box, he was in a position to suggest casually, "No reason why a man can't play a little solitaire while talking, is there, Mona, darling?"

He rubbed his fingers against his thumbs, with the air

of an experienced gambler, then shuffled the cards. Three different ways he shuffled the cards. Thumbs dug down, regular shuffle, and shuffle in the hands for the final cut. Then, with a subtle glance in her direction to see if she appreciated his skill, he began to lay out the cards for solitaire, making neat stacks, always careful to use his left hand to peel off each card and place it properly.

That done, with favorable reaction he was sure, he proceeded to ponder each move in the game while asking, casually he hoped, "Yes, my dear, you were saying?"

"Marvin and I," she began. Horowitz's heart began to sink. For it became clear to him what she had come to say reflected not only her decision but his son's as well.

"Marvin and I," she repeated, "have had several long talks in the past week."

"That's nice," he said trying to seem casual. "Your mother and I were always worried, that you living way out in San Diego and Marvin living in Washington you would lose touch. You know how it is, these days, in America, families only seem to get together at funerals. So you had a nice talk. Good. How is Marvin? And Florence? When I was sick, she was up here to see me once." He tried to divert the conversation.

Undiverted, Mona continued, "And we have decided that the most sensible thing is for you to come back to San Diego with me. We don't want you to be alone anymore. Where you have to go shopping for yourself and be exposed to muggings and slashing. If you get sick again you'll have family right there. And if you need it, there is the best Hebrew Home for the Aged in the country. Where Albert is on the board and we won't have the slightest difficulty getting you in. There are all sorts of advantages."

"Mona," he began, trying to interpose as many practical barriers as possible, "twenty-eight years, your mother

356

and I have lived here. It will take time to pack, to leave, to dispose of things. . . ."

"We looked into that. I already have a broker who'll come in and take over the whole place for a flat sum and dispose of everything. The few personal things you want, pictures of the family, or books, or little keepsakes, those we can arrange to have packed and shipped. In fact, if you like, we can do it now. Pick out the things you want and I'll see they're packed. Meantime tomorrow at ten the broker is coming up here to look the place over and make us an offer."

"Make us an offer?" Horowitz responded. His anger had overcome his fear and concern. "My life! My marriage! My home! And he is going to make us an offer? Absolutely not!"

"Dad, there's no sense being stubborn about this," Mona said. "Out in San Diego the weather is much milder. You'll love it."

"I love it here!" he protested.

"Did you love last winter?" she challenged. "The coldest winter in recorded New York history?"

"I didn't mind," he defended. "I like to take a brisk walk in the cold air. Makes the blood circulate. Very healthy!"

"Walking in the cold, especially against the wind, taxes the heart," Mona corrected. "Any doctor will tell you that. Out there you can walk as much as you like without damaging your heart."

"Out there you have spring? And fall? You have a Central Park, with the colors changing four times a year? I like it here!"

"Dad," she persisted, "it's not a matter of indulging likes. It's a matter of your health and safety. What if something happens?"

"What could happen?" he fought back.

"Another stroke, a big one this time," she warned.

357

"Believe me, out there you'll have the best of care. The Home has special provisions for stroke victims."

"I don't want special provisions," he protested. "I want my own home. I want my own way of life. I want . . . Mona, darling, I want my freedom."

"Your freedom to be mugged?" she asked bitterly.

"My freedom to come and go as I please."

"Dad, we have three cars. And a chauffeur who will be available at all times. He can take you anywhere you want to go. You'll have all the freedom you could want."

"Mona, darling," he began, pushing aside the cards, "let me explain something to you. What good is the freedom to go anywhere I want, if there's no place I want to go and no one I want to see. Here, I have places I know and love. A park. A synagogue. A few stores. A walk I will soon be able to take every day. Friends!"

He had to admit, "Of course, each year there are fewer and fewer friends. And, somehow, more and more widows. But there are still some. Like . . . like Liebowitz. He calls a couple of times a week to play pinochle. Who am I going to play pinochle with in San Diego? Who, in all of San Diego, ever even heard of pinochle?"

"At the Home there must be some men who know how to play pinochle!" she began to insist with that *fahrbissener* quality he knew so well.

"I don't want to play in any Home with a capital *H*. I want to play in my home, with a small *h*," he persisted, but his fear was beginning to undermine his resolve. He kept asking himself, is it this damned sickness? Has it left me so weak that I can't fight back against my own daughter? Am I sicker than I thought? Weaker than I thought? All the work, the effort, the extra exercises we did, Mrs. Washington and I, is that all going to be swept away by this iron-willed daughter of mine? When she was growing up, he would ask Hannah, such a child, where did she inherit such a strong will, such a stubborn

358

streak? And Hannah would smile and say, "Samuel, take a look in the mirror."

Well, if Hannah was right and the girl took after him, how come now she had such a strong determination and he was left with so little when it counted? It could be age, he admitted, it could be sickness. That damned sickness robbed you of more than you knew. Hadn't they told him in the physical therapy classes that parts of his brain also had to be reeducated? But they had not given him any exercises in stubbornness. So he was at a marked disadvantage in this battle of wills.

"Dad, you have to be realistic. This place is too big for you alone. And it can only remind you of Mother."

"I like to be reminded of your mother. She was the best thing that happened to me in my whole life!" he declared. Then he confessed softly, and quite sincerely, "You know, Mona, darling, in this world there are a lot more widows than widowers."

"I know the statistics," she said.

He had no doubt that she did, for Mona was a diligent digger into subjects of even the most remote concern.

"What I mean, Mona, darling, is not to be found in statistics. It is in a man's mind. Of course, there come times when a man feels lonely. No man who was married for forty-one years and loses his wife will not feel lonely. When he does, he thinks of all the lonely widows there are in this world. In this building alone. Nice women. Pleasant women. Anxious to be friendly. Because they are lonely too. So a man thinks, maybe I should encourage one of them, and maybe we could even get married.

"Then I say, no. Because it wouldn't be fair. *To them.* I would keep comparing them with your mother. And no woman on this earth can compare with her. She was a good wife, a very good mother, but most of all a very fine and special human being. I know no woman who could stand up under that comparison. So how can I do that to

359

some woman? Therefore, I say to myself, Samuel Horowitz, if loneliness now is the price you have to pay for having had forty-one years of life with a wife like Hannah, it's a small price. A very small price."

He turned to confront her, though he knew his eyes were filled with tears and she would interpret tears to be a sign of weakness.

"But, my dear, loneliness does not mean that the answer is to run away from memories, from the life I have lived. To some place I don't know, where I will be a stranger and maybe even more lonely. Where there will always be the threat that one day, when it suits you, I will be shipped off to a Hebrew Home for the Aged. In a big limousine, with a chauffeur, of course. But shipped off nevertheless. This is where I want to live, and this is where I want to die!"

"Dad," she began, and he knew at once that he had not softened her one bit. "Marvin and I . . ."

"It's a free country!" he shouted. "I have a right to vote too! And I don't care what you and Marvin have decided!"

At the sound of his voice, Mrs. Washington came racing out of the kitchen to the archway of the living room. "Mr. Horowitz? Something wrong?"

"Wrong?" he asked sarcastically. "There's nothing wrong, Mrs. Washington. Except they want to tie me hand and foot and drag me off to San Diego, that's all!"

"Dad," Mona remonstrated sharply, "you're taking an entirely wrong attitude. We're doing this for your own good!"

Horowitz turned to Mrs. Washington, "Tell me, you black people are experts in this kind of thing now. Isn't there something in the Constitution that protects a person from having things done to him for his own good? Or do we still need another amendment?"

"Dad, be sensible!" Mona found herself shouting now.

"This is no joking matter."

"Who's joking?" he countered, rising from his chair in such a precipitous, unthought-out action, that the gnarled cane slipped from his hand and he wavered, finally sprawling forward across the table, helpless. Mrs. Washington raced to his side to assist him. When he was able to support himself by holding on to the table, she retrieved his cane. He was once more able to stand fairly erect and steady. He tried to strike a pose of relative calm and dignity. But he could read the judgment in Mona's eyes.

"Well, Dad, I guess I don't have to say any more, do I?"

With the taste of ashes in his mouth, Samuel Horowitz had to admit, "I guess . . ." Inwardly, he cursed himself for having become so emotional that he had forgotten the one rule that Mrs. Washington had tried to drum into him for ten days now. Think first, move later. He had lost the battle which he and Mrs. Washington had planned so meticulously, rehearsed so carefully, so many times.

Samuel Horowitz, he accused himself, you are an idiot! You deserve what you get now!

He turned slowly to Mrs. Washington and admitted, "Sorry. I failed. In spite of all your hard work, I failed us both."

"I don't think so," Mrs. Washington said.

"What my dad means is that he is coming back to San Diego with me tomorrow. You will get the apartment in order for a secondhand broker to take over. Of course, you'll be well paid and there will even be a bonus in it for you."

"You don't understand," Horowitz tried to intervene, but realized that it would do no good to explain to Mona about Mrs. Washington, her grandchildren, her daughter's night work, and all the reasons he wanted this woman to remain with him. So he just shrugged and remained silent.

361

"If it would help, we could have Mrs. Washington come out and be with you while you're getting adjusted," Mona suggested, in what she thought was a gesture of magnanimous understanding.

"I'm afraid Mrs. Washington wouldn't be able to go," Mrs. Washington said. "But that's not the point," she said firmly.

"Oh?" Mona asked, resentfully, not used to being talked to in this way by service persons.

"If I may say so, the point is this should be a doctor's decision. I think before you force Mr. Horowitz to leave here . . ."

Mona interrupted sharply, "I am not forcing my father to do anything. After this last little demonstration, I think even he realizes what's best for him. Dad?" She sought his corroboration and acquiescence.

Before Horowitz could agree, Mrs. Washington intervened, "Just one minute!"

"Mrs. Washington, please," Horowitz tried to interrupt to protect her from any loss she would suffer if she incurred Mona's displeasure.

Mrs. Washington refused to be deterred. "There are some things about the patient that even the patient does not know!"

"Such as?" Horowitz asked, now indignant himself.

"Such as," Mrs. Washington continued, "the fact that he has made remarkable progress in the last ten days. So I think he shouldn't make any decisions until he's had a chance to talk to Dr. Tannenbaum."

"I've already talked to Dr. Tannenbaum!" Mona protested. "He favors the whole idea!"

"Dr. Tannenbaum has not seen the patient in almost two weeks," Mrs. Washington pointed out. "I think he should see him now. Before anyone does anything 'for his own good'!"

"Oh, I understand," Mona concluded. "You've got a

good thing going here and you don't want to lose it!"

"Don't you dare!" Horowitz interceded loudly, while cautioning himself not to become too emotional again. "She is a very fine woman! Sweet! Loyal! And very considerate!"

"I'm sure," Mona said acidly. "However, she does not give the orders around here. We both know what's best, Dad, and I think we'd better get on with it."

Mrs. Washington interposed herself between Mona and Horowitz, "I can't let anything happen to my patient without his doctor being notified and having a chance to express an opinion!"

"And just what do you propose to do about it?" Mona demanded.

"I am going to call Dr. Tannenbaum and have him come up and examine Mr. Horowitz!" Mrs. Washington said, as firm in her decision as Mona had been in her demand.

"It won't change anything, but do whatever you feel your professional duty calls for," Mona said. "Meantime, Dad, let's get on with picking out the things you want to save. Household things of sentimental value we can have shipped to San Diego."

Household things of sentimental value, he thought, and wanted to cry out, they are all of sentimental value! Each bit of china and silver your mother selected. Each piece of furniture over which she spent so many hours deciding. Each little bit of bric-a-brac.

Suddenly he remembered the mints! He had forgotten to offer the mints Mrs. Washington had so thoughtfully brought in this morning. But so many things planned this morning had been forgotten. Now he felt too tired to offer them, too tired to do anything but meekly follow Mona's orders.

As for Dr. Tannenbaum, Horowitz thought, he might be my doctor, but Marvin had brought him in, and Marvin had insisted on paying him despite Medicare. Tannen-baum would be a poor witness in his behalf.

So, Samuel Horowitz, go select, choose, pick up a bit of memory here, another there, consign the rest of this home to the hands of that secondhand dealer, whom Mona chose to call a broker.

In the old days, the days of Samuel Horowitz's boy-hood in Brooklyn, a man came along the streets, with a rolled up newspaper in one hand, sagging bag in the other, and several hats piled on his head. He called out, "Cash! I cash old clothes! Cash for old clothes!"

Women would come out of the tenements carrying shabby old clothes and worn-out shoes. The secondhand man would give them small coins in exchange. Then he would stuff the garments or shoes into his bag and continue on his way, calling, "Old clothes. I cash old clothes."

The words had changed, as had the method of solicit-ing business, but now Samuel Horowitz's entire life was going to be traded away like old clothes, for a handful of comparatively small coins. He would become a man without a home, a man without warm possessions, a man without existence. He would no longer be Samuel Horo-witz, human being, individual. He would be Mr. Horo-witz, Mona Fields' father, or Albert Fields' father-in-law. Or the man in room God-knows-what in the Hebrew Home for the Aged.

He had lost the war, and the defeated have no voice in their own fate. He might as well set about doing as Mona wanted.

PART
V

Chapter Twenty-six

For three and a half hours between the time Mrs. Washington called Dr. Tannenbaum's office and the time the doctor arrived, Samuel Horowitz applied himself to the slow, wrenching process of separating his belongings into those he would take with him, those he would give away, and those others, which, for size or lack of personal interest, he would put into the hands of the secondhand dealer.

Mrs. Washington assisted him, quite subtly, not wishing to offer help when he did not need it, but not wanting to run the risk of having him attempt to do those things he was not able to do.

With each item came a bit of memory, sometimes sweet, sometimes sad. But it was all painful to him.

"A man should not be forced to relive his whole life in a matter of a few hours," he said softly.

"You mustn't give up," Mrs. Washington tried to encourage. "The doctor will have the last word."

"The doctor may *think* he will have the last word. Mona will actually have it!" Horowitz insisted, on his knees, digging out of the bottom chest drawer an aging manila envelope. He opened it carefully since the paper had yellowed to the point of being brittle. At first its identity puzzled him but as the old metal clasp broke in his fingers he remembered, "Marvin! Marvin's *bar mitzvah*."

He drew out the artifacts of that momentous day. There was a discolored invitation, engraved on high-quality stationery.

"I remember, Duffy, the printer, did this job. He used to buy all his paper from me. Came Marvin's *bar mitzvah* and he was invited, he insisted on printing the invitations for free. This one I saved."

He showed the invitation to Mrs. Washington.

> *Mr. & Mrs. Samuel Horowitz*
> *are pleased to invite you*
> *to the Bar Mitzvah*
> *of their son,*
> *MARVIN*

As she read the details, Horowitz said, "In those days he was still Marvin Horowitz. Thanks God."

He slipped the invitation back into the envelope and laid it aside, on the pile of those things he would take with him. He continued through other memorabilia, graduation announcements, clippings from school newspapers about some play, concert, honors list or other mention of either Marvin or Mona.

The doorbell rang. Mrs. Washington rose from her knees to help Horowitz to his feet. "The doctor!" she said.

"Mrs. Washington," Horowitz began, as if in panic, but then said no more.

"Confidence!" she insisted in a strong whisper. "You can do it if you want to. But think first, go at it slowly, and you can do it!"

The look in Horowitz's teary eyes betrayed his sense of insecurity and failure. She raised her hand and gently wiped the corners of his eyes. "Those teary eyes of age may give the wrong impression," she said softly.

Suddenly Horowitz grasped her hand and, with desperate resolve, he said, "I'll do it for you. To save your job. And for Conrad and Louise. You'll see! I'll do it."

By the time they had come out of the bedroom, Mona had already admitted Dr. Tannenbaum, who was asking, "Where is he? What's the emergency?"

"I'm his daughter," Mona introduced herself, "Mrs. Fields. From San Diego."

"How do you do, now where's the patient?" Tannenbaum asked insistently.

"Coming, doctor!" Horowitz announced.

Tannenbaum watched Horowitz enter the room, leaning on his gnarled cane but walking in a smooth, if slow and guarded, stride.

"What happened? Another fall?" Tannenbaum asked, causing Mona to react in disapproving surprise.

"Have there been many falls?" she asked.

"More than one," Tannenbaum said. "But he seems all right this time. No abrasions, no contusions. At least no obvious ones."

"Doctor," Horowitz began under the prodding of Mrs. Washington's sharp black eyes, "we called you because we have a little difference of opinion here."

"You called me away from two other important cases to settle a little difference of opinion?" he demanded angrily. "I call that nerve. Sheer nerve! These days doctors, especially doctors who deal with the elderly who have Medicare, are too busy to go around settling differences of opinion!"

369

"You needn't worry, doctor. Send the bill to me! I'll pay it, and without Medicare!" Mona said crisply. "Now, the problem is this: I think, we think, my brother and I, that my dad should come back to San Diego with me. We have a large house. A couple in help. He will have his own room and bath. And Adam to assist him when it comes to dressing, eating, going out for air, and any errands. He'll be very well cared for."

"I don't want to be cared for!" Horowitz protested. "I am not an infant, or an animal in the zoo. I want to stay here and live my own life. Mrs. Washington and I get along very nicely, thank you!"

He seized her hand and held it tightly to demonstrate the unity that existed between them.

"Uh-huh," Tannenbaum declared thoughtfully.

To himself, Horowitz moaned sadly, Oy, those "uh-huhs" can kill you.

"Well," Tannenbaum began, brushing back the wings of his thick mustache, "if the patient has such a strong feeling, we have to take that into account."

Horowitz and Mrs. Washington exchanged glances of hope.

"On the other hand, this won't be the first patient who has overestimated the extent of his recovery."

At that warning, Horowitz's grip on Mrs. Washington's hand went a bit limp.

"Frankly," Tannenbaum continued.

Horowitz thought, There has never been any good news in this world that began with the word *frankly*.

"Frankly, the last time I saw the patient," and here the doctor turned to Mona and began to treat Horowitz in the third person, "his progress was not such as to give cause to be too optimistic. He seemed resistant to treatment. He was not coming along as well as one would expect."

"Exactly," Mona agreed.

"Well, now, let us see!" Tannenbaum declared. "First,

370

we must admit that the climate in San Diego is much milder and more conducive to easy living than the harsh New York winters. Where temperatures can run as low as zero and can stay below freezing for days on end, a patient's activities can be severely restricted. That is a factor to take . . ."

Horowitz interrupted, "Doctor, weather reports I expect on the eleven o'clock news. Right now 'the patient' would like your permission to stay here in his own home instead of being shipped off to the ends of the earth! What am I, an Indian, that you are going to send me to some reservation, even if it's a reservation for high-class Jews!"

"Dad, please!" Mona exploded.

"No more pleases, no more franklys, no more uh-huhs! You want to get me out of here, your dear Albert is going to have to buy this building and tear it down!"

"Mr. Horowitz, please," Tannenbaum started to say, but when Horowitz glared at him, the doctor quickly rephrased his interruption, "I only meant to say, we must not get excited."

"It's my life. And if I want to get excited, I will get excited. Now, doctor, you go into the living room and find a nice comfortable chair and sit down."

"I really don't have much time," the doctor protested.

"So start your meter running and charge me for waiting time!" Horowitz said.

"Dad!" Mona was shocked.

"Mona, my dear darling only daughter, you will also go in there and sit down!" When she refused to move, he glared at her. "Your father told you to go! And when you get there, sit!"

When they had both taken places in the living room, Horowitz came into the archway and said, "And now, my dear judges, I would like you to witness a little demonstration. First, notice that the patient is no longer using a wheelchair. He is not even using a quad cane. This patient is using a simple cane. What Riordan used to call a shillelagh. It has only one foot and yet the patient gets around pretty well on it. Watch!"

Whereupon Horowitz proceeded to walk back and forth in the archway, summoning up every ounce of determination while reminding himself to be constantly careful, think first, move later. In so doing he was able to keep his left foot from dragging on the thick pile of the carpet.

Oh, those days of double exercises, he gloated inwardly, they are paying off now. Watch me, Mona. Watch me, Dr. Tannenbaum. And, mainly, Mrs. Washington! Watch me!

He had walked back and forth several times, using his cane to good effect, and not once having to support himself by reaching for the walls at either end of the archway. Then he turned to them and said, "Doctor, a little exercise in proprioceptive neuro . . ." He could not recall the exact phrase.

"Proprioceptive neuromuscular facilitation," Tannenbaum supplied.

Graciously, Horowitz acknowledged the assistance with a courtly nod of his head. "Mrs. Washington! Buttons, marbles, and cards!" While she produced them, Horowitz proceeded to untie his tie, and then tie it again. When he had finished with that, he said, "Notice the shoelaces! Tied! Both shoes! And the shirt, every button buttoned. With these two hands!" He had leaned his cane against the wall to free both hands, and in so doing felt a moment of panic as he almost lost his balance. But he managed to regain his hold on the gnarled cane before his danger could become obvious to Mona or the doctor.

Mrs. Washington having laid out the paraphernalia on the leather-topped bridge table, Horowitz moved to one of the chairs that faced both his judges.

"What will it be, doctor? A little game of buttons. You wish to see a man, a grown man of sixty-eight, pick up a few buttons? Look!"

Horowitz proceeded to use his left hand to pick up each of a dozen buttons, favoring the small ones to demonstrate his newly acquired skill.

"There!"

Then he directed his gaze at Mona, "Mona, my dear, would you like to indulge in a little game of Chinese checkers? You don't know how to play Chinese checkers? Learn! Some day it may come in handy! Who knows? Some day when you are sixty-eight . . . you never can tell," he warned. Then he invited, "Mrs. Washington? For a quarter a game?"

She joined him at the table. While Mona fidgeted and the doctor kept glancing at his watch, the two older people played a game of Chinese checkers, with Horowitz using only his left hand to grasp each marble and advance it.

Mrs. Washington won again.

"Perhaps a little pinochle, Mrs. Washington?" he invited gallantly.

"Dad!" Mona tried to intrude.

But Horowitz was too busy shuffling the cards to pay any attention. He gave them the thumbs-down shuffle, and the regular shuffle, and then the hand cut. When he had demonstrated those, he proceeded to deal the cards, pack in his right hand, while his left doled out cards one by one, not missing a single one. He proceeded to arrange his cards, using his left hand to shift them around so they were in order of suits.

"Mrs. Washington?" he invited the first play of the game.

"Dad!" Mona insisted, rising impatiently. "The doctor is not here to watch you play games!"

"Games?" Horowitz disputed, turned to Tannenbaum,

373

"Doctor, do you call this games?"

Tannenbaum was forced to agree. "Not games, Mrs. Fields, exercises!" This time he seemed quite impressed. "How long have you been doing that so well, Mr. Horowitz?"

"The last week," Horowitz said.

"Uh-huh," Tannenbaum said, with special significance.

At the "uh-huh," Horowitz's heart sank.

"I don't think it's necessary to continue with the game," Tannenbaum said.

"Oh?" Horowitz asked, waiting anxiously now.

Dr. Tannenbaum was silent for a moment, then he turned to Mona, "Mrs. Fields, this is quite remarkable."

"It is?" Mona asked, puzzled.

"Two weeks ago, when I examined your father last, he was not making the kind of progress we like to see. Because patients who do not progress by the end of the second month or the middle of the third usually do not progress at all. Whether it's a lack of physical ability or a lack of will, by the end of the third month their future is generally sealed.

"That's why when your brother called me from Washington, I agreed that it would be best for Mr. Horowitz to go back to San Diego with you. But what I see today presents a quite different picture. He has regained considerable use of his left hand, arm, leg, and hip. I think he is quite capable, functioning well. If he wanted to, I think he might still carry on with his business. But certainly he is in a condition that makes it obvious he must be allowed to exercise his own judgment as to where he wants to live and under what conditions."

"But, doctor . . ." Mona started to protest, "we can do so much for him."

"Mrs. Fields, the real purpose of all our therapy is to prepare the patient to do everything for *himself*," Tannenbaum said firmly.

"Well, I never . . ." Mona said, but never finished.

"Mr. Horowitz," Tannenbaum said, "I don't know what made the difference, but your progress in the last two weeks has been remarkable."

Modestly, and with a subtle look to Mrs. Washington, Horowitz said, "Doctor, it's all in having the right incentive. When my dear Mona said she was coming East, I said to myself, do I want her to see her father a sick old man? So, out of concern for Mona's feelings, I decided to work extra hard and this is the result."

"Well, whatever the reason, you certainly succeeded!" Tannenbaum said enthusiastically. "I wish some of my other patients could do it."

To himself, Horowitz said, Doctor, if your other patients each had a Mona, they would do it, believe me, they would do it!

Horowitz did his best to pretend great sadness at Mona's departure. He nodded in agreement with everything she said.

"And you'll come out for the high holy days," she went on.

Horowitz nodded.

"Maybe you'll stay a while. The whole ten days. Or even longer," she insisted.

Again Horowitz nodded.

"Disneyland!" she exploded suddenly. "We could go to Disneyland! It's a fantastic place."

Horowitz nodded again, "I didn't know they observed Rosh Hashonah at Disneyland, but okay."

"And at Passover, you must come out. We have the most impressive seder in the temple. Six hundred people!"

"That's almost as many Jews as left Egypt. Except, of course, when Cecil B. De Mille made the picture," Horowitz said, trying to seem impressed.

At the door, Mona broke down and cried once more, as

375

she traced her finger along the healed scar on her father's thin cheek. "Oh, Dad, Dad!"

Finally the door was closed. Horowitz leaned against it, not because he needed support but to listen until the elevator door slid open and closed and he was sure that Mona was gone. Even then he did not trust his luck. He made his way to the living room window and looked down. Only when he saw Mona step into the waiting rented black limousine did he breathe his first real sigh of relief. He watched until the limousine disappeared out of sight up Central Park West on its way toward the airport.

He turned from the window, pivoting on his rustic cane, to find Mrs. Washington looking at him.

"Don't just stand there!" he cried out jubilantly. "Sing! Sing along with Mitch!" And he burst into, "California, here she comes!" Then he added triumphantly, "But without Samuel Horowitz!"

When he realized that Mrs. Washington did not join in his ecstasy, he insisted, "Cheer up! We did it! We did it! Mrs. Washington, this is as much your victory as mine! Together, we did it!"

Moving a bit more spritely than he had a right to, Horowitz advanced toward her, reached for her hand with his left hand. "You know what! Tonight we are going to celebrate! We are going to go out and have the greatest dinner anyone could have!"

"There are the children," she reminded.

"Bring them! Go, get into a cab right this minute and get them. We will all go out and celebrate. A big dinner. Maybe even a movie. Is there some movie the kids want to see? I hear on the TV about a new movie, *Star Wars*. They say kids are crazy about it. We'll go see it. Today I feel like a kid anyhow. So we'll go see a kid's movie!"

He invited her reaction with a big smile on his face, but she remained calm and said, "I think, you've had enough excitement for one day."

"I'm just beginning! I haven't felt this well or this free since . . . since Hannah and I sent the kids to camp and went away on our second honeymoon!"

"I think you ought to rest. Then we'll run through your exercises again. You'll have a nice simple dinner and get to bed early," Mrs. Washington insisted.

"Then tomorrow we'll celebrate, right?"

"I'll see," she said softly.

"Meantime," he said, thoughtful, his eyes twinkling with excitement for the first time in months, "I have to do something . . . anything . . . to express my feelings. I know! Liebowitz!" Repeating it as if it were a battle cry, he started for the kitchen phone, challenging, "Liebowitz!"

He dialed the number. "Liebowitz? Horowitz!"

"Sam! Sam, it's good to hear from you!" Liebowitz said. "I called and called and you never called back so I thought you didn't want to see me."

"Didn't want to see you? What kind of *mishegahss* is that? A man wouldn't want to see an old friend? It just so happens I was busy. Very busy. You know, when you're away for weeks there's a lot to catch up on. So I was . . . busy."

"I understand," Liebowitz said simply.

"Listen, Phil, I got to ask you a very important question," Horowitz said.

"Sam, whatever you ask, the answer is yes!" Liebowitz said. "And if it's something to do with the apartment, if I can't do it, Rose will be delighted."

"Nothing like that," Horowitz assured. "I only want to know if you remember how to play pinochle?" Horowitz aughed.

"Listen, Mr. Wise-guy, three weeks before you went into the hospital, who beat you for fourteen dollars? Do I remember how to play pinochle?" Liebowitz crowed.

"So how's about a little game?"

"Tomorrow afternoon?" Liebowitz suggested.

377

"You got it!" Horowitz sang out. "Be here at four o'clock. You see . . ." Horowitz sounded a bit less exuberant now, "I have some exercises to do first."

"Four o'clock on the nose," Liebowitz said. "Except if you want to come here, then Rose could make dinner for us. What do you say?"

"Dinner? At your house?" Horowitz wavered. It would be the first time he had been to someone's home for dinner since the thing had happened to him. Mrs. Washington was smiling and nodding her head. Encouraged, Horowitz said, "I'll be there right after I finish my exercises!"

He hung up. "You think that was the right thing to do?"

"Yes."

"Rose'll see me like this, the scar, the cane . . ." He began to feel uncertain again.

"Come!" Mrs. Washington said. "Come with me!"

She led the way to the bedroom where she indicated he stand before the full-length mirror. "Now, tell me what you see!"

He stared into the mirror, striking first one pose and then another. He held the cane close, and then held it off at a jaunty angle. He turned to catch a profile glimpse of himself. First hiding the scar, then revealing it. He practiced a solemn face, and then a smiling face.

"You know that young black doctor was right. When I smile the scar almost disappears into the crease. And with my nice tan, it doesn't look so bad. Not bad at all. When you take a good look, if not for the cane, you couldn't tell about the rest."

To prove it, he flexed his left hand, making each finger respond. The vestigial reminders of his incapacity were so slight now that an outsider would not have noticed.

With the pride of a young boy, he remembered, "And I dressed myself completely. Every button. Even the tie."

He looked back into the mirror and said, "Not bad, not bad at all."

Behind him he could see Mrs. Washington staring at him, her black face solemn, her eyes strong behind her silver-framed glasses.

"Can't you get even a little joy out of it?" he asked, as he turned slowly to face her.

"Oh, I have joy. And pride," she said. "I am very proud of what we've been able to accomplish."

"Then laugh or at least smile! Let me see a smile, Mrs. Washington!" he insisted.

She smiled, her straight white teeth contrasting strongly with her smooth black skin.

"That's better," he said, satisfied at last, for it was necessary to him that this woman share his feeling of triumph.

He looked at his wristwatch. "Just about now, Mona should be taking off. Let's go to the window and wave!" he said, laughing.

Chapter Twenty-seven

He had slept late. The night at Liebowitz's had been longer than he was used to. The dinner had been excellent, and it was obvious that Rose was fully aware of his dietary restrictions. Except that at the end of the meal she served a cherry cheesecake, which was the richest food he had had in many months. It was her way of celebrating, of welcoming him back. Not a word was said, but he showed his appreciation by the gusto with which he ate. And she understood.

Throughout the entire dinner, he did not drop a single utensil, even though it was a different kind of silverware and not balanced in the way he was used to.

The pinochle went very well. He won the first three hands in a row, and at the end of the evening had won seven out of the ten hands, putting him four dollars ahead for the night. By that time it was past ten o'clock and later than he had thought.

Liebowitz insisted on going downstairs with him to

make sure he got into a cab. Before he left the apartment, Rose insisted on kissing him. "Don't be such a stranger, Sam. We love to have you. And by the way, if you are not busy Friday night, my sister is coming for dinner. You remember my sister Estelle, the one who was married to the optometrist."

"Yes, yes, I remember," Horowitz said, at the same time saying a silent prayer, Please, God, make this widow a little less anxious so I might like her more.

He had arrived home and been greeted by the relief night elevator man, who had not seen him in many weeks.

"They said you were very sick, Mr. Horowitz, but you look terrific. And such a nice tan. You been to the country?"

"Just around town," Horowitz replied with great savoir faire.

He fell asleep almost at once, not even waiting up to get the weather and news on television. When he finally stirred, he knew it was bright out, later than usual, and he was aware of the bustle out in the living room. Mrs. Washington, good, kind, faithful Mrs. Washington. She is a gem, that woman! How lucky that Marvin found her. That may well have been the most outstanding thing that Marvin had ever done. He must do something to cheer her up. To symbolize their victory. A gift. Maybe today he would dare to go downtown and find something for her.

Tonight he would certainly insist that she fetch the children so they could all go out to dinner and a movie.

"Mrs. Washington!" he sang out. She came rushing to the door thinking he might need help. Joyfully, he held up four fingers. "Beat him! For four dollars! I gave him a lesson he won't soon forget! *Shpieltzach mit Mutke!*"

Then he realized and tried to explain, "It's a Yiddish expression like, don't screw around with Gene Autry!"

"Not exactly the same," Mrs. Washington said.

"Rosengarten?" he asked, deflated.

"Rosengarten," she confirmed.

"Well, whatever! I beat him! And did I have a delicious piece of cherry cheesecake last night? Terrific!"

"Cherry cheesecake?"

"Once in a while . . . once every three months . . . I mean, after all, a man is not made of wood," Horowitz justified. "Which reminds me. Tonight! Tonight is our time to celebrate! Don't forget! You get the kids around four o'clock. We go to an early movie—*Star Wars*—and we go to dinner. Maybe in the park! They say that restaurant there, the . . . what's called . . ."

"The Tavern on the Green?"

"Right! Since it's under new management they say it is very nice. For families, too. So, tonight, that's where we go!" Horowitz declared.

"Tonight?" Mrs. Washington considered.

"Don't tell me you're busy, you got something else to do," he said, disappointed.

"Choir practice," she announced.

"In the summertime?"

"God doesn't take any vacations," she reminded.

"I'm not so sure," Horowitz said. "I heard of a temple so reformed that on Yom Kippur they posted a sign, Closed for the Holidays."

"Mr. Rosengarten told that one fifteen years ago," Mrs. Washington informed.

"Did I say it was original?" he retorted, delighted to argue with her. It was part of their relationship, an enjoyable part. "Now, if it can't be tonight, what about tomorrow night?"

"All right, tomorrow night!"

"Good!" he sealed the bargain, at the same time thinking it would give him a chance to sneak downtown tomorrow after lunch and buy her a gift. He would find

382

some pretext to go alone. A meeting with his accountant, yes, a meeting with his accountant would do.

Horowitz slowly strolled the aisles of Tiffany's, making sure to keep his balance on the green carpeted floor, while at the same time glancing down into various cases where jewelry was displayed. He stopped from time to time to fancy a particularly costly piece of gold set with diamonds or rubies, but he did that only to impress the clerks. He began to seriously consider his purchase when he eased himself over to the simpler solid gold ornaments. There were pairs of earrings that appealed to him but he had never noticed Mrs. Washington wearing earrings. There were bracelets, some of thick gold links, some more delicate and displaying considerable artistry.

He remembered what Joe Gottlieb had told him once. Joe had been in the jewelry business with a store up on Fordham Road until the neighborhood went to hell and Joe went to Miami. "Sam, when you buy jewelry for Hannah, don't buy anything fancy. Handwork has no resale value. Buy simple pieces, with lots of gold in them. Gold by the ounce always has a market. If it feels solid and heavy, that's it!"

So Horowitz concentrated on the simplest, heaviest necklaces and bracelets he could find. Finally he asked to see and feel two bracelets. While he was admiring them, and weighing their heft in the hand, his eye caught a pin that was made of knotted gold rope. Despite Joe Gottlieb, Horowitz was taken by the intricate work in the piece. He could imagine how such a pin would set off one of Mrs. Washington's dresses, which were always simple and of colors like navy or dark maroon. He recalled Hannah used to say, "On a dark dress a little touch of color at the throat makes all the difference."

He would give Mrs. Washington a little touch of gold to wear at her throat.

383

"I would like to see that one," he said, deliberately pointing with his left forefinger.

The clerk set the pin down on the black velvet board. Horowitz felt its weight, which was impressive. He held it out to examine it from all angles. The fine work pleased him, the weight impressed him. He felt sure she would love it. Anything fancier would not be Mrs. Washington. Anything smaller or lighter would not adequately express his affection and gratiude.

Without his reading glasses he could not read the price on the tiny tag. So, at his most casual, he asked, "And how much is this piece?"

"Four hundred and seventy-five dollars," the clerk responded, adding, "Of course, that does not include the eight percent sales tax. Unless you send it outside the state, then there's no tax."

"No, this is going right here in the state," Horowitz said. "In fact I have to give it to someone tonight. So polish it up, put it in a nice box, take off the price and wrap it like a gift. With some red ribbon around it."

"Is this charge or cash, sir?" the young clerk asked.

"Check," Horowitz said. "Personal check."

"Then I'll have to have some identification, I'm afraid."

"Don't be afraid, I have plenty." He started to lay out cards beginning with his Medicare card, his Diners Club card, Master Charge, American Express, voter's registration, driver's license. Though the clerk protested, Horowitz continued, an Avis card, a Hertz card, four cards from four different oil companies, his social security card, his hospitalization card, his Blue Cross card.

"That's quite enough, sir," the clerk said.

But Horowitz continued until he had covered the counter top with cards.

"That's my identification," he said. "And, young man,

384

anytime you want to lose ten pounds in a hurry just leave your credit cards at home."

He had the treasured gift safely in his pocket, clutched in his left hand. Weeks ago, he recalled, he would not have been able to hold that package as securely. Now he stood on the busy, noisy, hot corner of Fifth Avenue and Fifty-seventh Street and looked to his right toward Central Park. He remembered the treeshaded path that began at Sixtieth Street. It was lined with green benches on both sides and was a cool resting place on such a hot day.

He waited at the corner for the light to change to green so he could walk north. He stepped carefully off the curb, and slowly but confidently made his way across the street. Before he had completed his cross, the light blinked its warning: Don't Walk, Don't Walk, Don't Walk.

Horowitz would not be hurried. Silently he protested, What do you want me to do, run? He kept his steady pace and when the light changed and an impudent young cab driver honked his horn, Horowitz turned and defied him with an angry glare.

The path was as shaded and cool as he had anticipated. There was even a light breeze. He sat down on one end of a long green bench and rested both hands on top of his gnarled cane while he watched children at play, children eating ice cream cones, children playing with newly bought balloons. He remembered when he used to bring Marvin here, long before his name was Hammond. Then a few years later, Mona, long before her name was Fields, before she had ever heard of a place called San Diego.

He watched with regret, and yet with a kind of nostalgic enjoyment. Some things had changed. The complexion of the people had changed. There were more blacks and Hispanics now than there had been. But life never seemed to change. Ice cream, balloons, and frosted pops do not change, nor does a child's enjoyment of them, no matter the color of the child, nor the racial origin. One day, he thought, one day we must bring Conrad and Louise down here to see the animals in the zoo. To see the animated clock which every hour and half hour played music for the gilded animals to dance to.

He was thinking of such things when a young black man sat down at the far end of his bench. Instinctively, Horowitz became alert, tense, planned his defense. He tightened his grip on his cane, vowing, If that bastard tries to mug me, I'll smash his head! At the same time, his left hand slipped into his pocket to protect his precious gift. He sat that way, stiff and alert, casting an occasional glance at the young black man who seemed not so badly dressed. In fact, on closer inspection, it turned out he was wearing a suit that matched, pants and jacket. Although under the heat of the day he was carrying his jacket. And he did not wear those thick-soled platform shoes Horowitz was used to seeing in his neighborhood uptown.

Horowitz felt a bit more secure, relaxed his grip on his precious gift, not wishing to crush the tissue paper in which it was wrapped, or the red ribbon he had insisted on. But he remained alert. Now the young black man moved a bit in Horowitz's direction.

Here it comes, Horowitz said to himself, I'll kill him before I give up this package! He must have seen me in Tiffany's. He must have followed me all the way here. Picked the same bench. Soon he'll want to strike up a conversation. So he's dressed respectably, so what? There have been cases in the papers lately where black men disguised in business suits and carrying attaché cases have gone into the best hotels and ransacked some of the rooms. He must be one of them. The sonofabitch, one more move and I'll split his head open with this cane. If he's got a knife or a razor he won't get close enough to slash me. Not this time, Horowitz vowed!

Now the young black man spoke, "Say, do you happen to have the time?"

Ho-ho-ho, Horowitz thought, one of their favorite tricks. They throw you off by asking the time. And while you're looking at your watch they make their move. *Nisht by Mutke*, Horowitz vowed. Time I'll give you, but take me by surprise, you won't.

"Quarter after four," Horowitz said, coolly.

"Damn!" the young black man said. "Should have been here by now."

Don't try to strike up a conversation with me, Horowitz warned silently. Keep your distance. One more move and I'll defend myself. The young black man leaned forward, rested his elbows on his thighs and covered his face with his cupped hands. He closed his eyes as if wanting to shut out the day and the noise of the city.

An act, Horowitz said. He is pretending to be thinking but he is really getting ready to make his move. *Boychick*, are you going to be in for the surprise of your life when I bounce this shillelagh off your black head. Just one move, just one more move, he warned. His hand tightly wrapped around his cane, Horowitz was ready!

Now the young man suddenly leaped up from the bench. Horowitz raised his cane ready to strike. But the stranger darted past him to embrace a light-skinned, young black woman. They held each other, kissed. While she was still pressed against him she asked, "Well? Did you get it?"

"They said they'd let me know," he admitted in a defeated tone of voice. "Every damn time it's the same. Get dressed up for the interview. A nice pleasant chat, And, at the end, 'We'll let you know.' Only they never do. Thank God, you have a job."

"You have to be patient, darling. One day soon . . ."

387

she said as they started out of the park together.

Horowitz did not hear the rest of it. He did not have to. If he had known, if only he had known, he might have helped. After all, he still had a friend or two in business; he could have called one of them. But at least, Horowitz consoled himself, I didn't do anything foolish, like hit him with this cane. What would Mrs. Washington have said then? It was most important to him these days what Mrs. Washington thought.

Such a movie, so much shooting, and flying around in space, who can keep up with the story, Horowitz was saying to himself. But when he glanced to his side he could see Conrad and Louise staring at the screen, wide-eyed, breathless with intensity and excitement.

He could remember his own childhood days at the movies. William S. Hart. There was a man. A real man, not a metal contraption. You always understood the story in those days. William S. Hart was the good man and all the others were bad. There was no sound, no noise, no loud shooting. When someone shot a pistol in one of those pictures it was only a puff of white smoke. Or sometimes a chord on the piano if the pianist was so inclined. But at least one understood the story.

These days, Horowitz lamented, it all seemed noise and confusion and no plot. But when he watched the rapt look on Conrad's face as the boy actually seemed to live the whole futuristic adventure, Horowitz felt all the noise and the confusion were worthwhile.

And when, in the moment of greatest dramatic tension, Louise instinctively seized Horowitz's hand and held on tightly, he was deeply touched. He covered her hand with his own and was reluctant to let go when she relaxed her grip once the action on the screen began to resolve.

He thought, There is something about the warmth and

the softness of a child's needing hand that cannot be found anywhere else. He used to enjoy that with Bruce and Candy when they were very young.

But now on the screen whole worlds had exploded and the villains with them. The young heroes had triumphed. The film was over and they were free to leave. Horowitz looked forward to dinner and his big surprise.

The maitre d' at the Casino in the Park showed them to a table that looked out on the courtyard where open-air tables were neatly spread under trees that wore tiny electric lights in their branches.

"A drink before dinner, or maybe a little wine?" Horowitz suggested. When Mrs. Washington appeared uneasy, he coaxed, "We are celebrating our victory. One drink can't do any harm. Better still, a little champagne! After all, except for you, I would be way out in San Diego tonight, alone, instead of with friends. So a little champagne for us, and two Shirley Temples for the children. They still have Shirley Temples for children, don't they? I used to get them for Bruce and Candy when they were young."

He beckoned the waiter, ordered, and then looked around. "Nice place," he said with considerable satisfaction. But in looking around he became aware of some diners who stared at the anomaly of Samuel Horowitz, his black friend and the two black children. Let them stare, he thought. Anybody asks, I'll say they're my grandchildren. Better still, my own children! Mrs. Washington and I have been married for some time and these are our children. The idea amused and delighted him.

Champagne in hand, he made a toast, "Children, before you drink, a word about your grandmother. She is a fine woman. The type of human being one is privileged to meet too rarely in this life. What Lincoln did for black people, she did for me. So let's drink to her!"

He raised his glass and sipped. The children joined in

with their colorful, cherry-crested ginger ale.

"And now," Horowitz said, "the surprise of the evening!" He reached his left hand into his pocket and brought out the small box in its tissue-paper wrapping. He fluffed up the ribbon to make it appear fresh. As he held it out, he said, "Notice, it's with my left hand, Mrs. Washington."

She stared at the box but made no move to take it.

He urged it on her, "Mrs. Washington."

"I really . . . no, I don't think I should."

"I bought it special for you," he said. "It's a thank you, and a token of a long-lasting friendship."

"I can't, really. . . ."

Horowitz smiled understandingly. "My fault. I shouldn't have surprised you this way. Not here. You're embarrassed. I'm very sorry." He turned to Louise, "Here, darling, you take it. Open it. Show it to Grandma."

The child looked to her grandmother for permission. But Mrs. Washington shook her head in a single slight negative command.

"All right," Horowitz declared, "then I'll do it!" He proceeded to unwrap the little package, carefully putting the ribbon and paper aside. He held the small velvet box in his hands for a moment before opening it to display it to her. "There!" He searched her face for a smile of delight and approval. When she did not react, except to betray a slight misting of her eyes, he said, "Please? At least try it? Pin it on? It can't hurt."

Mrs. Washington did not move, but Conrad, sensing Horowitz's hurt and disappointment, urged, "Grandma, won't you even show us how it looks on?"

She reached for it, held it at the top of her dress where the two sides of her collar came together. Against the simple navy dress, the gold stood out in elegant contrast; against her rich black skin, it gleamed.

"Very pretty, Grandma," Louise said.

"Gee, cool!" Conrad said, awed by the sight of the impressive gold rope.

"Aren't you going to put it on?" Horowitz asked.

"No," she said simply, though he could tell she was taken by the beautifully fashioned piece. Reluctantly she returned it to its velvet bed. He closed the box and handed it to her. But she said, "Really, no, I can't."

"Why not?" he asked, becoming distressed now. "I am giving it to you. All you have to do is take it," he urged. When he realized he had not convinced her, he confessed, "I never went to see my accountant yesterday. Those two hours? I was shopping. For this. I want you to have it."

"I'm sorry," she said.

"But why?" he asked. "I'm at least entitled to an explanation."

"Not now," she said softly. "Tomorrow."

"Tomorrow," he echoed. "All right, tomorrow."

Chapter Twenty-eight

He had wakened early. With a sense of urgency that gave him concern. Then he recalled last night, dinner, the gift, Mrs. Washington's refusal. He got out of bed and, cane in hand, made his way out to the foyer. There on the table lay box, tissue paper, and tangle of red ribbon, all of which he had shoved into his pocket last night after her rejection.

It would not be easy but he was determined to restore the gift to the same condition as when he first presented it. He sat down at the card table in the living room. With considerable effort he managed to wrap the gift in its tissue paper, folding it neatly. He had to force his fingers to work diligently and skillfully to smooth out the ribbon, then wind it about the small package so it looked neat and even. The most difficult part was making his left fingers perform properly with the very thin, slippery ribbon. But when he finished he had produced a most creditable knot and bow. He pressed it down, hoping to iron out the wrinkles caused by much handling. When he thought it looked neat enough, he took it back to the foyer table and placed it so conspicuously that it would be the first thing she saw when she opened the door.

That done, he went back to bed, deliberately refraining from picking up *The New York Times* from the doormat. He wanted no distractions. He lay abed, waiting for the sound of her keys, the opening of the door, and her response to the gift.

After what seemed an inordinately long and frustrating time, after consulting the small clock on the bedside table so frequently that its hand hardly seemed to move at all, he finally heard it. Her keys. One lock, then the second. The door was open. He listened for her steps. If she paused, he would know that she had seen and been affected by his gift.

Her sensible shoes came to a halt on the bare floor that surrounded the foyer rug. He was satisfied that his plan had worked. She had seen the gift, possibly even stopped to pick it up and reconsider.

He turned on his side and pretended to be asleep. He could hear her tiptoe to his door, peek in. She must have assumed he was still asleep, for she tiptoed away to go about her duties in the kitchen.

In minutes he rose, slipped on his robe, performed his usual morning bathroom functions, except that this time instead of shaving after breakfast, he decided to shave before. He ran the razor over his face until it was smooth to his touch. He slapped on an extra palmful of shaving lotion. He brought his pajama collar to a jaunty angle above his robe. He even fluffed the handkerchief in his robe pocket. Then, gnarled cane in hand, he walked to the dining room, where he found his breakfast waiting.

As had become their custom, while he was having his breakfast, Mrs. Washington brought her coffee in and sat at the end of the table. Most mornings she would talk freely, some item she had heard on the news, or read in the paper on her way downtown, or else some event of the day before concerning Conrad or Louise. Today, nothing. For a time, Horowitz remained silent, waiting for her to make the opening gambit.

When, after a time, she did not, he said, "You saw it, I know you saw it."

"Yes," she admitted, but said nothing more.

After a pause, he asked, "Did you like the way it was tied? A good knot, no? Neat? Even?"

"Yes, yes, it was."

"You wouldn't expect a man with a stroke to be able to do that, would you? I mean that ribbon is very thin and slippery. It's not easy even for a man who never had this kind of trouble. Right?" he asked, trying to entice her into conversation.

She only stared at him, her black eyes shining behind the lenses of her silver-framed spectacles.

"Well, just for your information, Mrs. Washington, it was not as difficult as you might think. It didn't take more than ten minutes." Her skeptical look made him admit, "Maybe fifteen. Certainly not more than twenty," he finally granted. "The important thing is, I did it. And the only reason I could do it was you, Mrs. Washington."

To make his point even more strongly, he poked the forefinger of his left hand in her direction. He held out his left hand, examined the back of it, and then the palm and said, "Two months ago I couldn't have done this."

When she did not respond, he continued, "So, as the rabbis of old would have asked, what is the point? The point, Mrs. Washington, is this. I have you to thank for this. You bullied me, you shouted at me, you embarrassed me. Sometimes I had the feeling that you even threatened me. And because you did, I did! Not threatened, but did what you wanted me to do.

"So," he continued, "after all that, if a man wants to express a little appreciation, how does it look for a woman like you to insult him? I ask you."

"Mr. Horowitz, I had no intention of insulting you," she said.

"You refuse my gift and you don't call that an insult?" he reproached.

"It wouldn't be right," she tried to explain.

"Wouldn't be right?" he chided. "What wouldn't be right? Am I a young man waiting at the stage door with flowers and jewelry? Are you a beautiful young chorus girl I am trying to seduce into bed? Although I understand these days flowers and jewelry are not even necessary. Just hello, how you doin' and into bed they jump. But as between us, what's not right? A simple act of appreciation. A way of saying thank you. Thank you for working so hard with me. Thank you for enduring all my complaints, my moods, which I must admit have not always been exactly delightful. Thank you for making me go out in the wheelchair for the first time. Thank you for the million times you made me do what I didn't want to do. Mainly, thank you for keeping me a free man. So I could say no to Mona.

"This is a trivial gift to discharge such a large debt. The only thing that wouldn't be right, would be for you to refuse." When she did not respond at once, he nudged, "Mrs. Washington?" After a long silence, during which he suspected that tears had welled up in her eyes, he asked, more solicitously now, and much gentler, "Mrs. Washington? What did I do wrong? Did I hurt your feelings in some way?"

"You're making this very difficult, Mr. Horowitz."

"What's difficult to accept a gift? Take it. Wear it. You don't even have to say thank you. I don't want thanks. This is my way of saying thanks. At least give me that little bit of pleasure," he pleaded.

"Look," he decided suddenly, "we'll make a deal! I'm not an unreasonable man. The package is out there. We won't say another word. It will stay there as long as you like. Then one day, whenever you feel like it, open it up, put it on, and when I see it on you, I'll know that you've accepted it. It can be a week from now, a month from now, a year from now. But it stays there until you take it. Agreed?"

"Mr. Horowitz . . ." she tried to explain.

"No discussions, no arguments, just say yes. Fair enough?"

"Mr. Horowitz," she began more firmly, "the reason I cannot accept your very fine gift is that you expect I will be here a year from now, or even a month from now."

He grasped the edge of the table with both hands, firmly, to brace himself, as he asked, "Mrs. Washington, are you trying to tell me something which I do not understand?"

"I'm trying to say that by the end of next week I will be leaving," she said simply and directly.

"Leaving? You can't!" he protested. "You have a duty, an obligation . . . a . . ." Suddenly he decided, "It's something to do with the children. There's something wrong. Tell me what it is and if money can fix it, consider it fixed!"

"It isn't the children," she said.

"Then what?" he asked, rising to his feet and making his way to her side. "What?" he asked again.

"I'm no longer needed here," she said.

"That's an excuse!" he accused. "I know what it is! I know!"

He made his way out to the foyer and into the living room to sit at his table where she had laid out his marbles, buttons, and cards. Deliberately, and obstinately, he sat with arms folded, staring out of the window at the playground in the park. When she came in to dust the living room furniture, he proceeded to talk, not directly to her, but to an imaginary third person.

"A woman should carry such a grudge all these weeks,

who would believe it? Just because that very first day I said a few things. . . . Okay, so they were not nice . . . and I didn't know she was already here . . . and when you think about it, I had a little reason to say them. After all, I had been attacked, slashed, had a stroke, a man had a right to be upset. So I said a few things about black people. But I also said nice things about Bernadine. Bernadine is a lady, a fine person. Believe me, Bernadine would not desert me this way. But Mrs. Washington, Mrs. Harriet Washington . . ." He allowed his protest to drift off into silence, only to renew the attack again.

"You would think that Mrs. Washington would remember those nice talks we had in the park. Who would I have to talk to in the park if she left? I'd have to sit alone. And that wouldn't go on for long. Just let those widows look out their windows and see me sitting there alone and, like vultures, they would be circling me waiting to strike. That's what she wants to happen to me. And why? Just because once or twice I called her a Hitler. Is that such a crime that she has to desert me? Leave me?

"Come to think of it, I don't think she has a legal right to leave me. I am going to call one of the lawyers in Marvin's New York office and ask him if a nurse, a professional person, mind you, in the line of duty has a right to abandon a patient. There must be a law about that. God knows they got laws about everything these days. Yes, desertion in the line of duty. Maybe it's even a crime!"

He glanced up slyly through his right eye, to see if he had made any impression on her. But that silent, stubborn woman was still dusting.

Suddenly he exploded, "I know New York is a dirty city! But there can't be this much dust in the Sahara Desert!"

"You are shouting at me," she said primly.

"Okay, I'm sorry. I didn't mean to shout," he apolo-

397

gized gently. "Now, if you can stop dusting, and take a few minutes of your valuable time, perhaps you might sit down and tell me what I have done to make you want to leave." He beckoned her to a chair across from the bridge table, the same chair she sat in when they played pinochle.

"Now, please?" he asked in as entreating a voice as he could manage. "What did I do? And know, in advance, that whatever it was, I am sorry. I apologize. If it's a matter of money, I will rectify it. If it's my attitude, I promise to change it. Or are you still remembering my outburst in the hospital when I accused Conrad of trying to steal? Is that it? Believe me, I felt worse about that than you did. I cursed myself all the way home. What a terrible thing to do. But if that was it, why are you deserting me now?"

"Not deserting," she corrected, "leaving."

"Okay, leaving. But why? We . . . we are so used to each other. We have come to understand each other. And, I hope, respect each other. You are a fine person, Mrs. Washington, a very fine person. In many ways you have the same qualities as my mother. That drive to see the children get a good education. The desire to see them neat and clean, to feel above their environment, to dream of accomplishing instead of complaining.

"And, Mrs. Washington, I can confess, there is some of Hannah in you, too. I don't know what you would call it, but sometimes I have read in books a word: *nobility*. I think that may be the word for you. Nobility. That day when you said to me, 'I prefer not to be called by my first name. Call me Mrs. Washington!' I admired you that day. And even on the days when you bullied me, I admired you," he confessed.

"If I were a younger man . . ." he started to say and did not finish. "But we are neither of us young anymore. Which, in a way, is a reason for you not to leave here. Not now. Not when your work here is going to be so much easier. You don't have to struggle with me over my exercises. I can do them without help now. You don't have to hover over me to make sure I do marbles, buttons, cards. You'll have more time to yourself. Even the meals. Now that I get around so much easier, we can go out for lunch a few times a week. So you won't have to be cooking or doing dishes so often. It'll be much better, much easier for you," he argued. "So, reconsider. Please?"

"Mr. Horowitz," she began, "I am not a housekeeper. I am not a cook or a maid. Or even a companion. I am a nurse. You don't need me anymore. But somewhere there is a patient who does," she tried to explain gently.

"I don't need you . . ." he started to contradict loudly, until she glared at him and he lowered his voice. "I don't need you? I? Samuel Horowitz, who depends on you, whose day begins when I hear you unlock those two locks? I don't need you? Me, who looks forward to our discussions in the park? Who likes to argue with you? Who would still like to hear much more about Horace? Who waits every morning to hear everything you have to report about Conrad? And Louise? What they do? What they say? Me? A man who owes you so much, I don't need you? That's ingratitude, Mrs. Washington, to say that I don't need you. Terrible ingratitude!" he accused.

"Mr. Horowitz, don't you understand?"

"Understand? I am trying to understand why a woman with everything to gain here wants to leave? Why she wants to desert a man who admires and respects her."

"Because," Mrs. Washington began, "by what you did two days ago when Mona was here you proved that you are able to get along on your own. So you don't need me. What you need is someone like Bernadine, to keep house, to cook, to clean up. But you do not need a nurse. Even Dr. Tannenbaum says so."

"Tannenbaum!" Horowitz disparaged with a wave of his left hand, until he realized he was proving her point, so he switched to using his right hand. "Tannenbaum is a horse doctor! What does he know about a poor man who has had a stroke and is still suffering the effects."

"He was able to convince Mona," she reminded.

"Mona!" he scoffed. "Anyone can convince Mona of anything!" When she stared at him, he admitted, "Well, almost anything. The important thing is how I feel. I'm the patient. I know what I need. And I need you! And if you have any consideration at all for another human soul you will not give any thought to deserting me!"

After a long silence, with his left eye closed and his right daring to steal a glance at her, he asked slyly, "Nu?"

"Mr. Horowitz, what you refuse to understand is that you are no longer a patient. You are well, almost completely well. You can function normally. You proved that. To Dr. Tannenbaum. To Mona. But most of all, you proved it to me," Mrs. Washington said stolidly.

"And this is the thanks I get? To be deserted? I would think you'd be proud of me. I am your prize patient. You can show me off to the world. Look what I did for Samuel Horowitz!"

Finally he realized that he could not change her mind.

"When . . . when did you plan to leave?" he asked.

"Dr. Tannenbaum spoke to your son. He spoke to Bernadine. She can be back on Monday."

"So you leave at the end of the week?" he asked sadly.

She nodded.

Horowitz picked up the cards and began to shuffle them, first thumbs pressed down, then regular shuffle, then cutting them. The sound of the whisking cards emphasized the silence in the room. Mrs. Washington resumed her dusting.

It was Sunday. A bright, cool Sunday, the sort of late

August day in New York that promises delightful September and Octobers. The park below was crowded with families with picnic baskets. Crowded with baseball teams, with walkers, joggers, lovers, and jogging lovers. The whole world seemed to be celebrating the end of a hot summer and the beginning of autumn.

Mr. Horowitz and Mrs. Washington strolled along the walk under green leafy trees that conspired to cast intriguing patterns of shadow and light. Horowitz used his gnarled cane but with far less effort than weeks ago. He concentrated on his left leg so there was no noticeable foot drag. He walked more erectly. He was trying to make her proud of him. Though she had always been grudging with praise, using it as the carrot to her stick of domination, she had to admit that she was proud. She had to admit, as well, that she had come to like this man. She even loved him, not in the way women love men but in the way that one human being can love and respect another human being. He was a tough man, with a strange kind of pride. As Horace had been. Though, in the end, the world had ground Horace down.

They had not said much during their walk, using conversation to refer only to some moment of interest that they chanced on during their walk. An unusually beautiful child. A pair of young lovers strolling hand in hand. A crying child whose balloon had got away and was caught up in the branches of a tree, so high that her frustrated father could not reach it. But they made no comment when they passed one pair of lovers of whom the girl was white and the boy black.

When they came on the ice-cream vendor, Mr. Horowitz invited, "A little ice cream, Mrs. Washington?"

She hesitated. "Yes, I think that would be nice."

"A sort of farewell party," Horowitz said pointedly. "Maybe I'll have one too. Is it allowed?"

"I guess, today, it's all right," she said.

They sat on one of the old green wooden benches under the shade of a large tree and ate their ice cream.

"From tomorrow on it won't be the same," he said, then hastened to intercept the trickle of melting ice cream that started down his cone.

"And yet," he continued, "it will be the same. The same as it used to be before. Before Mrs. Washington. There'll be Bernadine. And walks in the park. And widows. Always the widows," he complained.

"You shouldn't feel that way about widows," Mrs. Washington said.

"They're all so . . . so pushy . . . so . . . what can I say, like vultures."

"I'm a widow," Mrs. Washington said softly.

"You. You're different," Horowitz said. "Nothing I ever said about widows applies to you."

"I'm really not different," she explained sadly. "Widows, all of us, have a lifetime habit. We need someone to care for. Someone to do for. Someone to worry about. Someone to wait home for at the end of the day. You can't ever break that habit. So don't feel so angry with us."

"If I said anything to offend you, I'm very sorry," Horowitz said most sincerely. "Will I see you again? Can I call you? I mean, am I just one more patient from the past? Or can I consider that we are friends?"

"There's no reason we can't be friends," Mrs. Washington said.

"You mean I could call you from time to time? I don't mean so often that I would be a nuisance. But occasionally. Just to let you know how things are going."

"Of course, why not?"

"Like when sometimes I am stuck with a pair of tickets. You know how it is, there's always something in the mail about a theater party for a worthy cause. So how would it look a man should buy one ticket? For a worthy cause, the least you can buy is a pair. So what am I going to do, use the other seat for my hat and coat? You know what I mean?"

"Uh-huh," she said.

"Is that uh-huh, yes? Or uh-huh, no?"

"Uh-huh, possibly," she responded.

Realizing she was reluctant to make promises, Horowitz urged gently, "It's nice to have someone alongside who can laugh at the same things, and cry at the same things. And you are such a person, Mrs. Washington."

"Thank you."

"In any case, wouldn't do any harm you should call me. Only from time to time, of course. To tell me how Conrad and Louise are doing in school. Like for example when he gets some award or she gets skipped a class in school, would be nice to have a little party, to celebrate. You know?"

He hesitated before suggesting, "And also, if it happens that you should need anything, or the children should need anything . . ." He could tell that he had offended her. "I'm sorry, Mrs. Washington. I didn't mean to say that. You just call me from time to time so I know you haven't forgotten me. All right?"

"All right," she agreed, then added, "And it wouldn't do any harm for you to call Mona from time to time."

"I know, she's got an 800 number," he lamented. "And it doesn't cost anything."

"She may be a little domineering but she loves you."

"She is a little domineering like the Johnstown flood was a little damp," he scoffed.

"She's your daughter, she loves you, and that gives her some rights."

"Okay, I'll call her," he finally acquiesced. "From time to time." Then grudgingly he conceded, "Maybe I'll even go visit her. For the holidays. Yes, Rosh Hashonah and Yom Kippur, ten days, I could stand ten days with Mona. But not a minute more."

* * *

His dinner was over. Mrs. Washington had changed back into her Sunday dress and was about to fix her hat in place when he invited, "Mrs. Washington, for old times' sake, one last hand?" And he shuffled the pinochle cards.

She hesitated a moment. "It's Sunday. My daughter is home with the children. Yes, I think there's time for one last hand."

He dealt the cards, pack in his right hand, dealing with his left. Then he set down the stock and arranged his cards. Looking over them at her, he asked, "Double or nothing?"

Since he had yet to pay any of his gambling losses, she sighed and agreed, "Double or nothing."

"Good!"

Whereupon she took the first trick and melded eighty kings.

"No wonder you were so quick to agree double or nothing," he grumbled. He applied himself industriously to his hand but could come up only with forty jacks.

By the time the game was over, he had been routed.

"Mrs. Washington, if there was a Bible on this table, could you put your hand on it and swear that you never played pinochle before you entered this house?" he asked with considerable irritation.

"Yes."

"Remarkable," he granted in a frustrated whisper. "You aren't satisfied the blacks took over basketball, baseball, and football. Today it's pinochle! Tomorrow the world!"

She had her hat on, was ready to leave. Horowitz was in the bedroom. She called to him.

"Mr. Horowitz?"

"Coming," he called back in his singsong.

He came out of the bedroom carrying the gift box and a small envelope. At the sight of the box, her black eyes stared at him forbiddingly.

"For me," he said gently. "Take it for me. To make an old man happy. How would it look I should go back to Tiffany and say, 'I want a refund. She didn't like it.' It would be very embarrassing. So please?"

He took her hand and pressed the small box into it, then tried to close her fingers about it. When her fingers resisted, he chided jokingly, "If you can't do that, Mrs. Washington, we'll have to start you on marbles, buttons, and cards. Come to think of it, if you had lost at pinochle and had to deal as often as I did you wouldn't be having this trouble now." He pressed her fingers around the little box. "Please?" he entreated, his eyes growing a bit moist now.

She stared into them. Before she could say anything, he explained away, "The teary eyes of age. Pay no attention."

She took the box.

He handed her the envelope.

"What's that?"

"What's that?" he demanded, putting on his best pretense at irritation. "Nineteen dollars! Pinochle winnings! Blood money! You ought to be ashamed of yourself, Mrs. Washington! A card sharp like you could make a fortune on one of those cruise ships! And a perfect front, a grandmother who is also a nurse. Who could possibly suspect you? Well, I was taken. I admit it. But I am a man who pays his debts. So there is your pinochle money!"

When she hesitated, he insisted, "Take the envelope! So at least one of us can sleep with a clear conscience tonight!"

When Mrs. Washington arrived home, her daughter asked, "How was it, Mama?"

"He was very upset. He pretended to be angry. But he was upset, poor man."

She opened her purse and took out the box. "Open it,"

405

she said. "It's the pin the children told you about. I had to take it." Taking out the envelope, she smiled, "And this. Pinochle money." She ripped open the envelope. A ten, a five, and four singles fell out.

There was also a note. And a slip of paper affixed to it.

"Dear Mrs. Washington: Because you are a very proud woman I have to do this my way. The enclosed check is NOT *for you. It is for Conrad and Louise. Put it in a savings bank in their names. And by the time they grow up and need money for college or some other good purpose it should amount to something. Whatever you do, you can't send it back. You have no right. It belongs to the children. And you have no right to deprive them. So for their sake, and mine, please do as I ask. Your affectionate friend, Samuel Horowitz."*

He had signed his name with the same flourish as appeared on the bottom of the appended check for five thousand dollars.

Mrs. Washington stared at the check and her eyes filmed over.

"Mama?"

Mrs. Washington sniffled and said, "It's nothing. Only the teary eyes of age."

Chapter Twenty-nine

It was early summer. The twenty-fifth of June, the twentieth day of Sivan, on the Hebrew calendar. Samuel Horowitz, attired in a proper dark suit, wearing a white shirt neatly buttoned, and a dark tie fashioned into a solid knot, emerged from the building to stand under the canopy and feel the warm welcome sun.

"Cab, Mr. Horowitz?" Juan asked, smiling.

"No, thanks, Juan."

"A little walk in the park," Juan surmised.

"Not exactly," Horowitz said as he started up Central Park West toward Eighty-sixth Street, using his cane more as an affectation than a necessity.

He waited at the corner for the light to go green. He crossed the street and headed for the synagogue. At the door the sexton, always anxious as to whether he would assemble the required ten for the morning minyan, was delighted to see him.

"Good morning, Mr. Horowitz! Nice day, nice to see

you." Then he asked solicitously, "*Yahrzeit*, Mr. Horowitz?"

"*Yahrzeit*," he admitted.

Horowitz entered the sanctuary and walked down the aisle. He took a place in the front row. He looked up at the crimson velvet and gold embroidered covered ark which contained the scrolls of the Torah. It was not God, but a symbol of God, to which most Jews addressed their prayers and, sometimes, also addressed those who had departed.

Samuel Horowitz stared at it and thought, Hannah, darling, last year I was late. But there was a reason. This year, you will notice, I am on time. The twentieth day of Sivan. And not only on time, but I walked here. On my own. No chair, no help from anyone. So I want you to know that I am all right. Yesterday I talked to Mona on her 800 number and she is all right. And the grandchildren, too. Bruce switched over from Harvard and is studying physics at MIT. When he graduates he'll be able to blow up the whole world. And Candy is going into teaching brain-damaged children. I saw both of them on Passover. In San Diego. At a big synagogue seder. The gefilte fish was a little too fancy. From a caterer. But otherwise you couldn't tell that seder from the real thing.

The main point Hannah, darling, everything is fine, the family is fine. And if you were here that would really be fine. We have our *minyan* now so they're about to begin. Hannah, I love you and I miss you. Not just this day, but every day.

Since none of the ten mourners had volunteered, the sexton commenced to conduct the morning service, and the others responded as required. At the proper time, Samuel Horowitz recited the *kaddish* for his dear departed Hannah.

When the service was over, he left the temple and started down Central Park West back to the house.

Across the street, on the park side, on a green bench, unobtrusive in the shade of a large tree, a neatly dressed black woman watched.

He had done it, she said to herself, had observed his wife's *yahrzeit* on the required day and walked to and from the synagogue so smoothly no one would have suspected he had had a stroke a year ago.

Gratified, Mrs. Washington rose, went down to the subway, on her way to take care of yet another new patient.